Crazy Thing Called Love

"There is no stopping the roller coaster of emotion, sexual tension and belly laughs. O'Keefe excels in creating flawed characters who readers will root for on every page. Despite very serious subjects and tear-worthy emotion, the tone of the novel is a perfect balance of fun and heart."
—4½ stars, *RT Book Reviews*

"O'Keefe's newest romance hits the high notes with a storyline that tugs on the heartstrings, maintains a sizzling degree of sexual tension, and plays on realistic, authentic conflicts that keep the audience emotionally invested from start to finish. Gripping storytelling and convincing character-building allow the story to unfold in the present and in the past, offering windows into the psyches of a damaged hero and his restyled first love. An intense, heartwarming winner."
—*Kirkus Reviews*

"*Crazy Thing Called Love* has become my all-time favorite contemporary romance! . . . Don't miss out on O'Keefe's Crooked Creek series! These are the books you will still be talking about in twenty years!"
—Joyfully Reviewed

"There is nothing lacking in Molly O'Keefe's *Crazy Thing Called Love*. I am glad to say that it has every possible thing a woman could want in a good romance story. The Crooked Creek series is something that you will definitely want to get your hands on."

—Guilty Pleasures Book Reviews

"Wonderful story . . . unlike anything I have read before . . . Highly addicting."

—Single Titles

"This was an absolute joy to read . . . . Definitely a book worth picking up."

—Cocktails and Books

"O'Keefe keeps the momentum of the present story going at a breathtaking pace with well placed visits back to the past, providing insight into these characters."

—Fresh Fiction

Can't Buy Me Love

"Readers should clear their schedules before they pick up O'Keefe's latest—a fast-paced, funny and touching book that is 'unputdownable.' Her story is a roller-coaster ride of tragedy and comedy that is matched in power by believable and sympathetic characters who leap off the pages. Best of all, this is just the beginning of a new series."

—RT Book Reviews

Can't Hurry Love

"Using humor and heartrending emotion, O'Keefe writes characters who leap off the page. Their flaws and foibles make for an emotional story filled with tension, redemption and laughter. While this novel is not a direct continuation of the first in the series, it makes the reading richer and more interesting to devour the books in order. Readers should keep their eyes peeled for the third book and make room on their keeper shelves for this sparkling fresh series."
—*RT Book Reviews*

"Have you ever read a book that seeped into your soul while you read it, leaving you feeling both destroyed and elated when you finished? *Can't Hurry Love* was that book for me."
—Reader, I Created Him

"*Can't Hurry Love* is special. It's that book that ten years from now you will still be recommending to everyone because it is undeniably great!"
—Joyfully Reviewed

"An emotion-packed read, *Can't Hurry Love* . . . is a witty, passionate contemporary romance that will capture your interest from the very beginning."
—Romance Junkies

Wild Child

Wild Child

MOLLY O'KEEFE

BANTAM BOOKS • NEW YORK

A Bantam Books Mass Market Original

Copyright © 2013 by Molly Fader
Excerpt from *Never Been Kissed* by Molly O'Keefe copyright © 2013 by Molly Fader

Published in the United States by Bantam Books, an imprint of The Random House Publishing Group, a division of Random House, Inc., New York.

BANTAM BOOKS and the HOUSE colophon are registered trademarks of Random House, Inc.

ISBN 978-0-345-53371-5
eBook ISBN 978-0-345-53372-2

This book contains an excerpt from the forthcoming book *Never Been Kissed* by Molly O'Keefe. This excerpt has been set for this edition only and may not reflect the final content of the forthcoming edition.

Cover design: Lynn Andreozzi
Cover photograph: Claudio Marinesco

Printed in the United States of America

www.bantamdell.com

9 8 7 6 5 4 3 2 1

Bantam Books mass market edition: October 2013

To everyone who has faked it . . .
whatever "it" is

Wild Child

Chapter 1

Six months ago

Jackson Davies knew better. He really did. There were friends you could do free hard labor for, and there were friends you couldn't.

Sean Baxter was decidedly a friend you couldn't. And yet Jackson managed to be shocked when Sean sat down to watch TV while Jackson was still sanding drywall.

"You've got to be joking!" Jackson threw down the sandpaper. He was covered in dirt and grime and sweat. He itched. Everywhere. Agreeing to help Sean renovate his family's old dive bar, The Pour House, had seemed like a good idea four months ago—a little physical labor, some laughs with friends.

But so far Jackson and Brody, Sean's brother, were doing all the work.

Why are you surprised? It's grade school all over again.

"I just want to see this clip on *America Today*." Sean's face mask was pushed up into his red hair, revealing a clean circle of skin around his lips. No doubt Jackson and Brody looked equally ridiculous. Jackson needed to shower before heading to City Hall. "Monica Appleby is going to be on. You know, that writer—"

"You know, I've actually got work to do. *Real* work." Jackson took off his tool belt. Behind him, Brody kept scraping away at the mahogany bar he was refurbishing. Brody was in town for a week between jobs and he'd committed to slave carpenter labor for that time.

Jackson couldn't help the man.

"I'm sure Bishop will do just fine without you on a Friday morning."

"I'm mayor, Sean. I can't just take the whole morning off." And the truth was, working out here at The Pour House was easier than going into City Hall today and almost every other day.

Bishop, Arkansas, was dying. Slowly, from a financial wound Jackson didn't know how to fix. And Jackson took a lot of pride in being able to fix anything.

At least sanding walls made him feel like he was doing something.

"I'm out," Jackson said. "I've got a meeting with the city council, and . . ."

"Shhhhh, there she is!" Sean turned the volume up, and even Brody was forced to stop his relentless work and watch the screen.

Monica Appleby sat on the couch in the *America Today* green room. The reality-star-turned-author was everywhere these days. And every time Jackson caught a glimpse of her on a magazine cover or TV show, he thought the same thing: *that girl is trouble.*

Her black-haired, purple-eyed beauty was diamond bright but lined in smoke and sin. Something about Monica managed to put a spotlight on every single wrong and dirty thing he'd abstained from in the last seven years. Expensive bourbon, cheap tequila, beautiful women whose names he didn't want to know, steak dinners, the Las Vegas strip, unpaid parking tickets—all of it.

She was the human and stunningly gorgeous personification of everything he wanted and couldn't have.

It hurt to look at her.

"Remember her?" Sean asked. "From when we were kids?"

A terrified six-year-old, clinging to her battered mother's legs.

"Of course I remember her," Jackson said. That girl's brief nightmarish stay in Bishop was a low point, for him and for the town. It had turned them all into voyeurs, decent people with better things to do than lining up outside the police station for a glimpse of Monica and Simone Appleby and all their pain.

"I loved that show she was on with her mom," Sean sighed.

Jackson did not want to get into the reality-television horror show that Monica and Simone Appleby had inflicted upon the world, years ago. Monica had been a nightmare teenager, and Simone's inability to control her had made for hugely popular though short-lived television.

Simone had her own show now, by all accounts equally bad.

"I gotta go," Jackson said.

"See you later?" Brody asked, his black hair held back with a bandana. He looked badass, as much as his brother looked like a leprechaun with drywall dust in his hair.

"I've got to pick up Gwen after school. She's got an interview down at Ole Miss."

"I can't believe your sister is old enough to go to college," Brody said.

She wasn't. But she was smart enough. And he was just desperate enough to let her go.

"Can you guys cut the chatter?" Sean asked. "I'm trying to listen here."

"We'll talk with Monica Appleby right after we discuss one CEO's effort to bring industry back to small-town America," said Jessica Walsh, the *America Today* host.

"Oh, Jessica, I always knew you were a tease," Sean said, and he grabbed the remote to turn down the volume.

"Don't," Jackson said. Industry and small-town America were kind of his current obsessions. "Leave it."

Riveted, Jackson stepped closer to the TV, as a handsome man with sharp blue eyes and shaggy blond hair that made him look like a cross between a surfer and a movie star filled the screen. His teeth were like pearls. Little white Chiclets.

"Dean Jennings, CEO of Maybream Crackers, makers of Crispity Crackers and Maybream Crème cookies, is moving his factory from South America back to the United States," Jessica said, managing to make crackers sound sexy.

"Those cookies are gross," Sean said.

"I like them," Brody answered.

"You would."

Jackson grabbed the remote and cranked up the volume.

"But that's not all," Jessica said, working her long blond hair like a stripper dancing around a pole. "He wants to bring his factory back to small-town America. Can you tell us about that decision, Dean?"

"Maybream was started in a small factory outside of New York. Twenty years ago we moved it down to South America." Dean's earnest-salesman charm played well on the screen—Jessica could barely keep her eyes off the man. "But all across America right now there are factories lying empty and American workers are without jobs. And I just realized . . . I couldn't stand by and watch American industry vanish, not when I could do something about it. Now, I'm a small company and I can't change the economy, but I realized I could change one small town by bringing the Maybream Cracker headquarters and factory back to America."

"This is all really exciting," Jessica said. "But I think

the most exciting, and frankly, PR-savvy, part about it is that you are teaming up with us, *America Today*." Jessica smiled into the camera. "And you, our viewers, get to choose the lucky town."

"It *is* exciting and I don't know about savvy, but I thought it would be fun." Dean made it sound like saving a small town was a trip to the seashore.

"Tell us how it works." Jessica leaned forward across the desk, hanging, it seemed, on Dean's every word. Or perhaps just hypnotized by his teeth.

"The application to nominate a town is available on-line, and my staff and I will look through every entry," Dean said. "We will pick six that best match what we need in a factory and community. Once we have our six semifinalists, *America Today* will travel with me to take a good, hard look at those towns."

"That's an interesting aspect of this contest," Jessica said. "What are you looking for in a community?"

"Well," Dean sighed. "Since we'll be moving our headquarters and staff, we need a place where people would want to raise a family. Someplace wholesome but forward-thinking, with opportunities for kids and parents. With a factory."

Oh, God, it was like the man was singing Jackson love songs!

"That guy wouldn't know wholesome if it bit him in the ass," Sean muttered.

Jackson shot a scowl over his shoulder.

"What?" Sean cried. "The guy's a sleazeball—anyone can tell."

Behind him, Brody was nodding.

Jackson dismissed them both, because his heart was about to burst.

We're wholesome, we're forward-thinking.

And best of all, Bishop had a factory: an okra-processing plant that had been closed for five years. It just sat there, empty, on the south side of town. A reminder of what this town used to be. A graveyard to nearly one hundred lost jobs.

Jackson had been trying for three years as mayor to bring in new business, new industry that would keep this town afloat—but he'd never dreamed of getting the factory open again.

"After I narrow down my choices from six to three and make sure the top three have factories that can be retro-fitted for Maybream Crackers," Dean said, "I'm going to let America vote which town wins. And together we will change that town's future."

"Deadline for applications is the end of the month," Jessica pointed out. "So if you know a town that you think would be a good fit for Maybream Crackers, check out our website." A website address scrolled along the bottom of the screen.

"Give me a pencil," Jackson said, holding out his hand toward his friends. "Now. Now before it's gone."

"Christ, man," Sean said, slapping a small oblong carpenter's pencil into his hand. "You can google that shit, you know."

Jackson scrawled the information on the wall he'd just been sanding. It would be painted over, but that didn't stop Sean from moaning as if Jackson were defacing the Taj Mahal.

"Dean," Jessica continued, "thanks so much for coming in today and partnering with us on this great project. I hope more American companies take note and bring their factories back to U.S. soil."

"Me too, Jessica. Thanks for having me." One last movie-star smile and Dean Jennings was gone.

The show cut to commercial, and Jackson turned down the volume before facing his friends.

Their wary expressions bounced right off his ebullient mood.

"Did you hear that? It's like he was talking about Bishop!" He punched the air in victory. It felt so good, so right, that he did it again. There hadn't been a whole lot of reasons for fist-pumping these days. "This is it!" he cried. "This is exactly what Bishop needs."

"A TV show?"

"Someone to reopen the factory. Bring back jobs. New jobs. For Bishop!" Jackson was light-headed with relief and excitement. "Oh my God, can you believe that? It's perfect."

"It's a long shot," said Brody.

"I believe in long shots," Jackson said. "I am the king of long shots." Not entirely true, but he was riding a wave here.

Sean, who made being a cynic his life's work, frowned. Now Jackson's good mood was dented.

"Just because you don't like the guy after a clip on television—"

"Guys who look like that can't be trusted. It's a fact. They get everything they want," Sean said.

"Bishop is dying, Sean. *Dying*. We need this."

"But a TV show?" Sean asked. "And letting America vote? That shit is always rigged."

"You want people coming into The Pour House?" Jackson asked. "Not just the regulars, but new business? Young people? Hot girls?"

"Hot girls would be nice."

"You want your kids—"

"I don't have kids."

"But you will someday, and you're not going to want to bus them to school an hour away, are you? If we don't change our tax base, we lose the schools. That's it. A chance like this might not come again. The town is in a bad way, Sean. A third of our population has left—"

"You don't have to tell me." Sean held up his hands in surrender, but he didn't lose that scowl.

"Then what's your problem?"

If Jackson were the punching kind, he would have punched Sean Baxter years ago. In kindergarten, maybe. And probably another hundred times since. For that face alone. Always the doubting Thomas. Always the fly in the soup.

"Remember when we played baseball in high school?"

Jackson shot a "can't you help me here, he's your brother?" look at Brody, who only went back to sanding. "Of course I remember, Sean. We had the worst record in the state."

"We sucked. It's true. But you know what I remember about you?" Sean asked.

"I can't even imagine."

Sean leaned over the bar, through sunlight and a snowstorm of dust in the air, catching Jackson in the crosshairs of his light blue eyes.

"You swung for the fences, every time. Even when a base hit would have sufficed, you went after that ball like it had insulted your mother. Like the fate of the world rested on you knocking the leather off that damn thing."

"That's why I led the team in home runs."

"And strikeouts."

True.

"What's your point, Sean?"

"I thought you were nuts when you decided to run for mayor, but I supported you. But this show . . . this idea . . . It feels like you're swinging for the fences."

Jackson stepped forward and poked his old friend in the chest. "That's *exactly* what I'm doing, Sean. And I'm doing it right now."

He glanced at the wall and memorized the website he'd scrawled there.

The whole texture of his day had changed. He had to get on that application process, and quick. He wasn't even sure who had keys to the factory. Shelby Monroe's mother used to run it; maybe she had the keys. He grabbed his wallet from the windowsill where he'd left it and walked out of the bar into the bright Arkansas morning.

As mayor of Bishop, population 4,200, he'd been working hard to fix what was wrong with the community, all so that he could leave it.

And this show might just be his ticket out of here.

Chapter 2

Friday morning, when Jackson stepped into Cora's, the bell over the café door rang and twenty pairs of eyes swung toward him. Every morning, all week, they'd been gathering here, waiting for him to arrive with the mail. City council, business owners, Ben at the newspaper—they looked at him. Wanting. Waiting.

For this moment.

Jackson held up the letter, his smile victorious. "We're in!"

The diner erupted in cheers, his back was slapped, his hand shaken. Ben sat him down in the corner booth, while Cora brought him a piece of rhubarb pie.

"So?" Ben asked when the celebration died down. Everyone settled into chairs and booths with their backs to the counter, facing him. Jackson pushed away the pie; he hated eating while people were watching. "What happens next?"

"Well," Jackson began, tapping the edge of the letter against the table, a sharp snap. Definitive. He liked the sound, so he did it again. "In the next week, Dean Jennings and a camera crew from *America Today* will come to town. Dean will check out our factory, and the camera crew will be putting together a package to air on the show."

"What kind of package?" Cora asked. She had her arms crossed over her Don't Mess With Me, I Haven't

Had My Pie tee shirt. Her black hair, short and natural, was hidden under a wild silk scarf tied in intricate knots around her head. She looked equal parts ironic and tribal. A force of nature.

"A package about us. About Bishop. It says in the letter that it will tell our story." Dean's words from *America Today*—*a good, hard look*—made him sweat, but he couldn't let anyone see that. There were already enough skeptics in the room.

Morning sunlight poured through the big windows, making the chrome shine; the red vinyl of the seats nearly glowed. But the faces in the room were worn. Weary. Hope was in short supply in Bishop these days.

"Shelby Monroe's Art Camps, the Peabody, Cora's." He spread his arms, doing his best Vanna White, showing off the restaurant they all stood in. Its retro diner vibe and excellent southern cooking had been getting noticed in food magazines. "We're a good story. An amazing one."

"That's right," Cora said. "We oughta be proud of ourselves. We oughta be shouting how hard we've worked from the rooftops." Cora, bless her heart and rhubarb pie, had been one of his best supporters. She understood that winning this competition would be good for Bishop. And, considering the work she'd put in on the diner, she was heavily invested in the increased tourism this competition would bring to the town.

Jackson picked up the letter and read the next part.

"After they're done filming, all the segments will be aired on *America Today* at the end of July. Dean Jennings will pick three towns for the finals. Camera crews and reporters for *America Today* will return to the three towns for a live taping—"

"At Honky-tonk Night at The Pour House," Sean announced, always looking to drum up business for his bar.

"Honky-tonk Night will be put on hold until this

competition is over," Jackson said. It was a booze-fueled nightmare, and there was no way in hell it was part of their "story."

"Who are you?" Sean shouted. "Stellan?"

"You mean Stalin, and I'm not."

"What about the Okra Festival?" Gloria, the police chief, asked.

"What about it?"

"The festival is at the beginning of August. People are already getting their floats organized for the parade and the girls are getting ready for the pageant."

"I'm working on my chili recipe," Sean said, prompting most people to groan.

"I don't see why that has to stop," Jackson said. "In fact, it's probably a nice addition to our story. We should move it up to the last weekend of July."

People around the room nodded. It was the hundredth year of the town's festival and despite the fact that there wasn't a single commercial okra factory left in the entire state, it was a beloved tradition.

"So?" Cora asked. "What do we need to do?"

"Everyone get the cars off the lawns. Water the grass, plant some flowers. Clean up your porches." He stared at Gloria, whose husband couldn't walk by a garage sale without picking up a bike he was sure he could fix and sell. Their yard looked like a bike graveyard.

"It's not just us," Gloria said.

"No, it's everyone," Jackson agreed. "I need to repaint the trim on my house. I know a lot of you are in the same boat."

"Who is going to pay for that?" Jim Shore asked. Jim had been mayor when the okra-processing plant finally gasped its last breath and closed, putting half the town out of work. It had given him a heart attack. There were days Jackson was pretty sure he would follow in Jim's footsteps.

"Everyone . . . everyone just do what you can. Ask for help if you need it. I know Sean would love to help paint houses."

"Very funny, Jackson," Sean said, and everyone laughed.

"I don't know when Dean and the producer are going to show up, sometime in the next few days, but let's . . . let's show them our best face. The best version of ourselves. Let's show them that we are the right town for this second chance, that gimmick or not, we're worth noticing. We're worth believing in."

He'd been practicing that rallying speech for a few days now (modified slightly in case they didn't make the semifinals), and from the way the faces in the room had lightened, it had worked.

Mel Gibson in *Braveheart* had nothing on him.

"Thank you, Mayor," Cora said, lifting a coffee mug in toast to him. "For all you've done."

There was a smattering of applause. Even Sean put down his fork long enough to clap his hands.

Uncomfortable with the attention and accolades, Jackson sat back down in the booth and stared at the rhubarb pie. He loved rhubarb pie, and Cora made the best he'd ever had. A tangy, sweet, artery-clogging delight.

But surprisingly, despite the victory, he couldn't eat.

Please, he prayed. *Please don't let me fail them. Not now, not when it really matters.*

If this worked, the town would be self-sufficient and he'd be free. Free to walk away from Bishop and the sticky webs of expectation and duty. He could move to Vegas, look at beautiful women who wouldn't be prompted by the first sign of his interest to bake him a casserole and start talking about a spring wedding. He could have sex with a lot of women. A few at the same time if he wanted. He could sleep in, or even not sleep at all. Drink too much. Jump out of airplanes. Hell, get a tattoo.

He could do whatever he wanted.

But if this all failed . . .

It's not going to fail, he told himself, not feeling at all like Braveheart anymore. *You will make this work, like you have made everything else work.*

There were harder things than pulling a town back from the edge of bankruptcy.

Taking care of Gwen was harder. Giving up his life. Knowing that he couldn't fix what happened and being reminded of that failure every time he looked at her. That was much harder.

Cora slid in across from him, her brown eyes alight.

"What's wrong with the pie?" she asked.

"Nothing, not a thing." Jackson pulled the pie toward him and took a big bite, despite a stomach full of everyone's expectations.

"Is that a dog?" asked the girl behind the desk. She had the dewy skin of youth and apparently X-ray eyes.

"Heavens, no!" Monica Appleby, without hesitation, went right for the lie. "Why would you think I have a dog?"

"Because that's a dog carrier." Gwen, according to her name tag, pointed at the hot-pink bag with mesh sides that Monica, in her fog of grief and weariness, had put right on top of the check-in desk.

Monica stared at the bag as if she'd never seen it before, ready to follow this lie to the ends of the earth if that was what it took to get her within falling distance of a bed.

After the worst funeral ever recorded, a hellacious redeye flight (during which the non-dog in the non-carrier whimpered and cried like it was being tortured by terrorist cats), and an epic dawn drive to this backwater town in the middle of nowhere where years ago her life was torn apart by a bullet, she wasn't going down because of a *dog*.

"Is that what that is?" she asked innocently.

"It's okay. The Peabody allows dogs up to twenty pounds."

Of course they did.

"Well, if I *had* a dog," Monica said, "that would be a welcome relief."

The girl was on to her—her straight face gave Monica all kinds of shit—but Monica felt compelled to hold onto the story. *One thing. I need one thing to go my way tonight.*

Finally, Gwen nodded as if accepting the fact that Monica was just going to lie.

It said something about how low Monica had sunk that she wanted to hug the girl.

"What name is the reservation under?"

"Monica Appleby."

It took all of ten seconds for Monica to regret using her own name. Gwen looked up at her, mouth slightly open. The teenager stared blatantly at Monica's rather famous chest, her face, her hair, and then, as it all seemed to check out against that picture most of the world had in their head of her, squealed.

"Ohmigod, you're—"

She nodded, forcing her lips to curve past a grimace into a smile. "Monica Appleby, I just told you."

"Ohmigod!" Gwen lifted her hands, waving them in front of her face as if fending off the vapors.

"Keep breathing," she said, managing to smile in earnest. It was the face-wave thing, always an entertaining reflex. "We'll get through it together."

"I loved your book."

"I'm so glad."

"Did you really sleep with all those rock stars?"

"They slept with me, actually—an important distinction."

"Totally," Gwen sighed as if she understood. But Monica had her doubts. "You look different."

"Rocker goth chick is a hard look to carry when you're thirty." Even Joan Jett had cleaned up, after all. And Monica was no Joan Jett.

Again, Gwen nodded sagely, as if from her post behind the Peabody check-in desk she'd seen it all before.

"So . . . my room?"

"Oh right, sorry." Gwen clacked around on her computer and Monica turned slightly, put the dog carrier on the floor, and looked around. According to the website she'd used to make the reservation, the Peabody was not only the only hotel within a thirty-mile radius, but had the dubious honor of being the last standing antebellum plantation home in the state.

Even in her crappy mood, Monica had to admit the place was beautiful. The cut-crystal chandelier caught the sun streaming through the rose windows and sent it sparkling around the domed ceilings, across the paintings of dogs and horses and cotton fields at rest. Wainscoting was bathed in rainbows, hardwood floors were splashed with sun.

There were elegant cherrywood chairs gathered in small groups, just waiting for the chance to host high tea. An old-world drink cart was set up in the corner, where guests could help themselves from decanters of booze that glowed like amber in the sunlight.

There was no music piped in anywhere, and she could hear the sounds of birds. Of quiet.

It was beautiful, all that carefully restored antebellum detail.

And it made her skin itch, her lungs tight. Claustrophobia wasn't going to be far behind.

It will be okay, she told herself. *You did the right thing coming here.*

Not that she'd had much of a choice in the end.

The silence suddenly registered and Monica realized that Gwen was watching her, probably waiting for her to say something.

"It's beautiful," Monica said, pushing her sunglasses up higher onto her nose.

When in doubt, compliment. That particular piece of Jenna's advice had never steered her wrong.

"It's been a true labor of love," Gwen said, her voice as southern as pecans and peaches, as if she were suddenly reading the script of a southern belle. Front-desk staff probably had a speech they had to memorize.

"Whose?"

"What?"

"Whose labor of love?" It was hard to imagine someone loving this place like that. Her feelings about Bishop, Arkansas, were deeply, firmly situated on the other side of the spectrum.

"Jackson Davies." Gwen nodded, some of the teenage eagerness hardening. "He's the mayor. He got all these historical societies to invest. It was a real big deal."

"Cool." Monica pushed her sunglasses up onto her forehead, digging at her gritty eyes as if she wished she could just pull them out and be done with it.

"I like your mom's show," Gwen said. *Oh God,* this conversation was going from bad to worse. Monica wanted to tell her that watching Simone's reality show, *What Simone Wants,* was not only going to rot her brain with its sheer stupidity, but it would not endear Gwen to Monica.

The last forty-eight hours rolled over her and she sighed heavily. "Can I . . . just get my key?"

Gwen's face fell as if Monica had squashed a bunny right in front of her.

Monica hitched her laptop backpack high on her shoulder. She was being rude; she totally understood that. The sunglasses, her tone, lying about the dog, even the torn collar of her Sex Pistols shirt seemed boorish. But she had nothing left in the tank for a starstruck teenager who wanted to talk about Simone's antics.

I'm sorry I'm not what you expected, she thought. *I can't be what everyone expects every single second of my life. I'm tired and I'm sad and I just want to go to sleep.*

Gwen blushed to her eyebrows and started to fumble around, gathering keys and brochures.

"I'm sorry, Gwen. I'm just super tired."

"Totally, I totally get it." She waved her hand in front of her face to imply it didn't matter, but Monica felt like a capital-A asshole. "Oh, you know? I think this is for you." Flustered and bright red, Gwen held out a folded piece of thick ivory stationery.

Monica stared at the paper as if it were a snake. "Me?"

Gwen nodded, shaking the paper.

Monica carefully unfolded it, as if the wrong move might make it pop.

Welcome, the note said, *I would love to personally welcome you to Bishop. After you've settled in please accept my invitation for a light dinner at my home. Sincerely, Jackson Davies.*

Wow. Just . . . . wow.

"How did Jackson know I was in town?" she asked.

"Jackson?" Gwen shrugged, one of those eloquent teenage shrugs that spoke a complicated ancient language. "He knows everything. It's a small town."

It was that damn *Rolling Stone* article. She'd told the reporter that she was coming down here to write about her father, a jazz musician of very little success but, thanks to the way he died, some cult status. Jackson must have read the article.

Maybe he wanted to help her set up interviews. Get her the police files.

Or maybe her editor had called and paved the way with the locals.

Either way, it was the kick in the pants she needed to start working.

Thank you for the invitation, I'd be delighted, she scrawled across the bottom of the note before refolding it and handing it back to Gwen.

"Can you see that he gets this?"

Wide-eyed, Gwen nodded.

Monica grabbed the key and picked up the dog carrier. Inside, Reba barked once, the sound unmistakable. Gwen, bless her heart, ignored it.

"Top of the stairs to the left," she said, and Monica turned. But Gwen kept talking, clearly unable to let her just walk away. "Why are you here? I mean, no one like you ever comes here."

"I'm writing a book about the murder," she sighed.

Gwen's eyes went wide, the scent of scandal and heartbreak and blood in the air. "What murder?" she whispered.

"My father's."

Chapter 3

Monica took Gwen's blank-faced look of astonishment as her cue to leave and nearly ran across the rose-and-vine carpet, up the stairs, and to the far corner of the beautifully restored plantation home. She unlocked the door to her room and slipped inside the hushed dimness. The shades were drawn against the bright sunlight, and the bed, with its thick mattress and snowy blankets, beckoned.

Reba barked again.

"Hold your horses," she muttered, then went into the bathroom with the carrier. Carefully setting it down on the floor, she unzipped the side and waited for what had to be the most ridiculous-looking dog to ever walk the earth to come barreling out. But there was only a whimper from inside the carrier.

She's spoiled, Jenna had said. *Temperamental and demanding. You two are made for each other.*

Monica rolled her eyes and got down on her knees. In the shadows of the carrier the dog cowered, pink ribbons quivering, rhinestone collar glittering in the bathroom light.

"Come here, dog."

The dog didn't budge.

Monica sighed and prayed for strength. Jenna had asked her to take this dog as though she'd been asking Monica to take her child and Monica, already depleted, already worn raw by Jenna's illness and all the hospital bills, had agreed. She'd agreed as if she couldn't wait to care for another creature. As if the company of a hair-less Chinese Crested dog was what her solitary life was missing.

"I live in hotels. I don't like dogs. Jenna was desperate, or she never would have picked me," she told Reba, bracing her elbows on the white tiles of the bathroom. Reba crept closer, the white fur on her paws and ears shaking as she inched her way into the light. She blinked into the wilderness of the bathroom, looking past Monica as if searching for Jenna.

"I miss her too," she whispered, bracing her face in her hands. She blinked away the bite of tears; the days of grief were over. She had work to do, a book to write, and Jenna's medical bills to pay off.

Monica reached out to touch the pink ribbon nestled in the wild hair around Reba's head. That hair grew nowhere else on her skinny, spotted body. "You don't even know how ridiculous you are," she whispered.

As if affronted, Reba growled and snapped at her.

Monica stood, grabbed Reba under her tiny smooth belly (which was weird and intimate and kind of made Monica's skin crawl), and lifted her up to look into her little brown eyes, nearly buried behind the white fur.

"I don't know what to do with you."

Reba squirmed and Monica set her down. Delicately shaking out her legs, the dog ran across the bathroom into the dark bedroom. With one smooth leap she was on the bed, turning circles before curling up on the pillow closest to the window.

Monica hung her head, wondering how much more bizarre her life was going to get on this awful trip down memory lane in Bishop, Arkansas.

"That's my side of the bed," she told the dog, who didn't care.

* * *

After a four-hour nap, she fired off some reassuring emails to her agent and publisher that yes, she'd arrived safely. That yes, she was okay and she was totally thrilled, absolutely over the moon, to start work on Monday.

Which bought her a few more days before having to think about her father and the murder.

Was murder even the right word? Monica wasn't sure of the lingo when it came to things like self-defense. *Killed?*

Outside the window, a bird flew across a sky so blue it made her eyes hurt.

She was here to write about the night her mother killed her father in self-defense.

It wasn't quite as dramatic as murder, but it was far more accurate.

I'll go with that.

She went down to the front desk, now manned by a young man with slick black hair. There was a small indentation in his nose, a hole pierced for a nose ring. Nose rings were undoubtedly *verboten* at this job.

The boy caught sight of her and started to beam, nearly levitating with his sudden uncontrollable excitement. Some days she felt like she was the pied piper of the pierced teenage masses. The poster child for adolescent rebellion in all its forms.

You wrote the damn book on it, she thought. *What did you expect?*

None of it, was the answer. Not a single part of her life had gone at all as she'd expected, and the last two years had been so surreal, she hardly recognized herself or her place in this world.

"Gwen said you were here," he said as she stepped up to the desk, situated just beneath the wide, curving staircase. "I didn't believe her."

Monica, a new woman after the nap and some in-room coffee, managed a bright smile. "Here I am."

"Can I," the boy lifted his phone, "take your picture?"

"Here's the thing," she said, glancing at his name tag, "Jay. Let's say you take that picture and I know you mean me no harm, but you're excited and you put that on your Facebook page. Maybe you tweet it. And the next thing I know, there are assholes with cameras leaping out of bushes." She winced for effect, and Jay was already putting the camera down. Most people just needed the domino effect explained to them. How one picture could bring down her whole world. "I came here—"

"To write about the murder." Monica didn't correct him; it seemed like too much effort. "I know. Gwen said. My dad was at The Pour House that night, with my uncle and a bunch of his friends. I bet you could talk to him. I bet you could talk to all of them!"

"That's great, Jay," she lied. It wasn't great. The thought made her nauseous. But the reality was, talking to people who'd been there that night was exactly what she needed to do. In her last book, *Wild Child*, she'd just opened a vein and bled all over the page, but she was only six the night of the shooting. And her memories were hazy, most of them willingly buried. She was going to have to talk to some people who remembered the event better than she did.

And she had no doubt this town was going to love that. If there was one universal in this world, it was humanity's love of scandal and suffering.

"And I'll keep that in mind, but I came down to see if there were any messages. If anyone called."

"No calls. But here." Jay held out another folded piece of stationery. Notes. She was passing notes with a man named Jackson Davies.

Sometimes her life seemed weird even to her.

Dinner will be at six, the note said. *Please join me for a cocktail at five.*

His address was written at the bottom.

Thank you, I'll see you at five, she wrote, folded the note, and handed it to Jay. Who, as solemnly as if she'd handed him the Treaty of Versailles, took it from her, setting it on the edge of the desk.

"I'll have someone run this over to him," he said, confirming that, yes, she'd slipped down a rabbit hole and gone back in time.

Monica thanked him and left, wondering what she was going to wear.

And what she would do with the damn dog.

A half hour later, the doorbell rang, a gong that echoed through the house. Jackson sprinted down the stairs and slid across the foyer to check his look in the mirror over the buffet in the dining room. He patted down his hair and straightened his tie. It had been a drama picking out that tie, but in the end he'd gone for the yellow. Suddenly he wished he'd picked the blue.

For a moment, feeling strange and disjointed, he wished he could slip out the back. Across the garden to the fields past the trees. He'd just keep walking. Across the border into Mississippi. He'd change his name. Change his whole story. Get blind drunk, have sex with a woman he didn't know. Start a fight.

He'd never been in a fight. Wasn't that weird? Most men had been in a fight by the time they were twenty-nine, right? He was totally missing out.

The doorbell gonged again.

Right. Real life. Dinner and the salvation of Bishop, Arkansas.

He stepped into the hallway and through the warped glass of the windows framing the door he saw a thin figure, wearing a skirt. A woman. *Interesting.* And she was alone, it would seem.

Marianne, their housekeeper, had made way too much food.

He opened the door. "Welcome—"

The words died on his lips. It was a beautiful woman—more than beautiful, actually. She was erotic in her black skirt with the red belt and the green blouse that hugged her waist and her lush breasts, inviting his eyes and hands to do the same. It was a trick some women knew, how to stay totally covered, but utterly suggestive all the same. He loved that trick, highly approved of that trick. She wore red shoes, high heels with peeka-boo toes.

He approved of the shoes, too.

Jackson didn't spend a whole lot of time thinking about all the sex he wasn't having in this town that expected him to be father figure and monk, rolled into one. It would send him over the edge if he did. But looking at this woman, and the bright pink of her toenail polish, he was painfully, tragically aware of all the sex he wasn't having.

Her black hair was thick, nearly blue it was so dark, and in the humidity the curls were teasing her chin and the corners of her eyes. Something tickled in the back of his head. Some memory. Those purple eyes were familiar . . . very familiar.

"Monica Appleby?" His famous graciousness fled the scene. "What the hell are you doing here?"

Her heavy black eyebrows practically hit her hairline and her mouth fell open, revealing the tips of white teeth. The fact that he found *her teeth* erotic only proved how distressing his sex life was. "You invited me."

"You work for *America Today*?"

"The TV show? No."

"Then what—" He stopped, suddenly realizing what must have happened. "There's been a mix-up with the notes."

"If only there was a more reliable mode of communication."

He took her sarcasm in stride. "Good point."

For no good reason, he remembered the one time he'd seen Monica in person. Three days after the shooting. Jackson, at five, hadn't been able to put into words the sick feeling in his stomach, watching Simone and Monica, beaten and bruised and terrified, get into their car and drive away, but he knew he had no business seeing that private moment. It was why he'd never watched that horrible reality show Simone and Monica had been a part of sixteen years ago. Or Simone's more recent show. It was also why he didn't read Monica's blockbuster book, *Wild Child,* that everyone else on the planet seemed to have read last year.

Looking at her now, at her beauty and poise, it was hard to believe she'd been that girl—so lost and scared. It was even harder to believe that she was here, at his home. Beautiful and erotic, a postcard from the outside world.

Suddenly the night took on new dimension and he was thrilled that it wasn't Dean Jennings on his porch.

"Let's try this again, shall we?" he asked. "I'm Jackson Davies." He held out his hand and she laughed, though her tone was suspicious.

"Monica Appleby." When they shook hands, he found himself unwilling to let go of hers. It was soft, her palm warm in his hand. His blood began to pound through his veins.

"A pleasure, Ms. Appleby." He stepped to the side. "Perhaps I can better explain the problem with the notes over a cocktail."

For some reason his invitation made her frown, which set off a whole domino effect in him. Women didn't frown at him, as a rule. They smiled, and cooed. They ingratiated themselves with their casseroles and secret spring wedding plans.

"You're awfully polite, aren't you?" she asked. "Do they have a section in the Southern Manners Handbook about how to deal with guests when they aren't who you were expecting?"

"I haven't looked at the handbook in years, but I imagine they do." He smiled. "Does polite bother you?"

"It does. People rarely mean what they say when they're being polite. I find that they usually mean the opposite."

Jackson laughed, charmed and at the same time poised on the edge of himself, ready for anything. It was an intoxicating feeling. "You're not wrong," he said.

She snorted and he loved it. So disrespectful that snort, so honest. He loved it so much that he acted on impulse, stuck his toe off the path he'd so carefully created for himself and this town. There was no room in his life for detours; it was win the contest, get his sister safely to school, and get the hell out of Bishop. That was the path.

But when Monica Appleby showed up at a guy's door, he would be an idiot to turn her away.

He held out an arm, ushering her in.

"Please. Join me for dinner."

It took her a second to respond; whatever her misgivings were, they were serious, which was intriguing on a whole different level. Jackson was a man people trusted. It was exciting to be unknown to her. Perhaps dangerous.

"All right." She stepped into his stale and stagnant home loaded with duty and years of respectability, and immediately it was new.

As she walked by him, he caught the smell of something feminine and complicated.

The delicious aroma of trouble.

* * *

It took a few seconds for her eyes to adjust to the interior. But once they did, she felt as if she'd stepped into someplace familiar. As lovely as the Peabody was, there was something very . . . staged about it. A beautiful girl who knew her appeal.

But Jackson's house, as grand in scale as the Peabody, was a home, filled with the lovely and worn things that made it one. It reminded her, not in layout or scope, but in detail and feel, of Jenna's mom's house outside Nashville, where Monica had spent the last two months with her dying friend.

Growing up as she had, rootless and wandering, Monica had made a study of homes. And the difference between a house and a home wasn't anything you could point at; it was a feeling. A sense of a group of lives lived together, in tandem and opposition, messy and sweet and complicated.

She sighed, some of her tension dissipating.

From the hallway, there were two doorways on either side of her. Through the door to her left, she glimpsed a deep couch, squishy embroidered pillows tossed in its corners like spare change. One of the pillows declared "Family is Forever."

Hmmmm . . . a promise, or a threat?

Through the other door was a large walnut dining-room table, a bowl of humble pink tea roses at its center. A black dog, white around the muzzle, wandered through from the dining room into the hall. It brushed against her legs once, a warm hello, and then headed into the sitting room, where it sighed and flopped onto the hardwood floor in front of the couch. Its collar jangled as it settled.

"We're set up in the back," Jackson said.

His voice was masculine and low, the sound of dark chocolate with a hint of spice, of a California Syrah aged just right. It touched her spine, that voice, brushed across the nape of her neck, reminding her briefly that there was still pleasure in this world.

Everything about Jackson seemed built for pleasure. For elegance. He was lean, but broad in all the right places. His linen jacket looked tailored to fit his shoulders, and when he smiled at her, she couldn't help but frown.

It wasn't just his looks; she'd had a surplus of hot men in her life. Her mother, after all, was Simone Appleby. Simone, before the reality show—probably what *led* to the reality show—had become notorious for dating famous men. Sports stars, rock stars, actors. The only things required from them were good looks and an increasing fan base.

Monica had learned that good looks were a trap for the unwary.

And she had become very, very wary.

But still, even with handsome men, she could put forth the smile they expected.

Not with this man. He was disconcerting with all his contradictions. His lovely light eyes were shadowed by stern eyebrows. His lips—the top one sculpted, the bottom one lush—were held in a firm line. His blond hair curved away from his face as if scared to droop over that long forehead.

He managed to be both stern and beautiful.

And the twinkle in his eyes was utterly boyish.

"Is something wrong?" he asked in that voice that made her want to curl against it.

"No." She waved her hand, forced a smile. "Your house is lovely."

"It's been in my family since before the Civil War."

"Oh, then it must have a name, right? All the good southern manors do."

He blushed slightly, and she laughed. "It does! Spill it."

"They . . . I mean, it's always been called the Big House."

"That is astonishingly unimaginative."

"I agree."

She pointed toward the elegant wooden staircase that curved from the main floor up to a wide landing on the second. "Is Scarlett O'Hara going to make an appearance?"

"There are some days I wouldn't be surprised."

"Are you . . . do you live here alone?" she asked, half expecting a passel of blond children in seersucker to come charging from the shadows, a blond wife with perfect eyebrows she never had to wax to hang on his arm and call him darling.

Jackson had to be some woman's darling.

Though perhaps he was too young for all of that. He didn't look thirty.

"With your parents?" she asked, imagining a Tennessee Williams scenario brought to life.

"No, actually, my parents are dead. A car accident."

She blinked, stunned at the sudden revelation of such personal information from the polished man. He looked slightly stunned himself, as if he didn't know where the words had come from.

"I'm so sorry."

He tried to wave it away. "It's okay. I'm not sure why I brought it up. It's a long time ago, now."

Jenna used to do this thing when she was lying about the pain—she'd smile real wide as if everything were fine, but her whole body would stiffen as if braced for a punch. Jackson was doing the same thing, lying with his face, telling the truth with his body. However long ago it may have been, he was living with his parents' death every day.

Amazing, she thought—*we have so much in common.*

"Would you like a drink? We're all set up in the back."

"Sounds great," she said, falling into step with him as they headed through the rest of the house, past a white tiled kitchen with aging appliances.

The back garden was like a scene from a movie, or a magazine article about how to throw an elegant outdoor party.

"It's so beautiful," she sighed. The lights, the slight flap of the linens on the table—it was all so inviting.

"I'm glad you like it. Wine?" He dug a bottle of white wine from a bucket of ice and water, but she shook her head and pointed to the glass decanter of lemonade sweating in the humidity.

"Lemonade would be great."

He seemed slightly surprised, but there was nothing she could do about that anymore.

"So what was *America Today* coming over for?" she asked, accepting her lemonade. Her finger brushed his on the handoff, and something charged and slightly painful swirled through her. Awareness, sexual and sharp. She took a step back, her heel sinking into the grass. "Or do you often have morning shows over for dinner?"

Jackson poured himself a glass of wine and she couldn't help but watch him, the sharp line of his nose, the delicate lace of his outrageously long eyelashes. Why did men always get those kinds of eyelashes?

"*America Today* and Maybream Crackers are hosting a competition for small towns that have lost industry. Maybream will move its whole operation to the town that wins the contest. We've made the semifinals."

She blinked, eyes wide, a bunch of incredulous rude words springing to her lips, but she swallowed them.

Clearly, her experience in this town was not the norm.
This was a beloved home to lots of people; she'd be well
served to remember that. "Congratulations."

"Thank you." He inclined his head. "Though so far it
just means we have a suitable factory. The hard part
comes this week."

"You have to eat those cookies they make?"

He laughed. "No. At least I hope not."

"They are gross."

"That is the consensus."

"So how did I get the invite and not them?"

"I had left the invitation to dinner with the hotel staff
and told them to pass it on to the producer and crew,
who are supposed to arrive sometime in the next few
days to film. And considering how few celebrities we get
out here, Gwen must have thought you were involved in
some way."

" 'Celebrity' is a stretch."

"Your book has made you famous. I heard they were
talking about making a movie—"

A bee buzzed over her lemonade and she waved it
away, feeling its wings momentarily against her fingers, a
minor brush with danger. As close as she got these days.
"There's always talk."

"Still, from what I understand it's a very popular
book."

She eyed him shrewdly, delighting in the way he
seemed so obtuse about the book, talking about it in the
abstract. "Why do I get the sense you haven't read it?"

"Is it obvious?" He laughed, still gracious, and she
wondered what it would take for him to drop his guard.
As soon as the thought occurred to her, she was stunned
by how badly she wanted to see that. He was flirting with
her and he'd never read the book. Every man who flirted
with her these days looked at her as if waiting for the

show—the big sex rock-star show—which was probably why she didn't flirt much anymore.

"Afraid so—you haven't asked me any questions about rock stars."

"You caught me. One of the few people left in the world who hasn't read *Wild Child*."

"Well, it's a sordid tale. Not for everyone."

"Trust me, my ignorance doesn't make you any less a celebrity."

"I'm afraid that's exactly what it does." She was actually enjoying herself. Amazing.

"I read your first book. The one about groupies," he said. Her heart kicked at the reminder. That was how she'd met Jenna. A kindred damaged soul, Jenna had spent her formative years backstage making the same bad decisions Monica was making.

"So *you* were the one," she joked, pushing aside her grief.

"I read your book of poems, too." She groaned, putting her head in her hand, and he smiled, that half-boy, half-man smile that went right to her knees. They each took a sip from their glass as if rinsing out the end of that conversation.

"You're awfully young to be a mayor, aren't you?" she asked.

He stared down at his wineglass as if the liquid had something to tell him, but then he shook his head and took a long sip. "No one else wanted the job," he said. "And aren't you a little young to be a worldwide best-selling author?"

"Well, considering I was a sixteen-year-old runaway, I had a lot of room for improvement." Her heels kept sinking in the lawn and she pulled them out, lurching toward him by accident. His hand grabbed her elbow, the bare skin there warming on contact. The younger her, the damaged kid, would have gone bonkers to have this handsome man touching her in any way. On that kid's behalf, Monica memorized the sensation.

"I can't imagine that improvement was easy." He let go of her, one finger at a time, and the intimacy of the conversation, his touch—all of it was too much.

"Well, it made for good reading." She stepped away, popping that small inclusive bubble of intimacy around them. "It looks like you were going to entertain a crowd. I'm sorry I wasn't who you were expecting."

"I'm not. Sorry, I mean." His words did something to her heart, disturbed the mechanics, and she thought she was past all that: the blushing, the sweaty palms, the heart thumping. Those were things for another woman, lifetimes younger.

And yet here she was contemplating a girlish giggle.

Coy behavior was for the old Monica she had spent years burying, and so instead she stared right at him.

"Are you flirting with me, Jackson Davies?"

"I thought *you* were flirting with *me*." His smile was an invitation to deeper secrets, darker rooms.

"It's mutual, then," she said.

"I can't believe I'm so lucky."

Me neither, she thought. *The only man in the world who hasn't read that damn book.* They smiled at each other in silence, until Jackson finally blinked and turned away slightly as if the moment had been a little too much for him.

What are you doing? she asked herself. *What is the point of flirting with him? There's no way any of this will go anywhere.*

And that was the appeal. Flirting in a safe place, dropping her armor, revealing herself in glimpses and side glances. All the while knowing nothing would happen.

He was too much of a gentleman to pursue anything

without the right signals from her, and she was far too broken to even know what those signals would be.

"I remember you," he blurted, and then winced. "I'm sorry."

She nodded, bracing herself internally, but externally she laughed. A version of the trick from Jenna, only Monica was far better at it. "That day outside the police station? It looked like most of the town showed up."

"I'm sorry," he said, and that was shocking. The apology actually took a few moments to assimilate. "After what you had been through, you deserved better than people standing around to watch you leave."

She glanced at her lemonade and lifted it, as if to take a sip, but realized she had no taste for it.

"Thank you," she said, meeting his eyes again.

"So, Monica," he changed the subject with grace. "How long are you staying in our fair town?"

"Indefinitely," she said and he blinked and straightened, as if he'd been poked.

"The Wild Child is moving to Bishop?"

Her heels sank again and she jerked them out, uncomfortable with the nickname, a leftover from that ill-fated two-year reality show Simone had signed them up for when Monica was a teenager, ripe for rebellion. And while the moniker might have worked when she was sixteen, at thirty it was wearing thin. She hadn't danced on a table, started a fight, smoked drugs, screwed another girl's boyfriend, or any of the other things she did on and off the screen in years, though no one seemed to care.

Titling the book *Wild Child* had been her publisher's idea, and all it did was make sure no one ever forgot the girl she'd been.

She'd written two works of nonfiction, the first a pretty crappy exposé on groupies, the second a bestseller about growing up a wild child, a life lived on the

road and backstage, traveling around the world and
through the rocky and terrible terrain between girlhood
and womanhood.

She'd written bad poetry, waited tables, traveled the
world, and held her best friend's hand while Jenna died
in near poverty, too proud to ask for money until it was
too late.

But no one was interested in those things.

It was as though she were in frozen animation—a
wild child forever.

"Not quite. I'm here to write a book, and I'm not sure
how long it will take."

"What's your book about?" He eyed her over the edge
of his glass before taking a sip.

"The night my father was shot."

He swallowed and coughed. "The murder?"

Inwardly, she cringed. She really was growing to hate
that word.

"Yeah. I'm a little behind and my deadline is coming
up quick, so I need to do some interviews this week."

"Interviews?" He made it sound as if she'd said rectal
exams. "With whom?"

"Some of the people there that night."

"This has to be a joke," he muttered. "It has to be."

She laughed, awkwardly trying to fend off his tension, his increasingly obvious dismay. "Is this a problem
for you?"

"A problem? That you, Monica Appleby, are writing a
book about the night your father was shot dead by your
mother in Bishop, the most notorious crime in our history? And you want to talk about it with people here?
This week?"

She didn't like it said that way, the part about her
mother—it was like someone dragging a rake over a
chalkboard, and all of her internal organs cringed.

"I'm not sure why this is important to you, or why you're suddenly being an insensitive jerk about it."

"Oh Jesus." He put down his glass with a thump, his eyes widening as if he'd just thought of some new horror. "Is your mother coming?"

"No. And who the hell cares if she does?"

"I do. I have one week, Monica. One week to get this town to win that damn TV show, and I can't have any drama or theatrics get in the way."

"I'm not here to cause trouble."

"But isn't that what you do? Isn't that what you've always done?"

She stiffened and set down her own glass. All that lovely buzzing awareness, all that sweetness behind those eyelashes—it was all gone. "I'm going to go back to the Peabody. Thanks for the lemonade."

She took off across the lawn and left Jackson swearing under his breath. She was inside the house before he caught up with her. His touch on her elbow made her whirl. Life had not done her a whole lot of favors in the last few months. She was raw with grief and confusion, and more than ready to use smacking the daylights out of his handsome face as a reason to feel better.

He held up his hands. "I'm sorry," he said.

"Good." She continued walking; the sound of her heels hitting the oak floors of the Big House had a satisfying violence. If only she could punch holes through that floor.

"No, Monica, please." He stepped around her, barring her exit. She huffed to a stop.

"This is a little much, Jackson."

"I am deeply sorry for the way I was talking. Especially about your father's death. I extend my sincere regret."

"You can stick your sincere regret—"

"Please." He smiled, but it was careful again, strained—

that whole lying with his face, telling the truth with his body thing—and for some reason that made her pause. "I . . . I am heavily invested in the results of this show. The whole town is, as you can imagine. The okra-processing plant has closed, the recession has hit us particularly hard, and the town needs this competition. And it needs to win. And perhaps I'm paranoid, but I have worked very hard to make sure that nothing jeopardizes our chances."

"And you think I will?"

"I think . . . you," again he gave that careful smile as if he were trying to sidetrack her from the horseshit he was throwing at her, "and talk of the murder might be a . . . distraction."

"I have a book to write. A deadline. People are counting on me."

"People are counting on *me*." He shook his head, correcting himself. "On this show, I mean."

Total deadlock. They stared at each other.

"Just spit it out—what do you want?" she asked.

"Can you . . . leave? Just for the week?"

It took some effort to pretend her heart didn't take a dent after all that flirting to be told it would be better if she left. Another reason why flirting was best left to the young. She was not nearly as resilient as she used to be. She took this shit personally.

"Screw you."

"You asked."

"Well, I'm not about to leave and I'm not about to stay locked in my hotel room, Jackson."

"There's a compromise here," Jackson said.

She crossed her arms over her chest. "Sure."

"Can you just not . . . interview people for a week?"

"No."

He sighed, hard. "Do you know what 'compromise' means?"

For a moment she contemplated giving him nothing. Contemplated, in fact, setting up a booth in his precious downtown and inviting everyone to come and tell her their favorite story about her and her mother.

Maybe she'd organize some reenactments.

"Monica," he said, dropping all that charm for the moment, and she saw just briefly the strings he held, the control he was trying so hard to exert. It was so vulnerable she wanted to turn her head away; it was like watching a car crash on the highway. "I cannot express how important it is that nothing jeopardize this *America Today* contest. They'll be examining us closely this week, and that night . . . I don't want them to see that night."

Monica had very little practice in not doing exactly what she wanted, exactly when she wanted. Outside of taking care of Jenna, she'd spent the last few years answering only to her publishing house. And to what passed for her conscience. She was as spoiled as Reba. So her compromise was rusty and came out petulant.

"Okay, because I understand the situation, even though you're a jackass—"

"True. Very true."

"I'll interview people quietly."

"Quietly?"

"I'll be discreet. That's all you get."

"Then I guess I'll take it."

Sun fell through the window over the door in a box of light, right between them, filled with glittering dust motes and the stench of his judgment. They stared at each other, all pretense gone. That zinging awareness from the backyard had turned sour.

I see you, she thought. *All the parts you hide behind that smile. And they aren't all pretty.*

"I liked you better when you were polite," she said.

"I liked you better when you were flirting with me."
Like that is ever going to happen again.

"Goodbye," she said and passed through that glittering box of sunlight, through his judgment, to the other side and right out the front door.

Turns out The Big House—and Jackson—were a disappointment, like so many others.

Chapter 4

Twilight sank over Bishop, and the Big House always got dark the moment the sun slipped behind the oak trees. Jackson pulled his shirt on over his head and walked the shadowed hallways to his sister's room.

He knocked lightly on her closed door and since it wasn't latched, it swung open, revealing his sister on her bed, head bent over a book. Gwen's natural habitat.

Bubba, the old mutt, lay curled up at the foot of her bed, despite both of them being told dogs didn't belong on beds.

"Hey," he said, leaning against the doorjamb, keeping the bubble of distance between them.

The bubble.

A few months ago, when things got really dicey between them—that was when he noticed the bubble. The distance that lived and breathed between them. If he shifted left, she shifted right. If he walked into a room, she'd walk out. And it had seemed like a new phenomenon. But lately, at night, aware of the silence in the house and its slightly malevolent nature, he wondered if it had been there longer.

If it wasn't something he'd created years ago, coming home from law school to take care of his eleven-year-old sister after the accident. He'd been clueless and sad and resentful, and maybe . . . he created the bubble. Considering the most recent example of his dynamic and powerful people skills with Monica, there was a very, very good chance that the bubble was his fault.

And now he had no idea what to do about it.

She just needs to get to college, he thought. *Spread her wings.* And maybe she was picking up on the fact that he was ready to spread his wings, too.

The thought—and the guilt that came with it—gave him heartburn.

"Gwen?"

She glanced up, her wheat-colored hair slipping down over one eye. One black-rimmed, heavily made-up eye.

"What . . . what's on your face?" he asked.

She looked back down. "Nothing."

"That eye makeup. Were you wearing that at your shift at the hotel?"

She sighed heavily, the sigh of judgment. Condemnation. *Jackson,* the sigh said, *you're a total jackass.*

Yeah, he thought, *and you look like a freaking owl with that shit around your eyes.* But he didn't say anything. He wasn't her father, as she so loved to point out.

"Pick your battles" was more than just a catchy saying. It was going to be his very first tattoo. Words to live by.

"What are you going to do tonight?" he asked.

"Hang out."

"With anyone, or by yourself?"

It didn't occur to him until after he said it how the words might hurt her. At her age, his whole life had revolved around friends, being social. Her aloneness seemed unnatural. And her reluctance to try to socialize was even more troubling.

She shrugged, and he fought with superhuman effort not to march into the room, pop the bubble, and shake her.

"You should invite some friends over," he urged, worried, always worried.

"I like being by myself."

Right. It wasn't normal, it *couldn't* be normal to want

to be alone all the time, but if he pushed, she pulled, and then nothing would get accomplished.

"I'm going out to The Pour House," he said. "Text me if you're going someplace."

She hummed in her throat, her eyes still on the book, and he waited another second as if she might look up and smile at him the way she used to. But she didn't, and he knocked slightly on the door before walking away. He got three steps before he stopped and turned back around.

"You want to go see a movie or something?" he asked.

That made her stop reading.

"What?"

"A movie, get some ice cream . . ." He shrugged.

"It's poker night," she said.

"I know, but . . . I'd skip it if you wanted to go see a movie."

She looked at him for a long moment, and in her blue eyes, so like their mother's, he saw his sister and a total stranger. Gwen was a genius, reading at age three, completing complicated algebra problems in grade five. She'd finished the entire curriculum of her sophomore year of high school, including calculus and zoology, during two and a half months of summer school.

For about a year when she was twelve he'd been slightly scared of her, even went to Memphis twice a month so both of them could see counselors. The counselor he'd seen had told him to make sure Gwen was still a kid, that she did kid stuff.

So in between her reading the classics and taking on-line physics classes at the University of Tennessee, he took her go-carting, as well as mini-putting every weekend. He went fishing with her and to the movies. He invited kids her age, tried his best to make sure she had friends.

He'd worked hard at it, poured himself into it the way

he had law school. Normalizing his sister was a job, and it had been all-consuming.

Those, he realized now with a bittersweet pang, had been the best years.

"No thanks," she said, and bent back over her book.

He sighed, slightly defeated, slightly angry. Always baffled. "Then I guess I'll talk to you later," he said, and as he turned again for the hallway, Gwen shifted and he saw what she was reading. *Wild Child*. Monica's purple eyes stared up at him from the author photo.

Gwen glanced up and saw what he was looking at before he could pretend not to be.

Without a word his sister pulled the book into bed with her, hiding it in her lap, another secret to keep from him.

Monica searched through the pink dog carrier's gazillion pockets for Reba's leash. She found packets of dog treats. Hair ties and lip gloss. Gum. Two cigarettes. From the side pocket she pulled a long silver strip of condoms.

"Oh, Jenna," she sighed, fondness a bittersweet lump in her throat. She tossed the condoms aside to the bed, but a white note floated out onto her shoe. When she picked it up she caught a glimpse of Jenna's handwriting, and it was so unexpected, she couldn't breathe.

Monica, the note said in Jenna's girlish print, and the grief bit so deep, she had to sit or fall to her knees. *Don't let the haters win. And that includes you. You're special and you deserve to be happy. It goes so fast. Take happiness where you can find it.*

Ruined, she sat there staring at the note; the circles Jenna dotted her *i*'s with seemed so profound. A note from beyond the grave. About her sex life.

Only Jenna. Only Jenna would care.

Maybe in a few weeks she could laugh, but the best

she could do right now was not bawl and put the condoms in the drawer of the bedside table. Where they would collect dust.

Wiping her eyes, she stood again and dug until she found the small pink bedazzled leash in the side pocket of the dog carrier and advanced on Reba, who quickly dove under the bed.

"Come on, you can't live in this hotel room. I have work to do," she muttered, then got down on her knees to fish the dog out.

"It's a walk, Reba," she said as she grabbed the animal under her strange, hairless belly. "Not a forced march. We need exercise. Sunlight." She clipped the leash onto Reba's collar, grabbed her purse with her notebook and pen, and headed for the door.

After that terrible run-in with Jackson last night, she'd come home and, fueled by anger and that four-hour nap, wasted several hours on bad TV, before finally falling asleep near dawn. She'd slept nearly twelve hours.

So now she was wide awake, and there was work to do.

You, Monica Appleby, are writing a book about the night your father was shot dead by your mother.

Jackson's words, his incredulous horror, still sent prickling chills down her arms. Like the feeling she got when she caught herself from falling, or managed to avoid a car accident, or thought of her mother.

"Let's go see the sights," she said, shaking out her hands, hoping the prickly feeling would go away.

She dragged the unwilling and surprisingly hard-to-drag Reba out into the hallway. But once she was out in the world, Reba gave herself a nose-to-tail shake and began to prance down the hall beside Monica, who found herself smiling at the little dog's strut.

Outside the front door of the Peabody, all the flowers were in bloom, which made the air smell like lotion.

Bees the size of hummingbirds roamed the flowering bushes.

The sun she planned to soak up was sinking low behind the city buildings across the street, and the sky to the east looked dark and bruised. She didn't remember this town from when her mother brought her here when she was six. They'd been running away, and Monica had only seen the inside of the apartment Simone had grown up in.

An apartment above a bar.

The Pour House.

There had been neon signs in dark windows, she remembered that. Some of them had been broken.

She turned right at the corner down a residential street where the houses were smaller and closer together. Kids' toys and bikes lay in yards, dropped when the shout for dinner came. In one yard a dog, chained to a cinder block, chewed on a bone and eyed Reba.

Unintimidated, Reba worked her strut a little harder, shaking out her back paws as they passed.

It didn't take long to find. A few more lucky turns and she stood kitty-corner to a squat yellow brick building. The horizontal windows were black and long, filled with neon beer signs. Above it were the dark windows of an apartment.

The Pour House was the poster child of dive bars. It was the dive bar other bars wished they could be. The neon o's in the sign were still burnt out, the way they probably always had been and always would be.

Monica appreciated a good dive bar, the honesty of a place that knew exactly what it was and exactly the service it provided.

But this wasn't just any dive bar. It was her nightmare.

I've got some kind of fucked-up karmic relationship with this place.

It was there—well, actually behind The Pour House, in the damp alley by the stairs leading up to that apartment— that her mom shot her dad.

Monica shook her head, denying the memories. Not that there were many, but they were there, just under the surface, dark sharks circling a crippled boat. She was good at denying those memories. Had been doing it for years, pushing them away, drinking them away, fucking them away.

Not anymore, she told herself, her stomach opening up like a black hole to swallow the rest of her organs. *You're writing about it, remember?*

Reba barked once, staring up at her through the white fringe of fur around her eyes.

"I know. But what else have I got?" She'd accepted the advance. Her editor was "eager to see Monica's take on such a personal horrific and cultural event."

Awesome.

Before she could let the ghosts win and talk herself out of it, she stomped across the street, poor Reba running to keep up, and pulled open the door to The Pour House.

Only to stare—slack-jawed—with surprise.

If the outside was the same, the inside was a revelation. A dive bar reformed. The brass and wood of the bar gleamed in the low light. All the taps—a huge array, like a beer-tap fence across the top of the mahogany bar— sparkled. The dark green vinyl on the bar stools was all intact and showed no sign of duct-tape repair work. The copper lights overhead cast the room in a warm glow. And the blackboard on the far wall announced "Sean's BBQ, coming soon."

All in all, totally different from the dark, scary cave she remembered. This was a nice place, a welcoming bar hiding behind foreboding clothes.

Suddenly, she noticed how quiet it was, and she turned

to see a table of three men staring at her. Including Jackson Davies.

His blond hair picked up the lights and gleamed like gold, his long body was stretched out, his legs crossed at the ankles, and his eyes glittered as they watched her.

And she didn't want to admit it—wanted to hate it, actually, because he was a rude, judgmental asshole— but she liked his eyes on her. She wanted to preen under that icy gaze, show him everything he was missing out on because he was an idiot.

But she wasn't that girl anymore. She was a woman, a writer, with a job to do.

And he was not going to like that.

She turned toward the bar, smiling.

When Monica walked into the empty bar, the atmosphere changed. As if a storm were approaching, all the hair on Jackson's arms stood up. He was always a little loose at poker night and tonight more so than usual, because no one else had come out for it. So it was just him and his friends—Brody was in town, on a brief layover between security jobs—and the mood was so easy, he'd had two pints of beer.

Well, he corrected, glancing down at his half-empty glass, *two and a half.*

And looking at Monica—wearing those tight black workout pants women seemed to wear all the time now, and a loose green shirt that slipped over one shoulder revealing her collarbone, the delicate curve of her neck— he was fully aware that he needed to apologize for his behavior yesterday, and also painfully, completely aware that before he'd blown it, she'd been flirting with him. And he'd been flirting back, and the yard had been ripe with the kind of sexual awareness he'd practically forgotten about.

I want her. And before I acted like an idiot, she wanted me, too. Or at least was interested in wanting me.

"Hello, boys," she said, her voice like scotch, rough and smooth all at once.

The rat at the end of her leash barked.

"What the hell is that thing?" Jackson asked.

"Reba's my Seeing Eye dog," Monica said. "Who runs this place?" she asked.

"I do." Sean stood as if he'd been called out by the principal.

"You did all this?" She twirled her finger around the room.

Sean glanced behind him at Jackson and Brody. "I . . . . ah . . . had help."

Damn right you did. Jackson and Brody shared a manly fist-bump.

"Well, you did an incredible job." Her smile, without a word of exaggeration, was like the sun coming out from behind clouds.

"Thanks," Sean said, standing a little straighter. "I . . . *we* . . . worked hard on it." He hustled behind the bar, remembering his role as bartender. "You're Monica Appleby, aren't you?"

"I am." Again that smile, and Sean paused, mid-step. Jackson knew exactly what was happening to his old friend. The way his brain was struggling to catalog all her beauty in one go.

Sean leaned over the bar toward Monica as if they were Cosmo-drinking girlfriends. "I loved your book."

"I'm so glad."

"He only read the sex parts," Jackson said.

"Don't listen to him. I read it cover to cover. Though I might have reread the sex parts a couple of times."

"You're only human." She said it as if she were flirting, but he knew when Monica Appleby was flirting; he'd been the recipient of those sideways glances, the blush on her cheeks, the nervous dance of her fingers over her glass. This wasn't that. This seemed . . . practiced. Careful. Brittle. And he realized, watching her, how skilled she was at letting people think they were getting close while in reality she was keeping them at arm's length.

Something prickly ran up his neck, an awareness.

I do that, too.

Or maybe he was just experiencing some beer wisdom. Or maybe he just wanted that connection he felt to her to mean something. To mean he was special.

"So, can I get you something to drink?" Sean asked, slapping the bar. "I can make a Cosmo, or one of them froufrou drinks. I got some of those umbrellas around here. Or maybe you'd like something more rock star?"

"Soda water with lime."

Sean nodded sagely. "Very rock star."

Monica sat down on one of the stools, crossing her legs. The small rat/dog at the end of her leash curled up under her stool. Her shirt dipped farther down her arm, revealing the bronze sheen to her skin, the small dent of her muscle.

"Are you here for my world-famous Pour House poker night?" Sean asked, and Monica took a long, slow glance around the empty bar. "Well, usually we're a little more full, but Jackson's scared everyone away with reminders of all the freaking yard work they need to do." Sean shot him a disgusted look.

"It's important, Sean," Jackson repeated for about the hundredth time tonight.

"Hardly more important than community togetherness, not more important than tradition."

"I'm with Sean," Monica said, swiveling around to face him. Flirting again, or just angry? It was hard to say with that gleam in her eye, but the smart money was on angry. "Community togetherness is way more important than yard work."

"Luckily, authors just passing through don't get a vote," Jackson said.

"Too bad," Monica pouted, and Jackson shifted in his seat. There was something really obscene about how he reacted to that mouth of hers. "Why the yard work?"

"Haven't you heard?" Sean wiped down his bar like it was a vintage Mustang convertible. "We're going to be saved by a TV show." He raised his hands to the ceiling. "Saved!"

"Calm down, Sean," Brody said. His deep voice made Monica turn around.

She slipped off the stool and approached, her hand held out to Brody. "I'm Monica."

Brody stood. As all six feet four inches of him came up out of his chair, he had to duck under the low light over the table. Sean's parents hadn't been able to have kids, so they adopted Brody when he was six, but three months later they were pregnant with Sean—their miracle baby. Sean inherited all of his mother's Irish looks, but Brody had Filipino and African American bloodlines. He had dark hair, dark eyes, and something wild simmering just under a calm surface. He didn't smile at Monica; not that it was anything personal. Brody was just really an unsmiling kind of guy. Part of his job, Jackson supposed. Bodyguards didn't do a lot of smiling.

"Brody Baxter." Even his voice was badass.

"I like your mom's show," Sean said, pulling Monica's attention away from Brody. "*What Simone Wants*."

"And I will try not to hold it against you." Monica said it like a joke, but it rang with bitter truth.

"I liked the show you did with your mom like fifteen years ago. Remember that one?" Sean asked and whistled. "You were like the original Kardashians."

Jackson was watching Monica, unable to take his eyes off her, so he saw the small muscles around her lips flinch, as if just the memory of the show had the power to wound her.

"What was it called again?" Sean asked, obviously unaware that Monica was not enjoying this train of conversation.

"*Mommy Dearest*," Monica joked, deadpan.

"No, that wasn't it," Sean said, oblivious. "You must remember, you were on the damn thing."

Jackson stood and walked behind the bar, compelled to stop this conversation, all because of a lip twitch.

Sean let him back there with only a scowl; part of Jackson's payment for the blood, sweat, and tears he'd put into the bar was free beer. And Jackson liked to work the taps.

"So what brings you to town?" Sean asked, distracted from trying to remember the name of Monica's reality TV show.

"Working on a book," she said.

"More sex, drugs, and rock and roll?" Sean asked, his eyebrows wiggling.

"No. I'm going to write about my father's murder."

The buzz of the neon signs in the windows was suddenly deafening.

"Really?" Sean practically squeaked in surprise. He jerked his thumb at Jackson. "Stalin here is letting you walk around asking questions about your dad's murder?"

"I am . . . in fact." She reached into her bag and pulled out a notebook. Jackson gaped at her audacity. "I was hoping to ask your father a few questions. He ran the bar then, didn't he?"

"Yeah."

"Is he here?"

Was she nuts? She couldn't walk into this bar, with him in it, and just start asking questions. *No way.* When

Sean glanced sideways at Jackson, Jackson didn't even feel bad about shaking his head.

Monica saw it and jumped like she'd been bitten on the butt. "Jackson doesn't have anything to do with this. And I certainly don't need his permission to ask your father a couple of questions about that night."

"No, but you do need mine." Sean grabbed a napkin and a pen from behind the bar. "Here," he said. "I'll talk to him tomorrow morning. You call him around noon, before he starts watching the baseball game."

Sean slid the napkin across the bar toward her.

"Thanks," she said, folding the napkin and tucking it in her bag. "I don't suppose you remember anything from that night?"

"I was only five," Sean said, running a hand through his hair. Of course he had memories of that night. The whole town did. Jackson did. There had been camera crews, coroners, jazz music fans wailing in the street for a week after the murder. "But I remember all the cops around the kitchen table the next morning. My mom freaking out. I remember Dad was covered in blood when he got home."

Jackson got a crippling vision of how this week would go if Monica was able to walk around asking questions. People would line up to tell her their memories of that night. And he just couldn't have this town distracted from the vision they were trying to create—the "story" they were trying to tell, which was the polar opposite of the story *she* was trying to tell.

Jackson cleared his throat, and Sean got the message. "That's . . . that's all I remember. Really." He pulled himself a beer and walked back to the table. No doubt, Jackson would hear about Sean's restraint tomorrow.

Monica whirled to face him, her eyes shooting daggers. "What the hell, Jackson?"

"I could say the same, Monica." Jackson poured himself another beer. Probably a mistake, but he was kind of in the mood to make a mistake. It was Monica's influence. "You said you'd be discreet," he reminded her. "Walking into The Pour House on Saturday night is not discreet."

She twisted her lips, which he translated as a concession. "Fine," she snapped. "Perhaps . . . I was not the most subtle."

"So, we're both sorry."

"That's a stretch."

He smiled, unable to help himself.

She frowned at him, which didn't do a single thing to kill his smile.

"Are you going to warn the whole town to stay away from me?"

"No. Just the ones you want to talk to in public about the murder."

"What about telling people to do yard work on a Saturday night?"

"I didn't tell them anything. Truth is, poker night is pretty much a dismal failure. Two people came in, took one look at me, and left."

"I can understand the inclination." Irresistibly, she was both sweet and spicy at once. And as he was getting excited, she was relaxing, he could tell, the curve of those shoulders easing from indignant to . . . reserved.

"I can't imagine it will be a good time writing that book," he said. Thinking of the kind of scab that would grow over a wound like that and the pain involved in ripping it off for the world to see. Or . . . maybe he had it wrong. Maybe she'd had years of counseling and was totally at peace with it.

"It's not supposed to be a good time," she said. "It's a job."

"Do you like being a writer?" He reached over and topped up her glass. Gave her a fresh lime. Maybe when he left town he'd go to Mexico, get a job on a beach somewhere as a bartender. He had a knack.

"Sure." She tucked her chin, her fingers tracing the grain on the wood. Her fingers were long, pretty. The nails were naked, but pink and short. Looking at them felt intimate, as if he were seeing something he shouldn't through the crack in a door.

Everything about her felt that way. Illicit and naughty. Forbidden.

"Do you like being mayor?"

He laughed once, and it burned in his chest. "No. I don't." Surprised at his honesty, he took a sip of beer to keep his mouth busy so he didn't go spilling any more of his secrets.

"Then why do it?"

"A man's gotta eat." Not at all the real answer, but he'd already been more honest than he'd intended. "Why are you writing a book you aren't excited about?" As soon as he said it, he remembered once, when he was a kid, daring Sean to touch the electrified fence around the railroad switch south of town. Sean didn't do it; he was dumb, but not stupid. But the two of them had stood close enough to feel the current, the energy coming off the wires.

That was how she seemed now; it was as if he'd stepped too close to the wires around her.

"That's hardly any of your business," she snapped.

"I disagree," he snapped right back. This wasn't what he wanted; he wanted to look at her naked fingers, try to see down her shirt, but he couldn't stop this terrible energy. "This is my town and you're about to go yanking our skeletons out of their closets."

"Why don't you want me to write this book?" she asked, leaning in, sending his equilibrium spinning. He took another sip of beer. It was as if his friends were on the far side of the moon; it was just him and Monica. And the language of her body.

"It's the past," he said, wiping his mouth. "We're looking toward the future."

"We?"

"Bishop." *Me. Me most of all. The wide-open future.*

"Right," she said, her expression close to a sneer. "The TV show. The yard work."

Now he stiffened, everything set alight by her disdain. Her sarcasm fed his doubts, watered his worry.

"What's wrong with that?"

"It's very . . ." she pretended to mull it over ". . . polite." She dropped her voice, leaned in close. "And you know how I feel about polite."

There was something about her smart mouth, her irreverence, that made him want to bite her. It was a fire in his blood—a swift and sudden obsession. He'd start with that small, delicate cup of skin supported by bone and sinew right there under her ear. He wanted that flesh in his mouth, the heat and softness of her. And then he'd move on to the fat center of her bottom lip, so lush, so erotic. He wanted to suck that.

"You think it's bullshit," he said.

She touched her nose, smiling.

"You know what I think is bullshit?"

"I can hardly wait to hear."

"Writing a book about a man who nearly killed his wife with his bare hands, a woman you clearly don't like, and a past you put yourself in jeopardy to run from."

Like water draining slowly out of a sink, her smile faded. The color in her cheeks went white, her eyes diamond hard. Sensing the change in Monica, Reba, under the chair, started to growl. A partly bald guard dog in rhinestones.

She pushed away from the bar and got to her feet with a little hop. "Gentlemen," she said. "Have a good poker night." She glanced at Sean and then back at Jackson, her eyes the kind of hard that should have taken all the heat out of his blood, yet it didn't.

This is what happens when you don't have sex. Ever. You get excited by a woman who you can't stop offending. A woman who loathes you.

Cooler night air blew in the door as she left, and he pushed away his beer.

"What the hell did you say?" Sean asked.

"I'll apologize." He ran a hand through his hair, over his eyes. Again. *Again.* It's all he ever did with her. Piss her off and apologize.

"It's late," Brody said, ever the Boy Scout. "You going to let her walk home alone?"

Jackson looked up at the ceiling and sighed. "No."

He left his nearly full beer and his friends and walked out into the night to chase down a woman he'd be smart to leave alone. She tampered with his locks, his rules, and distracted him from the plan. She tampered with *him,* opened up a side of himself he didn't know.

But as he stepped out the door, he was smiling.

Chapter 5

Monica wanted to make a proper dramatic exit, but Reba was suddenly interested in sniffing every square inch of the sidewalk. Peeing on every blade of grass, marking her territory.

"Please," Monica muttered. "Who are you kidding?"

She heard footsteps behind her and yanked on Reba's leash. Without having to look, she knew who was coming. Could tell by the whiff of superior condemnation in the air. Could tell by the way her skin rose in goose flesh, attracted and repelled in equal parts. "Go away, Jackson."

"It's late," he said. "You shouldn't walk alone."

"Stuff it."

"Look, I'm sorry."

In the bar, he'd touched something awful, something searing and painful, and it obliterated her interior landscape, those things about herself that she'd created and honed. Her indifference, her strength, her hard-won acceptance of her past, her parents—all of it. He just stirred up a dust storm of doubt and anger. And now she was a quivering ball of pain, all over again.

And she wanted to return the favor.

She whirled on him. "You say that a lot, Jackson. But what exactly are you apologizing for? For treating me like a pariah one minute and a woman you want to fuck the next?"

He flinched at her language. *Good, yes.* Because that

was how she felt, like flinching under his attraction and his judgment.

"Yes. For all of it. For all of it, I'm sorry." Standing under a streetlamp, the starkness of the light did him no favors and she loved it. *Look at the mayor now. Wrinkled and ravaged and guilty.*

But it wasn't enough. She wanted him to bleed.

"You think you're special because you want to fuck me? Because you're not. You're not special. You're a boring, judgmental ass."

Okay, she stopped herself. *Enough. Just walk away.*

She turned, tugging on Reba's leash, but she heard Jackson's footsteps behind her.

"What!" She whirled again. They were in the shadows now, between the streetlights, and he kept walking until he was close enough for her to see him clearly.

"My poor manners aside, is it just me you don't like, or is it any man who wants to fuck you?"

She wasn't going to tell him how long it had been since she'd had sex. How long it had been since she'd even noticed when a man looked at her with real interest in his eyes. And she refused, absolutely refused, to remember how nice it had been in his backyard to flirt with him. Really flirt, not this crap she did every day, this mirror she held up to the world, reflecting only what people wanted to see.

With him, she'd been herself. As much as she was ever herself in the company of other people. And she found herself terrified by the honesty of the moment, of the honesty he seemed to require of her right now.

"I am sorry for how I've acted toward you. I . . ." He continued after a breath. "It has been a very long time since I've been interested in a woman like I am in you. And it's thrown me off. It's made me . . . rude. And I am sorry." She opened her mouth but he held up his hand. "I know how you feel about me being polite, but sometimes an apology is more about the person with regrets than the person being apologized to."

God, the things she knew about regret! The steam emptied out of her, leaving her rattled. "Fine. I forgive you, but I think . . . I think we should just stay away from each other."

He laughed. "It's a small town."

"I know. But . . . we seem to bring out the worst in each other and it's just not worth it. Nothing is ever going to happen between us."

The sound of his footsteps approaching was loud in the dark, a pebble skipped across cement. "I think something already has."

Oh, how young he seemed with his lines, his cocky assurance. She didn't have the heart to tell him that she'd seen it all before. "You know what the largest erogenous zone is for women?"

"Your skin," he murmured and her body responded. Amazing! Her body, which felt so little, so shallowly, felt his voice all the way down to her bones, pulsing in her womb.

"No. My brain."

"Are you saying I have to seduce your brain?"

"I'm saying you don't stand a chance."

"Do you like sex?"

"Oh my God." She turned, stomping away. "Leave it to a man to hear a rejection and think it's because I don't like sex."

The asshole had the balls to smile as he caught up to her. "No. I'm just asking because every other woman in my life who has told me I have to convince her brain to have sex lets her brain get in the way during sex."

She tripped over the edge of the sidewalk. "Aren't you a regular Dr. Ruth?"

"Hardly." He put a hand on her arm and it was warm and heavy. Real. She felt every callus at the base of his fingers, along his thumb. The mayor worked with his hands. And her body—weak, weak, weak—imagined him shirtless and sweaty, nailing shit together, his muscles ropy and ripped. A tool belt, some of those low jeans . . .

Agh! He'd gotten to her.

"I am a man who hasn't had sex in two years," he laughed, somehow so easy with this confession when every other man she'd ever known would never dream of saying such things, "and has spent endless, and I do mean endless, nights reimagining and replaying every sexual encounter I've ever had. The women I've disappointed, the way I would have done things differently, the women I've pleased and who have pleased me." He pointed to his head. "It's all right here."

She stared at him. "What am I supposed to do with that?"

"I don't know." He sighed. "But I do know that I have not felt the way I feel about you in years."

"It's just sexual attraction, Jackson. It's chemistry."

"I know. And it's awesome." He nearly fist-pumped. He nearly danced with his excitement.

She laughed, because he sounded like a kid and part of her . . . part of her had forgotten—if she'd ever really known—what pure chemistry felt like. She'd confused it plenty in her youth. Manufactured it. Mislabeled it. Pretended it was there when it wasn't. Faked it.

But what she felt for Jackson—it was real.

"I'd like to kiss you."

"Jackson—"

"Say no if you want. But I'd like to kiss you."

She didn't say no and he stepped closer. Still she was silent, and he moved closer again. The hem of his tee shirt touched her shirt and she shouldn't be able to feel that, but she did, somehow. She felt everything—the night air, his breath, the attention of his eyes. It was as if her skin had slipped away and all she had was raw sensation.

Flirting with Jackson, kissing him—it could be a problem, she understood that. But when was this ever going to happen again? A man who didn't expect anything from her? A man she really and truly—despite his idiotic behavior and perhaps her own idiotic behavior—wanted.

It was so rare in her life these days. Rare enough to make her throw caution to the wind.

If not now, when? she wondered. Time was creeping ever onward and she was more alone by the moment.

She put a hand against his chest, over the pale blue shirt that made his eyes look like the sky on a hot August day. Beneath the cotton she felt the warmth of his skin, the tensile strength of his muscles, and beneath that, the heavy pounding of his heart.

When he stepped forward again, their bellies touched. The most intimacy she'd had in years.

"I don't put on a show anymore," she said. A warning to both of them. It was real pleasure for her or it was nothing. She was done pretending. Done manufacturing something for a man, leaving her with nothing.

"A show?"

"If you're expecting—"

"Stop." His fingers touched her mouth, his thumb pulling the flesh of her bottom lip down, revealing the soft inside. She tasted the salt of his skin, and the taste pierced through her chest, into her belly and lower, where it started a thousand small fires, a thousand little licks of flame. "Expectations make me angry. I don't expect anything. Did you hear the part when I said it's been two years since I had sex?"

"I did."

"So, are you of legal age?"

"And then some."

"Are you willing?"

"Getting there."

A part of the night, his chuckle twined around them, the purr of it reverberating in her chest until she couldn't quite tell who was talking. "Then just . . . hold on tight."

And then he was there, his mouth against hers. His chest against hers. His arms, long and solid, swept around her, pulling her closer, and she was up high and hard against his body.

Despite wanting this, despite the flirting, her instinct, wild and desperate, was to push him away, put the distance back between herself and the rest of the world.

Mistake, she thought, her hands clenching the hard muscles of his arms, *you are making a mistake.* This was why she didn't flirt with men, because flirting led to *this* and she so rarely liked *this.* It was too much, too close; claustrophobia loomed over her. It reminded her painfully of that part of her life when she didn't have enough pride to see the choices hidden in the shadows backstage.

But then his hands, wide and smooth, slid up her back, to the neckline of her shirt, and slowly each of his fingers found its way to the edge of her shirt, and then under it. To the bare skin at the nape of her neck. Her knees melted like butter in a hot pan.

It was torture, waiting for each of those fingers. She couldn't breathe, and when finally the last finger slipped under her hair, she gasped, her open mouth an invitation.

Holding the back of her head, he turned her, positioned her so when his tongue swept in, it swept in deep. She moaned in her throat, a purr, really, and she couldn't even muster up any embarrassment. Those fingers had unlocked her, pulled her loose, and now she stood, weak in his arms. Her hands gripped around his biceps, over those sleek, deceiving muscles. Inspired, her own fingers curled under his sleeve; the smooth skin of his shoulders felt like a secret. Something so soft, just for her.

He was right: this was chemistry and it was unbearably exciting. Because this was rare. So rare, in fact, she couldn't remember the last time she felt liquid and fiery and floaty and dizzy and . . . hot. From one kiss.

She didn't notice the car lights coming down the street, slicing apart the darkness. She didn't notice anything but him, until a police siren wailed once and then stopped. They jumped away from each other, putting yards between themselves, only to get hit in the face with the searing white light of a flashlight.

"Holy shit! Mayor?"

Jackson, beside her, swore under his breath. "Hey there, Chief."

The situation was so hysterical, Monica nearly laughed.

"Mrs. Gosset called about two teenagers making out on her front lawn." Jackson glanced back at the house behind them. Monica turned and saw the silhouette of a woman in the window beside the front door.

"We haven't seen any teenagers," Monica said, trying to create a little levity, but no one laughed.

"Sorry to make you come out here, Gloria," Jackson said.

"Well, no problem. But maybe you want to . . . take it inside?"

Am I the it? Monica wondered.

"Yes. Of course. And Gloria . . ." Jackson stepped closer to the car. "I don't need to ask you not to talk about this, do I?"

You just did, Monica thought. But Gloria, Monica could see, now that the flashlight wasn't blinding her, was assuring Jackson that he didn't need to do anything of the kind. Yes, clearly Gloria was going to take the fact that she'd seen the Golden Boy Mayor making out with the Wild Child to her grave.

Yeah, right.

But Gloria drove off, wishing both of them a good night, and suddenly the night was cooler, the world a little bigger than it had been just moments ago. And she wanted to go back to just the two of them in the darkness. The two of them and the kiss, and the touch of his hands and the aching tension low in her body.

"I cannot believe that just happened," he breathed up at the stars.

She laughed, and at his murderous look she laughed harder. "Come on, Mayor. It's a little harmless necking. Hardly the end of the world."

It took a moment, and frankly, she wasn't sure if he'd ever smile, but his lip finally curled. "This has never happened to me."

"You've never been caught kissing?" How hilarious! She'd spent two years on that reality show making sure she got caught kissing at every turn. "Not even in high school?"

"I was . . . careful, then."

The implication was that he wasn't careful tonight. Because of her, because something about her made him act out of character, lose some of that tightly wound control.

Before it even registered, she squashed her emotional reaction to that. Because the fact that she cared, that she found deep in her chest some sort of feminine pride in that, was shocking.

It was just a kiss.

But she couldn't even buy her own bullshit. For other women it was just a kiss. For her it was the first step down a road she had no interest in retraveling.

It started off as being complimented, feeling a certain pride that he responded to her the way he did, but it ended—and she knew this—it ended with throwing away all her hard-won feminine independence. She didn't need a man to define her worth; she didn't need sex to be her compass. The attraction of men was a shit currency and she knew that better than anyone.

But one kiss from this man, one offhand comment about how she affected him, and she could feel herself tying her pleasure, her pride, her sense of self to a man's attraction to her.

How disappointing.

Now she was grateful for the wide world, the space between them. She needed a world's worth of distance between herself and her mistakes and this man who would take her right back there.

Monica's lips glistened in the lamplight, and it took everything he had to look away from her. His mind, thick and slow from the kiss, from being caught in such a position by the police chief of all people, ran around in circles, sure of only one thing.

Monica was a terrible distraction.

Despite the embarrassment of being caught like that— despite the town, the contest, his sister—she could make him forget every one of his thousand responsibilities. He would throw all of them onto the back burner just for more . . . of her.

Dangerous. So damn dangerous.

The beginning of that kiss had been tense. Despite her flirting, despite her willingness, he'd felt the fight in her. That moment of panic when he thought she'd run, push him away and vanish into the night.

He didn't like to think what that might mean.

But then, as if his fingers under the edge of her shirt, right at her spine, had unlocked her, she melted against him. Arched to meet him. It had been sweet and hot and about the most perfect moment in his life in as long as he could remember.

Whatever "show" she was talking about, he didn't know if that was it. All he knew was that she was viciously, sublimely exciting.

But she was staring at him, her eyes deep and dark, and he realized that whatever her reasons were, the kiss was a mistake for her, too.

Ironic that it stung.

"I'll walk you home," he said.

"You don't have to do that."

"Yeah . . . I do."

The night had taken some strange turns, but when he turned and walked down the road with Monica close enough that her shirt touched his, he was electrified all along the side of his body.

The dog pranced ahead.

Before he realized it, he smiled. A real smile, not his mayor smile. And he knew in a heartbeat that if Monica had come back to town just two months from now, after the contest was all over, things would have been different between them.

But then, he wasn't going to be here in two months. It was now or never for them, and it absolutely couldn't be now.

Which left them with never.

Jackson held open the front door to the Peabody and Monica slipped in.

"Good night." His voice curled over her shoulder and when she glanced back at him, his face was half-shadowed. His lips dark, his eyes bright. *Oh.* Those eyes . . . in those eyes she saw the echo of the loneliness that lived in her heart.

"Monica—" This was the start of a conversation she didn't want to have.

"Stop, Jackson—it was a mistake for me too."

There was nothing else to say, and he nodded in maybe grim, maybe sad concession. Hard to tell.

"Good night." Reba at her feet barked and she saw the upward curve of Jackson's half-smile. " 'Night, Rambo."

And then he was gone and she was walking through the Peabody with its golden lamplight beating back the worst of the Arkansas night. Behind the desk was Jay, who waved with one hand and seemed nervous, probably because of that photo thing yesterday. She gave him the warmest smile she was capable of at the moment and climbed the steps to her room.

Through the door, she heard the sharp ring of the telephone. *Weird*. Who would call her at the hotel? She thought of Jackson and despite it all, despite everything she knew in her head, she got a thrill in her belly.

The instant the door was open, Reba raced past her for the prime spot on the bed.

Monica crossed the room and grabbed the phone on the third ring.

"Hello?"

"Monica?"

That voice, low and feminine. Southern at the edges, steel at its core, it unlocked something in her head, a dark room that she loathed. A dark room full of dark stories and memories and snakes and every monster under the bed.

No. No. Not this. Not now.

Monica pulled the receiver away from her ear.

"Don't hang up!" the voice shot out of the dark, and she was flooded with fight-or-flight instincts. Reba watched her and, as if sensing her dismay, growled low in her throat. "Honey, please don't hang up."

The endearment moved her and, standing in the dark, the monsters breathing down her neck, she sighed.

"Hello, Mother."

Chapter 6

Monica used to love her mom. Not just in the generic way all children love their moms, but after the murder, after Simone had been acquitted, and she and Monica fled the United States and the press and the memories, Monica *cherished* her mother. Cared for her, as if Monica had become the parent and Simone the child.

Simone drank too much in London, started doing drugs with the rail-thin English models they were staying with.

So Monica dumped out the booze. Hid the drugs.

With their lips curled and their hands in bony white fists, Simone's friends called her—unkindly—the little mother. And they weren't wrong.

After it got cold in London they went to Greece.

They lived in a small room behind a house. Monica remembered that the room was blue, and the curtains had red roosters on them. Simone spent days in the bed, staring out that window. Monica read books on the floor beside the bed, unwilling to leave her mom's side. She made her mother soup and stood over her to make sure she ate it.

Monica was seven by then. Her birthday was spent begging her mother to get out of bed.

After Greece it was Paris, and Simone started to come back to life, only with harder edges, longer silences. But Monica remembered being happy because they used to get chocolate croissants and take naps along the Seine.

They spent the days together, out in the city, walking hand in hand along the cobblestone streets. Now, of course, she realized that Simone had to keep them out of the apartment during the day—the price of being able to sleep there at night.

But sometimes, even now, she dreamt of cobblestone streets and chocolate croissants and she woke up crying.

"How did you find me?" Monica asked, swamped by the memories brought in by the sound of her mother's voice. So powerful, she imagined the scent of Shalimar. As if Simone were there. In the room.

She imagined her in pieces, never able to fully see her mother as a whole. The famous cheekbones, the flawless skin, the cold smile, the calculation behind those famous purple eyes.

"I read the *Rolling Stone* article."

"Why are you calling?"

"I would think that was obvious."

Monica bit down hard on her back teeth. "Illuminate me."

"I want to stop you from writing that book."

"Now *that* is surprising." With her suddenly thick and clumsy fingers, it took a few tries for Monica to unclip Reba's leash. "I would think that you'd love me writing a book about you."

"You want to write a book about me? About that reality show I made you do when you were a kid? Fine. Do it. Tell the world how I screwed you up. But don't write a book about that night."

"*That night.* Listen to you, you can't even own up to it—"

"The night your father tried to kidnap you and strangle me, and I stopped him by putting a bullet in his chest."

The silence buzzed, like a sound system turned up too

loud without music. Monica swallowed. She took her time hanging the leash over the bathroom doorknob, making sure the weight was distributed just right so it didn't slide to the floor. Something about all those words put together like that made her small again. A girl.

"Have I owned up to it enough for you?"

"Why do you care?" Monica murmured, wishing her voice were stronger. Wishing she hadn't put all that hate from her teenage years behind her. She could use some hate; she could use something to keep herself grounded. Because she felt about as substantial as fluff.

"I have always cared."

Monica's laugh was full of poison, but Simone was silent.

"I'm not sure when I started giving you the impression that I didn't care, but I'm sorry you feel that way."

"This is very old ground, Mom. Tell me why you've tracked me down to try—far too late, I might add—to tell me what to do."

Simone took a deep breath, as if pulling herself together, bracing herself for impact, and it was so surprising, Monica stood still in the middle of her room, wondering what could make Simone unsure of herself. Everything Simone did was planned, staged. She knew the angles, the lighting, her best side. Nothing was unscripted; there was no room for chance in her life.

"Because if you write this book you can't go back. You'll let the whole world into the darkest corner of your life—"

"You're one to talk, Mom! You air your laundry every week on national television. And a fair amount of mine, I might add."

"But I have never talked about JJ. Ever."

Monica blinked, stunned to realize it was the truth. Simone might have spent two seasons auditioning young men to be her lover, but she'd never publically talked about JJ. Dad.

"It's a choice," Simone said, taking advantage of Monica's silence. "What I do is a choice. I choose what to show the world, and I have made the choice to never show them that."

It was on the tip of Monica's tongue to ask why, but she shook her head. She didn't really care. "You're worried about your reputation," she said, assuming the worst.

"No." Simone's denial was said with such power, with such precision, that Monica had to fiddle with the leash again, as if it were the most important thing in the world. "I'm worried about *you*. About what it will mean for you if you keep giving yourself away like this. Handing out your secrets and your pain and your mistakes as if they mean nothing. As if by putting it all down on paper it loses its power to hurt you."

"It doesn't hurt me!" she barked. "I barely remember that night. And it's too late. The contracts are signed. The deadlines are set."

"Send back the money. Get out of it."

Monica almost told her mother she was broke. Almost. But she stopped herself just in time.

"If you need the money . . ." Simone said, apparently with the sixth sense that comes with motherhood despite being shitty at it.

"It's an important cultural event." Her editor's words gave her a little bravado, and she lifted her chin. "And I have a personal attachment to it."

"It's scandal and gossip."

"Once again, Mom, you are one to talk."

"You are trying so hard to pretend that you're better than me because you write books with the word 'nonfiction' on the spine. But you're just like me, digging through your life for little shiny bits and scary bits and terrifying bits to show the world so they have something to talk about at work, so they can feel better about their own lives because ours are such a mess."

Monica shook her head, denying it. Denying *her*. Wishing all over again that there was nothing between them. No connection, not even blood. Wishing somehow that she could sever all of it. Monica wasn't blind enough to pretend innocence in the great rift between herself and her mother. She'd done her fair share of damage, but those years—those lost years when she'd felt unprotected and vulnerable, when the questions about what had happened with her father, to their family, had been brushed aside—those years were her mother's fault.

"I am nothing like you, Mom. Nothing."

"I know you want to believe that."

"There's nothing you can do to stop me from writing this book."

Even if she didn't need the money, even if she was squeamish about going back into those dark days, she'd still write the damn book just to piss her mother off.

Not healthy, not at all, but the truth. The truth dug up from the place where she kept it buried.

I guess I do still hate her.

There were silver sparkles at the edge of her vision—a headache approached.

"We're done, Mom. We were done fourteen years ago. Don't contact me again."

Monica hung up. Which she should have done the second she heard her mother's voice, the second she imagined the ghostly scent of her mother's favorite perfume.

Monica collapsed on the bed and Reba climbed up on her chest, licking her chin. It was strange comfort, but Monica couldn't afford to be picky.

"What a night, dog," she whispered.

She closed her eyes, feeling young. Unsafe.

Chapter 7

It was getting harder and harder to breathe.

Shelby Monroe opened the window, despite having the air-conditioning on. Despite the red Arkansas dust that swirled in through the window. She couldn't breathe.

Every mile that brought her closer to home, closer to her life, suffocated her.

"Don't be ridiculous," she said out loud in an effort to calm herself down. Every time she came home from the annual Teachers of Fine and Industrial Arts Convention held in Memphis, she felt this way. Like she was burning through the atmosphere as she reentered her world.

This year was worse. And it was all because of the thong.

How do women wear these? she wondered, shifting uncomfortably in the driver's seat of her Taurus.

For two years she'd been flirting with Eric Long, sitting with him at the bar, nursing a white wine spritzer while everyone else went to bed. For two years she'd thought, breathlessly, that he was going to ask her up to his hotel room. And she'd waited. And waited. Two years.

Which was why she'd decided that this year, if he didn't ask, *she* would ask *him.*

That had been her plan. To drink three white wine spritzers and ask Eric, a balding high school Agriculture teacher with sweaty hands, up to her hotel room. For sex. *Yep. Sex.*

But Eric had shown up this year wearing a wedding

ring. And showing everyone pictures of a honeymoon with a tiny brunette in the Ozarks. And Shelby had thought for one long, horrifying moment that she might actually burn to dust in embarrassment. As if everyone could see what she'd been planning. As if everyone could see that under her Land's End denim skirt, she was wearing a pink thong. Just one of a bunch of thongs she'd had to mail-order because she was too embarrassed to go to the mall and buy them in person.

All of her friends at the conference, not just Eric, were showing off pictures of babies and diamond rings and telling stories about honeymoon cruises.

And she was still living with her mother.

"Oh God," she moaned, hating her life.

It wasn't as if she expected some grand love affair to come her way. She wasn't the kind of woman who got swept off her feet; she fully realized that. Her feet were so rooted to the ground where she was raised, it was amazing she wasn't covered in kudzu.

Practicality had its own list of benefits, but romance was never included.

She topped a hill covered in willows and in front of her, on the long stretch of red dusty road, she saw Mrs. O'Hara's burgundy 1977 Cadillac El Dorado on the shoulder, steam rolling out from under the hood.

For crying out loud, how many times did that woman need to get hauled off the side of the road before she'd get rid of that piece of garbage? Shelby slowed down and eased in behind the El Dorado, so covered in dust that the license plates were obscured and the back window had practically no visibility.

Eighty-year-old Mrs. O'Hara was a menace in this car. Any car, actually, but this one in particular. The blind spots were epic, the radiator problematic, and she had no sense of how damn big the car was despite having driven it off the lot a million years ago!

Shelby slipped on the mint-green ballet slippers she'd taken off to drive, tucked her cell phone in her pocket in case this was more than just the radiator hose, and popped open the door to her car. Immediately the hot wind swept up around her, and her pink skirt swirled around her knees.

"Mrs. O'Hara!" she cried, rounding the back of the car, slapping her skirt back down. Mrs. Hara didn't need to get a glimpse of her naughty underwear. "You all right?"

From the front passenger seat a person emerged. But it wasn't Mrs. O'Hara.

It was a tall, very tall, powerfully built man, wearing khakis and a white tee shirt that were rumpled and smeared with grease.

Shelby stopped and took a step back. She held up the mace on her key ring.

"Stop . . . I mean . . ." He held up his hands, his voice low and soft. His blond hair was long, and he swept it out of his eye and then put the hand back up. "I'm sorry. I won't . . . I won't hurt you."

"Where's Mrs. O'Hara?" she asked, stepping back again. No one ever came down this road. Except for Gary sometimes on his tractor, but it was the wrong season for that. This man could rape her, kill her, and bury her body and no one would ever know.

"Who?"

"This is Mrs. O'Hara's car."

"No. It's the crap car I bought from a crook outside Little Rock. Doesn't go twenty miles without overheating."

She hesitated before taking another step, but then he shuffled forward and she leapt back, her butt hitting the hood of her car. Her cell phone was in her pocket. She fumbled through her skirt until she pulled it out. Brandishing it like a gun.

He stopped, those hands going back up. His features were sharp, his eyes a startling blue. "I'm sorry. I am. I have no . . . well, no intention of hurting you. And I have no idea how to fix this car. I was calling someone for help, but I don't get service out here. Do you?"

She noticed, belatedly, through the adrenaline haze of panic that his accent wasn't local.

"You're not from here?"

"I just . . . I just arrived from New York."

Oh, that was worse, wasn't it? Being from New York made him seem decidedly more dangerous.

"Why . . . why did you buy this car?"

"The rental place was out of cars, if you can believe it. And this car . . . well, it seemed sort of cool in the lot." He gazed at the car as though it was a friend who'd betrayed him. "Look, if you get service out here, can I use your cell phone? Call a mechanic or something?"

It was his smile, abashed and charming, that convinced her. He was embarrassed out here with his broken-down car, relying on the kindness of strangers.

"I can look at your car, if you like. But I warn you," she said as she typed in 911 on her cell and showed him the display, "I do get service, and any funny business and all I have to do is hit send—" Hit send and if she was lucky, maybe in twenty minutes Darryl down at the station would find his way out here. But this man didn't know that.

"Understood," he said solemnly. "But . . ." Sunlight hit his blue eyes and she realized they weren't all blue, they were also gray and green, a beautiful color, and in the sunlight they glowed.

And his teeth were the whitest she'd ever seen.

He looked like a movie star, that Bradley Cooper guy.

"You know cars?"

His eyes swept down her body, taking in her pink skirt and white shell, all pristine despite the dust and travel.

The breeze pressed her clothes to her skin, and his eyes took that in too, flaring slightly as he looked away.

It was hardly polite the way he looked at her, and something raced under her skin, a sort of giddy awareness that bloomed to life before she could squash it with her levelheadedness.

"I know enough." She smiled when she said it, and somehow she didn't sound like herself. She sounded flirty.

It was the way he looked at her, as if he knew what was under her skirt. And why she'd bought it and what she wanted a man to do with it.

"Who taught you how to fix cars?" he said.

"My mom." She cleared her throat, pulling herself together. "Daddy raised me to be pretty, but Mom raised me to take care of myself." It wasn't the whole truth, but it made for some good roadside flirtation.

"Your mother sounds like a smart woman."

His voice was rich and deep, laced with humor and a sort of understanding, as if he knew her. As if they were comrades of sorts. She wondered if he did that on purpose, and, glancing at him, the smile on his face, she realized he did. He knew his charm. She waited for that to turn her off. She didn't like cocksure men, but apparently this cocksure man was an exception.

"Hey," he said as she was looking under the hood. "Don't call 911, but you look pretty great, bent over the car."

That. That was sleazy. Very sleazy. She shouldn't like that. She should smack him. Leave him out here for the sun and the dust and Gary.

But heat pooled between her legs.

Oh, the blood climbed her cheeks and she looked down at the engine, light-headed and flushed.

The car had overheated, just like Mrs. O'Hara's always did. She could fix this. "Do you have any wire?"

"Wire? Are you MacGyver?" he said as he tucked his phone back in his pocket.

She laughed. No one admired her practicality anymore.

"No. But if we had a little wire, I could fix this."

"I have a wire-bound notebook."

"Perfect."

He ducked back into the car and she tried very hard not to stare at his body as he bent over, but then decided what the hell and stared all she liked. He was very tall, and his muscles were thick. He was either genetically gifted or he hadn't had a carb in years.

Tall herself, she often felt physically awkward around men. But she wouldn't with him. She'd feel small. Petite, even.

"Here," he said, holding out the wire he'd pulled from a small notebook.

"Great." She took the wire and bent over the engine, finding the radiator hose that came loose, causing all the coolant to spill. "Can you hold this?"

Suddenly he was right there, those shoulders pressing against hers, his fingers brushing her hand as he gripped the hose so she could tighten it with the wire from the notebook.

Her body shook with awareness, and she held her breath with a sort of panicked delight.

Once the wire was tightened around the hose, she leaned back, glancing down as he was still bent over. She stared at the twin ridge of muscles racing alongside his spine, pressed against the thin ribbed cotton of his shirt. Her fingers twitched with the sudden urge to touch those muscles, to lay her hands flat against his spine. His shoulders were freckled.

That's sexy too.

You look pretty good bent over the car, too, she thought but couldn't say. Could never say.

I should have had some lunch, she thought, slightly panicked by this utterly foreign turn in her thoughts.

"Do you have water?" she asked, and he leaned up.

"No," he winced. "I have half a bottle of apple juice."

Why in the world the fact that he'd been drinking apple juice so totally captivated her she did not understand; it was all part of the strange personality split she was experiencing.

"Wait. I have some."

She walked back to her car and grabbed one of the bottles from the backseat. She never traveled without water, a flashlight, jumper cables, flares, and some crackers. Somehow, looking at that little emergency kit tucked behind the passenger seat in the back of her car made her unutterably sad.

That emergency kit was why no one had passionate affairs with her. She was always prepared. Never spontaneous. And she knew how off-putting that could be. How it sent a signal of failure to those people who weren't always prepared.

Anger suddenly surfaced, lifting her free of that sadness, lighting something dark in her belly. Something . . . unpredictable.

She was more than her emergency kit!

She stomped across the dirt road to the stranger's car, the gorgeous stranger, who for whatever reason was attracted to her—she could tell. It had been awhile since she'd been so aware of a man's interest, but this man's filled the air like the scent of apple juice.

Rounding the corner of the giant car she found him leaning there, his legs stretched out, the flat muscles of his belly pressed against the white shirt, looking like he was waiting for someone to seduce him.

"I don't know how to thank you," he said, coming to his feet. He reached for the water and she, utterly adrift in this wild and strange current she found herself in, walked right up to his chest.

"*I* do," she said and kissed him.

"Wha—" he breathed against her lips, and she shushed him. For a moment she was very sure he was going to push her away, and that seemed about right. If *he'd* kissed *her, she'd* push him away—at the least. That seemed like the reasonable reaction to an utterly unreasonable event. Even as her lips memorized the fullness of his, she braced herself for his hands at her shoulders, setting her aside. He'd say something sweet and she'd laugh, but she'd die a little inside.

That's okay, she thought. She dropped the water bottle to better feel the wide white sail of his back under her palms. *I'll survive.*

His body coiled, but then she felt those arms, thick with muscle, curve around her, lifting her against him. Her mouth opened with a surprised gasp and his tongue swept in, tasting her, slipping along her lips, her teeth.

Her arms locked around his neck and she opened her mouth wider, pressed herself tighter against him. She felt desperate inside of her skin, desperate to not be herself, to prove that she wasn't just an emergency kit to the people in her life. That she was a woman. A woman worth wanting.

He pivoted, leaning back against the car, shifting her, pulling her until she was standing between his legs. His hands swept over her back down to her hips, his fingers curving over her butt in a way she'd had no idea she loved. But she did, and when he squeezed her, his fingers biting into her skin through the fabric of her skirt, she groaned, the sound loud in the silence.

"Not quite so prim now, are you?" he asked in a voice that made her wet.

No, she thought, she was none of the things she tried

so hard to be, nothing like the woman the world thought she was.

"I like that," he murmured, and she wanted to tell him to shut up, that talking was ruining the psychotic break she was enjoying. He shifted again and suddenly they were pressed chest and torso together and the thick ridge of his erection brushed her core.

She gasped, arching into the contact, wanting more. And he obliged, lifting her against him until the point of friction between them was hot enough to start a fire. She bit his lip, fighting to get closer, fighting to have more of this feeling, this wild, uncontrolled, running-down-the-hill feeling.

He groaned against her mouth, his hands lifting from her hips to find her breasts, small and aching beneath the sensible white shell she wore. He stroked her, rubbed her, and when she bit him again he squeezed her, just enough, just enough to send her one rung higher.

"Spread your legs," he breathed against her mouth, and it didn't occur to her not to. It didn't occur to her to have a thought in her head that would contradict this stranger and the feelings he was creating in her. She shifted her little green ballet slippers and his hand curved around the back of her thigh. Had anyone ever touched her there? she wondered. Because the skin felt new, brought to life by his touch. She moaned at the contact of his skin, callused and rough against the smooth, relatively untouched skin of her thigh.

"More," he told her and she did exactly what he said, unable to think of a reason not to. Wind blew past them, under her skirt, against the dampness he'd created.

His hand slipped up under her skirt, his fingers under the elastic edge of her underwear, until he cupped her ass in his hand, his fingertips just at the edge of the valley between her cheeks.

"Oh," she gasped, breaking their kiss but not flinching as his fingers traced that valley, curling deeper. It was dark and exciting, and she couldn't breathe for the pleasure of his touch.

No one had ever touched her there. She was sure of it. Something like this a girl would remember.

And then he found the electric center of her body where she was wet and hot and dying for him. Dying for him to slide inside of her.

"What—" She gulped air, unsure of what she was going to ask. *What are you doing to me? What are we doing?*

"Shhhh," he whispered, calming her. His eyes, sleepy and sexual, blazing beneath his lowered eyelids.

His other hand traced the front of her underwear, finding her clitoris through the silk, and it was erotic. His bare hand, the silk, the silence surrounding them.

"You're so beautiful," he whispered. "So in control. You scared me, you know." He was teasing her. Making fun of her, and she didn't care. Was too far gone.

"Please," she gasped and he smiled, so wicked, so knowingly wicked.

His finger from behind sank deep inside of her and his other hand picked up a heady, demanding rhythm.

This. This was happening. This man . . . this handsome stranger so far beyond her reach, her world, was going to make her come on the side of the road and she was doing nothing to stop it. She had started it!

"Yes," she sighed, pressing her forehead against his shoulder; the scent of him, sexy and sweaty and warm and real, was too much, and the world started to go fuzzy. As her body coiled and burned, she opened her mouth and bit that shoulder muscle.

He jerked against her and swore, his hands getting rougher. Another finger joined the first and he picked up the pace and she clutched at him, wrapping her arms around him, the only thing solid in a world flying apart.

"Come on," he groaned in her ear and she clenched hard, her body one giant spasm of pleasure, lifting her up and away from herself.

Her eyes blinked open only to find him still watching her, his wicked grin softened into something kind. Human. And that humanity suddenly embarrassed her. The dampness between her legs suddenly embarrassed her and she had to look away.

"Wow," she breathed and he chuckled, warm and low. His fingers, slowly, as if savoring her, slipped away from her body and his hands patted down her skirt, fixed the crooked hem of her shirt.

Considering she had started this little bit of exhibitionist behavior, her sudden shyness seemed ludicrous. He stood up from the car and she stumbled away, the distance between them clearing her head.

Oh. Oh God, what had she done? It was just an emergency kit. She looked at it a million times a day; why had she lost her mind now?

She put her face in her hands, horrified on a molecular level.

His chuckle only made things worse. "Don't," he said, his fingers stroking her face. "Don't be embarrassed. Don't . . . you're beautiful. Sexy."

Ludicrous. His words were outrageous flattery. Lies. She wasn't sexy. She was an art teacher who lived with her mother. Despite the thong, despite what just happened, she was the opposite of sexy.

Sad. That's what she was. Bordering on pathetic.

She opened her eyes only to see his erection making a mess of the front of his khaki pants. And the sight, the thought of it, just destroyed her. What did he think was going to happen next? What did *she* think was next? That they would just climb in the back of the Cadillac, or, *oh my God*, was she supposed to do the same thing to him, out here? In the open?

I'm not this person, she thought. *What the hell am I doing?*

"I have to go," she blurted.

"What . . . now?"

"Yep. Yes. I'm . . . ah . . . I'm late. So. You'll be fine." She grabbed the water from the ground and poured it into the radiator. Water splashed everywhere. "Just keep an eye on the heat gauge and the car will be fine. I mean . . . and I suppose—" she gestured toward the erection, because she was that stupid. "You . . . ah . . . will be too. I guess." Oh my God, where was an earthquake, a flash flood when you needed it?

"Is this a joke?" he laughed, but there was an edge to it. He was getting angry.

She nearly ran, embarrassed, and her thong was unpleasantly wet and uncomfortable and her pride all worn and ratty. The door of the car slammed shut, sealing her into its familiar blandness, its safety ratings and good gas mileage. *Yes.* This was right. Even the emergency kit in the backseat made her feel better.

She drove away in a plume of dust, not even lifting her hand in a wave. Not even honking.

It didn't happen, she told herself, turning up the radio, brushing her blond hair out of her eyes. *None of that happened.*

Chapter 8

Jackson braced his head in his hands and wondered why he scheduled budget meetings on Monday morning. It was like taking a sledgehammer to the day. To his own head.

"I thought . . . I thought we'd dodged the bankruptcy bullet," Jackson said. "We were in the clear."

"It's not bankruptcy, Jackson. Not exactly. It's just . . . reality. Look, you've done a great job, son," Brian Andersen, the city treasurer and undoubtedly the next mayor of Bishop, took off his half-glasses and folded them up as if he were ready to throw in the towel. "You cleared up the pension mess you inherited. I thought for sure that would ruin us. Frankly, we've held on longer than I thought we would."

"Let's walk backward," Jackson said, leaning back in the chair behind his desk. His hair was still damp from his morning swim, his body loose and boneless, his muscles unable to muster up a twinge despite the conversation. On a purely selfish note, thank God he'd managed to keep the pool open. Without his grueling workouts, there was no telling what would happen at these budget meetings.

He imagined turning into The Hulk and smashing desks.

With a sigh, Brian put his glasses back on. Gray was smattered through his dark black curls, and wrinkles creased his ebony skin—this job had aged him.

"Without a change in the tax base, next year we either close the library or we pay the fire chief's salary," he said.

"We can't not have a fire chief."

"Then we close the library."

"We can't close the library! What about volunteers? If we just have volunteers run it?"

"And how do we pay the utilities? Taxes? It's one of the biggest buildings in the city—"

"Okay. Okay." Jackson looked out the window and wondered, just briefly, what was happening in Rio de Janeiro at this moment. Dancing, probably. That hip-swervy Latin stuff. He wasn't much of a dancer but if he moved to Rio, he'd learn. He was probably great at it and just didn't know it.

"The contest—"

"We can't bank on the contest, Jackson. We can't."

Jackson knew that, he did, but he *wanted* to bank on it. He wanted to put aside all this anxiety over the town and start looking forward to the next part of his life. He wanted to move on.

"Two more months," he said. "Two more months before we make these big decisions."

"Jackson." Brian's sigh reeked of disappointment and censure, and Jackson bristled. "What happens if we don't win? This town needs to restructure. It's not the town it was before the recession, which doesn't have to be a tragedy. But I think if we really looked at reality—"

"You can restructure when *you're* mayor." As soon as the words were out, he regretted them. Brian didn't deserve that, but Jackson had started down this road and he couldn't change direction now. He was swinging for the fences here, damn it! "How are the Okra Festival plans going?"

"Great. We've made a little money on the parade permits. The street-fair vendor licenses are all sold—people seem to be excited."

"Good. That's . . . good." Good, but not enough. Not nearly enough and they both knew it.

Brian closed his books, which was the universal signal that the meeting was over. He stood and collected his stuff, and Jackson had to admire the guy. Considering they were the only two people with all their fingers in the dam, Brian kept his cool. Brian could quit, as he'd no doubt been tempted to do once he realized the mess they were in—Lord knows Jackson had been—yet he'd stayed.

They might not always agree, but he showed up at these meetings every week with ideas, ready to try.

"You'll be a good mayor," Jackson said.

"The election isn't for another three months," Brian said, smiling over his shoulder as he headed for the door.

"No one is running against you, Brian. Everyone knows you'll be good for Bishop."

Brian stopped at the door, his hand on the knob. "I won't have a magic contest to help this town out."

That felt like hard censure, and Jackson's back rose. "Should I have sat back and not tried?"

"No, but . . . not everything needs to be fixed. Some things just . . . are."

Jackson shrugged, angry and at a loss, because he didn't understand what Brian was talking about. *Some things just are? What things?* Everything was changeable; he knew that better than anyone. One minute a guy could have a life, a girlfriend, plans for the future, and the next that could all be gone. People could change— he had big plans in that department. And everything . . . everything could be fixed.

Brian shook his head and left, closing the door behind him with a definitive click.

Jackson stared at the intricately carved door of his office. *Honestly*, he thought, apropos of nothing, *who carves a door like that? What is the point of a door like that?*

Something restless roared through him and he wanted, ferociously, to see Monica. To bury his discontent in her discontent. To find, in all the expectations that the world seemed to have about them, the truth, as only they could define it.

But then the moment was over, and he got up and walked to the door.

One thing he had learned coming back to this town was that when things were really bad, when he wanted to close his eyes and drown in the problems that rose around him, nothing worked like movement. Forward motion. Not always the best thing, but sometimes the only thing.

Ms. Watson—not Pam, not Pamela, but Ms. Watson—the secretary who came with his job, who had worked at the desk on the other side of that stupid door through the terms of four mayors including his father, looked up expectantly.

"I'm going to go to Cora's," he said. "You want something?"

Ms. Watson declined; Ms. Watson always declined. Jackson shrugged. "I have my cell if anyone needs me."

Ten minutes later, as he crossed the street to Cora's, the front door to the café opened and Cora stood there, her eyes wide and lit with manic excitement. No scarf in her hair today, and she wore chef whites. Very professional. Something was up.

"He's here," she said.

"Who is here?"

"The cracker guy."

"He is?" He glanced through the plate-glass window. Inside, the café seemed filled with regulars. But all the regulars were staring at the corner booth, obscured by the door.

He followed Cora into the restaurant, and the expectations he'd felt on Friday were doubled at least. It was like walking into a giant web.

"Coffee, Cora?" he said, and she walked away nodding. He took a deep breath and turned to face the man in the corner booth. Dean Jennings, in the flesh, wearing an ordinary summer-weight suit and button-down shirt, but somehow making it look glamorous.

"Hi," Jackson said as he approached the tall blond man. "I'm Jackson Davies, mayor of Bishop."

"Oh, right." The man stood partially and shook Jackson's hand. "I was going to make my way over to your office in a bit. Dean Jennings, CEO of—"

"Maybream Crackers, of course. It's a pleasure to meet you, Dean." The man's handshake was firm and swift. *Chalk another point up for Dean,* Jackson thought.

"Well, I don't want to interrupt your breakfast—" He let it dangle, banking on the man's manners being as powerful as his own.

"No, please join me. I was getting a bit wigged out with all of these people staring at me while I ate."

Jackson sat. "You get used to it."

"I'm not sure why I would want to."

It seemed those moments that just put a pin in the way his life was lived here were coming in fast succession. Those things he took for granted as immoveable realities just got kicked aside by other people, as if they were nothing.

Why get used to people watching you eat, indeed?

"It's sort of a small-town thing."

"I wouldn't know." Dean looked back at the people staring at him, as if they were the ones in the zoo. It was effective; most people looked away.

"Where are you from?" Jackson asked.

"New York, born and raised."

The words came with a cool breeze, a whiff of the exotic. Skyscrapers and counterculture coffee shops. Good pizza on every corner, music spilling out of grungy clubs. A city that never sleeps. He imagined himself there in one of those slick skinny suits, going to art galleries with fashion-model girlfriends.

Cora arrived with his cup of coffee. "Usual?" she asked Jackson but stared at Dean.

"That would be great, thank you, Cora."

"And you?" she asked Dean.

"I'm fine," he said, and she left. Rather slowly, truth be told.

"When does the *America Today* crew get in?" Jackson asked, getting comfortablc.

"Tomorrow. They're finishing up the shoot in Alaska."

"Alaska?"

"One of the semifinalists. I arrived yesterday, drove in from Little Rock."

Jackson burned to ask about the town in Alaska but refrained. "Well, I hope everything has been satisfactory so far?"

Dean grinned down at his nearly empty plate as if he had a little secret. "No complaints."

"You're at the Peabody, right?"

"Yeah, I am. It's very nice. Inviting."

The conversation stalled into silence. Christ, this guy didn't make anything easy. "So, tell me about your decision to move your factory."

Dean rubbed his face. The bell over the door kept ringing as word got out that Dean was here and everyone in town suddenly got very hungry for Cora's. "I wouldn't call it a decision, really. I had to do something. Nabisco is trying to buy us out and the board of directors is breathing down my neck to take the deal. So, this is my last kick at the can."

Dean looked up and laughed at Jackson's slack-jawed

face. "Not quite the story of patriotic industrial leadership you were hoping for?"

"I guess not."

"Right. Well, the thing Maybream shares with every town in this contest is we're all in trouble. We're all—"

"Swinging for the fences," Jackson supplied.

"Exactly. So . . . when can I get a look at your factory?"

"Anytime, really."

Dean stabbed the last bite of his pancake and ate it, groaning. "Well, so far you guys have the best food of any of the towns."

Jackson's heart rate spiked, but he had excellent playing-it-cool abilities.

"Did you have the peach?"

"Pecan."

"Either way, you can't lose. You know, after the factory, I'd love to show you some more of the town so you can get a better idea of our community. Shelby Monroe's art camps—"

"Listen, Jackson, I'm going to stop you right there. I could give a shit about the community—excuse my language. That's the *America Today* angle. They force me to tag along to that crap. But I'm interested in the town with the factory that won't bankrupt me to retrofit and the state that will give me the best tax break."

Jackson blinked, stunned, trying to keep up with this sudden turn in conversation. The bell rang again and it set his teeth on edge. "But . . . what about your employees?"

"They'll go to Timbuktu if it means the company stays alive and they get to keep their jobs."

Thank God, Cora arrived with his breakfast sandwich on an English muffin, because he had nothing to say to Dean. Nothing good. He felt like he'd been duped.

"No pecan pancakes?" Dean asked.

"When Cora first opened I gained about ten pounds. She was doing this pulled-pork fried-egg thing. . . . It nearly killed me."

"Sounds good."

Jackson forced himself to laugh, to pretend his stomach wasn't sitting in his shoes. "It was."

The front door opened again, setting off the bell. Honestly, Jackson was thinking of starting a petition to have that bell removed.

"Jesus Christ, is that—"

Jackson looked up and there, looking like a slightly grumpy forties pinup star, was Monica.

Her black hair was pulled back in a bun and she had a wide blue-and-white polka-dotted headband on. She wore a man's short-sleeve tan shirt over black leggings. A very sexy Rosie the Riveter.

"That's . . . Monica Appleby, isn't it?" Dean asked. Jackson nodded and tried not to stare. He'd worked very hard not to think about her yesterday, instead finding about thirty very strenuous jobs to do at the Big House, but it didn't stop him from dreaming about her last night like a fourteen-year-old boy.

Jackson took a bite of his breakfast sandwich—the tomato exploded in his mouth, tasting like summer—and nodded.

"Is she . . . does she live here?"

"For the moment, I suppose," Jackson said after he swallowed.

Dean's mouth hung agape. "Oh. My. God. The book. The book about her father's murder. She's here to write it."

"No. No." Jackson shook his head but his denials had no impact; Dean was digging through his briefcase. "Where . . . where did you hear that?"

"There."

It was the Sunday *New York Times* book section. A small side piece. Jackson read it out loud.

" 'Can Monica Appleby do it again? *Wild Child* author to write nonfiction account of her father's murder at her mother's hands in a small Arkansas town.' " Jackson sat back; so much for keeping it a secret. It was in the god-damn *Times*.

Monica glanced over at him, her hand lifting in a half-wave, and he gave her a sick smile. It was not his finest moment, but there was a disaster looming. Cold sweat formed under his collar, reawakening the smell of chlorine on his skin.

"She's . . ." He wasn't sure how he was going to finish that. *Not a part of this town. A dirty secret. Every single thing I want and can't have right now?*

"Beautiful," Dean said. "Way more beautiful than in her head shot, despite that ugly shirt. Have you read her book?"

"No, I have not."

"Hot shit, man. That woman is seriously hot shit. And she's here! Now I find myself a bit more interested in your town." Dean bobbed his eyebrows like a cartoon lecher and Jackson dropped his sandwich. The firm handshake had been a ruse.

"Are you joking?" Jackson asked.

"Hey, don't look at me like that. You want people to vote for your town—she'll help. The world loves gossip and scandal, and her family has that in spades."

Some awful voice in Jackson's head said, *He's right. People would give us the vote just for Monica Appleby.*

"If just half the things in that book are true . . ." Dean muttered, his eyes running all over Monica's body with a hot, insulting sense of ownership.

"Then what?" Jackson asked, his voice hard. He might contemplate using Monica for his own gain, which truly was one of the more despicable things he'd thought of in recent years, but he wasn't going to sit here and listen to Dean speculate about what she might or might not have done in her past.

Dean blinked at Jackson and then smiled. "You want to duel over her honor? Hardly seems worth it. She threw it away years ago, along with her underwear. I'm just going to go have a chat with her."

Before Jackson could say anything, Dean stood and crossed the café to the front booth by the window where Monica sat. A few people at the counter twisted on their stools to watch.

Monica had her laptop open and a pair of headphones on, the big fancy ones that he thought only hip-hop artists wore. She glanced up when Dean approached and slipped the headphones off, pulling some of her hair out of the headband she wore, and a fat curl bounced down over her eye. Jackson smiled when she batted it away.

They shook hands, and Jackson was somehow relieved to see that fake smile she gave the world on her face.

Good, he thought, *let's see you get past that, Dean.*

She glanced over at Jackson, her eyes unreadable, and the world dropped away for just a moment. Just long enough for him to remember with painful clarity the loosening of her body against his the other night. It felt like a secret between them, something special, perhaps like her frowns. Just for him.

She looked back up at Dean and shook her head. She laughed and gestured to the restaurant. And he could practically hear her saying, *I'm not really a part of the town. I'm not a part of the competition.*

And he was hit by two waves of equal size, one of relief and one of regret. *Thank God, and what if she really is the key to winning?*

Christ, could nothing be simple?

He expected Dean, having been rebuffed, to head back over to rejoin him. But instead he kept talking and then, Monica was frowning. Frowning at Dean, and then Dean was sitting down across from her. Jackson watched as the man's knees touched Monica's and she shifted to accommodate their length.

Jackson had to look away, embarrassed by his jealousy. He was in no position to monitor her knees and whose knees they touched. He was planning his great escape. He was going to be an art snob in New York.

He dug into his sandwich, which no longer tasted like summer, but he couldn't leave it. If he was honest with himself, he couldn't leave at all, not until Dean did.

She threw it away with her underwear.

A different man would have punched Dean's face for those words. Jackson couldn't tell if that different man was better or worse than himself.

Again, the bell over the door rang and Jackson fought hard not to roll his eyes. But on a wave of sunshine and sweet air, Shelby Monroe walked in, wearing a green sundress, her blond hair pulled back in a tight, straight ponytail. She saw Jackson immediately and walked over, pushing her sunglasses to the top of her head. They were good friends, and for a brief period of time after he'd moved back, he'd planned on marrying her. It seemed like a no-brainer: she was here, she was solid, and she would have been hugely helpful with Gwen.

But one drunken kiss between them dispelled the thought for both of them. They had about as much chemistry as siblings.

"Hey, Jackson," she said. "How are you?"

"Good. How was your conference?"

For some reason the question made her blush, and she dug into her briefcase. "I have the final registration numbers for the camps. Better than last year. Not a whole lot, but still better."

"Good. Hey, since you're here, I need the factory keys

back from your mom. Dean Jennings is here and wants a tour."

Jackson pointed over at Dean and Shelby turned to look. Sensing the attention, perhaps, Dean looked over, a wide smile on his sharp-featured face, but when he caught sight of Shelby, the smile dropped almost as fast as Shelby's purse dropped from her arm.

"What—?" Jackson reached for the purse, then for Shelby, who seemed somehow unstable. Her face scarlet, she grabbed her purse.

"Sorry. I . . . . ah . . . forgot something." And then she was gone, the bell over the door ringing madly at her exit.

Jackson glanced back at Dean, who was watching her go, his mouth agape.

Did I miss something? Jackson thought.

And then Dean was on his feet, headed toward his table.

"That was Shelby Monroe," Jackson said.

"Really?" Dean looked far more stunned than the information warranted. "The art camp woman?"

"I think she prefers 'teacher.' "

"Right. Whatever. I'll just . . . well, I suppose it wouldn't hurt to get a sense of the community." He grabbed his stuff and tossed some money on the table.

"Tomorrow morning," Jackson said. "When the *America Today* crew comes in, let's meet in my office. I can help get you all set up."

"Okay," Dean said. "That . . . that would be great." And then he was gone, the bell over the door ringing in the silence his departure had created.

The restaurant seemed suspended in time for a moment, as if the drama had them all frozen. Neighbors glanced at each other, and then life resumed.

Jackson watched as Monica put her headphones back on.

Don't, he told himself. *It's not really your business. And she probably won't even tell you.*

But in the end, he couldn't help it. He got up and crossed the café to see what Monica and Dean had talked about.

Shelby knew he—the man from the side of the road, *the CEO of Maybream Crackers*—was following. Her skin told her and that was weird, a first for her. So weird in fact that she stopped, and the man from the side of the road caught up with her.

"Hey . . . hey," he panted, coming to stand next to her, filling the air with a certain vitality. A focused energy, focused on her. He was somehow even better-looking at this moment, chasing after her. "I can't . . . I can't believe it's you."

What do I do? she wondered. *Pretend like nothing happened?* That was hardly mature. Jackson—hell, the whole café—was probably still staring out the window, mouth agape after that little scene.

"Shelby," she said and put her hand out like a barricade. The tips of her fingers ran into his stomach and he stopped. "My name is Shelby."

"I'm . . ." He stepped back and glanced down at her hand before slipping his palm against hers. Strange, the ripple over her skin. Shocking, a little. She felt worry. And desire, yes. Lots of that. She couldn't stop thinking about where that hand had touched her. And as if the thought had flipped a switch, the back of her thigh pulsed with heat. If she looked, she had no doubt that there would be a glowing handprint on the back of her leg. "I'm Dean."

"Nice to meet you," she said, clinging out of sheer force of habit to her manners.

"I'd say." His smile was not polite, and now even more

of her skin was pulsing. It was sending trails across her neck and down her chest where his lips had touched, his fingers.

She was a light-up map of that sexual encounter.

"You . . . you're the CEO of Maybream."

"I am . . . and you're the art camp organizer."

"I am."

The conversation jumped off the cliff into silence.

"Look, Dean—" she said at the same time he said:

"Shelby, I'm—"

They stopped and he smiled, and that smile was nothing but invitation. He was going to ask her out, to coffee, to bed, to the backseat of his car, she wasn't sure where, but she was totally sure he was going to ask.

"Dean," she said, stopping him. "What . . . what happened between us was an anomaly."

"Is that what you guys call it down here?" he joked, the invitation still looming. Lord, how did she get into this kind of mess? Other women had flings. Indiscretions. Peccadilloes. Why did hers have to be with the man who could help save this town? That added some steel to her spine. This contest was a big deal and she couldn't jeopardize it.

"I'm . . . not interested in anything more." Was that how it was said?

Dean blinked. "What . . . do you mean a relationship? Because I'm not either, but what happened—"

"Won't happen again. Surely, as CEO of Maybream it would be a conflict of interest, wouldn't it? To have . . . something happen between us."

"It's not like I intend to broadcast it to the world." His voice was low, a murmur that made heat flare between her legs. She pulled her sunglasses over her eyes, wishing she had more to barricade herself from him. From the way he made her feel.

"I understand, but this is a small town." *And it's my*

world, and we probably just broadcast more than you know to everyone at Cora's. "And I would hate . . . I would hate to jeopardize our position in this contest, over a . . . fling."

"Fine," he muttered, "whatever . . . whatever you want. But you sure put on quite a show for a woman who isn't interested."

She smiled, but her face was burning. Anger and a weird shame tied her in knots. Thirty-two years old and she'd never done this before. *Sad. Sad. Sad.* Other girls had mapped out all the parameters of their sexual power by the time they were sixteen. But she'd been too busy praying when she was sixteen, forced on her knees to repent the most boring life ever lived by a teenager. Her father had been a zealot, unstable, and convinced of her sin.

Dean lifted his hand as if to shake hands again and she lifted hers, but then he just waved, defeated. She dropped her hand.

"Goodbye," he said, laughter in his voice, and she couldn't help but feel that he was laughing at her and she wanted to die, just die.

This was why she kept herself hidden behind her teacher voice and emergency car kit. Because getting hurt, getting laughed at, being rejected even while rejecting someone else—it hurt. Diminished her in ways she didn't need any help diminishing.

Chapter 9

Monica ignored Jackson as he slid into the booth across from her. First the Cracker dude and now Jackson. Good Lord, weren't the headphones a giveaway? Did she need to make a Do Not Disturb sign? This was why she so rarely went to coffee shops to work, preferring her own company and her own music. But her hotel room was still haunted by her mother's call.

"What?" she snapped, pulling off her headphones.

"Good morning to you, too." His hair was all disorderly, falling over his forehead in a way that made her fingers itch to push it away.

She frowned at him, just to let him know she wasn't buying his smile this morning. His charm or floppy hair.

"You met Dean?" he asked.

"Don't worry. I told him I wasn't a part of Bishop's 'community.'" She put extra sarcasm into the air quotes, making them especially insufferable.

He nodded and gave his sandwich a totally unnecessary and utterly telling quarter turn on his white plate, and she realized with a finely honed feminine instinct that he knew what she'd said to Dean about the contest.

And he was over here for other reasons.

"He wanted to talk about the new book," she said. "Apparently he's a big fan."

He groaned. "You said you wouldn't talk about it."

"I didn't. *He* did. I can't help it that the *Times* picked up the *Rolling Stone* story." He opened his mouth and she put up her hand. "Don't worry, I told him my book didn't have anything to do with Bishop or the contest."

"Did . . . did you get ahold of Sean's dad?"

She nodded. "I'm going to talk to him at his house on Tuesday. Discreetly."

His smile was a narrow flash and she was glad, in a way, that they could joke about it. Because honestly, she liked him. She did. And that was pretty damn rare in her life.

A question blazed in Jackson's eyes and she realized he wasn't over here just because of the town. He might have told himself that when he walked over here, but there was another fuel in his engine.

"He asked me out for a drink," she told him, putting him out of his misery.

At the very bottom of Monica's life, when it was its darkest and most awful, she was dating the drummer for a famous rock band. The drummer, when he wasn't drunk, was sweet. Well, sweet compared to when he was drunk, when he was a raving lunatic. His jealous tempers, the way he went after guys who looked at Monica too long, or asked her for a light or innocently inquired as to the location of a bathroom—she told herself, from her position in that dark dead end that her life had become, that it was flattering.

That it was love.

And when it became obvious that it wasn't love, she told herself that it was just the way guys were. That they were jealous, irrational creatures.

But watching Jackson absorb her words, she realized that he was jealous and totally rational. His eyes might have flickered out the window, his hands tightening on his coffee cup, but whatever dark instincts swirled in him, he resisted.

How interesting, she thought, how infinitely more attractive his restraint was than her old boyfriend's violent abandon.

"Do you want to ask me if I'm going to go?" she asked, for no good reason.

"Of course I do, Monica. But I also realize I have no right."

Oh. Such poetry!

She sat taller in her seat. *Damn straight,* she thought.

"He recognized you from the book," he bit out, his eyes hot when they met hers. As hot as his hand had been on the back of her neck. "You know what he wants."

"Of course I know what he wants. And I can handle him. But he said something . . . useful to me."

Jackson reeled back. "Useful to you how?"

"Apparently the producer *America Today* is using to tape all the town packages is freelance. And he offered to introduce me to her."

"Why would you care?"

"Well, I . . ." *Stupid.* The words had just fallen out of her mouth, unchecked because she hadn't had coffee and she'd been kept awake at night trying to figure out how to handle the effect this book about her dad was going to have on her life. "I had this idea of producing a documentary to coincide with my book. To help me control my message."

"Message?"

She didn't want to talk about this. Not in a coffee shop. Not with him. "Forget it, Jackson," she murmured, and she lifted her hands to put her headphones back on. But he pressed down the top of her laptop—not all the way, just enough so they could see each other with nothing in the way.

So minor, presumptuous really. But it made her realize how *no one* did that. *No one* made any effort to see her more clearly, literally or figuratively.

You're high on Shalimar, she told herself, but she dropped her hands anyway.

"Tell me how he can help control your message," he asked as if he cared. As if his motives had nothing to do with this town and its success in the contest. As if he cared about *her.*

"Well, he can't. He's just a blowhard trying to get in my pants. But the freelance producer might be helpful."

"Explain it to me, Monica. I'm not judging you. I'm interested."

She couldn't help but smile, flush with a strange tenderness for this man, for his innocence.

Perhaps it was her mother's call, the awfulness that Simone's voice dredged up in her, but she realized in painful, heart-smashing clarity that no one, no one alive, really knew her anymore.

Jenna, her best friend, the only person who had known her, warts and halos and everything in between, was gone. *Gone.*

Friends are mirrors held up to remind us of who we really are, she thought.

And she felt the lack, the terrible hole in her life, in a fresh and disturbing way. Without Jenna reminding her who she really was, she was in danger of losing herself to everyone's expectations. To everyone's opinion of her.

But this man with his beautiful eyes and his hair and his fingers—he *wanted* to know her. And that was enough. Enough to make her unlock some of her secrets. To let down her guard to be more . . . herself.

"Look, I wrote a book about the messed-up kid I was. I was brutally honest about the mistakes I made and what I learned from them. And then that book came out and . . . I'm grateful, I am, for its success. It has allowed me to do a lot of things I wouldn't have been able to do." She thought of Jenna and those bills, the pain her friend had been in. And how Monica having money made some of that pain go away. And that was worth a hundred books. "But people only want that messed-up, hypersexualized kid. They look at me and see the sixteen-year-old in the TV show. The twenty-year-old in the book. Men look at me and see the woman who had sex with famous rock stars. But it wasn't sexy. Or exciting. It was sad, and needy. Scary sometimes." He didn't say anything, he just watched her without judgment. Another gift he seemed to give her without realizing how valuable it was. Jenna had done that too, and she marveled at the fact that Jenna had died and this man stepped into her life all in the same week. It was as if Jenna was looking out for her. And the thought, while crazy, was comforting. "And even though that was the way I wrote it in the book, the world saw it differently. Or at least most of the world. Every question I was asked by reporters, by talk show hosts, made it sound titillating, and no matter what I said—"

"They saw what they wanted to see."

She took a deep breath. "And with this next book, I want to be more than the child of a woman who killed her husband in self-defense."

"If you're so worried about it, why write the book?"

She bristled, recognizing his tone, his backward coercion. "You can't convince me not to do it, Jackson."

"I'm not trying."

"Bullshit. And you know it."

They stared at each other, neither of them giving an inch. Why was that so attractive to her? *Because you're perverse and hungry and lonely, and getting a cup of coffee takes a million years in this place!*

"I want to understand why you're putting yourself out there for the world to judge and get wrong. If it hurt so much the last time, why do it again?"

"I don't have a choice, Jackson. I . . ." She took a breath so deep it shook at the bottom. "I had a friend.

My . . . my best friend, Jenna. And she had cervical cancer and no insurance. She was teaching music to low-income kids in Nashville. Her money was gone, and she couldn't pay for treatment."

"Monica," he sighed, the word loaded with pain and understanding.

"So I paid Jenna's medical bills." The words flung themselves from her lips as though they couldn't wait to taste freedom. "As much as I could, just to keep her comfortable. I mean, by the time I found out she was . . . well, it was bad. And before that, I took a hit with the stock market, a couple of them actually. And now I'm pretty damn broke and I took the advance for this book. And I can't pay it back, so all I can do is write it. I have no choice. None. Not that I expect you to understand that." She threw that last statement out there, in an effort to deflect his attention, to shift things into a more comfortable position.

He was calm in the face of her incendiary words. But he didn't respond; his blue eyes just watched her, and that movie-star face of his changed, became . . . older, somehow.

It shamed her, that face. Made her regret her small taunts, her even smaller motivations.

She held her breath, waiting. Sensing the beautiful, golden Jackson Davies was about to reveal something tarnished. Something not a lot of people got to see. And she thought about how odd that was, how strange her life had become, that people didn't reveal anything to her anymore. You didn't realize how precious that was until it never happened anymore.

"I haven't had a choice since I was twenty-two and my parents died, and I moved back here to take care of my sister."

Oh. Oh no. She blinked. Stunned. Unsure of what to

say, how to address all the potential pain in that sentence.

"I didn't know you had a sister," she whispered.

"She's twelve years younger than me, and when our mom and dad died, she was only eleven. Not that it's ever a good age to lose your parents, but . . . it was rough. For her. For us."

"I'm so sorry."

"I'm sorry, too. For Jenna." His smile was weary, bone tired. "I moved back to Bishop because it was right, because there wasn't a choice, really. But it doesn't stop you from resenting it at times. Or being angry to have had the power taken away. Loving my sister with all my heart doesn't make it so I don't wish things were different. I had just started law school. There was even a girlfriend . . ." He stopped, his attention caught on the salt shaker as if he'd glimpsed something important, but then he looked back at her, his smile working so hard to convince her that the girlfriend, the life just beginning, it was all inconsequential. The smile didn't succeed. No smile could have succeeded.

"I . . . I didn't know."

"I know." He leaned forward, his hands flat against the white table with the red specks. She looked at his long, wide fingers and thought of their touch, one by one, on her neck. "I think there's a lot about you I don't know. And before you tell me to read the book, I need to tell you I won't. Ever."

Why did that seem like a gift?

Stupid Monica, putting all your gratitude on the stupid things.

"But I also want to say that I feel like the first choice I've made that was mine, all mine, in a very, very long time was to kiss you the other night. Or maybe earlier, when I invited you in for dinner. Something so small and yet huge at the same time. That's strange, isn't it?"

"No," she breathed, because she understood down to her bones, down to her sinew and muscle, exactly what he meant. Because her life had gotten slightly off track when she'd accepted the invitation for dinner.

Jackson heaved a big breath, tilting his head to look out the plate-glass window beside them. The sky was achingly blue, the street outside charming and totally worthy of being on television. *He did that,* she thought, seeing this town and the contest and all of his efforts differently at this moment.

As noble, not silly.

When he glanced up at her again, the weariness, that intriguing depth to his face, the difference in his eyes, was all gone and he was shiny again. He wore his public face. And she hated it, wanted to do something to make it go away.

Kiss him. She wanted to kiss him again.

"And that didn't go so well. For either of us."

It was a mistake for me too. She remembered her words. So flip, so dismissive.

"So perhaps it's best that I'm not left to my own choices anymore." Jackson tapped the table, then picked up his dishes to clear them himself because he was that kind of guy. "I'll let you get back to work."

She didn't stop him. She let him walk away even though part of her wanted to pull him back. To make him tell her more about his sister, and part of her . . . part of her wanted to tell him about Jenna. But in the end she watched him walk away. She put her headphones back on and opened up her computer and stared, unseeing, at a blank page.

"What's with you?" Gwen muttered Tuesday morning, giving Jackson the hairy eyeball over her cereal bowl. Apparently his whistling was an affront to her teenage grumpiness. She sat, slouched at the counter, her body a long curve. Her long blond hair hung across half her face. It was as if she were always hiding. From him.

I'm not Dad, I know that, he thought but couldn't say. *But we used to be friends.*

"Optimism, Gwen. Optimism is what's with me." He didn't wait for the coffee to finish brewing before pouring himself a cup and toasting his sister with it. If he were the singing type, he would have sung in the shower. He would have sung making breakfast. "Today is the first day of Bishop's second life."

"As a Podunk town in the middle of nowhere?"

"No," he said carefully, refusing to let her kill his buzz. "That was its first life. Its second life is as a wholesome, forward-thinking community with opportunities for adults and children alike."

When he'd memorized those words from *America Today*, he wasn't sure. But they were running through his head like marathoners.

Gwen blinked her heavily made-up eyes at him. The day was hot already, hazy with humidity, the sky outside nearly gray. He doubted anyone wanted to experience the 100-percent-humidity part of the Bishop story.

"You really think we're going to win this contest?" she asked, before tipping her cereal bowl to drain the milk into her mouth.

"Yep," he replied, leaning against the old butcher-block counters.

Gwen shook the hair from her face.

There you are, he thought with a piercing fondness.

Her face was changing, slowly being carved out by maturity. Womanhood. The chipmunk cheeks were melting away, her jawline losing its little-girl roundness. Her blue eyes were so big even with that dark crap she wore around them. She was lovely, and if she would just smile more . . .

"I forgot to ask, how did that thing go with Monica Appleby?" she asked.

"What . . . ?" The kiss. That was all he could think about at the mention of her name. The touch of her tongue against his.

Nice, Jackson. So grown up. So fully adult.

"At our house? The notes? Remember?"

"Right." He pushed aside thoughts of that kiss, reminding himself that it had been a mistake for both of them. "Actually, the notes were for Dean Jennings and the *America Today* producers."

"You . . . you just said someone not from around here." She was so quick to be defensive. So quick to snap at him.

"I know, Gwen, it's no big deal. Don't worry."

"So . . . did she come over?"

"She did."

"And?"

And I insulted her and then kissed her and then insulted her again. "She had some lemonade."

"Lemonade? Jackson . . . that's so lame."

"She wanted it!" he cried in his own defense. "What was I supposed to give her? Heroin?"

"So, is she like . . . coming over again?"

"I doubt it."

"What did you do?"

Jackson blinked, surprised by the viciousness of her tone. She'd been aloof, she'd been moderately disrespectful, but never mean. A thousand words, just as mean, just as vicious, came roaring up from his gut, but he swallowed them.

"I didn't do anything, Gwen. She came over, had lemonade, and left. What did—" He stopped, realizing what this was. The eye makeup, the book. Her sister had a little hero-worship happening.

For the Wild Child.

Part of him, faulty and human, wanted to bundle his

little sister up and avert her eyes from the wreck that
Monica had made of her early life. *Don't be like her,* he
thought. *Don't idolize her mistakes, cast her heartbreak in heroic lights.*

Careful here, Jackson, he thought, all too aware of
the high wire he stood on.

"If you want to talk to her—"

"Forget it," she sighed and moved to stand.

"Wait," he said, putting out his hand, barely brushing her arm before she recoiled. He sighed. The bubble,
he'd forgotten about the bubble. "What . . . what's your
plan for the day?"

"I have a shift at the Peabody, and then Shelby's comic-
book camp started on Monday; she asked if I could help
out with that because she was going to be busy with the
film crew and stuff."

"We should grab dinner tonight," he said. "Fried
chicken at Cora's."

"I have pageant rehearsal."

"Really? Seems early to be getting ready for the pageant."

"You're the one who wanted me to be in this stupid
thing, now you're angry about the time?"

"No . . . no." He should be used to the fact that he just
couldn't win with her. Ever. "Go to pageant rehearsal.
This is your year, isn't it?" As the oldest girl in the competition, she was a shoo-in. Perhaps as his sister, too.
And even with this goth-chick phase, she was by far the
prettiest girl in town.

"Whatever," she sighed. "It's lame."

Yep, *Pick Your Battles* was going to make a stunner
of a tattoo, along his rib cage maybe, in fancy script.

"I have to go meet the film crew at the office," he said,
changing the subject. "Check in with me around noon,
okay?"

"I'm not a kid."

"You're my kid sister."

"What are you going to do when I go away to school, Jackson?"

For a second he had that sickening feeling of being caught in a lie and blood roared up behind his eyes. She didn't know about his plans to leave when she left and he realized there was a very good chance that she wouldn't care. But still, somehow he hadn't been able to tell her.

There was also the chance she would freak out, and he couldn't handle her freaking out any more than she currently was—not with the Maybream situation.

All of which was a cop-out. He knew that.

He was scared to tell his sister he was leaving. Scared to hurt her. Scared to tell her and hear that she didn't care. That she'd never cared.

But maybe it was time to face up to all that fear.

"What do you mean?"

She smirked at him, a dagger at his heart. "I mean, I won't be calling you when I'm at school."

He braced himself against the counter, his knees weak.

Or he could face up to it all later.

"You haven't left yet. Check in with me," he said and was out the door.

When Jackson stepped through City Hall's wide granite arches, built by Bishop's founding fathers in a delusion of grandeur a hundred years ago, he was both comforted and made to feel insignificant. A dot on the time line of this town.

That was the nice thing about city halls, no matter what size the town: they were built with a little pomp and circumstance. With one eye to the future, the other to the past and the unbroken road between the two.

It was to be respected, that was for sure.

"Morning, Ms. Watson," he said to his secretary.

"You have some visitors, those television folks," she said, standing up behind her desk, wearing the pink cardigan she always wore when the air conditioner was turned up too high. "I . . . I didn't . . . I didn't know what to do. I made them some coffee, I had some graham crackers in the kitchen, but that . . . that was all. I didn't . . ."

"It's great. Perfect. I should have told you, but I didn't think they'd be this early," he said, glancing at his watch; it was barely eight a.m. He'd take their early arrival as enthusiasm. *Good.* That had to bode well, didn't it? He stepped into his office, and Dean, accompanied by another man and a woman, stood to face him. A plate of graham crackers sat untouched on the side of his desk.

"Hello," Jackson said.

"Hi, Jackson, sorry we're early," Dean said.

"No, no problem. I see you got coffee." Jackson circled his desk. "Is there anything else I can get you?"

"Three more hours of sleep?" the woman asked.

"Sorry, Vanessa and Matt here spent the night traveling," Dean said.

"Alaska, right?" Jackson asked. "Long trip."

"Tell me about it," Vanessa said. Introductions were made and they shook hands. Matt was the sound guy, a large man with too-small glasses and sweaty hands. Vanessa, the producer, had purple hair and a bit of a snarl. Something about her reminded him of Monica and his sister.

"Well, let's get started," Vanessa said after everyone sat down. "I talked to Cora already. Today she's going to show us how to make two of her specialties. We were hoping to get some information on the windmill technology you've started."

"That's on my property, no problem."

"So what can you tell us about the Okra Festival?"

"Well, tonight we have a Miss Okra pageant rehearsal."

Vanessa laughed. "You're kidding."

"Nothing funny about the Miss Okra pageant. The community takes it very seriously."

"Well then," Vanessa said as she made a few notes, "so will we. Now, the Peabody is lovely, the last antebellum mansion left in the state? That's quite a bragging feature."

"Well, we're proud of it. I'm not sure if that's bragging."

"Jackson." Vanessa smiled at him, indulgently, as if Jackson were a child behaving in a way that was adorable but wrong. "Please don't tell me you plan to be modest with me now. I need you to brag. That's how the show works."

Right. Time to switch gears.

"Our summer art camps set up by Shelby Monroe are becoming internationally recognized."

"That's the spirit." Vanessa nodded encouragingly. "Tell me more."

"This is our fifth year, and Shelby has secured renowned artists to teach classes in glassblowing and sculpture. We have classes for adults and children, including a camp for kids with special needs. This year the artist in residence for the month of August is a street artist from New York; he's going to teach classes on graffiti. The New York Public Library is partnering with us in that class, sending down inner-city kids for a week."

"Very impressive," Vanessa said without any sarcasm. She turned her attention to Dean. "You have to go to some of these tapings, Dean. I'm not kidding," she said when he groaned. "I need you at the tapings and I need you to talk to these people. And not just about engineering factories."

Ah, Jackson thought with real fondness, *there's nothing like a no-nonsense woman.*

There was more discussion about the taping schedules and everyone scribbled in their notebooks while Jackson sat back, feeling pretty damn pleased with himself.

"So?" Vanessa asked, glancing up at Jackson. "What else?"

"That's not enough?" Jackson asked.

"Not to beat Alaska," Matt muttered.

"True." She leaned over her notes toward Jackson. "Why are people going to pick up the phone to vote for Bishop over Alaska? Alaska is memorable, a town of bachelors who created a dating website to attract single women."

"And they have a very modern but defunct salmon-canning factory. And the state tax breaks are amazing," Dean interjected.

Fucking Alaska, Jackson thought for no reason.

"But," Dean said, looking pointedly at Jackson, "you guys have something Alaska doesn't have." Jackson knew in a heartbeat who the guy was talking about.

Monica.

The silence created by his indecision seemed like acquiescence. Maybe it was.

He needed people to pick up the phone and vote.

"Monica Appleby is in town," Dean said.

Vanessa's eyebrows hit the purple tips of her bangs, and Matt whistled low under his breath.

"Does she live here?" Vanessa asked.

"For the moment," Jackson said, knowing he should weigh in.

"She's working on a book about her father, but was very clear that she won't discuss the book. At. All," Dean supplied.

Jackson felt a rush of gratitude toward Monica.

"So?" Vanessa asked. "What do we do with her?

Doesn't sound like she has any part in Bishop's story.
Which is too bad—she'd be a powerful addition."

Vanessa sighed the deep belly sigh of disappointment.
And the silence in Jackson's office after that sigh smelled
like failure. Tasted like a bunch of people giving up, and
he couldn't stand it. Couldn't let it happen. Not when
they were so close.

"Monica teaches at the art camps." The words fell out
of his mouth attached to a half-formed idea. A really stupid half-formed idea. Really. One of his stupidest.

Three heads swiveled to stare at him.

"She does?" Dean asked with the kind of familiarity
that put Jackson's teeth on edge.

"We . . . we're still working out the details."

"What does she teach?"

"Writing. Of course." He fought the wince as he lied.
Shut up, Jackson. Shut up. Just stop talking. "We're very
excited about it."

"That is very cool," Vanessa said, looking at Matt,
who nodded. Dean stared at Jackson, no doubt knowing he was lying.

"Yep," Jackson said; now he couldn't stop nodding.
"Very cool."

In the brief silence that followed he scrambled to
catch up with himself, imagined the conversations he
was going to have to have, the begging he was going to
have to do—both with Shelby, who would *not* appreciate Monica Appleby's presence in her little kingdom,
and Monica, who, after he'd asked her to leave, would
no doubt go apeshit at his asking her to get involved.

This could go wrong in so many ways.

What have I done?

"Well, having Monica Appleby, a number-one *New
York Times* bestselling author, teaching people how to
write should make you very competitive," Vanessa said.

Competitive. Very competitive. That had to be enough.

Dean shut his notebook. "Let's get started, shall we?"

The film crew filed out, discussing with excitement their morning at Cora's. Apparently she was making her pecan pie cake and her brisket with fried green tomato relish.

"Your life is going to change," he told them, standing at the door as they walked through. Smiling as hard as he could while his stomach tied itself in knots.

"When can I get a look at that factory?" Dean asked at the door.

"This afternoon," he said. "Let me just clear a few things off my desk."

Once they were gone he closed the door, bracing himself against it.

Carefully, he lifted his head and thunked it against the intricate carving.

What a mess!

Nothing to do, he told himself, but fix it.

This was going to require the big guns. He hoped Cora made fritters this morning.

Jackson, after stopping at Cora's, walked past downtown toward the dusty outskirts where Shelby lived. Her family owned an old farm, though no one had farmed the land for years. When Shelby and Jackson were kids, her father used the barn for a church of his own creation. Half salesman, half crackpot, her father had been a difficult burden for Shelby until he died. Probably still was, though Shelby never talked about it.

Through her mom's side, Shelby's family had managed the canning factory for generations. Her mom ran that place like a family business until Del Monte finally pulled the plug, and she'd been slipping—mentally and physically—ever since.

Though when they'd gone through the factory cleaning it up for the *America Today* application photos, she'd perked right up. Still, she'd insisted on keeping the keys again when they shut the doors that night, eyeing Jackson as if he were a vandal she'd caught sleeping in the factory.

Across the road from Shelby's, a white moving van sat in the dirt driveway of the Halarens' old place. The farmhouse had been for sale for years, but with the bad economy and the housing situation it hadn't moved. But now the sign was gone and the van was there.

The doors were all shut and there didn't seem to be any movement, but obviously someone had either bought or rented the Halarens' place.

I'm going to take that as a sign that things are looking up.

He bypassed Shelby's house altogether and went out toward the back, where the barns were. Five years ago Shelby got a grant from the state for the money to fix up the barns, one as a studio and the other as a dormitory. Using profits from the camps, she'd made the smokehouse into a kiln a few years ago, and now she had plans to turn the chicken coops into a woodworking workshop.

"Hello?" he called, stepping into the barn. Long tables were set up along one half of the big room, along with small burners for the glass classes. There were pottery wheels in the corner, and easels surrounded a raised dais on the other side of the barn. In the middle were shelves and shelves and shelves of supplies. Paper, paint, turpentine. Buckets of brushes and pencils. Long, thin cases filled with watercolors and chalk.

It smelled both sharp and soft in the barn. The paint and turpentine stung his nose, but then they were quickly followed by the sweet smell of hay that couldn't be renovated away. Swallows still lived in the rafters, refusing to leave while work was done to the building. Occasionally one of the birds dive-bombed an artist's head, which sent the kids into hysterics.

Shelby affectionately named the swallows "the critics."

"Anyone home?" he called, and for a moment only the swallows answered.

"Hey." Shelby came around from the sinks and bathroom she had built into the far corner. Behind that, down a long hallway, was her office. She was drying off her hands. "If you're looking for Gwen, she's not here yet. Camp doesn't start for another hour."

"No, actually. I'm looking for you." He held out the white grease-stained bag and the paper coffee cup from Cora's. "Here."

"Ooooh, coffee and . . ." She opened the bag. "Fritters? To what do I owe this honor? Oh, right." She threw the towel over her shoulder and dug into her pocket. "The keys for the factory. I put them in my pocket and meant to run them by City Hall today."

Jackson pocketed the keys. "Thanks, but I'm not actually here for the keys."

Her brown eyes flared wide, and then she closed them. "Shit," she whispered. "Shit, shit, shit."

It was weird hearing Shelby swear, like catching your parent farting.

"Dean told you?" she asked.

He blinked. "Told me what?"

"About us . . . about the side of the road."

All the apprehension he'd had about asking Shelby to take Monica on as a teacher got pushed aside as he remembered with very sharp clarity Shelby dropping her purse at the restaurant, and the way she and Dean looked at each other as if stunned to see the other—again.

Jackson folded his arms across his chest. "He didn't say anything."

"Oh . . ." It took her a second, and Jackson had to

give her points for trying, but she smiled and managed to wave aside the whole conversation as if it were nothing. "Great, then. What do you need?"

"I need you to tell me what happened on the side of the road with Dean."

"Jackson—"

"He's the CEO of Maybream, Shelby. If something happened that you think I should know about—"

"No one needs to know about it," she said, her cheeks red, her neck blotchy. "It was just . . . a *thing*."

"A thing?" Shelby wasn't the kind of person who had "things." And he couldn't quite believe that she meant *thing* in the way that the rest of the world meant *thing*. Like, perhaps to her, she and Dean did her taxes on the side of the road and that was the "thing." While . . . while he was imagining something totally different.

"Yes." She stood straight, aiming for prim, which usually came pretty naturally to her, but with the blushing it looked like a lie. "A thing."

"Like . . . a sexual thing?" He managed to say it with a straight face but she sensed his shock anyway, and he could tell by the way her shoulders fell that he'd embarrassed her. And that wasn't his intention.

"Shelb—" He reached for her, but she shifted away from the contact.

"I didn't know who he was at the time," she said with stiff and painful forthrightness. "And I've made it clear that nothing else will happen between us."

"What happened?" he cried.

"It's none of your business, Jackson." Her cool eyes shamed him and he held up his hands.

"You're right. But . . . are you okay?"

"Except for this conversation, yes. I'm fine. Now, why are you here?" She put down the white bag and took the plastic lid off the coffee before taking a sip.

While part of him was incredibly grateful to get out

of this conversation, the other part of him was dying to press her for more bizarre details. But he knew it would only embarrass her further, and he didn't want that.

"I need to ask you a favor," he said. "For the *America Today* thing?"

"Sure."

"You're probably going to want to get a few more details before you agree."

"I know how important this is, Jackson. And I know the pressure you're under. If there's something I can do to help, I'm happy to."

He sighed. "I'm not sure if you've heard Monica Appleby is in town."

"That . . . reality TV woman?"

"No. That's her mother. Well, I guess it's her, too. Monica is the writer. That book, *Wild Child*?"

Shelby's screwed-up nose gave a stunning literary critique of the book. "So why's she in town?"

"She's writing a book about the night her mother killed her father."

Shelby shuddered and Jackson wasn't sure which she found the most distasteful, the murder, the book about it, or Monica.

"So, what does she have to do with me?"

Jackson took a deep breath. "Just for this week, while the camera crew is in town, I'm wondering . . . hoping, actually . . . that you could find a way to incorporate her into the art camps."

"As what?"

"As a teacher."

Shelby was blank-faced for a whole ten seconds before she started laughing. "You're joking."

"I'm not."

"This . . . you . . . my camps have a reputation, Jackson. And they are successful because of that reputation. My faculty are professionals, they are respected and revered. They are not former reality TV stars and groupies with questionable backgrounds and morals! Oh my God, what parent is going to send their kid here if she's on faculty?"

"Shelby," he snapped. "You're not being fair."

"Me?" she asked. "That's what the world thinks of her."

That wasn't entirely true, but he wasn't going to split hairs with Shelby. "Well, the world is wrong."

She crossed her arms, mutinous. Shelby would die if she knew that she looked exactly like her mother when she did that.

"I don't have a writing curriculum."

"I'm sure you can make one up."

"Right. Because that's so easy?"

"No. Of course not . . . but maybe she'll have ideas."

"Does she have experience teaching?"

Somehow Jackson doubted it, but that didn't stop him from lying. "Of course. She's a professional."

"Jackson, you sure she should be working with kids?"

"Come on, Shelby. What's she going to do? You'll be like ten feet away the entire time."

"Okay," she said. "I'll see if I can make it work."

"That's all I'm asking."

He left without saying another word, stunned by the judgment in his old friend. Stunned by the ugliness of what the world thought of Monica.

The humidity and sunlight were intense, and he put on his sunglasses as he headed back into town, making another quick stop at Cora's before heading to the Peabody.

One down, one to go. And if he thought Shelby was difficult to convince, Monica was going to be impossible.

Chapter 10

The pounding on the door startled Monica so much she jumped, smearing red toenail polish across her big toe.

"Great," she muttered, wiping it off with a piece of toilet paper.

Again with the pounding. "Hold on a second!" she cried, pushing herself off the bed and hobbling across the floor, her feet flexed so her toenails didn't touch anything.

She yanked open the door only to find Jackson on the other side, holding a white bag and a cup of coffee.

"Jeez, Jackson, where's the fire?"

"I thought you might like some coffee. And one of Cora's muffins. Peach today, her best. She was out of fritters."

Men bearing gifts? Immediately she was suspicious.

"Why are you smiling like a salesman?" She grabbed the coffee. Salesman or not, she'd take the coffee.

"Can I come in?" His scales weren't balanced today; he was more careful today than charming. More man than boy. *Interesting.* Letting him in would no doubt be a terrible mistake. But she had always been very good at those.

"Give me the muffin," she said and stepped aside so he could come in.

Reba, sleeping on the edge of the bed, woke up when Jackson walked past, as if sensing someone new to show off for, and she leapt to her feet, shaking herself awake.

Jackson patted the dog's head and then gave her a good scratch under her ridiculous collar. Reba leaned into his big hand, sighing and wiggling.

Do not, she told herself, *be jealous of a dog.*

"It's really tidy in here," he said, looking around.

"I have some experience living in hotels," she said. "It's a slippery slope from untidy to disaster zone."

"You live in hotels?"

"It's stranger to have a home with a name that your family has lived in since before the Civil War."

Jackson laughed in his throat. "I suppose you're right."

"What are you doing here, Jackson?"

He closed his eyes for a second and tidal waves of doubt rolled off him, as if all his dams and locks had been overrun and he could no longer hold back what he kept hidden from the world.

Oh no, she thought. *Don't show me this stuff.*

It made her want to hug him. Tell him that whatever was putting those lines of stress between his eyes, it would be okay.

"I have to . . . I have to ask a favor."

"A favor? This should be good." She sat down on the edge of her bed again and took a bracing sip of her coffee before she set it down and grabbed her toenail polish. What this town needed was a decent manicure/pedicure spot.

She was getting ready to go speak to Ed Baxter this afternoon, and having her toenails done felt like a crucial part of her armor. As she'd worked on the questions she had for Ed, it became increasingly clear that she was going to need armor for the interview. Her emotional distance seemed to shrink with every question she'd written down.

Did JJ—my father—seem scared? Did he seem to know what was happening?

The question had stopped her in her tracks. Sent her spinning.

She didn't doubt that she could do this—she'd done harder things. But she was keenly aware that asking these questions was going to cost her.

Jackson cleared his throat and she gladly refocused on him. "I need you to teach, or at least pretend to teach, at a community art camp."

"Art camp?"

"It's quite cool, actually. Shelby Monroe teaches these camps in the summer—"

"Why?" Monica put her foot down on the floor, the bottle of nail polish clenched in her hand.

"Why does she teach? I suppose it's a calling . . ."

"Why do you want *me* to teach?"

He opened his mouth. Closed it. Glanced out the window and then back at her. She knew what he was going to say before he said it. "For the show."

Monica howled. "Oh, that's good, Jackson—"

"I'm not joking. I'm . . . I'm very serious."

She shook her head, unable to connect the dots. "Spell it out for me, Jackson, because yesterday, *yesterday* you didn't even want me speaking to Dean."

"Apparently, Bishop, as it stands, isn't enough to beat this town in Alaska."

"So I'm going to tip the scales?"

"You teaching at the camps will tip the scales, or at least, that's what the producer seemed to think."

He was so pained, standing there, backlit by the sun coming in through the sheer curtains. His hands were in fists beside his khaki pants. He wore a white shirt and a red tie, something she'd never seen him in before. It didn't quite make him look mayoral. He looked like a good southern boy on his way to church.

"You'll be lying?"

"The ends justify the means, right? I mean, if we win, no one will care. I doubt people will care anyway."

"This Shelby woman probably cares."

"She's agreed." The way he said it implied it wasn't easy, implied a whole lot of not really agreeing. For some reason, she immediately cast Shelby as a lonely old woman with a cat problem.

She laughed, feeling small, a commodity. A chip moved around on a board. "No."

"No?" he gasped.

"That's what I said." She lifted her heel up onto the edge of the bed again and unscrewed the top of the nail polish.

"I need you, Monica," he said.

That was no way to win her over—she wasn't big on being needed.

"Why?" she asked, stroking red polish across her big toenail, using her pinky to clear the runoff. "It's a show. A contest, Jackson. Probably—considering the way they're talking about this town in Alaska—rigged."

Jackson hauled her desk chair over to the corner of the bed and sat, his legs, his hands, his body so close to hers that she dropped her foot in surprise and found herself staring at him.

"When I took office this town was literally bankrupt. We couldn't pay the pensions of retired employees. Garbagemen, policemen, firefighters, people who'd worked for this town in good faith their entire lives and we couldn't *pay them*. That factory closed and one-third of the population moved away. The housing bubble burst and people were just abandoning their houses, just walking away rather than selling them. It was like the Depression around here."

Monica felt the hair on her neck stand up, something that always happened when she sensed people flirting with the edges of their control. It was a defense mechanism, a survival instinct, a warning of danger. And usually when all the hair on her neck stood up, she cleared out. She stayed far away from any emotional storm that wasn't her own.

But right now, looking at the pain in Jackson's face, she couldn't have walked away if she tried.

"I did what I could, robbing Peter to pay Paul, but there's nothing left. The city is out of money and if something doesn't happen fast, we're done. Bankrupt, and I will have failed everyone. Everyone."

"It's not you, Jackson. It's not your fault, or your responsibility to fix it."

"The hell it's not, Monica. Whose else is it? Who else is standing here?"

She could tell by the rock-hard way he held his body that she wasn't going to convince him. He'd spent years telling himself this was his job.

"So what's the show going to do? If you win it?"

"Maybream opens the factory. Moves its headquarters here. We're talking about at least a hundred jobs. The city—and I'm not exaggerating—will be saved. And I will do anything to see that happen, Monica. Anything. I will lie, beg—"

The nail polish fell to the floor and before she could stop herself, before she even realized what she was doing, she had his face, that strong jaw, those cheekbones, in her hands. His eyes, liquid and blue and beautiful, met hers.

"Okay," she said.

"Okay?" He gripped his hands over hers. "Really?"

"Yes, really. But I'm doing it my way, Jackson. I'm not causing a scene and I'm not feeding the gossip mill and I am definitely not teaching little kids. Or kids at all, really. It's adults or nothing."

"Good. Yes. No problem."

She eyed him skeptically, pretty sure he was making

promises he had no way of keeping. "And if this Shelby woman so much as looks at me funny, I'll snatch her bald."

Laughter, deep and resonant, thundered out of his throat. "Deal. Thank you, Monica. Thank you." He pulled her into his arms and perhaps she helped, perhaps she jumped when he pulled, but she ended up in his lap in the chair, their bodies flush. Their hearts pounding against each other.

Slowly, carefully, as if there were trip wires all over them and any sudden movements would blow them up, he leaned back.

"Are you always this good?" she asked. And as if she'd pulled one of those wires, his eyes went dark. And she knew what was coming; she knew this kiss in this hotel room wouldn't be stopped by the police chief or Jackson or her. Despite knowing there was a good chance it would end badly—for both of them—this kiss was going to happen.

It was fast, the kiss. Zero to sixty in no time. They went from lips, to careful breaths, to teeth and tongues and a deep, sawing need. A breaking pulse that hammered between them.

Want. Want. Want.

More and yes and there and *now.*

Her heart pounded with excitement. The long, slow, delicious build started in her body, in her core, under her skin. Her body, untouched by anyone else for so long, woke up to pleasure, but her brain—always her reluctant brain—struggled to keep up. It kept pointing out the trapdoors, the pitfalls and dangers.

He stood with her weight in his arms like it was nothing, and her panties were wet in a heartbeat. And while he crawled over the end of the bed she clung to him, her lips fused to his, her tongue memorizing the taste of him. Coffee and peaches and toothpaste. Honest tastes, real and good flavors.

Don't trust this, she thought, *don't get carried away.*

He broke the kiss, burying his face in her neck, where his breath feathered across soft and hidden places that carried the sensation all over her body, making connections in her hands and breasts and between her legs and on the bottoms of her feet.

It's not real, you know that; it's desire and it fades. It vanishes.

His hand slid from her waist to just under her breast, pausing as if to ask for permission. The gentleman. And she was suddenly furious with herself, furious with her apprehensions, all the rules that kept her alone and lonely because she was so scared of who she'd been.

This feels so good and I am not that girl, she told herself, and she arched into his hand. Her nipple pebbled and his thumb found it, hard and waiting. Smart man, he wasted no time, rolling it between his fingers. His other hand burrowed under her tee shirt, and the touch of his fingers against the skin of her waist was fiery and ticklish all at the same time.

She tried to pull his tie off and it got stuck, making both of them laugh as he made a strangling sound.

"Hold on," he breathed. *No,* she thought. *No pausing.* Pausing let in the cool air of doubt. And there was enough of it already, swirling around her.

She pushed him away slightly, just enough so she could wiggle her arms and pull off her Green Day tee shirt. He forgot his own shirt, lost in the sight of her breasts in the red lace of her least favorite bra.

"You're beautiful," he whispered.

"You're talking too much," she said, and pulled him back down to kiss him.

He came willingly, as she'd known he would. Those lips of his, as she suspected, were not nearly as stern as they'd initially seemed. They were full and sweet and they sipped at her lips, sucked at her tongue—ate at her as if he couldn't get enough. As if she was all he needed.

And that was really fucking sexy.

He eased down her body, kissing the skin where it rose out of her bra. He licked her through the lace. Kissed her. At the sounds of her approval, he bit her. Too much but at the same time, not enough. Never enough.

She gasped, eager to hold onto this feeling, eager to prove that she could do this, see this all the way through. That she wasn't ruined, somehow. She reached between them. Beneath his staid khaki pants he was hard and long. Big.

Really. Very big.

A noise escaped her, a coo of delight, and he groaned, then chuckled, though it sounded like it hurt.

She put both hands between them, holding him in her palms.

"Hey," he whispered, and he groaned as she traced the length of him through the twill fabric of his pants.

His buckle came apart, the button, the zipper. And then there he was in her hand.

He leaned aside, pulling away, or trying to, but she had ahold of him in such a way that when he moved, he was stroked, and he groaned again, his head kicked back, his body shaking. "We . . . if we start here . . . this might be where we end."

Two years, she thought. That was nothing. Not even half of her own five long years of celibacy. Self-imposed because she was tired of failing herself. Tired of trying and then proving how broken she was.

But suddenly, she was desperate. Desperate for plea-sure. Desperate to erase the loneliness that had grown up around her like walls. Jenna was right: happiness, pleasure—it was all so fleeting, she had to grab on to it while she could.

This time, she thought. *This time will be different.* She pushed him over on his back, following him as he moved. Straddling his hips.

"Monica," he breathed, but she was relentless. At first he resisted as she yanked his pants down around his hips. "I don't have a condom," he said, his hand on her wrist, his thumb rubbing the pulse there.

"Bedside table," she said.

He shifted, was stroked again but he opened the bedside table, pulling the drawer out so hard that it clattered to the floor. The silver snake of condoms gleamed in the corner. He grabbed one, set it on the bed, and reached for her just as she reached for the condom.

They were going to do this her way. And her way was now. Fast. Before all this pleasure went away. Before her brain caught up to her body and shut it all down.

He groaned and lifted his hips, letting her push his pants off. He kicked off his shoes like he was going to stay awhile and the thought made her pause for just a moment, her desperation clearing like clouds to reveal the landscape.

What are you doing, really? But then his arms were around her, his face between her breasts, his lips hot, his tongue clever, and she tried so hard to ignore her brain.

He held her with one hand against his body so he could position her beneath him. He shifted her, held her, moved her. He took off her bra, swore with reverence, and she smiled, but despite all her efforts, a chill was settling in her bones.

I've been here before, she thought, *so many times. How will this be different?*

The kisses he pressed to her belly created ripples of desire, but they were shallow and she closed her eyes and tried to feel them deeper, tried to feel *more*. He pulled off her pants, the sensible black underwear, and ran his hands down the outside of her legs and then back, slowly, inch by inch, between them. His thumb pressed into the dark cloud of curls, finding, after a moment of searching, the hard knot of her clitoris. She jumped, her hands reaching out across the bed as if to hold on, as if to grab onto something solid. His thumb rolled over her clitoris like it was a marble.

Yes. Good. There.

The pleasure trickled back, just enough. Enough to convince her she could do this. She closed her eyes, gathering the pleasure around her, a warm cloak against cold doubts. Her hand brushed against the crinkly wrapper of the condom and she grabbed it, opened it with her teeth, and with her old expertise reached down and slid it over him.

"Oh, God, you . . . you feel so good. You're so . . . good," he moaned, shuddering in her hands, his pleasure filling the air with a humming electricity that hit her skin . . . and stopped.

Just stopped.

And all that pleasure, all that desire, that she'd felt just *one goddamn second ago* was behind ice. Locked away. Her brain holding the key.

You're so good, baby. So good. There's nothing you won't do, is there?

How many times had she heard that? How many times had she let those words define her worth, dictate her actions?

He slipped a finger inside of her, and she knew she was wet, which was a miracle in and of itself, but it was over. Her brain had won, her body lost.

No, she wanted to moan. *No,* she wanted to cry. Why? Why her? Why was she so cold with men, so alone in their embrace? All the sexual pleasure she'd faked haunted her now, when she couldn't hold onto desire with a man. Couldn't . . . ever . . . come.

"Monica?" In his voice she heard him recognize her sudden reluctance. Her sudden detachment. This, in the past, was when the show would really get good and she'd moan and writhe and pretend, like an Academy Award–winning actress, or at least an above-average porn star, that she wasn't broken somewhere very important.

Her eyes blinked open to look deep into his—concerned pools of warm blue. His erection was still hard against her hip. His hand no longer between her legs but braced in a fist against the quilt.

"You okay?" he asked.

And now she was at the crossroads where she swore she'd never be again. She could fake it, spread her legs, invite him in—it had been so long for him, she probably wouldn't even need to put on a show.

Or she could ask him to leave. Which seemed hideously unfair considering her actions of a few moments ago. But she'd promised herself she wouldn't let herself get used like this anymore, even with a man as sweet as Jackson.

"I'm sorry," she whispered.

Jackson had no idea what was going on. None. And his brain wasn't doing a very good job of trying to figure it out. The only thing he knew for certain was that this woman, this gorgeous, sexy, *naked* woman, was not interested in sex. A second ago, yes. Now, not so much.

Shaking, literally shaking with the effort it took to not take what a few moments ago had seemed to be offered, he pushed himself off the bed. Carefully rolled up the condom over a penis so erect he could barely push it down. He snapped the rolled edge of the latex against his skin, just to try to cool himself off. He winced, but stayed hard. Finally, he got the damn thing off and threw it in the garbage.

Out of the corner of his eye, he saw Monica pull on the Green Day concert shirt he'd taken off her . . . Christ, two minutes ago?

Go, he thought, his brain fizzing and popping. *Don't look. Don't ask. Just go.*

Ridiculously, he still had his shirt and tie on. He pulled on his pants, shoved his naked feet into his shoes, and didn't worry about his socks or underwear. They were a sacrifice to getting out the door to where he could take a breath that didn't taste like her, where he could form a thought that wasn't about her stunning, full ivory breasts, the beautiful brown nipples—

"I'm going to . . . go," he said, looking at her for just a moment. Her long legs were tucked up underneath her, her black hair a wild mess around her shoulders. Her lips were red and puffy and delicious, and it was a sucker punch remembering their taste, their unbelievable softness.

He shook his head; he had to leave before he made a mess in his pants.

Unflinching, her eyes met his and he couldn't read a single thing there, not one thing. Was she disappointed? Was he supposed to stay? Was this some kind of sex game that he didn't understand because he was a celibate monk from a nowhere small town and she'd had rock-star orgies?

Good God, he'd play, he'd play any game she wanted, but she had to let him in on it. She had to give him the rules.

He waited for her to say something. A hint, anything. *Force me. Convince me. Make me beg.*

But she was silent. Her eyes a purple, bottomless mystery—all the way through.

His erection vanished as if it had never existed.

Grateful for small favors, he turned and left, shutting the door behind him with a hard click.

At the end of the hallway was an east-facing window and it was filled with light; white-hot and bright, it lit the whole corridor. He walked toward it, trying not to be angry. Trying not to feel like a fool. Or used.

He stopped. Turned and looked back toward her closed door.

No. The thought taking root in his head didn't make sense. He didn't want it to make sense. He didn't want it to be true.

He shook his head, walking toward that light. *You're not thinking clearly,* he told himself. *You want there to be a reason she acted that way. Some reason that had nothing to do with you.*

But at the top of the stairs he stopped again. This thought wasn't new; that night outside The Pour House, at the beginning of their kiss, she'd nearly pushed him away and he'd had this thought then.

Angry and terrified on her behalf, he turned around, running back the way he came.

Back to Monica.

Chapter 11

Monica stood with one hand pressed to the door, the other pressed to her heart.

You don't owe him an explanation, she told herself, the voice coming from that island she liked to believe she lived on. *You aren't friends, and you clearly aren't lovers. He's a mistake you can't stop making.*

But his face when he left, it was . . . pained and resigned. Angry a little. But . . . worried, too.

Just tell him that you're one of the millions of women who don't actually enjoy sex. Tell him he was right—you can't turn off your brain long enough to enjoy someone's touch.

"Frigid" was a ridiculous, dated term and it didn't really apply to her. She saw stars when she touched herself. She had epic masturbatory skills.

Just stay on the island, she told herself, pressing her forehead to the door. *You're better off there.*

Even as she thought it, she shook her head. She was only thirty, too young to give up. Too young to push aside everyone and everything.

The answer was obvious. A scream just waiting to be heard.

She lifted her head and put her hand on the doorknob just as someone hammered on the other side of her door.

Jackson, her body cried in hope and fear.

The door flew open under her hand and there he was, his tie skewed, his jaw set.

She opened her mouth to apologize but he lifted his hand.

"You . . . you don't owe me any explanation," he said. "I'm not here for that. And there's a good chance that I'm getting this all wrong. That you decided no because I'm shit in bed, or not what you want—"

"No, Jackson, that's . . ." *so wrong, terribly wrong.* "Please don't think that." It killed her that he doubted himself because of her problems. But of course what else could he think? "You're wonderful. Exciting. Gorgeous, really." *It was just bad luck that you fell into my bed.*

"That's a relief." His smile was brief. Hard. The skin under his collar was red. And she wanted to touch him so intensely, to ease some of this pain she could sense in him. But she'd sent him enough mixed signals. "I have a question, and you . . . you don't have to answer it. But considering what we were doing just a few minutes ago and the kind of pain I might have caused even unintentionally, I would . . . appreciate an answer."

"Okay."

"Were you raped?"

Oh. Of course he would think that.

Her breath blew out of her in a gust, leaving her limp. In an effort to shore herself up, she crossed her arms under her breasts. "No."

He jerked back at her answer. "Oh . . ." He seemed to run out of steam, as if he'd been putting all his money on the rape card. He rubbed a hand through his hair, making it stand up, rumpled in that way that was so human. So endearing.

"Come in," she said. "This isn't a conversation I want to have in the hallway."

He eyed her room as if it were a torture chamber he wasn't entirely keen on reentering. *I don't blame you,* she thought, remembering the days when any room with her in it felt like a torture chamber to her. But then he was in the room, the door shut behind him, and she had to tell him what she'd never told anyone. Ever.

"I wasn't raped," she said to his back, strong and wide under his white shirt. "But I was used." He started to turn and she put her hand on his shoulder, keeping him there, facing away from her. Cowardly, yes, but this was hard enough. She dropped her hand but didn't like how that felt so she put it back on his shoulder, where the muscles were tense under her touch.

"And I can't blame the men who used me. I was a willing partner—"

"Monica," he sighed as if to contradict her, but she stopped him. If she couldn't give him herself in that rumpled bed, she could give him the truth. Unvarnished.

"No, listen. I wasn't . . . I wasn't . . ." *It was outrageous to say it, to lay claim to such a lack. Such an absence, but there were no other words that fit.* "Loved. Or made to feel special. By my mom, my dad. By the time I was back in school after the murder I was so far behind kids my age that I felt . . . stupid. Useless. And then my mom became a superstar and signed us up for that stupid show and I felt compared, every minute, to her and to the kid people perceived me to be, and to the kid I could have been if my life were in any way normal. And in every comparison, who I was . . . wasn't good enough. So when I discovered sex, or maybe I should say when the boys discovered me, I decided to be good at that. It became my identity. The girl who loved sex, who would do anything, who never said no. Sometimes it was a commodity, and trust me," she laughed, "I know what that makes me."

He whirled around and grabbed her hand, his eyes fierce. "Don't."

"It's the truth, Jackson—"

"It's the *result,* Monica. Of an unimaginable childhood. Don't label it because it's easier than seeing the whole picture."

She blinked, knocked sideways by his words. Knocked off her righteous position of truth teller. And she suddenly realized that she'd had this expectation of disgusting him. She'd tell him this and he'd turn, unable to hide his revulsion, despite his southern manners. He'd say something polite and stumble out the door, grateful that he'd dodged sex with that particular bullet and she'd be left alone in her hotel room, convincing herself that it was all for the best.

But he held her hands and looked at her with fierce tenderness, as if he would grab a sword and hack to pieces the people who hurt her.

No one, not once in her life, had looked at her that way. Ready to rise up on her behalf.

Was this what other women got? she wondered. *Because this shit is good.*

"Anyway, I convinced myself that it was enough to be wanted by them. That their desire for me was more important than my actually feeling desire. And the great irony is that the girl who worked so hard to convince the men she had sex with that she loved it never felt a thing. It was all a show. All faked."

He blinked. "You never had an orgasm . . . with those men?"

"After about four years, my body was dead and my brain was so aware of how awful it was that I could barely feel it when someone touched me. You were right that night outside the bar—my brain always got in the way. And even after I'd grown up and stopped behaving that way, I'd date nice men, men whom I liked and who liked me, and I'd finally get in bed with them and . . .

nothing. So, I would tone down some version of the big sex show and fake my way through it."

"Every time?"

She nodded.

"Why? Why me, then?"

With a smile, she reached up and brushed back the flop of golden hair over his forehead and then she lingered there, at the soft spot of skin near his ear. "Because when you kissed me, I felt it. I really felt it and when you touched me, I felt it. Because you made me wet and hot and so excited and I thought . . . maybe I could do it this time. Maybe it would happen to me like it seems to happen to every other woman on the planet. And I want . . . I want so badly to be—"

"Don't say 'normal.'" He shook his head.

"Fine, I want so badly to be a woman who feels half of what she faked." She sighed, at the end of her adrenaline, at the end of her honesty. Then she stepped away, out of his reach. Clearing the way if he wanted to leave; Lord knows *she* did. She wanted to slip right out of her skin and vanish out the door.

"Do you masturbate?"

"Jackson," she sighed. "This isn't something you can fix."

"Just . . . just answer the question."

"Like a fiend. I masturbate like a fiend."

"And you come, when you touch yourself?"

"Is this a cross-examination?"

He smiled. "I was going to be a lawyer."

That she managed to be surprised by that small bit of truth in this onslaught of utter honesty was funny, and she smiled.

"Yes, I come when I touch myself."

She could see the wheels turning in his head, his eyes lighting up with the sparks of idea clashing and colliding with idea.

"Have you had a bath in this tub?" He pointed to the bathroom.

She shook her head, flat-footed by the question. "No. I mean, I shower."

"Wait here." He walked past her into her bathroom and she didn't stop him. She didn't have any strength, physically or emotionally. But when she heard the thunder of water running into the bath, she peered around the edge of the door only to see him inspecting the in-room toiletries provided by the Peabody. He picked the bubble bath and stood over the tub squeezing the creamy stuff into the water. Soon, a mountain of bubbles appeared under the faucet.

"What are you doing?"

"Running you a bath."

"Why?"

"Because I think you could use one. Now," he tossed the empty bubble bath bottle into the garbage. "I've never seen you drink alcohol. Are you in AA?"

"No. I just . . . I just don't like to lose control."

He shot her an ironic look. "You think?"

That she managed to laugh gave her hope. Hope for what she couldn't say, but it made her feel good and that was enough.

"You get in the bath and I'm going to be right back."

"Jackson," she sighed, unsure of where he was going with this. Unsure of what he wanted. He crossed the bathroom in two steps and cupped her face in his big palms. It felt so good to be touched after all she'd told him that she gasped, and when he kissed her—close-mouthed but slow, chaste but not quite—she leaned against him.

"Trust me," he said, and then slipped one of the room key cards she kept on the edge of the desk in his pocket. "I just want to take care of you," he said before vanishing out the door.

She stared at the shut door and tried to remember the

last time someone took care of her. Even she'd been der-
elict in that department, caught up in the tragedy of
Jenna, the drama of the book. She'd stopped doing all
those small things that gave her pleasure. Because she
so rarely felt pleasure—sexual or otherwise.

A bubble bath? Why the hell not?

Jackson sprinted down the hallway, took the stairs two
at a time, and slid to a stop when he saw the front desk.

Jay, one of those kids Jackson used to invite mini-
golfing when Gwen was younger, came in from the back-
room door.

Jackson waved, relieved it wasn't his sister, before
heading over to the small liquor cart set up in the sitting
area. He grabbed a crystal tumbler, poured a finger of
bourbon in it, and quickly sucked it back.

Good. Lord.

Despite it being morning, he poured himself another,
smaller this time, and downed it too. There was a minibar in Monica's room, but he needed a second to get his
head together, away from where she was at this moment, getting naked.

He was daunted, sad, and angry on her behalf. He
was turned on, just being near her. Returning to that
room might be the biggest mistake of his life, but there
was no way in the world he wasn't going back up there.

He grabbed another tumbler and a sugar cube from
the tea set and placed it in the bottom of the glass before
pouring the bourbon over it. Using a spoon, he muddled
it, making sure the sugar was dissolved. He gave himself another finger of bourbon in his glass and headed
back up the stairs, slowly, *like a mayor, for crying out
loud,* this time aware of Jay's eyes on his back.

He used the key he'd swiped from Monica's desk and

stepped into the room. It was steamy now and sweet smelling. Feminine in the extreme. Just walking into the room felt like entering a mysterious, womanly, and sexual place.

Any room with Monica in it felt that way.

"Jackson?" her voice called from the bathroom, and he took a deep breath before he went in. She looked, as he'd expected, delicious. Gorgeous. Her pale, strong shoulders rose from mountains of iridescent bubbles. They were freckled, those shoulders, and that was a surprise. Her black hair was pulled up into one of those sloppy knots on the top of her head, snaky, dark strands stuck to the side of her neck.

Her toes, the nails fire-engine red, peeked out near the faucet and he wanted to kiss them. Suck them.

"Here," he said, handing her the tumbler. "A drink."

"Thank you," she murmured, her eyes wary but somehow relaxed. She took a sip of his drink and sighed, and he could see the tension draining out of her.

Good, he thought. *This might just work.*

The dog he'd forgotten about came charging into the room and jumped, delicately, onto the closed toilet seat and from there onto the top of the toilet. Where she yipped once and then lay down to watch.

Jackson sat on the closed seat and gave the rat dog a scrub under its ridiculous bejeweled collar.

"What's this creature's name?"

"Reba."

"Like the country singer?"

"Don't you think she'd be honored?"

Jackson smiled. "And how did you come by such a noble beast?"

Monica was silent and he turned to look at her, watched her take another sip from her drink. "She was Jenna's dog. She asked me to take care of her."

"Does she just come this way?" he asked, petting her strange naked body. "Without hair?"

"It's the breed."

"It's strange."

Monica laughed, shifting down into the bubbles.

"But she's growing on me," Jackson said.

"She does that."

As if she disapproved of the conversation, Reba stood up and jumped down to the floor, giving herself a good shake before running out the door. Jackson leaned back with his own drink. The shots he'd had downstairs were already working on his muscles. He felt both mellow and hyperaware of her. And of the disappearing nature of those bubbles.

"So, Jackson, since we're clearly on the subject." Her lips, red and erotic, tilted up in a sexy, mysterious smile. He wondered if it was just her naturally, with that sexual spark undiminished by her disappointments, or if it was the way he saw her. Always beautiful. Always desirable, always just slightly out of reach. "Tell me why it's been two years since you've had sex."

"Oh," he laughed. "It's air-all-our-secrets time?"

"I showed you mine."

He crossed his legs at the ankle, counted the tile squares between him and her. Too many at any other time, but for this moment—just enough. "I'm not interested in getting married," he said.

"Perhaps the news hasn't gotten to you guys yet, but you don't actually have to be married to have sex."

"It's a small town," he said with a shrug. "And being mayor, it's not like I can just pick up women at The Pour House. For a while I dated, but every woman I was interested in looked at me and started making wedding plans. Two years ago, Sean was researching bars in other towns—"

She made a scoffing noise in her throat and he laughed. "I know. He took that research very seriously. I went with him and I met someone and it worked, casually, for a few weeks. But then it just felt like this dirty secret . . . and like I was lying to this woman who'd started talking about meeting her parents and her kids and I knew she was thinking permanent thoughts about me. So I broke it off."

"Well, you do seem like a permanent kind of guy," she said.

"I'm not, though. Not right now."

"What about the girlfriend . . . from school?"

"What about her?"

"She didn't want to come back here with you?"

"I didn't ask," he said, and took a sip from his drink. "But there was no way she wanted to move to Bishop and help me raise my sister."

"How do you know if you didn't ask?"

Monica sounded affronted on behalf of a woman she'd never met, and he smiled at her. "*I* didn't want to come back here. Why would she?"

"If she loved you—"

"We were young, Monica. Whatever we felt for each other, it probably wouldn't have lasted. And . . . honestly, I didn't want her to come. I needed to focus on my sister, figure out this new life I was going to be living. I couldn't . . . I didn't have time for her. That might make me an asshole, but it's the truth. It was one or the other."

She seemed to absorb his honesty, his failings. *How novel.*

"Your life got cut short when your parents died. You must feel like there's a lot you didn't get to do."

In comparison to the rest of the people in his life, whom he'd known since he was in diapers, she was a stranger. And yet when she said things like that, it was as though she'd pried open his head and taken a good, long look inside.

"Something like that," he agreed. *Exactly like that. Exactly.*

Her chuckle was low, suggestive, and her eyes when they looked at him over the glass tumbler were heavy-lidded. She was such a sexual creature, the way she dressed, the way she looked—he wondered, how much of it was a disguise? An act? And how much of it was real?

I guess you're going to find out, he thought.

"How are you feeling?" he asked.

She sighed. "Better than I have in a long time."

"Do you have any music?"

She stretched out a long, damp ivory arm, bubbles dripping off her elbow, and pointed through the door to the bedroom. "My iPod is in the speaker set on the dresser."

Quickly, he stood and found it. Using his thumb, he scrolled through her playlists.

Jeez! She had a lot of angry music. Rage Against the Machine. Ani DiFranco, The Ramones, Hole. Finally, halfway down, he found something that would work.

Van Morrison's "Tupelo Honey."

He hit play, and Van's Irish soul came through the speakers. He walked back into the bathroom only to find her with her head back against the wall tiles, her glass empty beside her. Her cheeks flushed, singing nearly silently to herself.

"If I didn't know better, I'd think you were trying to seduce me." She laughed, her eyes closed. Fishing, she was fishing, and he smiled in acknowledgment.

He braced his hands on the doorjamb over his head. Leaning slightly closer, setting up his own boundaries. "I'm not going to touch you."

Her eyes snapped open.

"I want you to touch yourself," he told her.

Her eyes opened wider.

He didn't say anything else and he didn't look away, and the room was thick with intensity. Apprehension and excitement and worry. Big emotions stole the air, but he just kept watching her, waiting for her. Dying a little.

"Touch myself?"

"The way you like. The way that makes you come."

Do it. Trust me. Trust yourself. Just . . . try. The moment lasted so long, her indecision so palpable, that when she finally lifted those long arms out of the water, he gasped for air, unaware that he'd been holding his breath.

In the tub the bubbles were dissipating, but not enough. And that was probably a good thing, because if he saw what he hoped she would do, he'd probably lose his mind. He'd just combust in the doorway. As it was, imagining what she was going to do with those hands, those fingers, was a sweet and painful torture.

Her eyes locked on his, unflinching and not shy, but somehow . . . wary. Somehow unsure. She ran her fingers from the sharp curve of her collarbone to the swell of her breast just above the bubbles and then down, lifting her breasts slightly. Those brown nipples, so lovely, so sweet, appeared briefly before she covered them with her fingers. She pulled. Twisted, her mouth opening on a gasp.

"Does that feel good?" he asked. She nodded. One hand stayed with her breast and the other, he could tell by the flex in her muscles, the way her body seemed to lift in the water, slipped down, over her belly. He imagined the softness of her skin, the way it stretched over her taut muscles, her smooth flesh.

And then she sighed, gasped, her eyes closed.

"Tell me." His voice sounded scorched. Burnt.

"I'm . . . wet. Hot."

His fingers were white-knuckled on the doorjamb. His blood pounding so hard in his ears he could barely hear her whisper.

Her eyes opened again. "You too," she whispered. "You touch yourself too."

He shook his head. "This one's . . . this one's about you."

I don't put on a show, he remembered her saying, and he wondered if she would think that was what this was about. Because it couldn't be further from the truth. He just wanted to share some pleasure with her. And if this was how she felt it, this was the way he wanted it.

And then she bit her bottom lip, her white teeth in the pink flesh. Honestly, her teeth were so freaking sexy. Was there any other woman in the world with sexy teeth?

"Tell me," he said, "what you're doing. How you like it."

Her cheeks were red, flushed, her eyes unfocused when they opened. "At the top. My clit."

He ducked his head, his body shaking.

"I squeeze it, between my fingers."

"Hard?"

"Soft, then hard."

This was going to be torture. He closed his eyes, and her breath, those small gasps, the half-moans high in the back of her throat, echoed against the tiles, inside his head. He'd die remembering how she sounded.

"Now a finger," she whispered. "Inside." She gasped, groaned.

He opened his eyes to see her sitting up; her breasts, gilded with light and bubbles, were wet and perfect. The small muscles in her shoulder, her arm, were tense, flexing and releasing as she touched herself under the water.

"It's so good," she gasped and her eyes swung to his. He smiled, even though it killed him.

"You're beautiful."

She stopped. He could tell she'd stopped.

"Don't—" he protested, putting out a hand.

"I want to watch you, too."

"Monica."

"It's both of us or neither."

It took a second, a second of wondering what was noble, before he realized he didn't give a shit. Bracing his feet wide, he let go of the door frame, amazed that he hadn't left finger dents in the wood. As he unbuckled his belt, he noticed that the small muscles in her arms had started working again. Her breasts, full and beautiful, shimmied with the motion. She leaned back hard against the tub, her eyes fixed on the zipper he was lowering.

Hard, so damn hard, he hissed when he touched himself, freeing his dick from his pants, pushing them down beneath his sac so she could see. He wanted her to see. This whole thing had quickly turned into the hottest, most erotic thing that had ever happened to him.

"Stroke it," she whispered.

He did. Softly at first, top to bottom and then harder, just at the top, so hard he bit his lips. It wasn't going to be a long show, that was for sure. He slowed down, not wanting to miss a single moment of watching her, waiting for signs that there was something building in her body, something under those bubbles that would climax.

It took awhile but he was patient, slowly stroking himself. She braced a foot against the wall, and bubbles ran down her leg from her toes to her knees to the pale three inches of thigh he could see before the bubbles detached and drifted across the water.

And then she moved faster, her breath sawing harder, and he stroked himself accordingly, making himself work, slowing down when he got ahead of himself, speeding up to catch up with her.

"Soon?" she gasped.

He couldn't talk, just nodded.

"Oh," she cried, her neck, her chest, her face flushing red. "Yes. Oh . . . God."

And in three more hard strokes, his heartbeat pounding in his hand, he cried out, saw stars, saw nothing, and came. His knees nearly buckled.

Done. God. Oh my God.

In the tub, her legs were pulled up and she had curled herself into a ball, shaking.

They sounded like Olympic sprinters after a race, gasping for breath.

Just like honey from the bee, Van sang from the other room.

That . . . that just happened, he thought, staring down at the mess on his hands.

"You . . . okay?" he asked. She nodded, her forehead pressed to her knees, her face hidden. That didn't seem like a good sign, but he walked to the sink, cleaned himself up. The intimacy of the last ten minutes seemed awkward now; he had no context for this.

The sound of his zipper was loud in the bathroom and there was another sound. In the mirror over the sink, he could see her shoulders shaking in the bath.

"Monica?" He whirled and stepped toward her, and then stopped when she brought her head up, smiling.

"I thought . . . I thought you were crying."

"No." The look she gave him was warm. Fond, even. But knowing. As though she'd seen his secrets, and liked him better for it. That look was totally different from the way every other woman in his life looked at him. It made him nervous. "I'm . . . laughing."

"I don't know if that's better."

She held out her hand and he grabbed it, let her tug him closer. "That," she said, "was the hottest thing I have ever done in my life."

He thought about making a joke about rock-star orgies, but he realized it was hot for her for the same reason it had been so exciting to him—because it was honest. And real.

"Me too." Her knuckles were slippery under his lips.

"Now go," she said, dismissing him as she leaned back in the tub. "I want to finish my bath."

He laughed, something unexpected rolling through him. Relief, maybe. He was pretty much talked out and if she had wanted to dissect what happened, it would have been tough. But there was something else in that mix. Something young and exciting, and he didn't want to think about it too hard.

He would call it chemistry and leave it at that.

"I'll leave a message for you regarding the camps once I know more information," he told her, tucking his shirt into his pants.

"You can just send me a smoke signal," she said, her eyes shut, a little smirk on her lips. "I know how you like to communicate."

She was irresistible, and he didn't even put up a fight. Leaning down, he braced one hand against the tiles and kissed her, hard, on the lips. Startled, she jumped but then softened into the kiss. What he meant as something short and sweet turned into something long and hot. She twined ivory arms around his neck, and his tongue found its way into her mouth, stroking hers, licking at her lips. Finally giving in to the urge he'd had from the moment he'd seen her on his front porch, he sucked her lower lip between his teeth.

She groaned into his mouth and slowly, painfully, he pulled himself just a few inches away so he could look into her eyes. "I'm just beginning to show you how I like to communicate," he whispered and before he lost his momentum, he kissed her nose and left.

He wasn't a guy with lines, but he had to admit that was a pretty great one.

In the hallway he checked his watch. He was drunk, sort of laid, and he'd saved the contest—again.

And it wasn't even noon.

Who says I can't fix everything?

Chapter 12

Monica stood on the sidewalk outside a small, yellow-brick bungalow and checked the address on the napkin against the address on the house.

This was it. Ed Baxter's house.

She shoved the napkin in her back pocket and walked up the cracked sidewalk toward the front door.

It was impossible to know how she would feel without having had that . . . experience with Jackson a few hours ago. But right now she was keenly grateful for having had it, because the edge of her anger was filed down and she was able to ring the doorbell without feeling trapped by the specter of the book.

Masturbating in front of Jackson, watching him touch himself, had set her square, somehow. Given her the distance—the armor—she'd needed a few hours ago and had been scared she'd never get.

But still, standing on that cement porch, three short steps up from the dying grass on the lawn, her knees shook and her hands were sweating and her nerves were on high alert. She was going to do this, open up this door so long shut.

When the storm door opened behind the screen door, revealing a small man who looked like an older version of Sean, she smiled.

"Ed Baxter?"

The man—Monica would put his age at about seventy—nodded, reaching out to push open the screen door. "Come on in," he said, and she pulled the door open the rest of the way so she could slip inside.

A sense of neglect hung over the house, which was clean enough, but sparse. Empty-seeming. A sea of shabby beige. Not dirty, just worn. The few frames on the wall were all cockeyed, the photos faded. There were no knick-knacks. No rugs. No blankets tossed over the side of the couch.

It was an eerie tableau.

The table beside the recliner was cluttered with prescription bottles, the only real sign of life.

"Sit," Ed said, walking toward the kitchen. "You want coffee?"

"Only if you're having some." She glanced at the photos on the wall. Sean showing off a gap-toothed smile on Christmas morning. A round, red-headed woman caught in a pensive moment. A couple of family shots with Brody standing a few feet away, his dark eyes like bruises in a very serious face. Looking at the photos, it was obvious Ed and his wife were older when they had Sean.

There's a story here, she thought, looking at Brody's little face in the pictures.

Ed came back out, carrying two coffee cups. His hands had a tremor, and the coffee was in danger of sloshing out of both cups. She reached out to help, but he handed her a cup before turning toward his chair.

"Sit," he said. "You said you had some questions." He collapsed back in his chair, the coffee splashing up on his already spotted shirt.

"Yes." She sat on the couch, which predictably sagged, and pulled out her notebook and her recorder. "Do you mind if I record you?" she asked. "It's only to make sure I get everything."

He shrugged. "Suit yourself."

She put the recorder on the edge of the couch closest

to him and opened her notebook. A strange calm enveloped her. The people she was going to talk about were characters. Just characters. She was researching other people's parents. Other people's tragedy.

"Your family has owned The Pour House for three generations, right?"

Ed nodded. Took a sip of coffee. She waited for more but he was silent.

Oh boy.

"Your father owned the bar when my mom was growing up."

Ed nodded again. "Dad hired Neil . . . your grandfather . . . I guess after he got back from Vietnam. Gave him the apartment over the bar."

"Neil was in Vietnam?"

She didn't know that. Not that she'd ever met her grandfather, but that explained the service revolver.

"Did you know Neil?" she asked.

Ed glanced at her as if he knew what she was trying to do, the way she was keeping this story at arm's length. *It won't work,* his stony face said. *Sooner or later those sharks are going to get you.*

"Neil was a good guy. He had a temper, some bad spells. But he was a good man." Ed took another loud slurp of his coffee, a strange period on the topic of Neil.

"Did you know Simone?" she asked. Her internal calm cracked at the mention of her name, revealing a waiting tremble.

Ed smiled, giving her the impression that whatever he was going to say was only part of the story. The far less interesting part.

"I was older than her by quite a few years. But she was a wild thing. Just wild." His chuckle sputtered into a cough. "Neil tried, but he was all alone and she . . . she just ran circles around him. The girl needed a mother, not a father with . . . well, Vietnam in his head, I suppose.

No one was surprised when she ran away. She was . . .
she was never meant for this place."

"And when Simone came back . . . ?"

"With you, you mean?" He seemed bent on reminding her that she'd been there. A witness. A victim.

Monica nodded.

"She'd been on a bus for two days," Ed said. "That's
what she said, and it was hard not to believe her. I was
running the bar then and the apartment above the bar
had been empty since Neil died, so . . . it's not like it was
a big deal letting her stay there."

"How did she seem?" Monica asked.

"Seem?" Ed laughed, a gurgle in his throat. "She
seemed like a rabbit being chased by a big fucking dog.
Pardon my language . . ."

"She was scared?"

"You . . . you were scared. A little ghost trying hard
not to cry. She was terrified. She was . . ." Ed shook his
head. "You're the writer. Suffice it to say I'd never seen
anyone at the end of their rope like that."

Monica nodded. She couldn't take a deep breath
without rubbing up against some emotion or dim memory she wanted to avoid. The bus trip—she'd forgotten
about that. And now at the mention of it, the memories
floated into place. Those long, exhausting hours. The
mountains outside the window. Endless games of Hang-
man. Fried food from gas stations. Falling asleep with
her head in her mother's lap. Mom's fingers in her hair.

Monica cleared her throat. "How long was she . . .
were we . . . there before JJ came?"

"JJ showed up the next night. Drunk. Angry. Came
charging into the bar screaming for his wife. Calling
her terrible names."

*You slut. You goddamn whore. Spreading your legs
for every fucking man who looks your way.*

Monica shook her head. Whether the memory was

from that night or some other night hardly mattered. There were a lot of nights like that. A lot of names. So many memories pushed away for so long were now crowding back.

"Did he know . . . where she was?" Monica asked.

"Must have—he walked right through the bar to the back alley. Started climbing the stairs."

"Did anyone try to stop him?"

"He punched Sid Bates to the ground. Kicked him like a dog when he tried to get in the way."

Monica looked down at her notes. *Kicked like a dog,* she wrote. She retraced the word *dog* a few times until it stood out black against the white paper.

"I called the cops," Ed said. "But when I heard you screaming upstairs—"

Monica's head came up, but there was no question to ask and Ed didn't seem to need one.

The crack was a chasm now and she found herself sneaking around the edges of it, terrified of losing her balance and falling in. *You thought you could keep your distance from this?*

"I grabbed my shotgun and ran out the back."

"What . . . what did you think was happening?" she asked.

Be quiet, honey. Just be quiet and no matter what, don't come out from under the bed. No matter what. Do you understand?

But when the hand reached under the bed and grabbed hold of her shoulder, she'd been unable to stop the scream. It hurt. Daddy was hurting her. And she was so scared.

"I don't know. I didn't know what was happening. I just knew I'd never heard anyone screaming like that. Like the world was ending, and when I went outside, JJ was dragging Simone down the stairs by her hair. His hand wrapped around her throat. She was already bleeding. Already all banged up." Ed swallowed, looked down at his coffee, lifted the cup, but then set it down again.

"Why the hell are you writing about this?" Ed asked. "I mean . . . these are bad ghosts."

Monica nodded, her notes forgotten.

"They are . . . aren't they?" she asked. Very bad ghosts. And she wished she could just close her notebook and walk away, but she couldn't. *Jenna. Debt. Mom.* She looked up at Ed's eyes, a faded blue underneath eyebrows as thick as caterpillars. Eyes that seemed old, weathered by all he'd seen.

There was nothing to say, so she just waited for him to keep talking.

Ed sighed. "They got to the foot of the stairs, and JJ was saying all kinds of shit. All kinds of terrible, terrible stuff and then out of nowhere, like a movie or something, Simone . . . Simone just pulled a gun from the back of her pants—the one her dad always had—and shot him in the chest. Point-blank. He must have flown back about five feet. She ran upstairs and I . . . I tried to help JJ. But . . . he was gone."

Ed stood up, startling the hell out of Monica. She gasped, knocking over the tape recorder. But Ed only shuffled over to the cabinet behind him. All the shelves were empty, but he pulled open a door and grabbed a bottle of whiskey. "I don't drink the stuff," he said. "But maybe you want some?"

It was tempting, but she shook her head. Ed put the bottle back in the cabinet. "Suit yourself."

"What happened next?"

"Next? Well, I told the cops what I saw. Went home, covered in your daddy's blood, and put my arms around my wife and cried. Cried like a baby for all of you."

A bitter, stinging tide of tears flooded her eyes and no amount of blinking could make them go away. When they threatened to fall, she swiped them away with her thumbs.

There were more questions, but she couldn't ask them. She was done. Quickly, she gathered her things and shoved them in her purse. She took one big, bracing sip of the coffee for no reason she could really think of.

"We done?" he asked, and she nodded.

"I might have some more questions," she whispered around the lump of emotion in her throat, but he shook his head.

"Not for me," he said. "There's other people in town who'd be happy to talk about it, I imagine. But not me. I told you everything I remember."

She stared at him for a long time, the ghosts and the memories a dark fog that swirled around her. Around the two of them. It made no sense that she was both angry at him and grateful to him for bringing back these terrible memories. She'd asked for it, after all.

"Thank you," she said. She bent as if to grab the coffee cup to hand back to him, but he waved her off.

"Leave it," he said. "My son pays some girl to come and clean up after me. You . . . you just go."

Outside, the sun was a surprise, and she slipped on her sunglasses and all but ran from the house.

Wishing she could just as easily run from the memories.

Jackson was inordinately proud of the fact that the windows, the hundreds of high square windows on the factory, were intact. At most abandoned factories, those were the first things to go. Kids used them as target practice.

Not at the okra factory.

Dean was taking pictures and measurements inside

the building, his footfalls echoing in the wide-open space.

"Where's the machinery?" Dean asked. "I mean, most of these old factories, the companies just closed up and left, leaving a lot of the mechanicals."

"Del Monte stripped it," he said, stepping across one of the many cracks in the cement floor. Between the cracks and the holes where the machines used to be bolted down, the floor was a mess. But the rest of the place was sturdy and thanks to volunteers, pretty damn spotless.

"So I guess it offers you a clean slate, doesn't it?" Jackson asked.

"Listen to you," Dean said, smiling over his shoulder. "Now you're a salesman?"

Jackson shrugged, but he couldn't keep himself from grinning.

Monica, his heart beat. *Monica. Monica. Monica.*

"But the truth is, it's a little small for our ovens," Dean said.

Jackson stopped grinning.

Dean took another spin around, looked up at the ceilings, the far corners. "I gotta talk to my engineers."

Dean walked out of the building toward Jackson's car, leaving him to lock up and worry.

Wednesday morning Shelby got up early to get ready for the filming. The film crew. Dean. Monica. She still couldn't believe that she'd agreed to that nonsense. The more she thought about it as she put some extra effort into readying the studio, the more of a nightmare it seemed, and a see-through one, too. No one was going to believe that Monica Appleby was here—in Bishop, Arkansas—teaching a course on writing.

Considering the last-minute nature of it all, the best "writing students" she'd been able to gather were some of the teenage camp counselors who helped her through the summer. Gwen and Jay had seemed particularly interested.

The only camps she had running at the moment were for the ten-year-old comic-book campers and moms with toddlers, so she spent a few minutes getting out the glitter and glue for the younger kids and pulling out the India ink sets for the ten-year-olds.

"Wow," a voice said from behind her and Shelby turned to see Monica Appleby in a denim skirt and a tee shirt with Tweety Bird smoking a cigarette.

"Really?" Shelby asked, pointing to the shirt.

Monica started, no doubt surprised to be attacked the moment she walked in the door, and Shelby wished she could just rewind her life. Try again.

But then Monica glanced down and shrugged, as if it didn't matter. "I didn't realize there was a dress code."

"There isn't a dress code," Shelby said, painfully aware of how she sounded, how breathlessly and tragically uncool she was compared to Monica, who just reeked of disenfranchised . . . hipness. "But there are standards."

Monica's eyes ran down Shelby's denim capri pants and the white men's shirt she used as a smock. It was shapeless; she knew that. It somehow managed to both hide her body and announce all the things she hated about it—her broad shoulders and belly.

She wasn't feminine in these clothes, she wasn't anything, and Monica saw all of that, her judgment clear as a bell.

This was immediately going badly between them. In the span of ten seconds they'd picked their corners.

"How about you spare me the lecture and just let me know what I can do to help?" Monica stepped closer, deeper into Shelby's closely monitored and cared-for domain, and Shelby had to look away or she'd growl. Bar the way. Pick up a paintbrush, poke at her, and tell her to "git," like one of the stray dogs around her property.

"I'm Monica, by the way." Her voice was heavy with irony, well aware she needed no introduction.

"I gathered. I'm Shelby."

From the drying racks she grabbed the comic-book pages that the ten-year-olds had been working on, laying them down in the spots the kids had claimed at their table. From the corner of her eye she watched Monica come closer, her eyes missing nothing. Not the Christmas lights Shelby had put up, thinking they would add something special, or the wires hanging low between the rafters with the toddlers' masterpieces clipped to them.

"So, how do we do this today?" Monica asked.

"Well, we're going to pretend you're teaching a class to teenagers—"

"I said adults only."

"Well, there was a serious lack of adults interested."

"How many?"

"None."

"How many did you ask?"

Shelby sniffed and turned away, putting the last of the comic-book pages down.

Monica's rich laugh only made her bristle harder.

"You know, this place is really amazing," Monica said, touching the white twinkle lights Shelby had put up around the coat hooks and cubbies. "If you're a kid who likes art, this must be paradise."

"I like to think so," Shelby said, nearly snuffing the praise under a cool tide of disdain. Monica continued to walk around, touching the toddlers' artwork where it hung from the rafters. Shelby couldn't stop watching her from the corners of her eyes.

"You know, I'm only here because Jackson asked me," Monica said. "Once the filming stops I'll get out of your hair. I have no interest in encroaching on your art kingdom. So, how about we stop circling each other like cats and just be civil?"

Well. Damn it! Shelby kind of liked this anger. It felt protective. But she'd been raised to take the high road.

"That sounds reasonable," she said. "Why are you here so early?"

Monica shrugged, hitching a turquoise purse, which honestly matched not one thing that she was wearing, farther up on her shoulder. She even broke all the fashion rules and still looked good. "This is when Jackson told me to be here."

As if beckoned, Jackson came in the front door carrying a small tray of coffees. His hair still damp from his early-morning swim, his face split in that wide smile of his that Shelby always loved the best. She was so relieved to see him; he'd balance the scales in this room. With him there, Shelby wouldn't feel quite so invaded.

But when Jackson's eyes fell on Monica, it was as if a silent and invisible bomb went off. The whole room changed. The chemistry. The air, even.

The two of them stared at each other, smiling like idiots, and then quickly glanced away, making a bit of a shuffle about the coffees. But Shelby stood there, in the ruins of the world she'd known before Jackson walked in, and tried to get used to the new reality.

Jackson and Monica were having . . . a thing.

How much of a thing, she didn't know. She wasn't that wise in the language of glances and smiles and fingers brushing fingers as they handed each other coffees. But *something* had happened.

And this, she thought, getting hot, getting good and pissed off, after that lecture Jackson gave her about not screwing up anything for the *America Today* show. The nerve! The nerve of both of them, standing there trying to pretend that they were truly that interested in Matthew Henshaw's comic book about a farting robot.

The *America Today* crew came in with their equipment and another little cardboard container full of coffee cups. The producer was a woman with purple hair who introduced herself as Vanessa, and a man wearing a vest with a ton of pockets started unloading small cameras and a microphone system.

Dean was there too, glittering in her barn. Larger than life. Glamorous in a totally masculine way.

Everything about him registered underneath her peevishness; it woke up her body. Just like it had the other day by the side of the road, and again at Cora's.

"How did the taping go yesterday?" Jackson asked the guy with the pockets, trying so obviously to keep it casual.

Vanessa answered the question, because apparently Pockets didn't talk much. "Cora's is amazing. Truly world class." Shelby smiled at the news. Cora deserved some success and happiness after all she'd been through. "And the pageant stuff was actually really cute, a terrific contrast to those horror shows we see on TV these days."

"Your sister wasn't there," Pockets said, looking up from the equipment in a box.

"She wasn't?"

"No. You said she would be. But she wasn't. Everyone seemed a little rattled."

The news rattled Jackson, too, and he glanced quickly over to Shelby as if she could corroborate the story. She shook her head. Gwen was going through something dark and strange, and Jackson would be smart to be worried. Wary.

"I'll, uh . . . have to talk to her."

But he wouldn't, Shelby knew. He'd try, but Gwen would brush him off and he'd walk away, frustrated. And Shelby could say something, as she'd tried in the past, but he'd ignore her, or divert the conversation, unable to accept help when he needed it. It was the pattern they'd established years ago.

Jackson's phone buzzed and he dug into his pocket to read the text. "I . . . I'm sorry, I have to head back to City Hall." He glanced up and put the phone back in his pocket, that smooth fake smile over his face. "I trust you have everything you need?"

"We're good," Vanessa said. "We'll be in touch with you later."

Before leaving, Jackson walked over to Monica and whispered something in her ear, which made her blush.

Hot with fury—with something worse than fury, something that felt like a tally of all she'd given up, every pleasure she'd denied herself because it didn't seem "right"—Shelby turned away.

Her counselors arrived. Gwen, with her new eye makeup that made her look somehow both older and younger at the same time. Tougher, but infinitely more fragile. Following her, Jay, so love-struck over Gwen he'd all but grown puppy-dog ears. And Ania, sweet, quiet Ania, who reminded Shelby very painfully of herself as a sixteen-year-old. So eager to please, so scared of being different.

Don't bother! Shelby wanted to yell. *You can be as good as you want and no one will care.*

A few minutes later the toddlers came in with their mothers, who had all put some extra effort into their looks this morning. Gone were the yoga pants and sloppy ponytails, replaced with skirts and dark blue jeans, coiffed hair and lipstick.

The ten-year-olds trickled in with so much noise and energy you'd think there were eighteen of them instead of just eight. They threw their backpacks into their cubbies and launched themselves at the table with their work. Jay and Ania met them there and slowed them down.

Her camps, her barn, her whole damn life was such a

well-oiled machine that everyone just fell into the places and the work that she'd meticulously prepared for them. She didn't have to say a word. Do a thing. It all just happened, spinning on without her.

"Shelby?" She turned to find Dean standing beside her. *You touched me on the side of the road. You kissed me. Put your fingers inside of me. Me. Shelby Monroe.*

"Hi, Dean," she said.

"This . . . this place is so amazing. I've never seen anything like it before."

She could say thank you. She could smile, acknowledge his sweetness, and go on about her life.

But her life was terrible right now.

"Come back tonight," she whispered.

He blinked. And then stilled . . . tautened.

"Here?"

She nodded.

"To talk?"

She shook her head, burning, burning from the inside out.

"Is this a tease, Shelby?" His voice was silky with innuendo, with heat and knowledge and sex. Her heart hammered in her chest, angry and demanding.

Unable to speak, she shook her head.

"Say it," he commanded, and she was instantly wet between her legs.

"It's . . . it's not a tease."

"What time?"

"Eight."

"I'll be here."

And so would she, despite the damage it could do to her business, her reputation, the contest, her relationship with Jackson—none of them felt half as important as how alive and dangerous being with Dean made her feel.

* * *

Monica didn't know what she was supposed to do. Help? The counselors and the parents seemed to have everything under control. The glitter situation with the toddlers was getting out of hand, but no one seemed to care.

And Ania, Jay, and Gwen, with the heavy makeup, were doing a great job with the graphic artists.

With nothing to do, Monica sat on a little chair in the corner, feeling vulnerable and slightly naked under the lights after her conversation with Ed yesterday. She watched the kids and thought melancholy thoughts about the fragile and fleeting nature of childhood.

"Are you crying?" Vanessa asked.

"No," she snapped, but a few seconds later Gwen handed her a Kleenex and Monica could have kissed her.

I'm a mess, she thought. *One conversation. One interview. How am I going to do this? I can't write a book feeling this . . . raw. I can't do anything but sit here and leak.* This morning she'd thrown in the towel with Shelby, unable to go twelve rounds with the woman, when days ago she would have relished a little verbal sparring with the stuck-up princess.

But not today. Today she just needed some peace. And to watch kids make a mess out of glitter.

"So," Vanessa said to Shelby, putting down the small camera. "I think we're ready for Monica."

Both of them looked at her. Monica couldn't even muster up enough fight to give them the finger or make a face. She just sat there and let them stare at her.

"I'll take the graphic artists," Shelby said with an overbright smile, looking down at the table of kids. She appeared slightly manic, probably with the adrenaline of being taped. "Ania, Jay, and Gwen, you go on outside with Monica. You can work at the lunch tables."

"Uh . . . ," Monica said, suddenly painfully aware of what she was supposed to be doing. Teaching them. She wondered what Shelby would think if she knew that she had only gotten her GED last year. On this planet there could not be a worse person for this job. "Get your bags," she said, grabbing her own, and then she led the kids outside, where there was a concrete slab and three picnic tables underneath a cedar roof. There was a storm of butterflies in the backyard. Large purple bushes behind the tables seemed to attract them.

It was just as magical out here as it was inside the barn.

"This is where everyone eats," Ania said, suddenly the most talkative of the three.

"It's cool," Monica said, putting her bag on a table, painfully aware of Vanessa and Matt behind her.

"So." She sat down and the three kids sat across from her, crowded onto one bench. *Ridiculous!* But she pressed on. "Did . . . ah . . . did you guys bring some writing?"

"I did," Jay said, eager. He pulled out a limp red notebook covered in doodles. Ania rolled her eyes. Gwen stared at the ground. "Just one of you?" she asked.

"I have a notebook," Gwen said. "Shelby told us to bring it. But I haven't written anything."

"I thought you teaching us what to write was the whole idea," Ania said, sounding panicked, as if she'd failed something.

"Right. Yes." *Calm down, you little overachiever.* "I guess . . . I guess I just thought maybe, if you'd written something . . . you might . . . you know, want to talk about it."

"I will," Jay said, casting sideways glances at Gwen, whose head was lowered as she painstakingly pulled a notebook from her book bag. Ania yanked a pristine pink notebook from her bag and no fewer than three pens, and then crossed her hands as if waiting for guidance.

Gwen did the same, watching Monica carefully as if she might jump at any sudden movement.

Talk about being set up to fail! There was so much

expectation in the air, she actually felt herself hyperventilating.

"Not that this isn't great," Vanessa said, her voice foul with the stink of sarcasm, "but we actually need some footage of you saying something to them. Something about writing."

Oh. Screw you. For a minute she thought about standing up, just pushing away from this table and the kids with their ripe expectations and their wounded serious eyes, and telling Jackson he was going to have to do this shit without her.

Jackson.

Just the thought of his name flooded her with gratitude. With excitement. With fondness and tenderness. After that experience in the bathroom yesterday, she wasn't lying to him when she said it was the most exciting thing she'd ever done.

Hands down. The dirtiest, kinkiest, most thrilling sexual act she'd ever been a part of in a history checkered with kink. And today, when he'd whispered that he'd like to see her later, she knew what he meant. What they might be doing. And it had felt—no joke—as if something had been unlocked. If she had sex with him, she didn't know if she would actually come. But she really, really wanted to find out.

And she couldn't walk away from this table and still have Jackson.

"All right," she sighed. "First thing we're going to do is work on who we are as writers."

Eager, the kids all nodded. "Figuring out who you are as a writer, or even who you want to be as a writer, will inform your work. It will give you a voice. And I'm not saying you should write down your goal—like 'I want to write a bestseller.' Or whatever. I want you to think about what is special about you that will make your work special."

Again the kids nodded. Ania and Jay flipped open their notebooks and started writing things down. Gwen stared at her hands.

"Who are *you* as a writer?" Gwen asked Monica.

Monica felt the painful eye of the camera, the attention of the kids. And suddenly her mother's words from the other night rang—loud as an alarm—in her ear.

You're just like me, digging through your life for little shiny bits and scary bits and terrifying bits to show the world so they have something to talk about at work, so they can feel better about their own lives because ours are such a mess.

She shook her head, rejecting the words. Rejecting her mother.

"I'm . . . ," she said, needing to find new words to fill the terrible empty void her mother had created in her. "I'm a truth-teller."

"Because you write nonfiction," Ania said, showing her stripes as a classroom keener. "Autobiography, right? You can't make it up."

"You wrote a book of poems, too," Jay said. "And a book about groupies and articles for a bunch of magazines."

"How in the world . . . ?"

"I googled you."

Of course, not even bad poetry could die in the computer age.

"No. I mean, yes, you're right. But when I say truth-teller, I mean that I tell the hard truths. The ones people don't want to look at, or are painful to look at. And you can do that in fiction, too."

"Do you write fiction?" Ania asked.

Monica shook her head.

"Why not?"

"I guess . . . because I never really tried. So," she said,

pushing them back on track, "everyone take a few minutes to write down who you think you are as a writer."

As they scribbled away, Monica pulled out her own notebook and stared at the notes from yesterday.

"Kicked like a dog" stood out in grisly detail and she shut the notebook.

A few minutes later, Vanessa swung the camera off her shoulder. "That'll work," she said.

"We're done?" Ania asked.

"For the moment," Vanessa said, and Ania started stacking up her stuff while Jay kept writing. "I'm going to need to interview you." Vanessa checked her watch. "Tomorrow, though."

"Interview me?" Monica asked. "About what?"

"About writing and Bishop, I guess."

"No one said anything about interviewing."

Vanessa stared at her. "What's the big deal? You've done it like a million times."

"Not about Bishop!"

Vanessa sighed and gathered her equipment. "I'm sure you can think of something. I'll meet you here tomorrow."

And then she was gone, leaving her with the three kids, all blinking and staring at her. Monica wondered if she clapped her hands together whether the kids would scatter.

"Are we doing this again tomorrow?" Gwen asked.

"No," Monica answered. *Nope.* Writing class was canceled. Indefinitely.

Jay looked like he'd been shot.

"It's not . . . you know . . . it wasn't going to be a real class," Monica said.

"Why not?" Jay asked. "I mean, we don't have a lot of camps right now. We could do it, just like a half hour or something for the rest of the week."

Monica laughed, so uncomfortable her skin felt like it

was too tight. "Guys, I'm not a real teacher. I mean . . .
I just passed my GED last year. I don't know—"

Gwen's black-rimmed eyes were searing. "I read your
book, you know. *Wild Child*."

It sounded like an indictment. "Uh . . . thanks."

"Do you remember the dedication?"

"Of course."

*To all the kids feeling lost and alone in the hopes that
you find someone to listen and something to do that
makes you feel in control. Help is always there, just
have the courage to ask.*

"So?" Gwen asked, her voice a sharp blade of accusation. She gestured toward Jay and Ania, who stood
there, frozen, aware something strange was happening
but not entirely sure what.

"Gwen," Monica said, carefully. "I'm not that
person—"

"You're a bullshit liar!" Gwen cried. "Just like every
other adult!"

Gwen grabbed her stuff, shoving it into her backpack.
Half of it fell out but she didn't seem to care—she just
stormed away, across the lawn toward the barn.

Damn it! Monica thought. Inside, she screamed, *I am
an island. An island!*

But she knew a cry for help when she heard one.

She stood up. "Gwen!" she yelled and the girl stopped,
but didn't turn around. "Fine. For the rest of the week."

Jay fist-pumped, Ania groaned.

Gwen kept walking.

Chapter 13

Jackson snuck in the back door of the Peabody. He didn't like the idea of sneaking around, but he didn't need the front-desk staff guessing why he was going up to Monica's room all the time.

He took a deep breath and then knocked on her door.

Behind the door he heard the squeak of the bed, and he smiled. She was home. She was here. He was totally unprepared for the wild rush of excitement that squeak unleashed in him. The door opened, revealing Monica, still wearing the skirt and Tweety shirt she'd been wearing earlier, and that, too, was in total accordance with his plan.

They grinned at each other for what felt like a full minute.

"What's in that bag?" she finally asked.

Having forgotten, he lifted it. "Dinner. Cora's fried chicken. I know it's late, but—"

"It's perfect. Come on in."

She stepped aside and he walked into her room, letting the door close behind him. Suddenly, the room was alive with what had happened the last time he was in here.

This is where we kissed. This is where she touched me. This is where I stood and watched her touch herself.

He tried to push away the memories so he could at least feed her. He wanted to finesse his way slowly into his plan, but the memory of the way they'd touched themselves, of those things they'd said, became another person in the room, taking up space and air, brushing up against them.

Turning him on.

Jackson was no longer hungry for food.

He was nervous and excited in a way that felt somehow new and yet very, very old. As though he'd been wanting this woman forever.

The silence seemed to pound against his skin and he finally had to say something or go crazy.

"I don't want to eat," he said, his eyes on her. Even though she was on the other side of the room, the distance between them shrank to nothing. She was next to him, around him.

"What do you want?"

He put down the chicken.

"You."

Monica watched, her mouth dry, her hands sweaty, as Jackson reached up and yanked off his tie, different from yesterday's. Yellow. It took a pretty masculine man to look sexy taking off a yellow tie—and he did. And he was. He opened the first few buttons of his white shirt and she caught a glimpse of his tan neck, the tendons in that neck, that divot under his Adam's apple. It was as if she memorized it in a glance. If she had to pick his neck out of a lineup, she'd be able to do it, after just that hungry moment.

And then he reached behind his head and an inch of his belly showed, a ripple of muscles, a thin line of blond-brown hair disappearing under his belt. He grabbed the collar of his shirt to pull it off and then the shirt lifted, revealing another inch of his body, more muscles, a stomach of them.

And then his shirt was off and she was dry-mouthed at the sight of him.

"I thought I'd put on a show," he said. "For you, this time."

Well, he was starting off right, that was for sure. He had a swimmer's body, tan and muscled. His khaki pants hung low on lean hips, and he put his hands to his belt buckle and paused. "You're . . . ah . . . getting to the good stuff," she said, waving her hand at him to keep going.

"Sit back," he told her and pointed to the bed, which she nearly jumped into, quickly stacking her book notes and happily setting them aside for the night. His chuckle followed her and she was delighted in her excitement, delighted that he was entertained.

So far, so good. Bracing her back against the headboard, she stretched her legs out in front of her and crossed them at the ankles. "You may proceed," she said.

It was the most perfunctory striptease she'd ever seen, not that she'd seen all that many. But she certainly knew how to do one. He didn't tease, he didn't wink or bend over. She didn't think he was even flexing his muscles.

He just slowly, his eyes on her, revealed himself. His long arms, masculine and dusted with blond hair. The wrists that were all bone and tendon. She liked his wrists. His handsome feet.

"Your second toe is longer than the first," she said.

"I am evolutionarily superior."

"A couple hundred years ago you'd be burned at the stake."

"You are not helping the show," he said, deadpan. Which made her laugh. Hard.

He took off his pants, the waistband of his light-blue boxers riding low on all the muscles of his stomach. Her laughter dried right up.

"You . . ." she whispered, her eyes following that light trail of hair to the obvious erection under the cotton. "Swim?"

"I do."

He left the boxers on and crawled up from the end of the bed toward her. He grabbed her ankle and with one strong yank, he pulled her down flat on the bed. It was slightly caveman, and she totally dug it. Abandoned herself to it, put her arms up over her head, and watched him watch her.

"I like your Tweety Bird," he said, looking at her shirt and no doubt the breasts under it.

"Is that a euphemism for something?"

One corner of his lips lifted, but his eyes stayed on her chest, his finger coming up to trace Tweety's outline, across her breasts, along the sides, over her stomach, and then finally up to that cigarette Tweety held—contradicting all zoological reality—in his wing. Her nipples beneath the cotton were painfully hard. These light touches were killing her, were coming at her sideways, lighting her up from the inside. She arched against him, trying to inspire him to fuller contact.

But he resisted.

"I like your skirt, too," he said, shifting slightly so those hands, those clever teasing hands, were at her knees.

"I could probably get you one," she said, arching her throat to get a better breath.

"You know what I thought about all day after seeing you in this skirt?"

His hands, wide and warm, were slipping under the hem of her skirt, up to the top of her thigh, the muscles jumping as he passed as if vying for his attention, but he kept on, inch by inch up her leg. Under her skirt.

Having no sassy comeback, she could only shake her head.

"Tasting you." His fingers reached the lace edge of her underwear and slipped right over it, to the damp spot in the silk. For a second she thought about being embarrassed. He hadn't even kissed her. Barely touched her and there was a puddle between her legs. She was hot and wet and dying for him. "Will you let me taste you?" he asked, his thumb pressing up, shoving the silk of her underwear against her.

Her hands gripped the headboard. "Yes," she sighed. "Yes."

"Good." He slipped the scrap of black satin and lace off her legs and feet and tossed it over his shoulder and then those hands slid back up her legs, pushing up her skirt this time until she was revealed to him. Half-clothed, half-naked.

Yesterday she'd been covered by the bubbles. Hidden from his gaze. But right now she liked the way his breath caught, the way his eyes dilated. Her body and the attention it got had long stopped being something of pleasure to her. And she was suddenly grateful to have that back. That pride in her body.

He shifted again. His muscles coiled as he slid down on the bed and then his breath was between her legs, hot and humid, and he moved her, slipped one of her legs over his shoulder, pushed the other out to an angle. It was his show, and he was utterly in control. And she gave in to it, her eyes drifting shut. She felt everything he did with painful clarity. His thumbs parting her, the first initial soft and sweet lick. Bottom to top, as if finding her boundaries. She arched when he hit the top, the nerves in her legs twitching.

She could feel him smile against her and he settled in, his touch growing surer. More confident. Harder.

"Yes," she sighed. "Like that."

"Soft, then hard," he whispered against her, making her twitch and gasp. He sucked on her, licked her, bit her—very carefully—and she saw stars, felt her bones melt. Her brain was silent, blessedly silent, and she was fully inside her body, living in every lush inch of it, aware beautifully and specifically of that sweet, slow build between her legs, in her belly and womb.

He shifted again, as if finding a more comfortable spot, and she was suddenly aware of time. That he'd been doing this awhile and it felt good and she would definitely come, but was it too long? In the old life, in those rare times a man actually took the time to go down on her, she'd have put on the show by now.

She lifted her head. "Is it . . . are you—"

His eyes met hers over the black curls of her mound. Pleasure spiked again, despite her misgivings. That was just really hot. And when he lifted his face, she could see his lips were damp. Glossy. From her.

Oh, that was hot, too.

"We're just getting started, Monica. It's my show." Those blue eyes were so *alive,* and they stayed locked to hers as one of his long fingers reached inside. Panting for air, she pushed against him.

Oh. So. Good.

"You like that?" he asked and added another. A long, slow slide that filled her. She nodded, breathless with this pleasure. His hand twisted, his fingers finding some secret hidden space inside of her and pressing.

"Oh!" She flopped back on the bed. "Holy shit."

He chuckled against her and his mouth went back to work. Fingers, lips, teeth. His thumb. It became a blur, one long, loud party of pleasure between her legs. There was no room for thought, or doubt. If this was taking too long, good. It *should* take awhile. This was her body coming to life under his hands. Under his patience. It should take days. Nothing had ever felt so good.

The headboard was cold under her hot hands as she pushed onto him, into him.

"Oh, yes," she whispered. The orgasm built, grew, rolled through her, pushing aside organs and muscles, blood and sinew. She braced her foot against his shoulder, arching and twitching, and he grabbed her hips, holding her, and then she broke. Splintered. Exploded.

She grabbed his head, holding him to her. Maybe breaking his nose in the process—she didn't care. She just wanted this pleasure to last. And it did. She shook and moaned for what felt like hours. The big blast faded, but there were aftershocks, pops and zings of pleasure ricocheting through her body.

Weak, shattered, she stared up at the ceiling. "That . . ." Her voice croaked and she tried to clear it. "That was quite a show."

He flopped down on the bed beside her, chuckling and breathing hard. They lay there for a moment. "Thank you," she said, still staring at the ceiling because the intimacy was too much. She doubted he really understood what just happened, what he'd managed to hand back to her, and she didn't have the courage to tell him. Not now, when she felt so raw. So new.

"Thank *you*," he said, and she could tell he was looking at her, at her profile, as if waiting for her to turn and share with him this very real and beautiful moment.

Too much, she thought. *Not going to happen.*

"You hungry?" he asked when she didn't move. "There's chicken around here somewhere."

He sat up, and only then did she have the courage to look at him. The muscles of his back were a thick, rippling fan under his smooth skin and finally, because he wasn't looking at her, she could touch him. She shifted, moved, curled herself around him. Her legs along the outside of his, her arms around his chest. Her face to his spine. She kissed him there, a dozen small kisses, and he arched against her.

Blind, her hands explored the territory from his chest, to the ridges and angles of his stomach, down to the waistband of his boxers. She slipped her hand inside and found him, unbelievably hard, the head of him damp.

He hissed, grabbed her hand, and pressed it hard against him.

"Sorry," he muttered and lifted his palm, bracing his hands against her legs instead. "I . . . oh, fuck Monica. Please. Touch me."

And she did. Hard, soft. With both hands. She squeezed his sac, teased the tip, listened to him groan and curse, and felt him shake against her. His head fell back, resting against hers, and she felt so connected to him just then. More connected to a man than she'd ever been and she couldn't bear to leave it at this. Couldn't bear to hold him off with one hand while jacking him off with the other. She moved, quick and sudden, sliding around to the front of him. There was no room on the corner of the bed his legs straddled and she fell to her knees on the carpet.

"What . . . ?" he asked, his eyes gone, his face flushed. He was so close and he would never have asked for this and so it became a gift, cheerfully given.

"This," she whispered and slipped him into her mouth.

He touched her cheek, her hair. Fell back against the bed and held her hand where it rested on his thigh. He twined her fingers with his and she didn't like that. Didn't want that. How totally fucked up of her that she could have his dick in her mouth but holding his hand was too much.

She slipped her hand away from his, building her speed and pressure, making him jerk and swear against her. It didn't take long; she knew he was painfully turned on, and within seconds he exploded in her mouth, his feet lifting off the ground, his body jackknifing and curling around her, a cocoon of heat and skin and affection and mutual desire.

The safest place she'd ever been.

So, of course, she sat back, breaking the moment. The connection. It took her a second to catch her breath, to put at least some part of herself back together in a way that was familiar to her. Recognizable to her. But finally, she was able to look up and smile, resurrecting all of her sauciness, her flippancy, while inside there was a cleanup crew sweeping up after the mess of all her walls coming down.

"Well," she said, bright and shiny, as if she'd just opened a bank account instead of having the most intimate moment of her life. "You said something about chicken?"

He laughed, a big deep belly laugh—the kind that blew back the walls and cracked the ceiling, while at the same time rebuilding that cocoon, locking the two of them into an experience, a shared moment. Panicked, she scrambled to her feet, pushed down her skirt, and found at the foot of the bed the underwear he'd pulled off of her.

"I didn't bring any drinks." He took his time getting dressed; stretching, smiling, totally comfortable. She looked away, averting her eyes from the golden skin stretched over sleek muscles.

Leave, she thought. *Please. Just leave.*

He opened the bag, unleashing a whole new wave of the fried-chicken smell, and then spread things out as if they were going to have a picnic.

"I got you a leg."

When he handed it to her, she thought about not taking it. About making up some lie about work and then sitting down at her computer until he got the message, but she was *starving.* Could she ask him to go but leave the chicken with her?

In a backlash of terrible memory, she remembered visiting a guitar player's room with pizza and a six-pack.

They'd had sex, rough sex. Something she pretended to like while the whole time she had been thinking about the pizza getting cold on the dresser. When it was over and she had pulled on her clothes, he'd told her to take a slice and go.

At the time, the pizza had been cold and she'd been pissed, but now, looking back on it from this new place where she was standing, the whole scene was horrible. Vile.

And there was no way she could do that to Jackson.

Begrudgingly she took the chicken leg, thick and crusty, still warm. She could feel the care that Cora had taken, the love that she'd fried right into the meat. "If I stay in this town too long I'm going to get fat," Monica said. She opened the minibar.

"There's beer," she said.

"Perfect."

She handed the bottle to him by the neck.

"We can share." He opened the beer, took a sip, and handed it to her.

"I'm good." She sat in the office chair at her desk and bit a tiny piece of crust off the chicken. It was delicious, of course. Without a doubt the best small bite of fried chicken she'd ever had, and her instinct was to set it down. Push it away.

Like anything good that might roll up on the shores of her island.

"How's your work going?" he asked, pointing at the stacks of paper beside the bed.

"You don't want to talk about that," she said, largely because *she* didn't want to talk about it.

"I find myself interested in all parts of you, Monica."

This was the reality of letting someone in, of the lesson Jenna's death had truly taught her. As hard as it might be being alone, it was hard learning how to be with someone, too. She just had to decide which was harder.

Being alone, her heart answered.

"It's going fine," she lied.

"You know, you can just say, 'I don't really want to talk about it.'"

He was grinning at her from the bed. So happily oblivious to all the land mines between them. The land mines in her.

I have never in my life been happily oblivious.

She was always totally aware of the broken edges in people and situations. All the silent and hidden expectations that waited in the dark for her to fail. For her to be too much herself, or not enough.

But he sat there as though whoever she was at this very moment was just fine.

There was a long, slow unraveling of what remained of her distrust. Her suspicion. It wasn't comfortable, sitting there, but she had the deep-abiding sense that it was necessary. For her. For her moving on with her life.

"Work is . . . it's fine," she said, taking tentative steps. "Well, hard, actually. Harder than I thought it would be." She took a bite of chicken, a big bite, the flavor bliss. "How was showing Dean the factory?"

"It might be too small for the ovens."

She winced. He shrugged, but she could see the tension scurrying back into his muscles.

"But I really don't want to talk about that," he said.

It was amazing how they could do what they just did on that bed—share that kind of intimacy—and still cordon off big parts of their life from each other. It seemed wrong, somehow. Like a lie, or worse than a lie. But she didn't know how to change it.

"How was your teaching debut?" he asked, skipping from subject to subject looking for one they could talk about.

"Good. They . . . they want me to come back tomorrow."

"Vanessa does? They didn't get enough footage?"

She shook her head, pulling a long white sliver of chicken off the bone. "Not to tape. The kids . . ." It sounded ridiculous saying it out loud. "The kids want me to come back."

"Really?" He laughed, but it wasn't at her, so she relaxed. "Shelby must have been thrilled."

"I don't know if 'thrilled' is the right word."

"You didn't . . . what did you say . . . snatch her bald, did you?"

Monica shook her head, focusing for a moment on her chicken. On the memory of Shelby's face going white when Monica had said she'd be back in the morning.

I'm watching you, she'd said. *Those kids are at a really impressionable age and if you say or do one thing you shouldn't as an adult and as an educator, you'll be done.*

Monica had burned hard at the words, biting her tongue to keep from giving a big, long "fuck you, like I asked to do this, you judgmental cow." But in the end, she was proud that she'd managed to just nod and walk away. Her tongue bleeding.

"Her hair is intact," she said.

"Look, Monica, I know you're both adults, but if she—"

She held up her hand. "It's fine, Jackson. The whole thing is . . . fine."

Monica thought about Gwen, about how frantic she'd seemed. So wild. There had been something painfully familiar about the girl in that moment when she'd accused Monica of being a bullshit liar. The anger, the eyeliner, the tears blinked away before anyone saw them.

It wasn't so hard to see herself in Gwen.

Monica wondered about the girl's family—the other

bullshit lying adults in her life—if they were the cause behind some of that pain.

"So, who did Shelby get to take your class?" he asked.

"Ania," Monica said. "And Jay and Gwen."

His head snapped up and his hand holding the beer bottle slowly lowered. "Gwen was there?"

"Yeah."

"That's weird, she didn't tell me anything about it."

Monica laughed. "Does she usually?"

Jackson blinked. "Gwen is my sister."

Oh. No.

Chapter 14

If day one of teaching the teenagers was uncomfortable and strange, day two was an unmitigated disaster. She'd had this half-thought of just coasting in and talking some more about point of view. Perhaps using some words like "voice" and "author authority."

And if that didn't work, she'd tell them about meeting Jay-Z and Beyoncé.

But Jay had come armed. With poetry.

Monica should have known it was going to be a disaster when both Ania and Gwen rolled their eyes, but instead she had thought that if Jay was brave enough to want to share with them, they could be brave enough to listen.

Two minutes in, Monica clued in to the fact that Jay's poem was about Gwen. About ten seconds after Gwen clued in to it.

"Jay," Monica said, after Gwen gasped so hard oxygen became scarce out at the picnic table. "Perhaps we should—"

"I'm almost done." Jay rolled on; having worked up the courage to publicly declare his love via poetry, he was not going to be stopped.

"This is a joke, right?" Ania asked.

"No!" Jay snapped. "It's not, but you can't tell that because you're a soulless—"

"This class," she said, very pointedly at Monica, "is lame. It's not even for credit. I'm going to go eat my lunch." And then Ania gathered her stuff and was gone, which left Jay shuffling his papers, the fight draining bit by bit out of him.

Monica saw his chin tremble. "Break time," she declared, and Jay shot off.

Which left Gwen.

"Oh my God," Monica said. "Gwen, I'm sorry, if I'd known—"

"You suck at this." Gwen shoved her things in her bag.

"I don't want to do this," Monica snapped back, like the teenager she'd been.

"Whatever." Gwen's sigh managed to be both inflammatory and admonishing. Tricky for a sigh.

Monica reined herself in, remembering why she'd agreed to do this for a second day.

"Now, hold on a second, Gwen, before you charge out of here all pissed off. I'm a shitty . . ." *Oops, maybe hold off on the swearing.* "A bad teacher, I get it. So, how about I don't teach and instead we could just . . . talk?"

Beneath the goth makeup Gwen's face softened, lightened a little, making the black eyeliner even more garish.

"Fine." Gwen put her hands in her lap and stared at Monica. *Right,* Monica thought. *I'm the adult. I should act like I know what I'm doing.*

"Do . . . you want to be a writer when you grow up?"

"I like writing," Gwen said. "But I don't want to be a writer. I'm not sure what I want to be."

"Well," Monica laughed. This girl was barely out of diapers. "You've got some time yet to decide."

"I'm going to college in September."

Monica nearly dropped the laptop bag she was putting up on the table. "Aren't you . . . young?"

"I'll be seventeen in two months. I'm . . ." Gwen looked down at the picnic table and used her thumb to peel off some of the splintered edge. "Smart. I guess. I skipped some grades."

"It's good to be smart," Monica said, but Gwen rolled her eyes. "It is. You can take it from me, as someone who isn't, it's better to be smart than stupid."

"You're not stupid."

"You don't do the stupid stuff I did without being at least a little stupid."

"But at least you've done stuff," Gwen said.

"You will too," Monica said. "I mean, hopefully much smarter stuff and far less dangerous." This was probably not the right avenue of conversation between a pseudo-teacher and pseudo-student. "Where are you going to college?"

"My brother is making me go to Ole Miss. It's where he went. And my dad."

"Family tradition, that's cool."

Gwen rolled her eyes again and Monica, in what had to be one of the least smooth moves she'd ever executed, rested her head in her hand and fiddled with the zipper on her laptop bag and said, "So . . . your brother is Jackson."

"Yeah?"

"He . . . ah . . . he seems like a nice guy."

As soon as she said it, she wanted to hit herself in the head with her laptop.

"Nice. Sure. Everyone thinks he's nice."

"You don't?"

Gwen's silence was utterly and totally damning.

Poor Jackson, Monica thought.

"You don't like your brother?"

Gwen shrugged. "I don't think he likes *me* all that much."

Monica was swimming into seriously deep waters here and she had no idea what to say. "Sometimes it feels that way with adults," she said. "They're so busy telling us what to do, or what not to do, that we forget they're doing it out of love."

"Maybe other adults." Gwen swung her backpack

over her shoulder and before Monica could ask any more questions, she was gone. Back into the classroom.

Monica put her head down in her arms. She'd known this was going to be a disaster—this teaching thing. She should never have agreed, no matter what filthy things Jackson provided for her.

"Monica!" She looked up to see Vanessa crossing the lawn, camera in hand. "You have a few minutes for me?"

Just when she thought things couldn't get worse.

Jackson was going to owe her some serious sexual favors for this.

Jackson had himself fully convinced that he was coming by the Art Barn to pick up Gwen and take her home and personally escort her to pageant practice. Wanting to see Monica had nothing, absolutely nothing, to do with it.

But when he walked in, just as Monica was getting ready to leave, he was floored by excited relief. Relief that he hadn't missed her.

"Hey," she said, those purple eyes cagey, but her lips gave her away—they curved into a happy, loose smile before she could stop them. He knew now that he could trust her lips. Her eyes were experts in camouflage, but her lips were on his side.

"Hey yourself," he said, leaning against the kids' now-empty cubbies. "You're still here."

"Vanessa wanted to interview me about my long and successful teaching career."

Jackson winced. "How did that go?"

"Lucky for you I am an accomplished liar."

That wasn't the only reason he was lucky, and she seemed to read his thoughts because she looked away, a red stain on her cheeks. "How was class?" he asked.

She laughed, and he loved it. That laugh of hers was dirty and bright at the same time. Like a shot of tequila, it woke him up. Sent his blood pounding. "Ask your sister," she said.

"Ask me what?" Gwen approached and Jackson, as he had more and more lately, didn't recognize her at first. It was as if her features had been slightly rearranged over the few hours since he'd seen her.

"About what an amazing teacher I am," Monica joked.

"You're not," Gwen said.

It was so rude. So unlike Gwen that he actually flinched.

"Gwen," he chastised. "Apologize."

"Sorry you're a shitty teacher," she said.

"Hey!" Jackson said sharply. "Go wait in the car."

Jackson braced himself for more fireworks, never sure what his sister was going to do at any given moment, but Gwen was just a baby hardass, and she folded under the sharp tone of his voice and meekly went out the door.

"Monica," he said after his sister was gone. "I'm so sorry. She's . . ."

"A teenager," Monica supplied. "I remember what it was like. She's clearly going through something right now."

Jackson bristled. His sister was his business and Monica, though well intentioned, didn't understand what Gwen had been through. And while he might not understand what she was going through now, he would figure it out.

He didn't know how to say, *Stay out of this part of my life; no one comes in here.* But Monica was looking at him as though she understood. And maybe she did. They seemed to understand a lot about each other without having to say a word.

The other day, they'd walked wide circles around the parts of each other's lives that the sex didn't allow access to. It had been strange, but truly the kind of strange he understood.

Intimacy was weird.

"I'm . . . I'm just going to go get my stuff," she said, walking toward the darker hallway.

Jackson watched her go, wanting to say something, make some kind of plan so he could see her again back in her hotel room. It felt, decidedly, like there was unfinished business—sex business—between them, but perhaps there was just too much of themselves they were keeping private. Maybe there were too many unsaid things between them. Too many dark places the other couldn't go. His sister, his parents. Her trust issues, her book. Her mother.

Perhaps they'd been right initially and it was all just a mistake.

"Jackson," she said, looking back over her shoulder, caught in the dark of the doorway to the hall. "See you later?"

As far as codes went it was impossibly simple. And he was gutted with desire. Gutted with impatience and gratitude and excitement.

Not a mistake, or if it was, he didn't care.

"Yes," he said. Because, really, there was no other answer he wanted to give her.

As soon as he stepped out to the car, the sight of his sister in the passenger seat crushed his excitement.

He opened the door and slid in but didn't start the engine.

"What is going on with you?" he asked, not looking at her, unable to look at her.

"Nothing. She said it, she's not a very good teacher—"

"Do not," he breathed, turning his head to stare at her, "treat me like an idiot. You're being rude."

"There's no one here," she said. "No one is watching you, so you can stop pretending like you care."

"Of course I care!" he cried. "Your behavior reflects on me, Gwen!"

"Right." Sarcasm was heavy in her voice. "Can't have the mayor look bad."

Oh, for fuck's sake! He couldn't step right with her. Everything was a fight. Exhausted, he started the car. "You're grounded," he said.

"Right," she laughed.

"I'm not kidding. Grounded. For a week. And you'll apologize to Monica."

She blinked at him, as astonished as he was.

He had no idea if any of that would actually do anything, but it felt good to do *something*.

Shelby pushed down her skirt and pressed away from the wall but kept her hand there, her fingers splayed against a child's drawing of her under a rainbow, holding a fish, of all things. Her legs were weak. She braced her forehead against the wall, the push pins holding up the pictures in her office catching at her hair.

That's it? she thought. *I'm jeopardizing everything for sex that's getting worse?*

"Vanessa is waiting for you," Dean said from behind her. The sound of his zipper being pulled up caused her to straighten her spine. She lifted her head. "Every time you say you're going to film, you get distracted." His laughter made her bristle, it was so knowing.

This has to stop. It has to. What kind of woman does this? What kind of woman keeps having sex like this? And now, where I work?

If the sex was amazing, as mind-blowing as what had happened on the side of the road, she might understand it. Might be able to rationalize it. But the sex was getting worse, as though the farther they got from the side of the road, the colder she was. The slimier he was.

Yet some desperate ache in her to find that wild woman who had kissed a stranger on the side of the road drove her to say yes to Dean when she should say no. When she *wanted* to say no.

And instead she kept doing *more*, and trying sex acts she'd only read about, all in an effort to feel something.

"I told her I'd meet her outside," she said, though she knew Vanessa was taping Monica first.

She turned and found him smiling and honest to God, she had no idea what that smile meant. She had the sense that it was supposed to be fond, a fond smile, as if she were a pet who had performed well, but all she saw was a sort of smarminess. *Those teeth,* she thought. *Too white.*

I'm having mediocre sex with a man I don't like. What the hell is wrong with me?

"I need to go," she said when he didn't step away. Didn't let her pass.

"How about I come back again tonight?" His expression was hopeful.

Last night he'd taken her down on the floor, on her hands and knees, her skirt pushed up around her waist. In her office.

"No," she said, because honestly, someone had to.

"I do like it when you play hard to get." The texture of his voice implied that she amused him. That because she'd let him put his dick in her mouth he understood her. But something had happened to her in this affair, something strange. It was as if she'd splintered off into pieces. There was the woman she'd always been, watching this other piece of herself having sex with a slightly despicable man. And the woman who watched was marginally repulsed at the acts she performed, desperate to prove . . . what? That she wasn't herself? That this wasn't her life? That the years weren't marching forward and she was more alone every single minute?

And that repulsion was spreading. *It's over,* she told

herself. *The mental break is over. Time to get back to regular life.*

"I can't meet you tonight," she said. "My mother has a doctor's appointment." That was a lie. Her mother refused to go to the doctor, but he didn't know that. He didn't know anything about her, really.

"Well, we're leaving tomorrow afternoon."

"Which is why I need to go tape with Vanessa now," she said.

He laughed. A little mean, that laugh. "Baby, I don't want to put too fine a point on it, but you look like you've been properly fucked."

She straightened and gave him her iciest glance. The idiot! Honest to God, she was never going to have sex with him again. Ever. That part of her that was weak and desperate and needy was getting locked away.

Fed up, she pushed past him and pulled from the bottom drawer of her desk her purse, her makeup bag, and her hairbrush.

As she walked past him toward the door, he grabbed her arm. And she was reminded, stupidly, horribly, that things with Dean always *started* exciting. Her body liked it when he touched her like that. Firm. In control. Part of her, when he did that, shrank down . . . waiting with pained and bated breath for whatever he was going to do next and couldn't wait. *Could. Not. Wait.* For it to come.

Too bad it was turning out to be such a disappointment. She pulled her arm free.

"I'll see you out there," she said.

Face burning, she opened the door, only to run into Monica. They both stopped as if held in place by a repellant magnetic force. They couldn't get closer, nor could they leave.

"What are you doing?" Shelby asked, because she was so off balance, so turned around, and Monica was truly the last the person she wanted to see.

Monica's eyebrows went up at Shelby's tone and Shelby knew she was doing this wrong, but she was doing everything wrong these days—it was as if she were a train without brakes.

"Getting my bag." Monica lifted the laptop case in her hand. "What are *you* doing?"

Shelby nearly rolled her eyes. Honestly, with the chip on that woman's shoulder, it was amazing she could walk. Despite what had just happened in her office, Shelby managed to say, without any compunction, "Vanessa is going to interview me outside. I just need to get ready." She pointed at the bathroom door behind Monica and they did an awkward shuffle getting around each other in the narrow hallway.

"How did it go today? With the kids?"

"It was terrible," Monica said.

"You know the filming is over tomorrow," Shelby said. "The crew is leaving. And it's Friday."

"So, I'm fired?"

"You were never hired."

"Right. Then one more day and I'm done."

"I guess so."

Shelby pushed open the door to the bathroom and at the same time, Dean stepped out of her office. He grinned at her, a dirty, knowing grin, before he realized Monica was there.

Shelby could feel herself blushing. A red tide of blood spreading from her heart, across her body. Across her face.

If Monica was even a little intuitive, she'd know exactly what was going on.

"Monica," Dean said, a little too loudly. Shelby wondered, painfully, if the guy had any tact.

Shelby could tell Dean was looking at her and she tried, insanely, to act normal but she wasn't entirely sure what normal was in this situation. So she stood there. Frozen, staring at Monica. "See you out there, Shelby," Dean said, and he was gone.

"You have got to be kidding me," Monica breathed.

"It's not what you think."

"No? It's not you and the—" She stopped. Shook her head. "Never mind. It's not my business."

Shelby wanted to die. She wanted to burn to cinders with mortification and let the wind blow her to the sea. But instead she had to mutter, vaguely pleadingly, to Monica Appleby, "Don't tell anyone."

Monica nearly laughed, Shelby could tell. But in the end she said, "I won't," and walked away.

Taking the last of Shelby's pride with her.

Chapter 15

Later that day, Monica watched Jerome Hennings push his coffee cup back and forth between his hands. The white porcelain mug covered the five inches of Formica with a whirr and a click and then it hit his palm with a fleshy smack.

Monica, notes forgotten, couldn't look away. It was as if Cora's, the sinking sun outside the window—all of it was gone. Just gone. And her life was reduced to that coffee cup, the five inches of Formica, and Jerome, who had been the first officer to arrive the night Simone shot JJ.

A young officer, fresh out of training. Up until then, he said, he'd mostly been handing out speeding tickets. Breaking up the odd fight. Nothing to prepare him for the murder scene.

"I had to follow Simone to the hospital," he said. "I mean, it was obvious what happened . . . what JJ tried to do, but she needed care and I had . . ." He cleared his throat. "I had to question her."

"Of course," Monica said, because the guy seemed to be asking forgiveness for doing his job.

The mug stopped its cross-table journey and Monica looked up at Jerome's dark eyes. Dark and sympathetic. The sympathy made her want to rear up, tell him to fuck himself, and walk out of there. Maybe smack that cup against the wall, just to be awful.

To just be awful was the first instinct of the hurt and angry kid she'd been.

You are not that kid anymore, she reminded herself.

She was rebuilding herself from the ashes of Jenna's death and this was a test.

"She wouldn't let go of you," he said. "She was all beat up, bruised . . . it was nuts . . . She was like an animal fighting to keep you close. You were crying, she was screaming and trying to kick anyone that got close. She bit the paramedic. *Bit* him. Broke the skin on his hand. Anyway, I didn't want to hurt her more so we put both of you in the ambulance. But once they got her to the ER down in Masonville, they had to separate you." Jerome blinked. "I've never heard anyone scream like that."

"Me?"

"Your mother."

Oh.

"One of the nurses smacked your mom across the face. Swear to God, we all just about tackled her, but . . . your mom stopped screaming. The nurse got right into your mom's face, looked right into her eyes and told her to be quiet. That she was scaring you." Jerome ran a hand over his head; the dark curls sprinkled with gray didn't move. His wedding band flashed in the light.

You're a good man, she thought. *I'm sorry I'm making you remember this. I'm sorry.*

"She shut right up. Closed right down. Never seen anything like it. Bruised, bloody, broken, and then . . . just not there. Just—" He shook his head. "I can't explain it."

"Inside herself?" she asked, remembering her mother on that bed in Greece, her open unseeing eyes.

"Yeah. That works. Inside herself. Like as far away as she could get." Jerome took a deep sigh and gave the coffee cup one last nudge. "You get enough? Because I'm running late for the parade meeting over at The Pour House."

"Yes. Of course. Thank you." Monica made a good

show of stacking her notes, turning off her recorder. *Look at me, I'm a professional writer, totally okay with everything you just said.*

Jerome laid one big black hand over hers. "This is a weird job you got."

She laughed. "Tell me about it."

"You know, you should come to the parade meeting. Have some fun, forget these terrible things for a while."

"Parade meetings are fun?"

"Ours are. It's in the big garage beside The Pour House. Come. It would be good for you."

Jerome tapped the table once and headed out the door, making the bell ring as he went.

Monica looked around, surprised to see an empty restaurant. Cora stood behind the cash machine, counting money.

"Oh my gosh, Cora, I'm sorry," Monica said, shoving her stuff in her bag. "I didn't realize you'd closed."

"Well, you were talking pretty good there. I didn't want to interrupt you."

Clearly, talking about her mother had put her way off balance, and she suddenly found herself blinking back tears. Grief was a tourniquet around her throat and she could barely breathe.

"But if you're done," Cora said, "I'd like to get going to that parade meeting too."

"Of course." Monica managed to smile while she stood. She took a twenty-dollar bill over to Cora, who only stared at it.

"For our pie," she said.

Cora shook her head.

"No, Cora, come on." She pushed the twenty a little closer. Cora ignored it.

"I heard some of what you were talking about with Jerome," she said, in that utter no-nonsense way she had. "And we got something in common."

Monica's hand fell to her side. *No,* she thought, with grief for this woman who put so much love into her food, who'd created such an enviable business. Monica didn't want Cora to have any experience with the conversation at the table.

"Abusive asshole fathers," Cora clarified.

"My . . ." Monica cleared her throat. "My father never touched me. Not once." *Always my mom,* she thought. *Every single time.*

Cora stacked her twenties, then put a rubber band around them. "Then you're lucky," she said.

And never looked up.

Monica walked back to the Peabody on leaden legs. She let herself into her room and Reba stood up from the corner of the bed, shaking herself so hard she fell over.

"You are ridiculous," she told the dog for about the thousandth time.

Reba barked, once. A succinct "screw you."

Monica put down her bag and picked up the leash from the doorknob. There was no way she could sit in this room, not with the ghosts and the memories having a party in her head. She recognized this feeling from her misspent youth—this anxiety, this impatience, this anger mixed with grief—it had driven her to awful places. Dangerous men, stupid decisions. It was a hole in her that could not be filled. Could never be filled with the junk she'd tried to fill it with.

I have to find a new way to cope, she realized, staring at Reba, who only stared back. *I can't pretend it isn't there. I can't ignore it or wish it away.*

"Let's go for a walk," Monica said.

* * *

Jackson dropped the plastic spoon back in the bowl of red meat that Sean was calling chili. "This is awful," he said.

Cora, next to him, nodded. "Really bad."

"No, it's not!" Sean tried in vain to defend his concoction. He took a bite from his own bowl and made a big show of chewing it and swallowing it down. But his eyes were watering.

Jackson wiped his mouth, wishing he could use the napkin to wipe off his tongue.

"You know I'm entering the cook-off," Cora said.

"So what?" Sean demanded, red-faced. "We should all just not enter? Just crown you the winner?"

Jackson was aware of the cameras rolling behind him and he walked away from the arguing duo, hoping the cameras would follow.

They didn't. *Damn it.*

More than the usual suspects had shown up to the parade meeting because the camera crew was there. Sean, always looking to make a buck, was selling beer alongside his terrible chili and since people were nervous around the cameras, they were drinking it. A lot of it.

Jackson was doing his best to steer Dean, Vanessa, and Matt away from the crowds who were just there to gawk and drink, and so far he'd been pretty successful, but he had doubts about his ability to keep up the show for long.

And frankly, looking around the room, he realized that no one seemed to be actually working.

Including his sister. After dragging her to the meeting, she sat in the far corner near the old Chamber of Commerce float that had been stored here since last year.

Alone.

After the scene at the art camp, he'd dragged her to pageant rehearsal and confiscated her phone. All of which she'd accepted silently. Contrite and belligerent at the same time.

And now she sat alone and he felt . . . bad.

He'd taken three steps toward Gwen when the side door to the old garage creaked open and Reba the mutant dog made an entrance, followed by Monica.

Her eyes immediately found him, as if she were a compass and he was True North.

And all that shit they didn't talk about, those big black spaces they kept secret from each other, from the world—none of it mattered. Seeing her, it wasn't just that the night got brighter, or the room warmer, or any of that. It was that finally inside the building filled with people he'd known since he was a child there was someone who *knew* him.

She was more than a friend, really. A comrade. A kindred spirit.

Nearly thirty years old and that had never happened to him before. He scratched his chest, suddenly uncomfortable with the feeling; it was like being handed one too many things to carry.

"Hi," she said, almost shy. "I'm crashing your party."

"It needs crashing."

"I can see that." She glanced around. "Are you actually making the floats tonight?"

"The Chamber of Commerce one, yes. Vanessa's request."

"Vanessa has a lot of those."

"Can I tell you a secret?"

"Please do."

"I'll be happy when Vanessa is gone."

She smiled and her purple eyes danced, and he was taken aback by how they seemed to be in accord with each other. Her smile and her eyes told the same story about Monica this evening and it was a good one, as happy as he'd seen her outside of her hotel room. Entranced, he stepped a little closer. Reba danced around his feet. "We still on for tonight?"

Her lips parted and a breathy gasp escaped. God, he loved that. He really did. Lust roared through him, a wave obliterating everything but her. Everything but how she made him feel.

"Yes."

"I need you to do exactly what I say," he whispered, his eyes never leaving hers. She nodded. Spellbound. He knew if he touched her, she'd be hot. Growing damp. Cautious and careful in her desire, she didn't fling herself into it, didn't rush into sex. It felt like such a goddamn privilege to turn her on.

He wanted to roar, throw her over his shoulder, and run away with her back to her hotel room.

"When you go back to your hotel room, leave your door open."

She nodded.

"Have a drink."

She blinked.

"Turn off the lights."

"Now you're getting pushy."

"Take off your clothes and touch yourself."

She gasped. A soft small sound that turned him on so hard and fast he got dizzy for a moment. Lost in her eyes.

"Can you do that?"

She nodded, her pupils dilated. The purple nearly all swallowed up by the black.

"Can you do that and think of me? Of what I'm going to do to you?"

"Yes," she whispered, her lips curving into a sly smile. *Just for me,* he thought. *That smile is just for me.* And it was so much better than her frowns.

He stepped back from the cocoon they had managed to make between the wall and the door and his back to the room. They weren't alone. No one was listening, but they weren't alone.

He took a deep breath, to center himself, to pull himself together, and turned only to see Vanessa halfway across the room, holding a camera on them. She held up a thumb, her eyes alight with excitement.

"I'll . . . I'll be right back," Jackson told Monica.

"I don't need a babysitter, Jackson."

"Okay, but don't try Sean's chili." He fought the urge to kiss her, to press his lips right to that place on her forehead revealed by the black sweep of her hair. He ignored the urge, unsure of what to do with it, and walked over to Vanessa.

"Now *that's* a twist," Vanessa said. "The mayor and the Wild Child?"

"It's . . . it's not what you think. There's nothing between us."

"Well." Vanessa grinned knowingly. "The important thing is that on tape, it looks like there is. And that stuff plays, my friend. It will be eaten up—viewers will be breaking their thumbs to vote for Bishop."

Here he stood once more at a divide in the road. What exactly would a better man do? He didn't want to use his relationship with Monica for votes. But he needed to win this contest.

In the end, he did nothing. Vanessa walked away knowingly and Jackson told himself he was just trying to take care of the town.

She won't care, he told himself, but knew it was a lie.

As a rule, in Bishop, Monica had encountered only kindness and some mild celebrity worship. Shelby had been the only one ready with her judgment and her upturned nose. And walking around the garage, she got a few more nods and careful smiles, as if people were unsure how to approach her. A few men watched her with something altogether different in their eyes. Those were the men who had reread the sex parts in her book. And how odd, after years of becoming inured to men thinking the worst of her, that now she wanted to shrink away from it.

Her armor was dented. Rusted. Full of battle wounds. She could no longer pretend to be a version of what they expected.

But Jay waved when he saw her, using his whole arm to do it. Ania brought over her parents to meet her, and they were both very kind, if slightly embarrassed. The younger kids who recognized her from the art camp made her a part of an elaborate obstacle course they were running around the adults.

She wasn't alone, and her soul, though barbed and over-sharp, was . . . quiet.

Reba drew a crowd of people, for whom she twitched and preened. Monica found herself no longer annoyed telling people about the breed.

All in all, it wasn't awful.

And every once in a while, she looked up and saw Jackson watching her. Smiling at her. Every single dirty thought in his head right there in his eyes.

I'm in trouble with him. Real trouble. The kind of trouble she'd never, ever thought she'd be in.

Luckily, Sean was a fantastic antidote to all of it.

"Hey!" he called, standing behind a folding table, a Crock-Pot in front of him beside a bunch of plastic bowls and spoons. "You here to try my chili?"

"Absolutely," she said, grateful for his cheerful and easy acceptance.

"Don't do it," Cora warned as she went by, her arms full of tissue-paper flowers that people were tucking into chicken wire on the float. "Nearest doctor is thirty miles away."

"Hilarious, Cora," Sean said as the woman swept right on by. "Don't listen to her. She thinks she owns the market on food in this town."

"I'd love some chili," she said, and Sean beamed as he spooned some up for her.

"So . . . this garage," she said, looking around at the soaring ceilings and cement floors. It was about as big as a house. "This is yours?"

"Yeah. I bought it a year ago thinking I would start brewing my own beer, you know. Microbrew style."

"Great idea."

"Yeah, but my brother Brody hasn't been home long enough at one time to help me set it up."

"There isn't someone else you can have help you?"

Sean looked at her for a moment, as if gauging whether or not to trust her with a secret. In the end he shrugged—choosing not.

Sean handed her a bowl of chili. "Bon appetite," he said with absolutely no attempt to pronounce the words correctly. She smiled at him, inexplicably fond of the man at this moment. He wasn't pretending to be anything.

And then she took a bite of his chili.

"Oh my God," she said, choking it down, because she couldn't actually spit it out. "That . . . that's awful."

"Come on!" he cried.

"No, it is. I'm sorry. Is the . . . is the meat even cooked?"

Sean grabbed the chili bowl and scowled at her. "Get," he said. "Go away."

That was clearly her cue to leave, and she was all right with that. She'd broken up her loneliness, managed to brave a few steps off her island.

But Jackson, over by the float, lifted his hand, calling her over.

"Didn't I tell you not to try the chili?"

"You did. I wish I'd listened."

"Well, I need your help. What do you think?" he asked, holding two tissue-paper flowers. "Light green or dark green?"

"For what?"

"For the okra on the float."

She laughed. "You can't be serious." Reba ran in circles around her. Vanessa swung her camera over toward them.

"Stay," Jackson whispered, glancing sideways at the camera. "Just stay for a little longer."

She wanted to stay. With him. *Oh. Oh no.* She was in such trouble. And helpless to get out of it.

"Dark green," she said.

And stayed.

Jackson stared at the gold safety lock popped backward out of the hotel-room door, keeping it cracked.

She did it. She actually did it.

He'd rushed here. After Vanessa had left and Gwen walked home, Jackson nearly ran out of that garage. Desperate to see Monica. Desperate to have her.

And she'd done what he'd asked. The door was open.

Want was a twitch in his muscles, a fire under his skin, and he pushed open the door and took a step into the hushed darkness of her room. The air was warm and faintly damp and he thought of her in the bath, those freckled shoulders. The three inches of thigh above the water, covered in drippy trails of bubbles.

His foot made a soft noise on the carpet and he heard her breathing on the bed.

There were a dozen things he could say. Dirty words. Kind words. A joke or two, but something compelled him to be silent. The trust of that cracked door—that trust, it just wrecked him. Left him stunned and humble.

And so, silent, he came to stand next to her. The moon came through the sheer curtains just enough that he could see the gleam of her bare skin in patches. Snapshots. Her thigh. Her belly. The slice of her left cheekbone. Her arm came out of the shadows, and the glass in her hand glittered as she set it down on the table.

This felt . . . inevitable. Whether or not she'd worked up the courage to tell him her secrets, whether he'd worked up the balls to try to seduce her out of her own head—this moment felt unavoidable. Like a destination they would have come to no matter what detours or wrong turns they might have made.

The bedsheets rustled as she bent her knee, revealing the dark shadow of curls between her legs. Drawn, powerless, he touched her knee, running his hand up the outside of her thigh to her waist. She arched into his hand, curved and curled under his touch. Open-handed, his palm slipped up her rib cage to cup her breast. She was warm, trembling in his embrace.

He felt an impatient tug on the hem of his shirt and in answer he ripped it off, then pulled off his pants. He stood naked over her. Her fingers, soft and cool, touched his erection. Curled over him, around him. Pulled.

They hadn't kissed. They'd barely touched, and he was hard as stone. His blood pounded beneath his skin.

This . . . this wasn't how he'd imagined it happening. He'd had this image of him controlling things tonight. Of being the big-man seducer and not giving her a chance to think, to talk herself out of what she felt. But here she was with her own control. Her own agenda.

Fuck. That was hot. Surprising and beautiful.

"Condom is on the table," she whispered. Even in the dark he found it without a problem. Tore it open with his teeth, slipped it over his skin, hissing because it felt so good. His own touch burned.

He put his fists on the bed near her shoulders, braced his knee beside her thigh, and held himself over her, the heat filling the inches between them. He felt so close to breaking, so near his own edge; he'd felt that way every time he walked into this room. She sent him there with her trust, with her skin and scent. Taking his time, trying to pull himself under control, he slipped his fingers between her legs, his thumb finding the heat and dampness of her. She gasped, groaned, pushed herself against him.

"Please," she whispered.

Oh Christ, if she was going to start begging, he'd never last. She made room for him between her legs, curled her arms over his neck. That touch seared through his skin, down to the marrow of his bones. No matter where he was, years from now, he'd remember the exact and specific sensation of her arms around his neck, her breath in his ear.

But still he hesitated.

"Are you . . ." *sure, ready, okay?* He shook his head, struggled to pull himself together to not be just a bag of dumb lust and blind sensation. She deserved far better than that.

She shifted under him, found his erection with her hands, and positioned him, there. Right there where he could feel through the latex, through his skin, the answer to his questions.

Yes. She was sure. *Yes.* She was ready. *Yes.* She was okay.

And then, still holding him, she arched and he slid inside of her.

She was the instrument of her own glory, her own pleasure.

Incendiary. He couldn't breathe for the heat and squeeze of her.

"Here," she sighed, pulling him tight against her, slipping her legs up over his knees. She arched her back and lifted herself, using him, dragging herself over him. "Just . . . just like that."

Still no kissing.

"Monica," he breathed.

"Yes." It was a sigh. Acceptance. Invitation. "More."

Fine. No kissing. She was pliant against him, a willing shore for him to break against. And he took her, with long, smooth, hard strokes. She braced her hand against the headboard, pushing against him, chasing him down. He sat back on his heels, pulled her legs higher up over his, used his hands at her waist, pulling her, pushing her, lifting her.

She dug her heels into the blankets beside him, shifting him off balance, and he caught himself against the headboard, driving high and hard into her.

"Yes!" she cried. "Oh God. Yes." Her legs curled around his waist, her strong, muscular thighs holding him tight against her. "There," she breathed as her hands came around his back, under his arms. "Right . . . right there."

Her head kicked back, her hair an ebony splash across the pillow. He watched her as he pushed into her, all the way down, all the way in. He would touch her heart if he could. Captivated by her, by the twitch of her lips, the long sweep of her eyelashes, the way her body squeezed him. The coil of her muscles, the way he could feel . . . there . . . at the bottom of his stroke . . . her tremble.

It built, they built. The walls could have come down and he would have been unable to look away. Unable to stop.

"Jackson—"

He bent his head, bracing his forehead against hers. They were sweating, breathing hard. He licked her throat, sucked at the skin near her ear, and it was good. So good. And he couldn't control it for much longer. He slipped a hand down her body, over her breasts. She gasped when he touched her nipple and he pulled it, squeezing it harder, to hear her moan. He wanted her in pieces in his arms. He wanted her screaming. Crying his name. Driven suddenly by the ticking clock of his own orgasm, he bent his head to pull a nipple into his mouth, and his fingers found where he was sliding into her. He touched her stretched skin that accepted him with such beautiful grace.

She bucked against him. "What . . . ? Oh God, again. Do . . . do that again."

He smiled against her breast and used his fingers against her, against himself. He shuddered, holding on by only a thread.

"Come on, come on," he breathed, prayed really.

And then suddenly she was one long contraction. He felt every muscle in her body seize and he was caught in the grip of her thighs. He closed his eyes, braced his hands against the headboard, and rode it out.

The sigh of his name, the sudden languid nature of her body—it told a story. He looked into her eyes and saw it there too. Not a show. It was real.

"You're magnificent," he told her without hyperbole.

"Your turn," she whispered.

Unleashed, he thrust into her, holding her, positioning her so he felt her from base to tip. A growl roared out of him, the orgasm rolled through him, and he exploded.

Chapter 16

He was a sweaty, heavy mess on top of her and she delighted in it. Curling her arms around his wide swimmer's back, she let him shake and twitch against her, sighing her name.

She relished it—the tickle, the sweat, the squish between her legs—the messiness of it all. The messiness was real. Honest. And how beautiful it was. She blinked away the prick of tears behind her eyes, not because she was embarrassed by them, but because she didn't want him to be wounded—to think the worst. And maybe she didn't want to talk about it just yet. This feeling—this buoyant gratitude—she wanted to keep it to herself for a while.

"I'm sorry," he murmured, pushing himself up and away. "I must be crushing you." A bead of sweat dripped from the damp edges of his hair onto her breast. He touched the drop with his thumb and she quaked, just quaked with ticklish pleasure. "I'm sweating on you."

"You are," she murmured, smiling up at him.

He rolled to the side, turning away from her to handle the even messier reality of the condom. He stood and tossed it in the trash.

"I . . . brought up the bottle," Monica said, pushing herself up on the bed. She reached to the side and grabbed the decanter she'd snuck upstairs. "There's a coffee cup in the bathroom you can use."

"Great," he sighed, as if still trying to catch his breath. She could relate. Her heart had stopped pounding, but she still felt somehow behind herself, unable to catch up with all that had just happened.

Shamelessly naked, he came back into the room holding the coffee cup. He stopped to look at her, and she felt his gaze up her legs, across her belly, her breasts. She wanted to stretch under that gaze, invite him back to stroke her.

"That was—"

"Great," she said. She wasn't sure if he had misgivings, or doubts, but she wanted them gone. What had happened on that bed was spectacularly authentic.

Like a jungle cat, all sleek and coiling muscles, he crawled up the bed but then ruined the image by flopping down beside her, pushing his messy hair off his forehead.

She filled his coffee cup with more than the recommended serving size of scotch and settled up against the headboard, too happy, too relaxed, to be worried about her nudity or about these dangerous foreign feelings taking root in her chest.

"I was surprised to see you tonight," he said after a long sip and a sigh, as if the scotch was just what he was missing. "I didn't know you were interested in the parade stuff—I would have made sure you knew about it."

"I wasn't interested." He laughed, and she realized how bad that sounded. How blunt. "No, it was fun. It really was. But I think . . . I think the truth is, I didn't want to be alone."

That seemed like a confession. A declaration. She was putting a flag in the ground and was deeply uncomfortable doing it. But it felt so necessary. She turned her own coffee cup in quarter-turns in her hands.

"I talked to Jerome Hennings today. He was the first officer on the scene the night my dad was shot." She shook her head. Her memory of that night was so cloudy and while she might not remember the events so well, she'd had a stance on them. A point of view, a way of referencing them so that they made sense in her head. *Dad was shot. Murdered.* But now . . . all this new information. These details that knocked her down and pushed her around, shaking that stance. "I don't even know what to call that night anymore. I used to say the night Dad was murdered. But that doesn't seem right anymore. And maybe . . . maybe it's the night my mom was almost killed. Or the night I was nearly kidnapped." She was suddenly tense. Angry even, the sweetness from moments ago gone. It was as if she'd pushed them up against one of the electric fences that encircled the things she just didn't want to talk about.

I don't want my life to be like this. Full of relationships so shallow because she was scared to talk about the things that mattered, the things that kept her up nights. The things that made her Monica.

Who will know me if I don't let them in?

"It can't be easy talking about that night," he whispered, giving her an out. *It's okay,* his voice said. *We don't have to talk about it.*

"You know," she laughed, to cover the dark bruise forming on her psyche, "it's not. It's not at all. It's awful. But it's helped me see where some of this 'I am an island' bullshit I've been telling myself came from."

"You are an island?"

"Or a lone wolf, depending on how I feel that day." Joking about it was a defense, she knew that, but she was opening herself up in baby steps here.

"What about Jenna?" he asked. "Your friend."

She ran a hand through her knotted hair, the small snags distracting her from the larger ache memories of Jenna brought up. "We were very close while I wrote the groupie book. We pulled each other out of the lowest points of our life and then, once we had our acts together . . . we drifted. I think the memories that each of us carried for the other were really painful, so it was easier to let each other go so we wouldn't have to be reminded of that part of our life. But then she came to a signing in Nashville and we had dinner. And she told me she was sick and . . . everything kind of snapped into focus. I realized how alone I was and how alone she was, and I didn't want that for her at the end."

"You're a good friend," he said.

"I think . . . I think I just did what I would want someone to do for me."

He ran a finger across the back of her hand. "I understand feeling alone."

"Oh, please," she said. "You're surrounded by friends. By people. Everyone in this town loves you."

He stared at her for a long moment, a kind of bewildered surprise on his face, but then it was gone, vanished behind that smile he wore so easily.

"You're right," he said and took a drink, waving her off. "I'm just addled by great sex."

Immediately she realized what an asshole she sounded like. Who the hell was she to shrug off his loneliness just because it didn't look like hers?

"I'm so sorry, that was unfair of me."

"Well, trust me, I know how ridiculous it sounds but sometimes, like tonight, I can be in a crowd of people who are my friends, who have known me my whole life, and I feel . . . alone. Part of it is my own fault, I know that. When I first moved back, everyone wanted to help and I held them all at arm's length, you know. I just circled the wagons and concentrated on my sister."

"You isolated yourself."

"Well . . . I don't know how much of it was a choice, and how much of it was just the way things turned out."

She wanted to ask if he really believed that, but she could tell by his face that he did. He was somehow distanced from all those choices he'd made and the long-term ramifications of them.

"How did you become mayor?" she asked.

At his sudden tension, she guessed she'd brushed up against one of his electric fences. And she wondered if he'd brave it out to answer her, or if he'd even consider that brave. But then he relaxed, his leg resting against hers. The hair above his knee tickled, so she pressed harder against him. Past the tickle, until it felt . . . right.

"I had a degree and a year of law school. When I moved back, there was nothing for me to do. Besides, obviously, take care of my sister. But I was living in a house that smelled like my mom. Pictures of my dad were everywhere but I had nothing of my own. What twenty-two-year-old does? After the initial shock wore off and Gwen got a little more settled, I did some odd jobs for the city. But I was just . . . passing time. I wasn't *doing* anything. Dad was mayor when I was a kid and I remembered watching him walk through town . . ." The smile he gave his coffee cup was beautiful. Sad and sweet and young and a million years old, all at the same time. "Well, it seemed like it would be an all-right job. So, I ran for mayor and walked into that office to a disaster. I mean, a disaster. And I tried to contain it as much as I could."

"Contain it?"

"It's not like it's a secret, but the details and how bad it really was, I tried to keep under wraps."

Of course he did, she thought.

"So who knows?" she asked. "Who really knows how hard you're working to keep this town afloat?"

"You." He kissed her shoulder.

"I'm serious, Jackson. Who else knows?"

"The city treasurer. City Hall staff. Shelby. I don't know, why does it matter?"

"Your sister?"

He shot her an incredulous look. "Why in the world would I tell her?"

It said so much, that look on his face. About his relationship with his sister. The town. The distance between him and everyone else in his life.

"This is a bad heavy secret and you shouldn't have to carry it on your own." Secrets were isolating, she knew that. Had been locked behind her own for years.

He made a face, clearly uncomfortable, and she knew she should stop pushing him. But she had this strange knowledge on the other side of her own secret. This delicious weightlessness.

"Tell me what you're going to do after you save this town. What does Superman do for an encore?"

"I'm leaving."

"What?"

"I'm leaving town."

"Forever?"

"If I can. Yes."

Monica blinked at him, stunned. She couldn't even pull her mouth closed.

"What?" He laughed—he actually laughed. "Gwen's going to college, so there's no reason for me to stay."

"Where will you go?"

"I don't know. Maybe I'll backpack through Europe. Go to Vegas. Hide out on some beach in Mexico."

"When?"

"Election's at the end of August. Seven weeks away."

"And then . . . you're gone?"

"Gone."

Ah, she thought, bundling the sting in her chest in the comforting embrace of sarcasm. *And here I was starting to feel something for the man.*

"Don't make that face at me, Monica." She realized she was making a face, something between shock and horror. The current between them got colder and she pulled the sheet up her body, suddenly aware of her nudity. "It's not selfish. It's not juvenile. My life got cut short. You said it yourself. There were things I wanted to do. Places I wanted to see and now, with Gwen going to school, now I get the chance."

"Does she know you're leaving town?" He turned away, color on his cheeks. Monica gasped. "You haven't told her."

Jackson stood and began pulling on his clothes.

"She won't care. She's independent. That's what every single counselor said. She's older than her years." So much of what Gwen had told her about the adults in her life made sense now. Even if Jackson hadn't told her, she clearly knew he was keeping secrets.

"Don't you think it's weird you haven't told her?"

"No. I've just . . . I've just been waiting for the right time. She's been in this mood, and now with the show there just hasn't been the right time."

"A mood?" Oh, she was so offended on Gwen's behalf. "Don't trivialize her because you're a coward!"

"She's leaving!" he cried. "Why should she care what I do?"

"Because you are her home, Jackson."

That made him pause, as if he didn't quite understand what she was saying or didn't want to, but then he shook his head.

"We don't have that kind of relationship." He pulled his shirt over his head.

And whose fault is that? she thought.

"Have you ever talked to your sister about your parents? The accident?"

"All we did was talk," he said, sitting on the edge of the bed to pull on his socks. "For like a year it was endless counselors. Endless talking. We processed the fuck out of Mom and Dad dying. How long are we supposed to talk?"

"I think forever, Jackson."

He glanced at her over his shoulder, pausing for a minute in his readiness to flee. And when he stood she saw a new edge to him, something defensive and angry, and she braced herself for the slice.

"You learn that on your island, Monica? Two bullshit writing classes and you think you know my sister? You think you know us?"

Being prepared for it didn't make the pain any less intense. She breathed through the sting.

"I know what not talking does," she said. "I know the wounds that fester. Look at your sister, Jackson, and tell me something's not festering."

His silence was all the answer either of them needed. Jackson might be a fool, but he wasn't an asshole, not quite.

"I'm sorry," he said, standing like razor wire at the foot of the bed.

"No. You're not."

"Monica—"

"Thank you for the sex, Jackson. Go talk to your sister." The shame in this situation wasn't hers, and she met his eyes for a long time.

"This . . . this isn't how I wanted it to end," he told her, his hand flung out toward the bed with its wrinkled sheets, the smell of their sweat drying in their folds.

"Me neither. But you can't insult me and think you're welcome back in my bed."

If only she'd had this strength ten years ago. It was so damn astounding to stand here on her own terms, despite the pain, despite the part of her that wanted him back in her bed no matter the cost to her.

"Go, Jackson," she said, lying back down. The sheet slipped, revealing her breast, a nipple puckered in the cool air, and she let him see it, a reminder of what he'd just thrown away. Never in her life had she played hard-to-get—never had she held herself out as a prize to be won. "You're not the man I thought you were."

* * *

The next morning, Jackson wanted to wake up relieved that Dean and the film crew were gone. He wanted to walk through town, proud of himself. Confident that he'd done all he could. But instead he'd barely slept, and his alarm clock rang while he was staring up at the ceiling—Monica's words in his ears.

You're not the man I thought you were.

He kicked off the sheets, tired of this endless argument he'd had with himself since walking away from Monica last night.

An hour later, Gwen came shuffling downstairs in baggy shorts and her Bishop Swim Team tee shirt, her black eyeliner smudged under her eyes. Bubba, the dog, a black shadow behind her.

"Sleep well?" he asked, trying for a joke but landing near sarcastic. He opened the kitchen door and let Bubba out in the backyard.

She ignored him as she opened the cereal cupboard.

"We're out of Fruit Loops?" She grabbed a box of Cheerios and sat down in front of the bowl he'd put out for her. "That sucks."

Jackson bit his lip, her attitude rankling so hard on his doubt, his sleepless night. But starting a fight over breakfast cereal wasn't what he wanted.

"Hey . . . can I talk to you about something?"

She stiffened, eyeing him warily.

"When you go away to school, I was thinking of . . . of leaving town."

Her breath went in, hitched, and he found himself holding his own breath, waiting. It was like being lost, that held breath, but still believing the next turn would lead him home. That everything would be okay.

But then she exhaled on one of those head-exploding

sighs, implying everything about him was just one big burden for her to bear.

"Where are you going to go?" she asked, shaking cereal into her bowl.

"I'm not sure yet."

"Well, have a great time."

"I don't want to fight—"

"Who's fighting?"

Try again, he told himself. *A different way, this time.*

"It's not like we're not going to be in touch or—"

"You going to sell the house?" she asked, not looking at him.

"I'm . . . I'm not sure."

Her eyes rose to his, quick and furious, an opinion burning in those blue depths.

"No," he said, quickly, wanting to squelch that angry hurt on her face.

"I don't care," she said, the angry hurt morphing into bitter indifference in a heartbeat. So fast she hid her heart from him! "Do what you want."

"I won't sell the house, but do you care if I leave?"

Quickly, she stood, the stool screeching against the tile. "I don't give a shit what you do, Jackson."

"Hey!" he cried. "I know I'm not Dad, but you don't talk to me that way."

"Whatever," she sighed, and it was like a match to kindling. He hated that word; he hated that tone in her voice.

"Don't brush me aside." He put a hand on her arm and she pulled herself away so violently, she stumbled. And in the air she left behind, the small current created by her body, he smelled alcohol. Stale beer coming out of her skin. "Have you been drinking?" he asked, stunned more than angry.

"So what if I have?"

"Gwen, come on. Drinking, the makeup . . . this isn't you."

She took advantage of his slack-jawed astonishment and pulled her arm free.

"How the hell would you know?"

His sister ran upstairs before he could think of what to say.

The impulse to heave her bowl against the wall was nearly uncontrollable, but he turned toward the sink and held onto the ceramic lip as if his life depended on it. Outside, his mother's tea roses bloomed in direct opposition to the ugliness in this house. The ugliness in his life.

His sister.

Monica.

How was he going to fix this?

Monica stared at the flowers held in Jay's hands.

"They were delivered for you," he said, thrusting them toward her, over the open threshold of her door.

She didn't have to ask who they were from. They were the same fragile pink tea roses that grew in such abundance outside Jackson's house.

"Thanks," she said and took the thin branches, tied together with a white ribbon.

Jay vanished back to his post at the front desk and Monica slowly shut the door, taking in the pleasures of getting flowers from a man for the first time in her life. She touched the edge of a pink petal, slightly crumbled, slightly yellow.

A lifetime ago she would have sneered at such romance. Such an old-fashioned, trite apology. As if flowers were going to be enough to get him out of the doghouse and back into her bed.

But it was easy to laugh at something you'd never experienced. Easy to disregard something the rest of the female world took such pleasure in, when she had no idea what that pleasure felt like.

She imagined Jackson taking the time to cut the flowers for her. Finding the ribbon, walking over with them and leaving them with Jay. It was an apology, sure. But it was also . . . a whisper in her ear. A hand against her back. *I'm thinking of you*, the flowers said in subtext. *I took the time to do something that would bring you pleasure.*

She put her nose in the blooms, inhaled their sweetness.

It wasn't enough, but it was a pretty good start.

She put the blooms in a water glass and set them on her desk where she could see them as she got ready for her day. It was the last day of her fake writing class and after that, she had to take some time to answer the worried emails her agent and editor were sending her.

But first, she thought, grabbing Reba's leash, *coffee*.

Fifteen minutes later, Sean turned to look at her from his seat at the counter at Cora's.

"You're becoming a regular around here," he said, wiping his mouth with a napkin.

"Good coffee is good coffee."

"Even if it comes with attitude," Sean said, casting Cora a poisonous glance.

"You don't like it, make your own damn omelette at your own damn house," Cora said, pouring coffee into a to-go cup.

"It's kind of nice not having the film crew around, isn't it?" Monica asked. It was as though the whole town had been sucking in their bellies for three days and now they were finally comfortable again.

"I've had enough of cameras in my face for a while," Cora said.

"Well, if we make the finals they're coming back," Sean pointed out. "Hey, did you hear? Next Tuesday morning we're having the *America Today* party at the garage next to the bar. We'll watch the results live. The whole town's invited."

"Sounds like fun," she said.

"Then you'll come? We're going to have specials on Bloody Marys."

"I'm making fritters," Cora said.

"What a disgusting combination," Monica said. "I wouldn't miss it."

Cora handed Monica her coffee and Monica held out a five-dollar bill, but Cora put up her hand.

"Oh come on, Cora, not this again."

"It's not on me," she said, pointing over Monica's shoulder to the far corner of the café. "Talk to *him*."

Monica turned only to see Jackson, his head down over a notebook. A cup of coffee steaming at his elbow.

"Standing rule as of this morning," Cora said. "He's buying whatever you're having."

"Then give me one of those peach muffins, too," she said, unable to look away from him. The roll of his shoulder, the way he rested his head in his hand, scribbling away in that notebook.

He was the picture of dejected. Of burdened.

Cora handed her the bagged muffin and Monica approached Jackson, who didn't look up until she stood nearly beside him.

"Hi," he said, the light in his eyes flaring for just a moment. And she felt like a spider caught in his gaze. Caught in him. Caught in the memory of the pleasure he gave her. The soft wilted edge of those flowers.

"I understand you're paying my way around here," she said.

"The least I can do," he said.

"No one's ever given me flowers before." She had no idea why she told him that. What was the point of revealing yet another piece of herself to him?

He ducked his head, humble and earnest. "Then I am especially glad I picked them for you."

"Christ, Jackson, you are so polite," she breathed, both charmed and then angry that she was charmed.

His smile was different from all his others. This one was worn. So terribly depleted, yet she refused to be swayed by that smile. She knew, with the sixth sense that came with the intimacy that they had shared—and not just the intimacy of their bodies, but of all they had inadvertently revealed about the parts of themselves they usually hid from people—that whatever was weighing on his mind was heavier than her.

"Sadly, Monica, I can't find it in myself at the moment to be rude, just to please you." That he tried to make it a joke broke her heart.

"I'll . . . I'll talk to you later," she said and again he nodded, before running his hands through that thick curl of hair over his forehead and looking down at the notes he was making.

She got as far as the fire hydrant she'd tied Reba to, the sunlight glittering and sparkling, causing her to squint against the dazzle of the day.

Jackson had come back for her. Despite the disappointments of yesterday, she had to remind herself that he was also the guy who came back to her hotel room after she'd rejected him and pushed him away with no explanation. He'd been so concerned for her that he came back. Asked her if she'd been raped, for crying out loud. He'd sensed her wounds and returned to see if he could help. And he had. He'd helped her immeasurably.

And in that back corner booth, he was wounded. It was obvious, despite his efforts to pretend otherwise.

And she could accept his flowers, and his coffee. Bilk him for a free muffin every once in a while, and eventually let him back into her bed—but walking away from him right now would be a betrayal. She'd be using him the way all those men had used her.

And she didn't want to be that kind of woman.

She had no idea if he would feel that way. She really wasn't even sure if he would talk to her, but for herself, for her own peace of mind, she had to try.

"I'll be right back," she told the dog and walked back into the café, heading right for Jackson's booth. He looked up, startled, when she slid onto the bench across from him.

"Are you okay?" she asked.

It was obvious he'd been putting all his energy into pretending he was fine. She waved her hand. "Don't answer that. Just . . . just tell me what happened."

"What are you doing?" he asked.

"I think . . . I'm trying to be your friend." It was hard work being honest. Being vulnerable with all her clothes on. "Because you need one. And I need one, and something is clearly bothering you. I don't think just being unkind to me yesterday would make you act like you've been gutted."

"Is that how I'm acting?"

She nodded.

"I'm sorry I was unkind."

"I know."

"I told my sister I was leaving," he finally said.

"Good for you."

"Well, I wouldn't go that far. We got in a huge fight. She said, and I quote, 'I don't give a shit.'"

"A fight is better than nothing, right?"

"I don't even know. I've screwed things up so bad." He ran his hands through his hair, gripping the ends as though he'd pull the whole mess out if he could. "Before our mom and dad died, I barely knew Gwen. I was so much older than her. I was barely her brother, and then suddenly I was in charge of her. I couldn't be her parent, there was no way. So I tried to be her friend, but she . . . she was so smart. Just. So. Smart. And I remember so clearly, after the funeral, after it had all settled down and it was just her and me . . . she looked at me with these eyes, these old-woman eyes in a little girl's face, and she needed me. I . . . I don't know, I just freaked out a little. She needed me so much. *So much.* And I had no clue how to help her, how to be what she needed. How to meet these unmeetable expectations she had. I couldn't . . . I couldn't fix things for her. I couldn't make things right. So I backed off. And all the doctors tried to tell me to make her life normal and I . . . I didn't even understand what that meant for her, you know? So I just kept inviting these kids around, because I didn't have to look into her eyes when we had a bunch of kids around."

Never had she heard anything so pointedly honest. So terribly cowardly and brave at the same time. She felt torn in two by his words.

"You're probably not all that different from her, Jackson."

"I feel like either I'm an alien or she is, that's how different we are."

"Come on," she laughed, but he wasn't joking.

He sighed, putting his hands down on the table as if he could shove it all away. Which, she realized, was probably what he'd been doing for years.

"I don't want to talk about it anymore."

"Okay," she said, knowing it wasn't a reflection of how he felt about her. He'd probably revealed more to her than anyone else in his life. "Do you want me to leave?"

His eyes pierced hers. "No."

Well, that didn't leave them much, did it? She opened her bag and split the muffin, putting it back on the bag before pushing it into the no-man's-land between them. It took him a second, as if he were some wild animal she was trying to tame with crumbs. A ridiculous notion, but still. She acted normal, ate a little, sipped her coffee. Nodded to people as they passed, until finally he reached out too and took a piece of the muffin.

Piece by piece, they ate the muffin in silence.

Chapter 17

Other than Jay watching Gwen like a puppy dog, the third and final installment of Monica's fake writing class was relatively uneventful. The assignment for the first part of class was for the students to write a letter to someone who had hurt them. Gwen kept her head bent, her blond hair hiding her and her paper from view.

She'd been manic all class. Fidgety and snappy. She'd yelled at Ania already, called Jay an idiot.

And she sat there writing so furiously, it was a wonder the pages didn't burst into flames.

Monica hoped she was getting some catharsis over Jackson.

In the second part of the class the assignment was to write a letter to themselves, pretending they were the recipients of the first letter. Basically, switch places with the person who had hurt them.

"What?" Ania asked.

"The whole point of books, of art in general, is to experience empathy. To allow ourselves to walk a mile in someone else's shoes. And as a writer, you've got to do that. You have to learn that." She tried not to look at Gwen, but she couldn't help it. Vicious unease radiated off that girl like fumes. Even if Monica weren't aware of what had happened between her and Jackson, she'd be worried about Gwen's behavior.

"Ania doesn't understand empathy," Gwen snapped, flipping the page in her notebook so hard it ripped. "All she understands are grades."

"That's not fair!" Ania cried.

"It is, kind of," Jay said.

"Stop," Monica said. "Everyone just stop arguing and start writing."

"But what if the person we're writing to did something really bad?" Gwen asked.

"Even villains think they're heroes," she said, and Jay gasped.

One mind blown, yay me.

"Go ahead," she said. "Try. No one has to read this if you don't want."

They split back up and kept writing until Shelby came to the back door of the barn.

"Time!" she yelled across the lawn to the picnic tables that had become Monica's makeshift classroom, and the three teenagers started collecting their things. Jay reluctantly stopped writing.

"That . . ." he sighed, "was epic."

Delighted, she laughed. Almost clapped her hands—this feeling, of being important, of making even a little impact on these kids—it was pretty great. She suddenly envied Shelby, who got to have this feeling all the time.

"I'm so glad," Monica said. "And since this is the last of these classes, I just want to say . . . it was fun."

Gwen snorted.

"It was. It . . . I mean, you may not have learned anything, but I did, and I appreciate that."

Jay gave her a fist-bump before leaving. Ania asked hesitantly for a letter of recommendation for colleges next year, but Gwen took off across the lawn and back into the barn without even a backward glance.

Alone at the picnic tables, Monica sighed, feeling like a big stone had been rolled off her back.

But she kind of missed the stone.

She took a few minutes to use Shelby's wi-fi and opened her laptop to answer her agent's and editor's slightly frantic emails. Her agent wanted a sample of what she'd been working on, just as a sign of faith for the editor, and Monica struggled to put together a couple of brief character sketches. A loose scene between JJ and Simone, when Simone was a teenager and JJ was committing what was in all actuality statutory rape.

What a beautiful family I have, she thought, poisoned by the story all over again.

She glanced up, suddenly aware that the sun had shifted behind clouds. Glancing at her watch, she realized she'd been here for two hours.

"Holy cats," she breathed, and put her things away. She was surprised Shelby hadn't been out here with a pitchfork, kicking her off the property.

Inside, the classroom part of the barn was mostly empty. Except for Gwen hanging up art on the drying wire.

"Hey," Monica said softly, aware that the girl was deep in thought and practically coated in radioactive ill will.

"What are you doing here?" Gwen asked with heavy suspicion.

"I was just . . ." She pointed behind her toward the outside. "Just working on some stuff. I lost track of time. The campers are gone?"

Gwen nodded, putting the last of the comic books on the wire. "Everyone's gone. Shelby's in her office. Jay had a shift at the Peabody and Ania . . . Ania flew away on her broomstick."

Everything about Gwen screamed that she needed someone to talk to. She had a cosmic neon sign over her head saying "Don't leave me alone."

"Well," Monica said, fighting her instinct to help. Because she'd probably screw it up and Jackson would hate it and really, frankly it was none of her business. "I'll see you—"

"Can I ask you a question?"

"Yes." Eagerly, Monica put her bag back on the floor, relieved that Gwen was going to make it her business. Another reason intimacy was so weird—it showed up in the strangest places without visible boundaries. It was like the Bermuda Triangle. "Shoot."

"Are you mad at your mom for killing your dad?"

Whoa. Talk about unexpected. And . . . and not anything she'd really ever thought about before.

"It was self-defense," she said. "My dad was going to kill her. Probably hurt me. My mom was doing her best to protect us. There are plenty of other reasons I'm mad at my mom, but that's not one of them. Are you . . . are you mad at your parents for dying?"

Gwen shrugged. "What's the point, you know? They're dead. I can't be mad at them."

"But you're mad at someone?"

Gwen held herself very still for a moment and Monica recognized a glass about to shatter. She had been in that position more times than she could count, keeping it together until it was impossible. Until it hurt too much to try.

She decided to nudge. "Your brother?"

"Brother," she scoffed. "I'd hardly call him that."

"What would you call him?"

"I don't know—babysitter?"

Monica winced before she could help it. Gwen saw it, and it launched her on a tirade. "You don't know what it was like. Before the accident I barely remember him. I mean, like nothing. He was always off at some big swim meet or some other cool high-school-kid thing. And then he was gone and it was just Mom and Dad and me. But he was still kind of there, you know? I could feel them watching me and thinking—why isn't she more like him? Why isn't she normal? And popular?"

"Gwen, you don't know that," she whispered.

"Well, it felt like it. And then suddenly . . . he was in charge of me. And he used to do all this shit, you know—invite my classmates over for movies. Or to go miniature golfing, and they only went because he was paying. They weren't my friends. And he didn't ever see that. Those kids were laughing at me because I didn't know how to talk to them. I never knew what to say or when to say it and he . . . he never saw that. He just kept setting up these stupid parties. Without ever guessing how awful they were."

"I think your brother just wanted you to be happy."

"Yeah, well, total fail. And now he's going to be all over my ass because he smelled beer on me this morning."

"Is that . . ." Oh, she had to be careful here. "Do you drink a lot?"

"Never. But I went to a party last night."

"Parties can be good." From the look on Gwen's face, she could guess the opposite was true.

"It was awful. Totally awful. All these idiots standing in a field getting drunk and making out. And I thought . . . why can't it be easy for me? Why can't I want to do this?"

Monica sat down on one of the low tables, suddenly so aware of how different Jackson and his sister were on the outside, but on the inside, how similar. Jackson just knew how to hide his discomfort behind a wide smile. A friendly demeanor.

"You know," Monica said, "I totally get what you're saying. Those party situations . . . they suck. Unless you want to be there. Unless you feel comfortable. I used to pretend I wanted to be there, and I wasted a lot of years being someone I didn't like very much."

Gwen sat down on the other table, her flip-flops dangling from her clenched toes.

"But once I stopped that and wanted to be friends with someone—I mean, actually be close to someone—I had to force myself to do it." She thought of Jackson that day in her hotel room with the chicken. It had been so uncomfortable, so truly painful to share those moments with him, but it was something that had to be done. Like tearing off a bandage long after the wound was healed. And she was glad she'd done it, no matter what situation they were in now. Otherwise, truthfully, she'd probably never be able to have this conversation with Gwen. Opening one door had opened a lot of her doors.

"What are you saying?" she asked.

"Start small. Start with someone safe, who you know won't hurt you or make you uncomfortable or ask you to stand in a field and drink beer and make out. And just . . . talk to them. About yourself. About them. About movies. Stupid stuff." She thought about how smart Gwen was. "Or genius stuff, whatever." Monica thought she might pass out from relief when Gwen smiled. "What about Ania?"

Gwen rolled her eyes. "She's the queen of the beer parties."

Really? Monica would not have guessed.

"What about Jay?"

"He's so annoying."

"Boys his age are. It's unfortunate. But he likes you, and he seems like a nice guy."

"I guess." Gwen nodded. "Just talk to him?"

"Just talk. He likes you, so you could probably talk about anything and he'd pretend to be interested."

"Pythagorean theorems?"

"The language of love."

Gwen laughed, pushing the blond hair out of her face. Monica considered saying something about the makeup, but decided she'd played After School Special enough for one day.

"You going to tell my brother about this?"

"No," she said, adding it to the pile of secrets she was keeping for people around here. "I won't tell your brother. But, give me your phone." Stunned, Gwen reluctantly held out her phone. Monica typed in *Taxi* and her cell number. "I have a car here, and if you're somewhere drinking and the choice is to get in a car with someone who has been drinking or call me, I hope you'll make the right choice."

Gwen took her phone back like it was the holy grail. "Thanks," she said. "It's nice to have someone to talk to. Someone who understands."

Oh. God. Oh no. She was not role-model, not confidante material. She'd made every mistake in the world; no one should look up to her.

But there was Gwen, looking at her. Waiting for her to say something, to validate this incredible risk she'd taken, to offer up some modicum of respect for what it had cost her to open her mouth and talk about why she felt so different.

"My pleasure," she said. "I'm glad you talked to someone and I'm really honored that it was me."

Gwen walked to the cubbies and grabbed her book bag before heading out the front door. She looked back over her shoulder, lit by the powerful southern sun behind her. "You're not a bad teacher after all."

"Well, let's not go overboard."

Gwen lifted her hand in a small wave and left, the door closing behind her. Monica collapsed, folded right over, her hands on her knees, the strength totally drained from her body.

She turned, looking for a chair she could die in, only to be brought up short.

Shelby stood in the hallway leading to her office, and from the look on her face, she'd seen everything.

* * *

Shelby watched Monica pull herself together, gather all her armor and her fuck-you attitude, and stand there with her chin out, pretending to be so tough.

But Shelby had heard most of that conversation, and Monica had nothing to be defensive about.

"Wait here," Shelby said.

"Why? So you can call Jackson?" Monica grabbed her bag. "Read me the riot act for giving her advice? No thanks."

Shelby stepped up to the low table and put down the bottle of bourbon one of the parents had given her for Christmas about a zillion years ago. The coffee cup she'd been planning to drink out of landed next to the bottle with a thunk. "I'm going to get another glass. Wait here."

When she came back in the room with a second mug, Monica was sitting in one of the small chairs, her body curled up as she rested her head in her hands.

Shelby quickly poured the bourbon into one of the mugs and handed it to Monica.

"I don't drink," Monica said, staring at the cup.

"Me neither," Shelby said, but she poured her own shot and, in total disregard for the bourbon's fine sipping qualities, drank it back in one swallow.

"Ahhhh," she winced. "That hurts. Come on," she insisted, pointing to Monica. "Drink up."

Shelby had woken up this morning feeling as if the clouds had parted, the rain had passed, and she could get on with her life after the three-day meltdown she'd engaged in.

Dean was gone. *Gone.*

But in the three hours he'd been gone, he'd emailed her twice.

Dirty emails, about missing her. Missing her taste.

She'd deleted them. But she was unsettled. Rattled.

"I wouldn't peg you as a drinking-in-the-workplace

kind of woman," Monica said, sipping the bourbon like a teetotaler.

"Well, it's a day for surprises, isn't it?" Shelby poured herself another shot and sipped it. She was already slightly light-headed from the first.

Monica laughed bitterly. "You were listening to us talk?"

"Only the last part."

"And you didn't step in?"

"You had it handled, and truthfully . . . you handled it way better than I would have. *Way* better."

Monica seemed shocked at the praise. As shocked as Shelby was at handing it out, but she'd stood in the shadows, terrified, worried, feeling utterly inadequate to the scene she'd walked in on.

"I would have lectured her about the drinking, missing the point totally. And giving her your phone number? You were brilliant. In fact, I wish someone had talked to me like that when I was growing up. When I felt different. You have a knack," Shelby said, looking at the dark-haired woman who seemed so exotic next to her own ordinariness.

"Thank you, Shelby," Monica said after a moment. "That means a lot from you. You are a really good teacher."

Shelby nearly snorted, doubting Monica's sincerity, but Monica wasn't being sarcastic. She meant it. *Oh. Well.*

Monica reached over and poured them a little more to drink.

"So Dean is gone," Monica said, staring down at the bourbon in her glass.

"You're keeping a lot of secrets for people these days," Shelby said.

"Not my choice, trust me."

Shelby had no shortage of friends. Book club friends.

Work friends. High school friends. Parents of some of the more gifted kids she'd had. Jackson. But none of them knew what this woman knew about her. That didn't make her a friend, exactly, but Shelby couldn't find another word for it.

"I had an affair with a man I detest."

Monica shook her head like a cartoon character who couldn't believe what she'd heard.

"I put my whole life here in jeopardy for a man I could barely say two words to if they weren't dirty."

Monica choked on the sip of bourbon she'd taken and Shelby, having uncorked herself, couldn't shut up. "And he's emailed me. Twice. It hasn't even been a day and he's talking about missing me. It's . . . gross."

"Why did you do it?" Monica asked.

"Because I'm lonely. Because no one I know would ever treat me the way he did. Because being respected and liked can be sad substitutes for being desired."

"Did he hurt you?" Monica asked, looking like she would form a posse if one was required. Shelby was touched by her venom.

"He didn't hurt me," she said, unable to really put into words what had happened. And she was ashamed of why she'd liked him, at the nature of the sex between them. "But the sex was . . . not great. I think I had a psychotic break."

Monica tipped her head back and laughed, full-throated, all out. Uninhibited. Shelby had never laughed like that—not once in her life—and she took a sip of her bourbon, made sour by her jealousy.

"I understand psychotic breaks," Monica said emphatically.

"Jackson?" Shelby asked, perhaps pointedly. Monica sobered. Shelby would not have been surprised if Monica walked out. It was a personal question, and just because Shelby had offered up her own mistakes didn't mean Monica was going to offer up hers.

"How did you know?" Monica asked.

"It's pretty obvious when you're in the same room. The atmosphere changes."

Once, a few years ago, Shelby had told a high school student that the only reason he was a smartass was because he was so smart. And the look on his face had been this sort of dubious pleasure, as if he wasn't sure being proud of himself was the right thing in that situation.

Monica had the exact same look.

"Never mind," Shelby said. "It's none of my business."

"It will end," Monica said, "soon enough. I'll leave town. He'll . . . do whatever he's going to do, and it will all be back to regular life."

Shelby wondered if Monica knew how sad she sounded about the prospect of her regular life.

"Back to regular life, huh?" she said, happy about the idea, ready to shelve this person she'd been for three days.

Monica leaned over to clink her coffee cup to Shelby's. "To real life." They both sipped and stared up at the comic books hanging from the ceiling. "You know," Monica said, "I really like that kid's farting robot."

For some reason Shelby thought this was the funniest thing ever and she bent forward, laughing.

Full-throated.

Uninhibited.

Chapter 18

Monica had gotten in the habit of waking up early and walking Reba around town along the bike path. It was gorgeous in the morning, with the mist and the sunrise and the silence. She'd taken her words to Shelby to heart and had gotten back to regular life with a vengeance. She had pages—lots of them—to send to her editor. They were full of vitriol and hurt feelings and opinions on her parents' poor choices, and as much as she tried to take herself out of it, she couldn't.

The story was about her, after all; it was why people would pick up the book. And so she just stopped listening to the misgivings about her work, and late last night she'd emailed her editor her first three chapters.

She circled back through town, heading toward Cora's for her coffee, when she remembered it was Tuesday, the *America Today* show day, so instead she headed toward The Pour House, hoping that besides Bloody Marys, Sean would have had the good sense to make coffee.

Or better yet, let Cora make it.

Walking into the garage next to The Pour House was like walking into a wall of sound. A wall of smell. Sweat and fritters and coffee made for an interesting perfume— Eau de Bishop. The place was packed. The chairs were full, people lined the wall, and kids were sitting on the floor in front of the TV. A commercial for a credit card company was on, but the second it was over Jessica Walsh was back on the screen—beautiful in the fantasy way of beauty pageant contestants—and the room went silent.

Reba barked, no doubt her doggy brain confused, and everyone turned around to shush her. A few hands reached out to give her a pat, which Reba accepted as her due.

"Sorry," Monica mouthed, creeping around the edges of the group over to where Sean stood behind a card table, a cooler at his feet, a coffeemaker steaming beside him.

"Hey, Sean, can I have some coffee?" she whispered. Silently, he poured her a Styrofoam cupful.

"No milk," he said. "Or sugar. But I can make it Irish coffee if you like."

"Black is fine. What's going on with the show?" she asked, tilting her head toward the TV, where the weather was being discussed.

"Four of the towns have been on already. It's just us and Alaska left to show."

"Have we got any competition?"

"This town in Michigan. They got a good story. Real sad and shit."

Oh Sean, a student of the human condition.

Because she couldn't help herself, she glanced around, looking for familiar blond hair held rigidly away from blue eyes. "Where's Jackson?"

Sean pointed to the very far corner, where Jackson stood. Alone, but surrounded by people. *That's exactly what his loneliness looks like.*

She'd avoided him all week, easing away to give him room, or maybe to give herself room. Because the friendship thing had been surprisingly harder than the sex thing.

But looking at him now, there was no place she'd rather be than filling that empty space beside him.

Reba and Monica circled the crowd again and got over

to Jackson just as on the screen, Jessica started talking about the Maybream contest again.

"You okay?" she asked.

He shrugged, but she saw his fear in the set of his shoulders. The way he held his arms folded across his chest. Despite keeping some safe inches between them as she leaned against the wall beside him, she could feel his anxiety. Like low-level electricity.

"It's Alaska," Cora said, and someone turned up the volume as the package started.

Monica couldn't see the screen, but the audio was enough. She could imagine through the voice-over's description soaring snow-capped mountains crowding around a small sea inlet. A remote fishing village along the coast of Alaska that was settled during the Gold Rush. And now, the population was almost predominantly men.

"What we need," a new voice said from the TV, "is women. We need families. We want families."

"In preparation for the families they want," the voice-over said, "the men of Gershaw have gone to drastic measures."

"We've built a new school and community center, and a women's health clinic. We've got a doctor who lives here now, full-time."

"All of this," the voice-over continued, "was done through volunteer labor and community donations. But perhaps the most drastic thing they've done in their efforts to attract wives and families"—music played, the kind of music one usually heard in the background of porn movies—"is create a website. The Men of Gershaw."

The people of Bishop watching the TV burst into laughter and hoots, and, unable to resist, Monica stepped away from Jackson until she could see the screen.

Big, burly men, most of them in beards, were stripped down to their work pants, doing a variety of tasks. Building the new school, hiking through the forest. Fishing. Tending dogs. One guy was baking, half-naked under an apron. As the porn music played he licked a whisk and a giant dollop of batter fell into his chest hair, which was hilarious, and when the guy laughed and tried to get it out, it was only funnier.

Monica had to smile, she really did. The men looked good. But silly. And okay about being silly. All in all, it was pretty damn attractive. The website apparently had information not only about the single men, but the jobs that were available, ranging from nurse to teacher to lumberjack camp cook to fishing boat captain to police officer to mayor.

Monica walked back over to Jackson.

"It's good?" he asked.

"Only if you like half-naked men."

He groaned.

"You should have taken off your shirt more," she said, which barely made him smile.

Hidden from view, she took Jackson's hand. "It will be okay," she said.

He opened his mouth to argue but then shut it, and instead squeezed her hand.

Intimacy, she thought, feeling that squeeze all the way up in her heart. *So weird.*

The citizen of Gershaw kept talking. "We're a small town and we're pretty remote, but there isn't another place in this world that's as beautiful. And the families that we have up here, they are happy. But we need more, more women, more kids. More families to make the winters warm and the summers happy. We're a tight-knit kind of place and we want to grow."

The voice-over went on to discuss Gershaw's factory—a salmon-canning plant that closed before it really even opened.

The segment ended, and Sean across the room said,

"A website? That's all they got? Some half-naked fishermen? Please."

Everyone in the room argued about it through the commercial break. It was obvious the women in Bishop thought the website was pretty appealing. And Monica had no doubt that right at this moment, it was probably spreading across Twitter and Facebook like wildfire.

For a cracker company seeking out great PR, the town in Alaska was a dream.

"I missed you." Jackson's whisper sliced through the noise of the garage and stunned her.

"I missed you too," she confessed.

"I'm sorry," he said. "I . . . I'm not sure how to do this."

"Me neither," she admitted.

"Quiet!" Sean cried. "It's us."

"Our last semifinalist is Bishop, Arkansas," the voice-over said. She saw people in the audience holding hands. Mrs. Wiggins in the back bent her head in prayer.

"You don't want to watch?" Monica asked Jackson.

"I think I'm going to throw up." The fact that he was holding onto her hand in a death grip meant she wouldn't be watching either.

"Another small town hit hard by the economy, Bishop is struggling to meet the demands of the future, while still holding on to the heritage of its past."

"Wind energy for a small town like us is a huge benefit." It was Jackson's voice on the TV and half the room glanced over at him. He raised the hand that wasn't holding hers in a salute, and his smile would have been convincing if she weren't aware of his sweaty palms. "First of all, government grants pay for the whole thing, and as of 2014, our entire town's energy will be provided by windmills. Moreover, by 2015 our surplus will be plugged back into the grid and the state will be paying us for the energy we provide."

The segment went on to cover Cora's, and everyone cheered. And then the art camps.

"I think what the art camps provide is a way to help a school system with limited arts availability, but it extends beyond that." At the sound of Shelby's voice through the speakers, the kids in the front row sat up straighter. *That woman's got powerful mojo*, Monica thought. "Adults taking art classes, teaching the art classes, bringing their kids, sticking around to help—it's not about how good you are, but your willingness to try. What an important lesson, don't you think?"

"Art is a way of giving the things you are scared to say or embarrassed to say or too big to say a voice." Monica blanched at the sound of her own voice. "The kids and adults who take part in these art camps, they're lucky people. I wish this camp had been around when I was a kid. Maybe I could have found a better way to say all the things I needed to say. And I'm really proud to be a part of it."

Across the room, Shelby met Monica's eyes and she nodded. Monica pretended to do a little curtsy, and Shelby smiled.

The voice-over continued to discuss the Okra Festival, and Monica realized at one point nearly everyone in the room started looking at her and Jackson.

"What?" she asked.

Sean pointed at the screen, and Monica jumped forward in time to see a shot of her and Jackson at the float build, talking in the corner, eyes only for each other.

It was obvious something was going on between them. While they'd never said they were keeping things a secret, it was a pretty safe bet Jackson wouldn't love the whole town knowing she and the mayor had a thing.

It seemed awfully messy for a guy like Jackson. She looked back at him and winced. "Sorry," she mouthed.

"Shhhh!" Cora shouted. "They're judging."

She felt Jackson come up beside her and the whole room held their breath while Dean, in a slick suit, talked about his top three choices. Monica glanced over at Shelby, who was looking at the screen as if she were slightly sick to her stomach. Monica felt bad for the woman. Dean was a seriously good-looking sleazeball.

"The first finalist," he said, "is Gershaw, Alaska. My company employs a lot of women and they were pretty excited by those fishermen." Jessica Walsh laughed, and the citizens of Bishop groaned. "But it's not only because of the website, which is brilliant. Truly, it's probably already viral, and I can only hope those men find love in cyberspace. But it's also because of the environment they live in and how they care for it. I've been to Gershaw and the man wasn't lying—it's one of the most beautiful places on earth. And the factory would work great for us.

"The second," Dean shifted on his stool, "Is Ludlow, Michigan. When you think of areas hit hard by American manufacturing leaving the country, you think of towns like Ludlow. Their tire factory and the skilled labor in the town makes it a shoo-in."

Shoo-in seemed dire. Monica felt all her organs contracting and she was suddenly shocked to realize she was invested in this outcome, not just for Jackson, but for everyone in the room. Sean and Shelby. Gloria and Cora.

It was painful caring, but it was too late to stop it.

"And your third choice?" Jessica asked.

"Bishop, Arkansas," Dean said with a shrug and laugh. "Beautiful town, beautiful people, a factory that will suit us, but really it comes down to Cora's café. They had me at pecan pie cake."

The room exploded. The sound was deafening. Jackson behind her wheeled back, as if suddenly light-headed, and she grabbed his arm, only to be pulled into a hug so tight she couldn't breathe. And then she was let go and Jackson was high-fiving and shaking hands and hugging people. Cora, across the room, stood stock-still, tears running down her face. Sean lifted the woman in the air.

"Let me down, you idiot!" she cried, but she was laughing.

It was like standing in a room filled with helium. Never in her life had she been a part of so much joy and relief. It was astonishing. She was humbled.

And she was really, really glad for everyone.

"Thanks, Monica."

Monica turned to find Shelby, her face pink, her eyes damp. "Those were lovely things to say about the camps."

"Well, they were true. You should be very proud of yourself."

"The whole town should be." Shelby laughed. "I can't believe we made it to the finals."

"Okay!" Jackson yelled over the noise. "All right. First of all, congratulations. All of you. I'm so . . ." His voice broke, and Monica had never in her life been attracted to a man more. "I'm so proud of all of you. I really am."

Cheers roared through the room.

"But," he added, lifting his hands, and the room quieted again. "Now we've got two weeks to get ourselves together for the Okra Festival and the live show. We're ahead of schedule, but let's not get lazy. Let's make it the best festival ever and win this thing!"

More cheers. Sean opened up a bottle of champagne only to realize he didn't have any more Styrofoam cups. "Everyone," he cried, "let's go next door. First round is on the house."

No one seemed to mind that it was barely ten a.m. They all turned toward the door only to freeze.

Silence settled over the room.

"Well, will you look at this. A party, and no one invited me?"

There, surrounded by a camera crew, dressed in angelic white and looking more beautiful than any woman should, was Simone Appleby.

Mom was back in town.

Chapter 19

It was as if everyone had been jerked backward. People stared, openmouthed, shock chasing the celebration out of the room. All of which was enough to piss Jackson off, but the look on Monica's face, the stone-cold fear and disbelief, as if she were watching a nightmare become real, drove him to action.

"You can't film in here," he said, pushing through the crowd toward Simone and her crew.

"Yeah, she totally can!" Sean said, no doubt thinking of free publicity on her reality show.

"Not . . . not without permits." Jackson met Sean's eyes and jerked his head backward at Monica, who was still rooted to the spot. Sean shut up. Shelby stepped out of the crowd to stand beside Monica.

Simone's eyes missed nothing. "Permits? Really?"

"Yep," Jackson said, improvising as he went. "Lots of them. Very expensive, too."

He was just a few feet from her at this point and honestly, her beauty was a tangible thing. An aura that surrounded her. She was ageless. Her blond hair and white pantsuit gave her an angelic air. But those eyes were dark and full of sin. He knew it was ridiculous, but he actually thought if he got too close, he'd get caught in some web of hers.

"You're joking," she said, trying to call his bluff, but Jackson had been gambling so long and so hard with every single aspect of his life that she had no chance at winning.

"Mom," Monica said, obviously coming out of her shock. He felt her approach to stand near him, close but not too close. "What the hell are you doing here?"

"Filming," Simone said, her eyes cold, her smile practiced. Monica's mother was a stone-cold shark.

"Is this how you think you're going to stop me from writing the book?"

"Please, honey, I am just here to film." Simone was all innocence and Monica stepped forward, lunged actually, like she was about to snatch her mother bald. As Jackson put up his hand to stop her, he felt the fabric of Monica's tee shirt and then the taut muscles of her belly underneath.

She was trembling. Shaking. And the whole situation felt one word away from being out of control.

"You do need permits, actually." Brian Andersen stood up, smiling, and Jackson could have kissed him. No doubt, Brian was thinking about how much he could charge this crew to use their cameras in town. "If you'll follow me to City Hall, I'll get you set up."

Simone's eyes flashed over Jackson's shoulders toward Monica, and he got so angry so fast that for a moment, he was worried what he might do to this woman on Monica's behalf.

But Monica was back in full form, and she needed no one to fight her battles for her.

"Get out of here, Mom," she said. "You're not welcome at this party."

"Well, you've certainly made yourself at home here, haven't you?" Simone asked. "Talk about a twist I wasn't expecting."

He felt Monica ramping up behind him, and the only way to stop a good, old-fashioned screaming match in front of camera crews and most of the population of Bishop was to get Simone out of here.

Braving her aura, he stepped closer until Simone turned

her purple eyes to him. Physically, those eyes were so much like Monica's. The color, the shape, the fringe of black lashes. But Simone's were empty of all the things Jackson had grown to admire in Monica's eyes—the fire and heart. The intelligence and wit. The deep-seated pain that this woman had inflicted upon her.

"You want to talk to your daughter, now is not the time," he whispered. "Go, or I'll get my police chief to escort you out."

She blinked, the shark flinching for a moment.

"Aren't you clever," Simone said and then nodded at her cameraman, who swung the camera off his shoulder. "Let's go."

Simone and her crowd left, taking with them the oppressive tension that had filled the garage, and everyone behind Jackson started to buzz again, but a pin had been stuck in this town's victory. And he couldn't stand for that.

"Let's go over to The Pour House, second round is on me!" he cried, and people rolled past him out the door. Smiles were back on their faces but he could tell they were rattled, focused on Simone Appleby and not their victory.

"Weird day, huh?" Sean asked on his way out the door. "You want to give me your credit card for that round?"

"You know where I live," he said, then turned back around to see Monica surrounded by an almost empty room. Shelby stood next to her at a respectful distance, a surprising ally if not a friend.

Reba sat looking up at Monica, all the hair on her body twitching.

Shelby and Jackson shared a brief look and Shelby walked out the door too, pausing first to squeeze Monica's arm. Monica seemed startled at first to find someone next to her, but then smiled—unconvincingly, but she gave it a shot.

"I'm . . . I'm sorry," Monica said, when they were alone. "She totally . . . totally ruined the party."

"No. It's fine. The party is just getting started, I'm sure."

It was awful seeing Monica so beaten. So outside of herself. It was like seeing Sean when his mother died—all the fire in him had been banked. Lost. And now Monica sat in this empty garage looking like she'd been kicked in the stomach.

"I'm going to walk you home."

"No, no, you should go . . . go celebrate."

Oh, those eyes, they just killed him. The truth was, he *should* go celebrate, because he wasn't the man she thought he was. He wasn't the man *anyone* thought he was.

Avoiding her, as he had for the last few days, was undoubtedly the right thing to do in the long run. The safe thing. Because the closer they got to each other, the worse it would be when this was over. What had started as sex had turned into something well beyond his control.

But he couldn't look in her eyes and leave her like this.

"I'd rather walk you home," he told her with a smile, and he found it to be unalterably true.

It was shock. It had to be shock. This numb feeling, as though her feet were in ice and her head was floating off her body. It felt . . . like she'd been caught without her shell. All her doors had been thrown wide, her windows open. She'd been vulnerable and . . . happy. Standing in the corner of the garage, holding Jackson's hand, watching the show and everyone celebrating, and feeling a part of that. Feeling that she had something to do with it. And to have Simone walk into a moment so sweet, so pure, and destroy it with her blackness—Monica had been unprepared.

Once they got to her hotel room, she couldn't stand it. She couldn't stand the room, the memories, the fact that her mother was somewhere in this town waiting for her. That she'd come here to ambush her. To force Monica to bend and twist and change so that Simone would get her way.

Monica tossed her key on the desk and walked over to the window, cranking it open, letting in a hot breeze that didn't make the room feel any bigger.

"How long has it been since you've seen your mom?"

"Years. Three. Maybe four years."

"You okay?" Jackson asked quietly.

"Okay?" she cried. It was as if he'd pressed play on the internal monologue building in her head and heart. "No. No. I'm not okay. I'm *never* okay when she's around. I should have known. I should have known she would do something like this."

"How could you have known?"

"She called," she said, realizing she hadn't told him this. They'd shared so much, and yet somehow not much at all. "After that night at The Pour House, I came back here and she'd called the hotel. Tracked me down. She asked me not to write the book. Told me it would ruin my life."

His eyes opened wide.

"But I think what she meant was that if I tried to write this book, *she* would ruin my life." She stared at the curtains, the sheers, fluttering in the sticky breeze. There was only one thing to do. "I'm going to leave."

She grabbed her suitcase from the closet and flung it open on the bed.

"Leave?"

"I have enough to get the work done. I don't need to stay here, and it would serve her right."

"You're going to run away again?" Something in his voice infuriated her.

"Run away?" she asked. "From what? I wasn't going to stay here. This wasn't going to be my home. I don't have one of those, Jackson. I was here for a job. That's it."

He flinched and she knew how she sounded, how she'd reduced him and what they'd shared—the same way he'd reduced her the other day. For something that was supposed to be easy, they kept screwing it up.

"I'm not talking about Bishop, Monica. I'm not even talking about me. I'm talking about your mom. You're going to run away from your mom again? You're thirty years old—how many times do you think you can do that?"

"As many as it takes."

"You're tougher than that. Smarter than that."

No! she wanted to cry. *I am exactly this stupid. Exactly this weak.* But his eyes saw right through her.

"You don't know me," she said, railing against him. Against the truth in his words. "And you don't know my mom. If I stay, she stays. How is that going to go over?"

"Well, I imagine right now Brian Andersen is making them pay a pretty hefty price to film here, so I'm okay with it."

"What about the Okra Festival? If she's here, she'll ruin it. She ruins everything."

"It's two weeks away. We can deal with that then."

Jackson reached over and touched her arm, which, because she was angry and wound up, she pulled away. "You called me a coward, remember?" he asked. "When I wouldn't talk to my sister?"

"Are you calling me a coward?"

"I'm saying you have a whole lot of unresolved issues

with her that I think, for your own peace of mind, you should resolve. What if she finds you someplace you don't want to leave? Are you going to let her chase you around all your life?"

She wanted to say yes; she wanted to hold on to this grudge, this anger. She wanted every protective shell she'd ever crafted to keep her safe and warm. But the truth was a very sharp spear, and it cut through all her bullshit.

When she collapsed onto the bed, her suitcase toppled to the floor. Jackson sat next to her and she groaned, embarrassed by her inability to keep her shit together.

"Go ahead, Monica," he breathed in her ear. "Go ahead."

He put his arm around her, his big hand cupping her shoulder, his fingers touching the skin of her arm beneath her shirtsleeve. The solid warmth of him made it worse, and her face crumpled in an effort to keep from crying.

Silently, he kissed her forehead, pulling her close. And Monica, her face averted, broke into tears.

Loud, messy, awful tears, and Jackson didn't say anything. He didn't shush her or calm her or in any way try to comfort away the storm that raged in her heart and head.

These new memories that had resurfaced while she was here, talking to people about that night Simone shot JJ, had made a mess of her. Of her strength and her anger toward her mom. They turned everything she knew by heart on its head. And she hated that.

Jackson seemed to understand, and he just let her rage until the rage was gone. All gone. And then she sat there, limp, next to him, held upright by his big hands. His strength.

Another first, she thought.

Orgasms, flowers, friendship, and now this. Jackson was her conquistador, the first foreign man on all her untouched shores, and he didn't even know it.

"Thanks," she whispered, using the hem of her shirt to wipe at her eyes.

"Thank *you*," he said, and she laughed, all snotty and messy.

"For what?"

"For this morning, during the show. Standing beside me."

She glanced up at him, somehow both embarrassed and emboldened by it all. Weird how vulnerability was addicting. It was so freeing not to pretend all the damn time. "You looked like you needed a friend."

"I needed you, and you were the only person in the room who knew that. Thank you."

"I've been avoiding you the last few days," she confessed.

"I know. I . . . I've been avoiding you, too."

She leaned away from him, from the intimacy and this budding . . . need of him.

"Maybe we should . . . stop, you know?" She gestured limply toward the bed.

"I don't want to stop. I want to be with you, however long it lasts."

In her lap her hands were knotted together, the knuckles like white flowers. A bouquet of bones.

I want to be with you.

Was there anything more lovely?

"I want to be with you, too," she said and his hand covered her knuckles.

"You're a bit of a mess, you know that, right?"

"Must be why we get along so well."

He laughed, his thumb stroking her cheek. "You're right." Their broken edges seemed to fit together in a way they didn't fit with anyone else.

Tired of talking, of thinking, she kissed him. It was familiar, that kiss, but at the same time unknown, as if beyond a familiar room there was a new wing and she was just stepping into it.

"Thank you," she said against his lips, thinking of the way he'd handled her mother, how he'd backed her up, how he'd walked her home, talked her off the ledge, and let her cry with her pride intact.

"For what?"

"For being you." Slowly she climbed up onto his lap, her legs straddling his hips. He put his hands on her ass, pulling her closer, and the heat between them built.

There was something about this man that turned her inside out, that made her . . . not herself. Or a different version of herself. And she was somehow grateful and horrified at the same time. But when he lifted her shirt over her head and looked at her with such adoring lust, it just felt so right.

Whoever she was, whoever he was—they worked together.

And she would take it while she could get it.

Wednesday morning, Monica had an appointment to speak to Mrs. Blakely, her mother's sixth-grade teacher. She wanted to cancel the meeting because the outside world felt vaguely dangerous, as though her mother would pounce on her at any moment.

But instead she decided to practice a little fake-it-till-you-make-it confidence and headed out early to grab some breakfast before meeting Mrs. Blakely at the library, where she was a volunteer.

At Cora's, the mood was still high from yesterday's news. Cora had a free coffee special, and plenty of people were lingering at the counter. Monica even saw some strangers. An older couple sat at a booth by a window, taking pictures.

"Who are all these people?" Monica asked when she ordered.

"Folks from Memphis, mostly," Cora said. "Came down because they saw the show."

"Congrats, Cora—I didn't get a chance to say anything yesterday, but you should be so proud of yourself."

"I am. I am real proud." Clouds passed over Cora's eyes and Monica wondered if she was thinking about her father. Not wanting to bring up any bad thoughts on a day that should be just about celebrating the hard work the woman had done, Monica ordered what had become her usual, and when it was time to pay, insisted on paying.

Jackson had more than made up for the fight they'd had.

Monica sat in a far corner booth with her muffin and coffee and opened up her notebook to go over her questions for her mom's sixth-grade teacher.

"Can I sit down?"

Monica froze at the sound of her mother's voice. She'd been prepared for this, in a deep internal place. But that didn't quite stop the panic from taking root in her lungs and heart.

"Where's your camera crew?" Monica asked, surprised to see her mother alone, carrying a small teapot and mug. Nearly everyone in the restaurant was watching them; some were trying to hide their interest, while others blatantly stared.

"Yesterday I paid huge fees in permits to apparently be unable to film just about everywhere in town. Including here."

Monica smiled, and Simone mistakenly took that as invitation enough to sit. As soon as the teapot hit the table, Monica began gathering her things. The instinct to flee her mother's presence was deeply ingrained.

"I have to go," Monica said. "I'm actually interviewing your sixth-grade teacher today."

Simone's face made a powerful and stunning transformation, and for one long heartbeat she actually looked her age. It was so astonishing that Monica stared for a moment, her notes forgotten.

"Then you *are* working on the book."

"Sent the first three chapters to my editor yesterday."

Simone slowly filled her teacup, and the pale brown liquid steamed into the air between them. Monica didn't know her mother drank tea.

"And it's going well?" Simone asked.

"People have plenty to say."

"Why don't you interview *me*?" Simone asked. Monica gaped at her mother, her internal plates shifting and grinding to accommodate her astonishment. "Your book is about getting an accurate portrayal of the events from that night. It seems remiss of you not to interview me."

"You're actually willing to talk to me about it?"

Simone opened her mouth and shut it again, staring at the steam from her cup. She nodded.

"You've never—"

"I know."

Silence rippled and pulsed between them. Talking to her mother about the night she shot JJ would be like running to the closet and letting out all the monsters. Those events, those memories, that pain—all of it would be let loose on the world, and that could only bring disaster.

But there were other answers she wanted, answers to the questions born in the years after the murders. In those hours alone beside her mother's bed, under those fluttering curtains, so scared nothing would ever be right again.

"Can I ask you questions about the years after the murder?"

Simone looked up, a wrinkle between her eyes as if she didn't remember an "after."

"London," Monica said. "Greece. France."

"If you'd like."

Monica laughed, not holding back on the scorn she had for the woman across from her. "Yes. I'd like."

"Then fine." Simone stiffened at Monica's laughter. "Come over today."

"Tomorrow," she said, giving herself a day to put together her thoughts. To assemble a battle plan. But mostly, to keep her mother waiting. To punish her in whatever large and small ways she had available. "Here."

"I won't discuss it in public. You can come to the house I've rented. Across from those art camps you spoke so highly of on *America Today*. A *teacher*, really?"

Her mother actually sounded . . . proud. And Monica didn't know what to do with that, so she ignored it. "All right, what time—"

"You can come for lunch."

"This is not social. Or friendly. I'm not interested in having lunch with you."

Simone, already so pale, went a bit lighter; even her lips paled. "Fine, come at four. So I can have a drink and you can judge me."

Monica wrote it down and gathered her things. "I'll see you then."

Without another word she left, rattled that she'd agreed to this, worried about what it might mean to her, unsure of how to handle the interview, and feeling, all in all, pretty upside down in the wake of her mother's arrival.

But at the door she turned, for no reason she could name, and looked back at her mother, who was looking down into her teacup and smiling.

* * *

Wednesday night, Jackson waited up for Gwen to come home. He'd been doing that more often than not. Initially it had been to check if she was drinking, but now it was becoming a habit, and it felt good to see her before going to bed. Obviously, he'd let too much distance grow between them and he didn't know quite how to shrink it, but he would do what he could to keep it from growing.

So he sat in the front parlor, trying to get comfortable on the really uncomfortable couch there, and texted Monica while he waited.

What are you wearing? he texted.

What you saw me in not five hours ago.

He shifted on the couch, remembering what they'd been doing five hours ago. And exactly what she *hadn't* been wearing.

Correction, she texted, *what you saw me in before you took it off me.*

I really do love that Tweety Bird.

It was a Metallica concert tee shirt, dummy, and you just like what's under any shirt I'm wearing.

He smiled, his big fingers inaccurate on the keypad, but he was learning. He was learning lots of things, thanks to Monica. Before he could hit send on the dirty text he was sending to his non-girlfriend girlfriend, the front door opened and Gwen walked in.

When she saw him, she sighed. "Again? I told you, it's not like I'm an alcoholic."

"And I told you, trust is something you have to earn back."

She rolled her eyes as she shuffled into the room. "I liked you better when you barely paid attention."

For some reason, the words blew holes through him. Giant holes where his heart had been. "What do you mean?" he asked. "I always paid attention."

She laughed outright and if it hadn't been at his expense, he would have been happy to see her smiling. But since she was laughing at him, he only got angry. "You know," he said, "if you didn't keep secrets, I wouldn't have to check up on you."

"*Me?*" she cried. "*I'm* keeping secrets?"

"You were drinking, Gwen."

"Yeah, and when were you going to tell me about Monica?"

He blinked. "What about her?"

"Please—the whole town knows you guys are like together. I had twenty people ask me today if you guys were getting married."

"Getting . . . *what?* That's ridiculous."

"You were on TV, Jackson, practically making out!"

What Vanessa had taped at the float meeting was making its way through the gossip mill. This was the second edge of that particular sword. Using Monica for votes was one thing, but admitting it, in light of their real relationship? Tricky.

"Then there's nothing going on?" She crossed her arms over her chest as if she were in charge of his inquisition, and he didn't like it.

"There's nothing going on that's any of your business."

For a moment she looked like she'd been punched in the stomach, and he realized how awful his words sounded. How ostracizing.

"Gwen—"

"No, it's fine. Totally fine. I get it." She walked up to him and blew in his face. She smelled like gum and Doritos, a slightly nauseating combination. "Not drinking, see?"

She turned and walked away through the shadows, and she was almost gone before he found his voice. "I don't know what's going on with me and Monica," he said, and she paused by the stairs. "She's leaving, you know. She's not . . . she's not going to stay."

"Neither are you," she said, her eyes unreadable, glittering gems in the half-light.

"No, you're right."

"So it's just a thing?" she asked, somehow giving "thing" all kinds of weight and meaning, but not the right kind of weight and meaning.

"Yeah," he agreed, though it didn't quite feel right. "It's just a thing."

She shrugged and went up one step. "Hey," he said, suddenly desperate to stop her. Suddenly desperate to turn back whatever clock he could. "You need a dress for the pageant, don't you? Why don't we go shopping tomorrow?"

"No thanks, I've already got an idea. Shelby's helping me with it."

Anyone but him. That used to be a relief to him, but now it hurt. "Oh, well, you know, if you need shoes or anything . . ."

"I'll let you know." She smiled at him, and for a moment the bubble between them burst and they were as close as they ever had been, and he realized—painfully—that wasn't all that close.

Chapter 20

Thursday at four p.m., Monica stood on the gravel path outside the white farmhouse her mother had rented armed with her laptop and questions, her belligerence and anger. All the slights and hurts from her childhood she had shored around herself like a barricade.

She'd even brought Reba in her fanciest collar.

Try, Mom, she thought, *just try and get past this*.

But somehow, with all that stuff, she couldn't quite make it up the stairs.

Beside her, Reba barked.

The front door opened and Monica's skin broke out into a heavy sweat. It wasn't Simone standing there, but a short man. Balding, with glasses. He looked like a turtle. A small turtle.

"Hello Monica," he said.

Because she was marginally poisoned by her own venom, Monica sneered. "Who the hell are you?"

The man glanced over his shoulder and then back at Monica. "I'm Simone's husband," he said.

And that was enough for Monica.

"Tell her the interview is canceled," she said and turned on her heel, walking away from . . . *holy shit*, her stepfather.

She couldn't go back to her hotel in this mood. It was too much to go to Jackson now, asking too much after the other day with the tears and the sex. And every day since, with the sex and the talking.

But she didn't want to be alone.

Unable to do anything but keep moving, she walked right across the street to Shelby's place. Past the house, with the rusting gutters, to the barn in the back.

Where she hoped there might be a drink. And a friend.

Late Thursday afternoon, Shelby stared at the email from Dean on the screen. *I don't like that you haven't responded to my emails.*

Quickly, she deleted it, feeling dirty and threatened. But getting rid of the message didn't make the feeling go away.

You're overreacting, she told herself, pushing away from the computer and then standing up from her desk because she suddenly needed more room, more distance between herself and that email. And that stupid, stupid mistake she'd made.

There was every chance that Dean was trying to just be friendly. But those words echoed in her head with Dean's patronizing tone, the vaguely threatening way he spoke. But maybe that was all colored with the way they'd had sex.

Oh, what is wrong with me? she wondered. And now she was late for the pageant meeting. It was dress-fitting night, and she'd promised to come help hem and make minor alterations.

She grabbed her sewing kit from her supply closet.

"Shelby?" Shelby, who thought she recognized Monica's voice but couldn't quite believe it, nearly sprinted into the other room.

It was Monica. But Monica as she'd never seen her. Gone was the bravado and the attitude, leaving just the hard life she'd lived up until this moment.

"Are you okay?"

"No."

"Do you need a seat?"

"No, I need a drink. You still have that bottle?"

"I do." She ran back into her office, grabbed the bottle from the bottom drawer of her desk, and texted Janice that she was going to be a little late for the fittings.

"What's going on?" Shelby asked, pouring Monica a shot into her Best Teacher in the World mug. She had about seventeen of those mugs.

Monica knocked back the shot and blew out a wild breath. "I'm a mess," she said, and then shook her head. "And I'm sorry. I shouldn't have come barging in here. I just . . . I was across the street and I couldn't . . ." She sighed heavily and managed a very weak smile. "I just couldn't talk to my mother. And the stepfather I never even knew about. Sad, isn't it?"

"Not so sad, considering your mother."

Monica smiled. "You know, you're not so bad, Shelby."

"Neither are you, Monica."

The silence between them was pregnant, and Monica pursed her lips and blew out her cheeks as if she was struggling to keep something inside.

"I'm falling in love with Jackson," she blurted.

It wasn't a surprise, but it was strange that Monica chose to tell *her.*

"I know that's not anything you probably care about but I wanted to say it, just once. To someone. Someone should know how I feel."

"Shouldn't that someone be Jackson?" Shelby asked.

Monica looked so threadbare, Shelby could see right through her. This love she had for Jackson brought her very little joy. Shelby leaned down and poured her another drink.

"He's very loveable," Shelby said, which was only half the truth. The good half.

"Yes, he is. He's very good at being loved. He might not like it, but he's good at it."

Shelby nodded, wondering how well Monica knew the man she'd fallen for.

"But who does he love?" Monica asked, and Shelby's heart cringed. "Who does he let in?"

"Not . . . many people." No one. Not even his sister. He managed to gather people close, earn their trust, their affection—sometimes their love. Without ever investing back in them. He was closed off. In some respects, totally untouchable. And from the look on Monica's face, she knew it.

"Maybe I'm wrong," Monica said. "Maybe it's not love. Maybe it's just gas."

Shelby laughed, and Monica blew out a long breath. "Well, you going to join me in a drink?"

"I can't. I have to go to a pageant meeting. The girls are being fitted for their formal dresses."

"Oh!" Monica put the cup down, suddenly flustered. "I'm sorry. I didn't mean to keep you."

"You didn't . . . I was just leaving. You want to walk out with me?"

"Of course, sure."

Shelby turned off the lights and locked up while Monica waited in the waning daylight with Reba by her side. Reba was a ridiculous dog, but she liked how Monica didn't look alone with a dog by her side.

I need a pet. But then she quickly imagined herself with four cats, and the jokes that would go around town about the spinster teacher with four cats.

"Have you had a lot more interest in the camps after the *America Today* clip?" Monica asked as they started walking on the gravel shoulder of the road.

"About two hundred percent. The website went down after the clip aired. We broke the Internet."

Monica's laugh was distracted. She seemed very focused on the white farmhouse across the street.

"You know," Shelby said, hoping to pull Monica's attention back to this side of the road, "most of the interest was in you. If you're interested in teaching a course . . ."

"I'm not a teacher," Monica laughed. "You know that."

"Well, you fooled the kids. We could work on a curriculum, get it put together?"

"Shelby, I appreciate the thought. But . . . I'm not sticking around."

It wasn't surprising. Monica probably had a life waiting for her with far more exciting things than could be offered here in Bishop. But it was too bad. Against all odds, Shelby liked Monica. The town liked Monica. "When are you leaving?"

"After the Okra Festival." They passed under the oak trees into the square. Mrs. O'Hara sat in the park watching her grandson, and Shelby waved.

"You've got everything you need for the book?"

Monica sighed, watching the kids splashing in the water fountain. One kid stripped naked and Monica laughed—the woman had the bawdiest sense of humor. Shelby turned left away from the center of town, toward the high school. "I do. I can make it work."

"You know," Shelby said, "it's not really my business to say, but if you were ever interested in writing books for young adults, teenage girls . . . you'd be good at it. I think your wisdom and your experiences are wasted on adults. It's titillation to adults. Kids, though . . . kids you might be able to help."

"That's a very nice thing for you to say."

Shelby laughed, knowing a brush-off when she heard one. "Well, here we are," she said when they reached the entrance to the high school.

"Right." Monica looked up at the stone façade. Small but grand, like most of the public buildings. "This town has real delusions of grandeur, doesn't it?"

"I suppose so," Shelby said. "But I like it. Why not go for grandeur, right?"

The parking lot was half full, and the high windows

of the gymnasium were filled with light. "What's going on here?" Monica asked.

Shelby knew a thousand stray-dog looks. People from all over three counties dropped dogs out on the road past her house and barn. Abandoned dogs showed up on her porch all the time, and Shelby had to call Animal Control in Masonville to come handle them.

Monica had a stray look about her. Not the look of the angry strays, the ones who tried to bite the hand she held out to them, but the sad ones who wondered how they got so alone in the cold, dark night.

"You should come in," Shelby offered, unsure of what Monica would do with the invitation but feeling like it needed to be made. No one should seem so alone. "The girls will freak out. In a good way."

"Freak out, you say?" Monica asked, surprising Shelby. "Why not?"

Monica remembered with a potent mix of fondness and embarrassment her first forays into fashion as an extension of her personality. Her rebellion. There was the ripped flannel phase, followed quickly by the safety-pin year. And then there were the various and subtle variations on stripper clothes. Corsets with combat boots. The fakest black leather pants with white tank tops. But as she walked into the gymnasium, the dresses were variations on one theme: princess.

And for a moment, it was so simple, so exactly as it should be, that she felt emotion well up in her throat.

The girls did freak out, running over to her—only because she was the closest thing to a celebrity they'd encountered—in a rainbow array of sequins and sparkles. They tripped over their fluffy skirts, waddled in their too-tight skirts. It was a very awkward stampede.

"You guys all look amazing," she told the crowd.

"All right, everyone spread out," Shelby said, taking control of the situation. There were a few mothers there and they started unrolling elaborate sewing kits. "If you need hems, stand over here," she said, pointing to the area under one of the basketball nets. "If you need straps adjusted, stand over there. Everyone else, hang out in the middle."

The sea of satin parted, and Monica glimpsed sitting on the end of the bleachers a girl still wearing shorts and a tee shirt, her long blond hair hiding her face.

"I'm going to go talk to Gwen," she told Shelby, who nodded in quick agreement, her mouth already full of pins.

Gwen, when she heard Monica approach, looked up and immediately blushed. "What are you doing here?" she asked, and Monica did not try to tease out the various strains of embarrassment in her voice.

"I'm the fashion police," she said, sitting beside her. Monica finally shrugged out of her laptop backpack and it felt like she was dropping a thousand-pound stone off her back. Her tee shirt was stuck to her skin with sweat. Reba jumped up on the bleachers beside her. "Why aren't you in your dress?"

"It's . . . it's lame."

"Oh, how about you let me be the judge of that?" Monica joked. "It's why I'm paid the big bucks."

Gwen sighed and unzipped the black garment bag beside her just enough that Monica could see a cream strapless tulle dress embroidered with chocolate, mocha, beige, and metallic gold flowers. A pleated gold ribbon circled the bodice and waist.

"Oh my God," Monica said, reaching out to touch it. "Is that vintage?"

"It was my mom's. I found it in the attic."

"Oh, oh wow." Monica was actually starting to hyperventilate as she unzipped the rest of the bag, revealing a full skirt with two layers of tulle underneath, one of them a full crinoline.

"It's old-fashioned," Gwen lamented.

"It's amazing," Monica gasped. "And you . . . oh, honey, you will look amazing in it."

"But all the other girls—"

"Who cares?" Monica demanded. "Honestly, Gwen, do you care what the other girls are wearing? You're different and you know it. *They* know it. You're wearing that eye makeup so the whole world knows it. Why stop now? Let your freak flag fly, my friend, in this stunning dress."

Gwen smiled shyly, and Monica nudged her with her shoulder. "Go put it on. I'll be right here."

Gwen left and was back in about five minutes, slinking along the edge of the gymnasium so no one could see her. But she was impossible to miss. The dress was a little too short, but that could be fixed. And a little too loose up top, but that could be fixed, too.

The color made Gwen's hair look like gold, and her tanned skin was bronzed.

And while all the other girls looked like children pretending to be women, Gwen looked like a woman. A brand-new, beautiful woman with nothing but the best of life ahead of her. She looked like feminine hope brought to glittering, sparkling life.

"I look like an Academy Award statue," Gwen said, as if that were a bad thing.

"You look like a woman," Monica said, and Gwen's eyes lifted to hers. Monica spun the girl around and zipped up the rest of the dress. "Like a beautiful woman. Gwen, you are gorgeous."

"She's right." Shelby came up behind her, armed with pins and big office clips. In record time she had Gwen's hem down and repinned, and then the bodice fixed with the clips.

Gwen transformed under the efforts, standing straighter and lifting her chin. Monica could feel the attention from all the other girls in the room. "You look awesome," Ania said, wearing a sea-foam green mermaid dress that made her look like a little girl playing dress-up.

"Thanks, Ania," Gwen answered.

"Here." Shelby turned the girl around and force-marched her across the wooden floor over to the mirrors leaning against the Bishop Bulldog painted on the gym wall. Monica followed, happy to see Gwen beaming at her reflection. "Tell me you don't look great."

"I . . . look pretty great," Gwen said.

"I'm going to keep pinning," Shelby said, then walked off toward the crowd of girls with straps hanging down their arms.

"But it's really old-fashioned, don't you think?" Gwen asked, turning sideways.

"Vintage tends to be that way."

"Do you think . . . do you think there's a way to make it look more modern?"

Monica lifted her eyebrows and looked over Gwen's shoulder at the girl's reflection. "Gloves," she said, and Gwen nodded. "Maybe the kind without fingers."

"Cool," Gwen sighed.

"And I have this set of three brooches, very glittery, very fake, but we could put them right here . . ." She touched Gwen's waist, just above her hip bones. "That would be pretty funky."

"Funky would be awesome."

"We could do a modern beehive look, too, and some smoky eyes and nude lipstick. Very James Bond Girl."

Gwen clapped, looking more her age than Monica had ever seen her, and Monica got caught up in the excitement. "I'll go and get the pins and see what I have for earrings."

"Can I come with you?" Gwen asked.

Monica nodded, and she unzipped the back of the dress a little so Gwen could do the rest of it in the bathroom. "Go change real quick, and don't knock loose any of those pins or Shelby will kill you."

Within ten minutes, Monica and Gwen were punching open the back doors to the school and stepping out across the football field toward the Peabody. As they walked through the tall grass, bugs buzzed up around them.

"So how are things going?" Monica asked, feeling stuffed full of feminine bonhomie. Honestly, nothing like a little dress-up to lift a woman's spirits.

"Jay wants to have sex."

Monica lurched to a stop in the grass and whirled to face Gwen, who was staring intently at her feet. "It's been like a week and a half."

Gwen shrugged, her fists shoved into the pockets of her cut-offs.

"You're not thinking about doing it, are you?"

Gwen blushed bright red, and Monica realized she probably could have been a whole lot more diplomatic on that topic. "Are you . . . I mean . . . Do you even like him?"

"I don't know if you know this, but you don't have to love someone to have sex with them." The sarcasm was unmistakable, and the words were so similar to what Monica had told Jackson about sex and marriage that she had to laugh. She started walking again, out of the grass and onto the track.

"Well, you should at least really, really like him."

"Do you really, really like Jackson?" The girl wasn't fishing. She knew, the same way she'd known the first time Gwen and Monica met that Monica was lying about the dog.

"How did you know?" Monica asked.

"Everyone's talking about you guys on the *America*

Today clip, and Jay saw him sneaking up to your room a few times."

With no idea of what to say, Monica started walking a little faster. Gwen skipped to catch up.

"I'm not mad," Gwen said.

"It's not really your business to be mad," Monica said. "Your brother and I are adults. And yes. I like your brother very much."

"Why?" The word was loaded with such bias and confusion that Monica stopped again. Was Jackson blind, she wondered—did he really have no clue what the distance between him and his sister was doing, the alienation Gwen felt?

"Your brother is a really good man. But he has a hard time letting people close."

"He let *you* close."

Not close enough. "Let's get back to the important topic here. You are talking about having sex with a kid that a week ago you didn't like very much."

"He's nice, and . . . I'm curious."

"Curious is a bad reason to have sex. And trust me, I know all the bad reasons there are to have sex."

"I . . . like him. A lot."

"How do you know that after a week?" As the words were coming out of her mouth, she realized she'd known Jackson for only two weeks. Oh man, she was so over her head with this conversation! And part of her wanted to brush Gwen off, to play it safe and tell her to go talk to Shelby or something. But the truth was, Gwen had come to her.

And Gwen didn't have a mother. All she had was Jackson, and there was no way Gwen would bring this up with him.

So Monica took a second and remembered what it was like to be sixteen, running away from her own mother and right into some bad sexual decision-making.

What would have helped her? she wondered. What advice might have saved her some heartache?

She stopped walking and put out her hand, and Gwen stopped too. "Are you really serious about this?"

Gwen shrugged.

Monica fought the desire to roll her eyes. Those shrugs, honestly—who was she kidding? Tortured teenage angst rolled off the kid; she was the farthest thing from indifferent.

"Do you know anything about your body? I mean . . . do you know how you like to be touched, or more importantly, how you don't like to be touched?"

Gwen turned beet red and stepped backward, away from Monica. "Never mind, forget I brought it up."

"Oh," Monica said, smiling. "It's only gonna get worse."

She pulled open the door to the Peabody and there was Jay behind the desk. How incredibly fortuitous! Now she could say to Jay what someone should have told the boy she'd had her first sexual experience with.

At the sight of Gwen he just beamed, sunlight and adoration spilling out of the kid. That was a very good sign.

"Wait here," Monica said and went up the stairs to her room. She grabbed the jewelry from her bag, as well as some clip-on fake diamond earrings she got from a thrift store in Chicago, and then from the bedside table she grabbed a strand of condoms from the box she'd bought a few days ago.

Downstairs, Gwen and Jay were deep in conversation. Or rather, Gwen was talking and Jay looked like he might spontaneously combust.

"Okay," Monica said, approaching the pair. "Here are the pins and some earrings that might work." She set them on the front desk and then put the condoms down next to them. Jay jumped away as if she'd fired a gun. "Do you know what those are?"

She glanced between the two silent teenagers.

"Someone needs to say something."

Gwen quickly gathered the condoms and shoved them in her pocket, looking around as though she'd been caught stealing. "They're condoms," she breathed through immobile lips.

"If this is the way you act at the sight of condoms, there's no way you're ready for sex," Monica said. "But I also know that my opinion isn't going to change things. I hope . . . I hope you guys take the time to get to really know each other and really know each other's bodies—"

"I want to die," Jay breathed, staring at his shoes.

"Now, should you ignore me and this amazing advice I'm giving you and decide to have sex: You. Must. Use. A. Condom. You must. Got it?" The kids nodded at her, unable to make eye contact, but that wasn't good enough for Monica. "Jay, look at me."

He groaned as if lifting his eyes to hers hurt. "Got it?" she asked.

"Got it," he said.

"Me too," Gwen said, and then she nearly ran out of the building.

Monica watched her go.

"Monica," Jay said. "Can you . . . can you please leave now?"

She laughed. "See you later, kid." And then, just to torture him, she lifted two fingers to her eyes and then pointed at him. A little Robert DeNiro, for *I'll be watching you.*

Jay vanished into the back room.

And my work here is done.

* * *

Years ago, after Monica ran away, putting the kibosh on that horrible reality television show, Simone had been the darling of the tabloids. Monica couldn't go into a store, or walk by a TV, without seeing a picture of her mother pretending to be heartbroken or comforting herself on the arm of some handsome man. Eventually, her star had faded enough that no one cared where she ate lunch, and Monica's name was only referenced in a "Where Are They Now?" context.

But after Monica published *Wild Child* and it started to become successful, Simone found her way onto another reality show. And sure, that might have been just coincidence, but Monica didn't believe it. Monica saw her mother on the tabloids and on TV and she burned with resentment.

But instead of sleeping with bad boys and running away, Monica showed her mother by getting on better shows and in better magazines. She dragged that press tour out as long as she could, just to shove it in her mother's face.

Not her finest hour. Or two years, actually.

But then Jenna got sick and Simone became background noise.

But now . . . just when Monica had decided to get her life together, to step off the island, her mother shows back up. It was as if she had an instinct for when Monica was in the midst of change and just wanted to screw it up.

But this time, Monica wasn't going to play.

Everyone was talking about the fact that Simone was in town, and they seemed compelled to tell Monica where they'd spotted her. Cora saw her at the grocery store. Sean saw her at the post office. Mrs. Blakely apparently had a strained reunion with her at the library. After the vitriol-filled interview Monica had with Mrs. Blakely, Monica imagined the woman sprinkling Simone with holy water and making the sign of the cross.

But Monica wasn't going to retaliate; she wasn't going to show her mother how much she didn't care about her by ignoring her at Cora's. That was what the old her would have done.

The new her was hiding.

She was ordering in, making do with the horrible in-room coffee. She tried to train Reba to pee in the sink so there would be fewer walks. But Reba was untrainable. So she paid Jay a few bucks to take Reba around the block twice a day.

She told herself she was keeping to her room because she was working, which she was—the book had to be written. But that was an excuse.

For a week, she'd been using Jackson as a distraction. Just as he was undoubtedly using her for distraction from the Maybream contest. And it worked—spectacularly—most of the time.

"You're not actually here, are you?" Jackson asked, looking down at her. His face was folded and creased into lines of worry and strain.

"It's good, baby," she lied, pushing her hips up at him, gasping when he settled deeper inside of her.

Hold the phone, she thought, *there's hope for orgasm yet*.

"If this is the show, I'm disappointed." He grinned at her and kissed her nose before pulling away and sliding out of her. She was immediately cold in his absence and sorry that she was so distracted.

"Jackson," she said, putting a hand to his back. "It's okay. I'm just . . ."

"Distracted. I . . . understand, and don't worry." He tossed the used but empty condom in the garbage and leaned back against the headboard, his erection pink and hard.

"Your mom, right? You want to talk about it?"

She howled with laughter. How ridiculous! "You want

to talk about my mom." She lifted her eyebrow, glancing at his damp erection. "With that?"

"It's got a lot of tricks, but it doesn't talk."

"Jackson, honestly, this is just too weird."

He stroked her arm, pulling her toward him. It should feel awkward—the stopped sex, her distraction, his erection. It was a mess of an afternoon, but somehow, somehow it was okay. He made it okay with his largesse, with his kindness.

He pulled the blanket up over his groin. "I'm a man, Monica. Full grown. Not a kid or an asshole who will have sex with a woman who isn't really interested. Just ignore it—it will go away."

Was it any wonder she liked this man? Any wonder that every minute they spent together sent her spinning toward someplace new—someplace she'd never been before? She was giddy and sick and . . . falling in love.

"Have you left this hotel room?"

"Today? No."

"You can't hide from your mom forever."

"I'm working!"

His lifted eyebrow denounced her as a liar. She was waiting to hear back from her editor on the work she'd already submitted, and he knew that.

"Fine," she sighed. "But . . . what's there to say to her? Honestly, what will change if we talk?"

"You don't know until you try, right? I think you'd be crazy not to be worried about talking to your mom. It's okay to be nervous. Or scared, or whatever it is that's distracting you from my awesome sexual powers."

And that was the moment—that was when she knew. It was as though all the dams burst and she was flooded with knowledge. It was done. Over.

I love him. I really love him.

And instead of freaking her out, it blew her open. And she realized that every other feeling she had for any other man in her life was dirty compared to what she felt for him. It was in fact the purest thing she'd ever felt for anyone.

Loving Jackson was the best thing she'd ever done. Ever.

Immediately she doubted it, because that was her nature. Because she'd been conditioned not to believe that good things could happen to her. There was a chance that this was just another coping mechanism for dealing with her mom. Instead of press tours and drugs and bad sex, was she filling the holes in her life that her mother left behind with Jackson and good sex?

She tested the edges of that theory and found it to be false. What she felt for Jackson was totally and utterly free of her mother. It was about *her.* About who she was and who she wanted to be.

How . . . amazing! Liberating. She wanted to shout it from the rooftops.

Delighted by her discovery, she squeezed his face, beloved and handsome.

"You all right?" he asked, his lips pursed.

I can never tell him, she realized, turning cold. She dropped her hands. *I can't. He won't . . . understand it. Or accept it.* She imagined his face, the way he would close it down—become polite.

Oh God.

She would tell him she loved him and he would be *polite.* Because she would be one more set of expectations on his shoulders—her emotions would be something he would try to handle, try to make right.

He would try to fix it.

And that would be awful.

"You okay?" he asked. "You've gone pale."

She realized she had her hand over her heart, as if she could protect it from the hurt coming her way. Because it was coming, and it was going to be bad.

"I'm fine," she said, grappling with both this new heavy love and the equally heavy heartache loving him brought.

But the realization that she loved him couldn't come without notice, without commemoration. Because she'd never loved anyone before. Not really. And the fact that she could, that she'd grown up enough and grown past her mistakes enough to be vulnerable in the face of another person—that deserved commemoration.

She deserved some commemoration.

It took no effort to push away thoughts of her mother; Simone had already been sidelined by these new realizations. So instead she concentrated on him. On the way he made her feel. How whole and desirable and perfectly flawed.

"What are you thinking about?" he asked with a smile—a slightly confused smile, but a smile, nonetheless.

"I'm thinking about how good you make me feel." She ran her hand down her breast, over her nipple. As he watched, she pulled her nipple, twisting it in a way she'd never realized she liked until he'd done it.

She pulled aside the quilt, and his erection, which had flagged momentarily, revived, and she ran her fingers down it, tracing the veins from the top down to the base.

"I love your dick."

"It feels warmly toward you, too." Unable to wait another minute, she leaned over and slipped him into her mouth. He tasted like latex and her and she loved it. She pressed her nose into his skin, taking him as deep into her throat as she could.

"Ah, God, Monica," he breathed, brushing aside her hair so he could watch.

"Tell me," she said, lifting away from him, looking up at him, breathing over him. "Tell me how I make you feel." She kissed him once, hard, before putting him back in her mouth. She would settle for this, settle for the dirty words spilling out of his lips about how sexy she was, how exciting. She pushed him in so deep, she felt tears burn in her eyes. Part of her, from the old days, the old her, told her to be ashamed, but she couldn't muster up that emotion.

Loving him made all of this right. Made all of it okay.

He pulled on her hair, lifting her off of him. His kiss was wild, wet. His control was breaking and she loved it, loved being on the receiving end of a passion slipping out of its restraints.

"On your stomach," he whispered and pushed her down onto the mattress. She was drenched between her legs, wanton and hungry, and she lay across the bed as he'd demanded, the sheets rubbing her nipples. She spread her legs a little so he could see what was waiting for him.

He groaned just before he covered her and she felt tiny under him. He lifted her hips and in one smooth thrust buried himself deep inside of her, deeper than ever. He pierced her heart.

She braced herself as best she could, curling up and into him, using everything she had to pull him along with her, to break that control.

"Monica," he breathed against her neck, across her cheek. He braced a hand by her face and she sucked his thumb into her mouth and bit it. Hard. Wanting him wild. Wanting him to be changed, if by nothing else then by this magic they shared.

He braced his thighs wide and lifted her hips, holding her as he thrust heavy and fast into her.

"Come on," he breathed. "Come with me."

She slipped a hand between her legs, using her fingers to catch up, to stay with him.

"Yes!" she cried as it all started to coalesce. The love

and pain amplified by the fact that this was all he wanted from her, this was all they would really share. And it was so good she could almost convince herself it was enough.

Crying out against her pillow, she exploded, broken by her love.

Chapter 21

Monday morning, Monica was ready to venture out into the world, emboldened by her secret love. Proud of herself for being brave enough to feel it, if not express it. It made her feel new. Powerful.

It kind of made her feel like singing.

Only to be brought up short by the sight of her mother and Turtle Man sitting near the windows in the hotel lobby, reading the newspaper in sunlight so perfect, so bright and solid, it looked fake. Like they were on a movie set.

In a heartbeat, anger eroded her pride. And she knew hiding out in her room had not brought her any closer to dealing with her fury and resentment toward her mother. Just the sight of her slammed shut all her doors and locked all her windows, sealing her inside her head with all her demons—all her worst instincts.

As she approached their little sunlit scene, she caught the scent of Shalimar and it produced a whiteout in her head. "This is harassment, you get that, right?"

Simone looked down at the stack of papers in her lap. "It's the news."

"Don't be cute, Simone. This is bullshit."

"Join us," Simone said. "We'll discuss it."

"No," she said. "There's nothing to discuss."

"Your mother has a lot of things she'd like to say to you," Turtle Man said, and Monica spun.

"I don't care who the hell you are," she lashed out at the man. She stood at the edge of the rug, as though the hardwood floor had a repellant property. "But you don't know me. And you don't know *her*. Not really. So stay out of it."

"You blew off our meeting," Simone said.

"Well, you blew off my childhood, so I guess we're even." Monica took a lot of comfort in being awful. Being awful made her feel strong around her mother, as if those purple eyes would never see her, really see her.

Simone carefully folded the paper, running her thumb along the crease. "I think we should meet. I think . . . there are a lot of things we need to say."

"I'm not very interested in what you have to say. I think I've made it pretty clear. You can hang out in this town and hang out in my hotel and talk to my friends, but it's not going to change anything. We're not going to talk."

"What about London?" Simone asked. "Greece, France? You don't have questions about those years anymore?"

The red roosters, the blue room. The dreams of croissants and the tears on her face.

"It won't change anything. We can talk about it, I can ask you all these questions, but it won't change me. The damage . . . the damage is done."

"Oh." Simone swallowed. Her hand reached out and then fell back to her lap. "You're not damaged," she said.

"How the hell would you even know?" Monica asked and then stopped. She held up her hand, forcing herself to calm down before her head started spinning. "Why are you here, honestly? What do you want?"

"I want . . ." She glanced at Turtle Man, who nodded, as if giving her permission or supporting her, and Monica wanted to gag. "I want you to be happy, and I think maybe . . . if we talk . . ."

"It's too late, Mom. Too late."

The inevitability of it all suddenly crushed her. The rock of her reality was an immovable force. Loving Jackson when he didn't love her back wasn't new. Or special. This was what she did. She loved people who could never really love her back. It was the lesson she'd learned from her mother, repeating itself. Monica stormed out of the Peabody like she was being chased out of her own skin, with nowhere to go. Homeless all over again. It was as if all the work she'd done in the last years, to be her own woman, to bury that child she'd been, was gone. And the wild child was back.

Or maybe she never really left.

"Businesses have seen a twenty percent increase in revenue," Brian said. It was Monday morning again, four days until the Okra Festival started on Friday morning, and the town was electric. Walking down the street felt good. Cora's Café was full of smiling faces and miraculously, for the first time since Jackson had taken over the job as mayor, this budget meeting didn't suck. "The Peabody is sold out for the next month of weekends and Cora has started taking reservations," Brian continued.

"The Okra Festival has gotten more attention than it's ever gotten. Businesses as far as Masonville have reserved booths," Jackson said, thrilled about that fact, if for no other reason than that it would make good television. "The chili cook-off actually has five entrants. A restaurant from Memphis is coming to challenge Cora."

Brian laughed. "Well, good luck to them. I've had some of Cora's chili and there's no way it's getting beaten."

"We've had to reorganize some of the events," Jackson said, flipping through the calendar, "for the live taping. The parade and street festival will start Friday morning, eight a.m., instead of Saturday."

"When does the crew arrive?"

"Thursday night. We'll have the pageant that night, too. We've sent out fliers and the schedule will be in the newspaper on Wednesday."

"Well, then, let's keep our fingers crossed that the Okra Festival goes off without a hitch."

Jackson was past crossing his fingers. He was considering offering Sean as a sacrifice to the gods to ensure the Okra Festival went smoothly.

"You know I doubted the validity of this contest," Brian said, gathering up his files. "But even if we don't win the contest, with the increased tourism the town is already winning."

It felt that way; it really did. The town had new life, but without the new factory it would fade away. Vanish as soon as the parade was over.

When Brian left, Jackson turned back to his computer. Only to stare at the dark screen.

It was happening; all the work was paying off.

Soon there'd be a factory working in this town again. Jobs. A tax-base increase. The schools would be fully funded, and everyone would be okay. He imagined the future and it was bright, brighter than he'd ever dreamed.

He heard the door shut and he was dragged from that fantasy back to his office.

It was Monica standing there, her back to the wall, fire in her eyes, a different kind of fantasy altogether.

"Hey!" He jumped to his feet, happy to see her.

"Hey yourself," she said, dropping her laptop backpack into the chair Brian had just vacated.

"What's up? You seem . . . tense?" She seemed wired to blow, surrounded by thunderclouds and twisters. Dangerous.

"I am."

"Your mom—"

"I don't want to talk about Mom." Monica reached over and locked the door, the click loud in the silence.

"What do you want to do?" The blood getting hot and thick in his veins knew the answer.

"Fuck the mayor." She pulled off the ancient Duran Duran tank top she wore, revealing a utilitarian white bra. His lingerie-loving lover obviously hadn't gotten dressed this morning planning to seduce him, which made him wonder, briefly, distantly, what was going on.

Her denim skirt landed in a heap at her feet. She wore black panties, a tiny vee between her legs. "Sit down," she ordered.

He had no choice; his free will had vanished. He was hers to command. He sat in his chair and wheeled away slightly from the desk, giving her space to slip in. She pushed aside the paperwork and his keyboard and sat down on the blotter, putting one leg up on his chair, her other foot pressed against his crotch.

He wasn't a foot fetish guy, but still, he saw stars. She tossed a condom at him.

"Like this?" he asked, meaning with the strange current between them, the anger that rolled off her in waves.

"No," she said and hopped off her perch, turned around, and braced her hands on the desk. She waved her ass at him. "Like this."

Something was wrong. But he was a man and he was devoutly in love with her ass, so he stood, though in the back of his head he knew better. His pants dropped faster than he thought possible. Through the cotton of her underwear he felt her, already damp, already hot.

"Hurry," she breathed, pulling down her underwear, kicking it under his desk.

Right. Hurry. He tore open the condom with his teeth and slipped it on. He touched her hip, then reached around to find the sweet, luscious weight of her breasts, encased in white cotton. "Don't," she whispered. "Just . . . fuck me."

She pushed back into him, the curve of her ass a terrible tease, a delicious torment. *Fine. Yes.* A quickie, that's what this was. Somehow, that made it . . . okay. He reached down, positioned himself, and thrust deep into her.

Damp she might have been, her words hot, but she wasn't entirely ready, and he felt her resistance and stopped. "Monica—"

"Don't. Just let's go . . . come on." Again she pushed back against him, and he felt her loosening. Holding her hips, he thrust into her, slowly, carefully, working to get her caught up.

"No," she snapped, looking at him over her shoulder. "Hard."

"I'm not going to hurt you," he told her, aware in some part of his brain that that was what she wanted. She wanted pain with her pleasure, and usually he could get into that, but not like this. Not with the scales so weirdly out of balance.

She bent her legs, taking him deep, working herself against him, and he felt the tide coming, the tide he wouldn't be able to resist. "I need . . . I need hard, Jackson. Please. Hard and fast."

He was done. Washed away. Whatever anger had pushed her here to his office for this strange and degrading fuck, it spread to him and he found himself angry with her. With one hand he pushed her head down onto his desk, holding her there, while with his other hand he held her hip in a punishing grip as he thrust high and hard into her.

She was wet now, moaning against his desk. Lifting up on her toes to take as much of him as she could, and it was so exciting and so awful at the same time, he closed his eyes. Not wanting to watch himself have sex with her like this—like they had no kindness between them. He felt her come and then he followed her over the edge.

It was anticlimactic. Over, mostly, before it even started.

If he weren't such a simple, stupid machine, he probably wouldn't have been able to muster up the orgasm.

"That what you wanted?" He panted, pulling away, yanking off the condom with no finesse.

"Yes." Her voice was small as she stood up. She winced, and he wanted to kick his own ass. It didn't matter that she'd wanted it. He didn't like his sex mixed up with that much anger.

"Well, happy to serve."

"It wasn't . . ."

"Don't say it wasn't like that." Jackson jerked up his pants, unable to look at her. "It was exactly like that."

"Okay, fine, so what if it was?" She pulled on her underwear, walked around the desk, and yanked on her clothes.

"I don't like being used."

She laughed. "But isn't that the whole nature of our relationship, Jackson? We are using each other. We're not dating. We're not going to last past the next two weeks. We're fucking each other to pass the time."

He was trying not to get angry. Not to rise to her bait, because clearly she just wanted to fight. "Look, if you're mad about your mom—"

"Not everything is about my mom."

"Well, that certainly wasn't about us." He pointed to the desk, where everything had been scattered in their haste.

She yanked on her tank top, pulled her black hair back, and started to tie it up in a ponytail. "It was about sex, Jackson. That's all."

"Bullshit." He wasn't an idiot and he wasn't going to be treated like one. "You want to be mad at someone, be mad at your mother. Or better yet, do what you said you were going to do and go talk to her."

"Oh!" she cried, stepping toward him, and honestly, he had no idea how this had happened. How in less than twenty minutes he'd gone from being so happy to see her, to bending her over his desk like a whore, to fighting with her. "Really, you're the expert on talking."

"What's that supposed to mean?" he asked. He thought they'd been really honest in their relationship. He'd talked to her more than he'd talked to anyone since the shrinks after his mom and dad died.

Monica grabbed her bag and unlocked the door. Jackson could see Ms. Watson in the hallway, trying very hard to appear busy and as though she hadn't been listening.

"It means talk to your sister."

The door, that stupid door, slammed shut behind her.

Two hours later Monica sat at her desk, her world in shambles around her, staring at an email.

While the writing is strong, its tone is problematic. I understand if it isn't possible to create an emotional distance between yourself and the events of that night, or between yourself and your parents, but for the sake of the book, and the success of the venture, you need to try. These three chapters are intriguing, but they sound like they were written by an angry teenager. I want the woman we met at the end of Wild Child *to write these books. I want the woman I know you are to write these books. Can you try again?*

Monica closed her eyes and slouched back in the chair. Uncomfortable fucking desk chair, she couldn't get a good slouch on. She tipped sideways and crawled up onto her bed.

Worst. Day. Ever.

How did I get here? she wondered. *How did I get so empty?*

The scene with her mother. The scene . . . oh God, that awful, angry scene with Jackson. She had no idea

how she was going to make that right. How was she
going to explain that being unloved by the people she
loved made her angry? Made her want to hurt herself.

And that was why she'd gone to Jackson's like that—
to hurt herself. To prove to herself that she didn't deserve happiness, that it wasn't for her.

She thought of how angry she'd been today seeing her
mother, how it had driven her to act like the child she'd
been and not the woman she was. And she was suddenly so angry at herself for always reacting. Always
bouncing off and away from people, instead of being a
fixed object secure in who she was. Secure in the right-
ness of her feelings.

Her love for Jackson had been so clean just yesterday—
it was the best thing she'd ever had—and then she'd
gone and messed it up, dragged it down through the
dirt. So that at the inevitable end, when he left her hurt
and miserable, she could comfort herself with the idea
that it hadn't been all that special anyway.

But it *was* special.

In the drawer of the bedside table was a note from the
only person who ever really knew her, all the *i*'s dotted
with circles, and Jenna knew she was special.

She was special.

And she deserved some goddamn happiness.

Enough.

Right now, right here, she fixed herself to solid ground.
She tugged and tore and pushed and pulled the anger
away from the love she felt. The person she was.

Spurred to action, she grabbed her laptop and started
making some notes.

What happened in his office with Monica haunted Jackson all day. He felt dirty and angry and worried, and

when he went home that night he was ready to pop that bubble between him and his sister forever.

"Gwen!" he shouted as he pushed open the front door. "We need to talk."

Silence greeted him, but that wasn't strange. He went upstairs to her room, but it was empty. So were the den, the TV room, and the kitchen. He even checked the never-used sleeping porch. But she wasn't there.

He grabbed his phone. *Where are you?* He texted.

At pageant practice. Going out with Jay after. Will be very drunk, so be sure to wait up.

Furious, bent over the sink, he ate pork chops left over from who knows when.

At eight o'clock he texted her again. *No going out with Jay. Come on home.*

He stared at the screen, waiting for her angry answer, but it never came.

Bullshit, he thought, and he walked around his empty house getting angrier and angrier. At his sister. At Monica. At his parents for dying in a car accident. At the world for not being controllable.

At nine o'clock he found himself outside his sister's bedroom door.

Knowing he was crossing a line, but somehow unable to stop himself, he opened the door.

What exactly he was looking for he didn't know. Something. Anything. A small clue into what was going on with Gwen.

Parents do this all the time, he told himself as he stepped over the threshold.

Her room was a mess. Maybe every teenage girl was this way; he didn't know. But it bothered him to see it now. She constantly complained about not having clean clothes to wear, but if she never put them down the laundry chute, how were they supposed to get clean? He grabbed the first few things off the floor, a tee shirt and her cut-offs, and stuffed them in the hamper. But as he did so, something fell out.

It took a second for him to even recognize the silver strip as condoms. Condoms in his sister's shorts. He picked them up off the floor.

Lubricated, ribbed, magnum, and the dead give-away . . . glow-in-the-dark.

It had been a joke a week ago when Monica had pulled out these condoms. Glow-in-the-dark seemed dubious. But they worked, and at the time they found that out, he hadn't been laughing.

And maybe Gwen just happened to have the same kind. But he didn't believe it.

Monica was giving his sister condoms.

His sister was having sex.

It was enough to make him light-headed. Light-headed and furious.

Chapter 22

It was close to midnight when Monica knocked on the screen door of her mother's house. The light clicked on over her head and all the small moths leapt into action.

Turtle Man pushed open the screen door, wearing a robe and a disgruntled expression.

"You know what time it is, don't you?"

"Of course."

"You want to speak to Simone?"

She nodded.

"Come on in. I'll make some coffee."

The inside of the farmhouse was a surprise. Richly decorated. Homey, even. One room was filled with a big brown leather couch with bright orange pillows facing a big-screen television. A knitting basket sat on the floor near the edge of the couch. Knitting needles skewered red and yellow balls of yarn. There were beautiful rugs on the polished wooden floors and decorative tables with knickknacks.

Must have come decorated, she thought. But then in the hallway filled with pictures she saw photos of her mother. Turtle Man. And two young men.

"My kids," Turtle Man said, watching her from the kitchen on the other end of the hallway. "Jake and Charlie."

Stunned, Monica looked back at the picture of Simone with her arms around one of the boys. Simone was smiling. Beside the man was a young woman. A pregnant young woman.

"We're expecting our first grandchild." Turtle Man watched her carefully.

Her throat throbbed, ached.

"What's your name?" Blind to the rest of the photos, she walked down the hallway. "I can't keep calling you Turtle Man."

That he smiled was surprising; she was doing her best to piss him off. "Charles."

"Chuck?"

"Charles. Why don't you have a seat and I'll go get Simone."

He pointed to the white chairs surrounding a circular distressed wooden table.

It was the kind of table that spoke of family dinners and happy memories. She couldn't imagine what Simone was doing with such a thing. Perhaps the version of Simone in those pictures out there, but not the one she knew. Not her mother.

Monica sat, then took out her recorder and notebooks. Her three favorite pens. When she was organized, she reached out a hand for Reba, who jumped up in her lap and licked her chin.

Monica was immeasurably comforted.

"Hello." Her mother's voice, rough with sleep, preceded her out of the shadows from the stairs. But then she was there, in the white kitchen, a splash of green. Bright green. Monica blinked, disoriented. It had been so long since she'd seen her mother in anything but white, but now here she was in a bright green jersey robe.

Her hair was a mess. A wild, white-blond cloud around her head. She wore no makeup and was still beautiful.

"Charles made coffee?" Simone asked and as if in answer, the coffeemaker on the counter gurgled and hissed. "Would you like some?"

Monica shook her head, her lips shut. Locked against the river of questions that were suddenly filling her mouth. This had to be calm, had to be controlled. She had to be removed and distanced. Not the girl she had been, but the woman she was.

Simone poured her own coffee into a china cup with pink flowers and then sat at the table, carefully crossing her legs, pulling the green robe closed around her knee-caps.

"What's all this?" She pointed to the recorder.

"I'm going to interview you," Monica said.

Simone nodded, as if everyone who showed up at her door at midnight did the same thing. Maybe they did; Simone's life was a mystery. "All right."

Monica pushed Reba down onto the floor and pressed record on her machine. The click was epic, the sound of something big and irreversible starting.

"How old were you when you met JJ?"

"Monica, you know this."

"I'm not . . ." She was about to say "I'm not Monica," but that would sound ridiculous. So she just said, "Answer the question."

"Fifteen."

"How old was JJ?"

"Twenty. He was playing in a band down in Masonville. I snuck out of the house every weekend for a month to see him."

Monica created a time line in her notebook.

"And how old were you when you got pregnant?"

"The first time? Fifteen."

Monica's head shot up and Simone smiled, sadly. "You didn't know? Well, I had a back-alley abortion that nearly killed me. When I got pregnant with you two years later he wanted me to get another abortion, but I couldn't do it. After what I'd gone through before, you seemed like a miracle."

Simone had been seventeen and pregnant. For the second time.

"How old were you when he first hit you?"

Simone set down her china cup with a small thunk. "Seventeen. He didn't like that I wouldn't terminate the pregnancy."

Right. She took a deep breath that shuddered at the top. The cold, hard facts didn't feel all that cold and hard. They felt hot, searing and alive. "Why did you stay with him?"

Simone pursed her lips and tilted her head as if trying to find the answer where she'd hidden it. "I was alone. Daddy wouldn't have me back—he made that clear when I ran off with JJ in the first place. I had no money. And, after you were born . . . well, my body changed. I was curvier, womanly. While still looking like a little girl. And people seemed to notice. A talent scout saw me at the Santa Monica pier with you one day and asked me to come in to see him. JJ was on tour at the time and I had a girlfriend look after you and I went in. Within two weeks I was booking national commercials. Print work. *Playboy* had contacted me."

"JJ didn't like that." It wasn't a question; it was a memory, and Simone's eyes flared.

"No. He didn't. His career was a . . . disappointment to him. And the constant touring was very difficult. And watching me start a career with a little success made him crazy. But he liked the money."

"So, he'd let you make the money and then knock you around when you got home."

"I had always hoped you didn't remember that."

Monica shrugged, her notes consisting of scribbles at this point. "It would be nice not to." Simone blanched at her words, lifted a trembling hand to her hair, and Monica had to look away from the chinks in her bright armor.

"What made you finally decide to leave?" Monica asked.

"I'd left a few times when you were smaller. But he always talked his way back. JJ . . . JJ was good at that. At promising that he'd be different. That he wouldn't hurt me again. And I was good at believing him. But when you were six, you tried to stop him one night from hitting me and I realized . . . I realized I had to make a change."

"That's when you decided to come back to Bishop?"

"I took all the money I had saved and got us on a bus. I thought . . . I thought I'd buy us a house. Something small, and you could have a regular childhood."

Monica ignored it—the allure, the vision of a regular childhood.

"Did you think he'd come after you?"

Simone stared into her coffee cup. "I'd hoped not. It was naive of me to think that, I realize." She shook her hair back, managing to pull herself back from some dark internal brink.

"What do you remember from that night?" Monica asked.

"What do *you* remember?"

Stay under the bed, honey. Don't get out for any reason.

"Nothing," she lied.

"I remember hearing him on the steps. I remember putting you under the bed and then . . ." Simone ran her hand over the hem of her robe, over and over again, as if there were something there she couldn't wipe off. "I remember grabbing Dad's gun and thinking, 'Oh, Simone, you're overreacting. You're being ridiculous.' But . . . I'm glad I had that gun. The second he walked through that door, I was sure he was going to kill me. I was sure he was going to hurt you. I was . . . I was just sure of it."

"The people there that night agree with you."

Simone nodded, still so regal, and though they were long gone, Monica imagined the bruises and the scratches and the blood on that perfect face. It was as if they were still there, just beneath the surface.

"What do you remember from afterward?" Monica asked. "From London and Greece and France?"

Simone smiled. "I remember you were so fierce in London. So protective. A guard dog. Pouring out all the booze, hiding the drugs."

"Your friends didn't like it."

"My friends." Simone waved her hand, dismissing the women, the notion of their friendship. "I remember being so glad that you were strong. That you could bark and bite at those women, not just because it was on my behalf, but because I had no bark and bite. None. I never did. And I thought it would protect you, that fierceness."

Monica almost said that it did. That it both saved her and got her into a lot of trouble. But this was an interview, not a conversation.

"I don't remember Greece at all," Simone said, and Monica blinked. Astounded. "I was . . . in hindsight, it's easy to see that I was dangerously depressed. I didn't ever think about those months there until Charles . . ." Simone smiled, glancing over her shoulder to the shadows and the stairs. Monica wondered if he was listening. "Charles told me if we were going to be together, I needed to see a shrink and talk about some of the things I liked to pretend didn't matter. Greece was one of the things we talked about."

Monica remembered with photographic clarity the sight of her mother's hand slung over the side of that thin bed. *Mom,* she remembered crying, *Mom, please get out of bed. Please talk to me.*

"You must have been terrified," Simone said.

"It was a blast." The sarcasm didn't make her feel better. "What about France?"

"France was . . . scary."

"Really?" Monica asked.

"You didn't think so?"

You had come back to me. You smiled, laughed, held my hand as we walked along the river. Monica found herself unable to say those words. "I'm interviewing *you*," she said instead.

"We had no more money. I'd spent all our savings. Used up everyone's goodwill. And I knew we had to go back to the States. I'd been hiding for three years. We got back and I struggled to get work, crappy sitcoms and B movies, and game shows. And then *Playboy* called, and after that success, my agent told me about a reality TV show and I agreed."

"Did you like doing *Simone Says*?"

"No. God, no."

"Then why the hell were we doing it?" she yelled. She hadn't meant to yell. She picked up a pencil, put it down. At loose ends inside herself.

"I was thirty-three years old, Monica. I didn't even have a high school diploma. We had no money. None. The only other job offers coming my way with any real money attached were for adult films. I was just trying to make a living for us. A home. I wanted a chance to start over."

"It must have been a relief when I left," Monica said. The interview was slipping away from her, devolving into memory and accusation, and she was trying to rise above her feelings, but there was no getting away from them. She started to gather her things, ready to leave. To find Jackson and punish herself on him. To make this bad feeling acutely more painful.

This is what you do, a quiet voice whispered. *When it gets too painful, when it gets too hard, you run away. Or you make things worse. It's what you did with Jackson yesterday. It's why you will never be happy.*

Simone slipped her hand over Monica's and she was so stunned, she didn't move.

She forced herself to stay, to sit and be there in this painful, awful, honest moment. It was like holding her hand in a fire. She had to open her mouth to breathe through the pain.

"In a way, Monica, it was. I know how that sounds, but I was scared and you were so angry. And I made a lot of mistakes. More mistakes than I can count, but I should never have let you go."

"You didn't *let* me do anything . . . I ran away."

"I could have dragged you back. I could have tried harder to keep you. But . . . by the time I tried, it was too late."

She remembered her mother showing up backstage at random shows, asking her to come home, inviting her out for a meal, slipping her some money. All of which she refused. And then came the paparazzi blitz.

"Why the paparazzi, then?"

"You ran away from me, you wouldn't come home. Wouldn't speak to me and I . . . I knew what you were doing. The trouble you were flirting with, and I thought . . . if I could be everywhere, everywhere you turned, you couldn't run. But . . . all I did was push you farther away."

"Why are you doing this show now?" she asked. "This reality thing again."

"Same mentality, I suppose. After you had so much success, I just wanted . . . I wanted you to know I was there."

Monica didn't want to understand. She had no interest in understanding this twisted, narcissistic behavior. But she did—because she'd behaved the same way. She'd retaliated against her mother using the same means.

Charles came back in the room, still in his robe, and he looked very pedestrian next to Simone's slightly rumpled beauty.

"Why are you two together?" Monica blurted, apropos of nothing but trying to find some anchors in this new landscape.

Simone didn't even flinch. One thing she could count on her mother for, she was pretty unshockable in the face of Monica's shitty behavior.

"Why is anyone together?" Simone asked. "Why are you with the mayor? Oh, don't look so shocked, Monica. It was all over the television in that *America Today* clip. He seems like a very nice man. Very protective of you."

Done. This interview was done. Simone had just walked into a whole lot of none of her business. Monica gathered up all her stuff.

"That's it?" Simone asked.

"That's it." Monica turned to Charles, who watched her with unreadable eyes behind his glasses. "Sorry to keep you up so late."

"No." Simone stood, her eyes flashing. She looked desperate, which was strange. Sort of alarming. "No. We're not done."

"What were you expecting? A Hollywood ending? We'd get all this out in the open and I'd fall into your arms, a little girl again, grateful? It doesn't work that way in the real world."

"Well, when . . . when can I see you again? There's more I could tell you. For your book."

"I have enough." There was no further need to see Simone. No more ghosts to chase.

"Monica!" she cried, sounding stern, her attempt at a mommy voice. Monica turned back around and saw her mother, tears swimming in her eyes, her face red with anger and remorse. "Please," she whispered.

Oh, if only she'd said that when it really mattered! She thought of all the years she'd imagined her mother begging to have her back.

And here it was, just after she'd stopped caring.

It was as if the ropes that had been holding her in the same place all these years were cut at once and Monica was set free, set loose from the anger. The memories, the child she'd been. Even the woman she'd been just days ago.

She drifted away from all that weight dragging her down.

She took a deep breath, gasping at the pleasure of being free of all that pain and anger. And then gasping again at the unexpected ache of it.

"I'm not leaving," Simone said.

"Then I guess I'll see you around." That was all Monica could give her.

She walked out the door, Reba trailing behind her. Outside the screen door, the summer night was quiet. It was after midnight, and even the bugs were asleep. There was nothing but black velvet silence out there.

"I'll walk you home." The screen door opened behind her and Charles came out, wearing a dressing robe and boots.

"No." She smiled, because he looked so ridiculous and it was—at its heart—a nice thing to do. And she could recognize that now. She felt chagrined for her earlier anger. Turtle Man, honestly. "Thank you. I'll be fine."

"It's late."

"I'm a big girl."

"At least to the end of the street." He started walking past her, and she had nothing to do but start walking herself.

"I won't apologize for Simone," he said.

"I don't expect you to. I don't expect anything from you, Charles."

"I know. But I do want to say this. We learn how to be happy from our parents. We learn how to treasure it and work for it, how to sacrifice for it. We learn how precious happiness is from the example our parents set."

"Simone didn't set much of an example," she said, feeling sad for both of them.

"I know. She didn't learn from her father, who probably didn't learn from his parents. But . . . you could break that cycle. If you wanted."

"I don't have any children. I'm in no danger of passing on my family's shitty legacy."

"But you could be happy," he said, his voice soft in the night. His boots kicked gravel and somewhere along the ditches, bushes rustled. Reba growled in her throat.

"You're not making my mother happy?" she asked. "Shame on you."

"Some days are better than others, but I love her. And she loves me, and she tries. But happiness . . . happiness isn't her natural state. There are days, and she'd tell you this herself, she is just too scared to try."

Monica found herself smiling, a surprise. "I understand that all too well."

"Then you know it doesn't take any courage to expect the worst. But to try . . ." He whistled, as if there were just no words for how hard it was to try to be happy.

Isn't that the truth, she thought.

She stopped at the edge of the road, the streetlights of the square just up ahead. "I'm okay from here," she said.

"I hope so," he answered and vanished back into the shadows, leaving her to walk toward the light by herself.

Chapter 23

At dawn Jackson was on the front porch of his house. Waiting. Phone in hand, condoms by his side. Fear and anger a snarling, snapping beast at his back.

Gwen hadn't come home last night.

She hadn't returned his texts.

His only comfort was that if she were lying dead in a ditch, he'd have heard about it by now.

When he saw her again . . . he shook his head, unable to even finish that sentence.

He braced his elbows on his knees and held his head in his hands, but at the sound of the front gate creaking open he lifted his head, like a dog catching a scent.

"Gwen?"

But it was Monica, holding paper coffee cups and a bag from Cora's. The pink of her shirt, of her lips, glowed in the half-light. "No," she said with a smile. She looked about as rough as he felt, wan with dark circles under her eyes. Somehow, though, she managed to be the most beautiful woman he'd ever seen. And he found himself so susceptible to that right now, he wanted to put his head in her lap and let her tell him everything would be okay. "Just me. Where's Gwen?"

"She didn't come home last night."

"Oh my God." As she walked up the stone path toward him, the smell of fritters and coffee and . . . *her* pulled the trigger on the worst of his volatile emotions and he remembered the condoms beside him on the stairs. "Do you know where she is?" she asked.

"With Jay." He grabbed the condoms. "What do you know about this?"

"She gave those to you?" Monica asked as she set down the coffee cups and grease-stained pastry bag.

"No. I took them from her shorts."

"Jackson—" That she dared to sound reproving made him furious.

"Don't. You. Dare lecture me on morality when it comes to teenagers. I'm not running around giving them condoms."

"You think that's what I was doing? Running around just handing out free condoms?"

"It sure as hell looks like it."

"Your sister came to me, Jackson. Talking about having sex. What should I have done?"

"Told her to come talk to me."

Calm, she watched him.

"What?" he demanded. "You have nothing to say?"

"Why would she come to you, Jackson? You don't talk to her. You don't talk to anyone."

"This isn't about me, Monica. It's about you getting involved in something that's none of your business." She kept pushing herself out of the corner she was supposed to be in. She bled into the edges of the town, his relationship with his sister, his plans for his life after Bishop.

"In the interest of full disclosure, she mentioned you caught her drinking, and I gave her my cell phone number and told her it would be better for her to call me for a ride than get into the car with someone who had been drinking."

The top of his head felt like it had been blown off; he could only gape at her.

"I was only trying to help," she said. "But you're right. I should have told you."

"This is how you help?" he snapped. "You learned this on that island of yours?"

She blinked at his viciousness but he couldn't curb it. His whole life had started to fall apart the minute she blew into town like a hurricane, blowing apart the boundaries, the lines, the paths he needed.

"This isn't your business," he breathed, shaking the condoms in her face. "None of this is your business."

Her lips went white at the edges, the small muscles flinching just like they had so long ago at The Pour House. *I am hurting her. And I don't know how to stop.*

"What *is* my business, Jackson?" She stuck her chin out, as if asking for his best shot, and he didn't think twice. He gave it to her.

"I think what happened in my office yesterday answers that question."

The memory of her tipped over his desk, his hand holding her down, rippled through him, shaming him. That he brought it up like this—blaming her for it—made him even sicker.

She closed her eyes for a moment, as if gathering herself for another round. But when she opened them, there was a ghost of a smile on her beautiful lips and he was disarmed.

"This . . . this isn't going the way I thought it would." She stepped closer, looking up at his eyes, her body a breath away from his. And despite everything between them, he wanted to touch her. He curled his fists against the urge. Awareness that there was something different in the air didn't sit well with him at the moment. He was raw. And his instinct was to circle the wagons, push her away.

"I came here to be brave," she said. "I came here to try for happiness. I came to tell you I love you. I love you, Jackson."

For a moment the words didn't sink in. They didn't

mean anything. They were gibberish spoken in a foreign language.

"I . . . What?"

"I love you. I didn't want it or expect it, but I love you."

He opened his mouth—but there were no words he could apply to what ached in his bones. *I didn't want to hurt you. I don't know what to say or do. I can't see myself out of this.*

"You don't have to say anything," she said, as if she knew just what the storm was inside of him. "I just . . . I just wanted to say it. I've never said it before."

The front gate screeched open and there was Gwen, running up the front walk. The relief was painful, as though all his blood was falling through his body to his feet, leaving him numb and light-headed. "Jackson, I'm sorry," she panted. "I fell asleep in Jay's basement—"

"Go to your room." He couldn't even look at her, so he spat the words at her shoes.

She jerked to a halt, her eyes darting from him to Monica, and he wanted to scream at his sister not to look at Monica. That *he* was in charge. He was her family.

He held up the condoms.

"Did you tell him?" Gwen asked Monica, daring to act as if she were the affronted party.

"No. He . . . found them."

"Found . . ." Gwen's eyes swung to him. "You went through my room?"

"We'll talk about it later."

"I'm not a little kid and you have no right—"

"I'm in charge!" he cried. "I didn't ask for this, Gwen. But you're here and I'm here and Mom and Dad aren't. I don't know what you want from me! What more am I supposed to do for you?"

"What have you done for me?" she spat.

"I gave up my life!" The second the words were out he knew it was a mistake. He didn't have to see her pain-filled face, her angry eyes. He didn't have to hear Monica's gasp of censure.

"You should just leave now," Gwen said, stepping away from the hand he reached out to her. "Go, get on with your awesome life. I don't need you. I *never* needed you. You were just too stupid to see it!" She stomped up the stairs and ran into the house. Into her room.

He watched her go, his bones aching.

I never needed you. You were just too stupid to see it.

God, if only he'd been that stupid, but he'd known she didn't need him, not really, all along. All along.

Just as she probably knew how much he resented her for being the reason he had to give up his life.

"She didn't mean that," Monica whispered, trying to make it better. Trying to make it right. "Just like—"

"Like I didn't mean it?" He looked up at her, his anger fading to grief. "We meant it, Monica. Those are the things we've always known and have just never been able to say."

Her lips went hard. "Then shame on you."

A tidal wave of exhaustion and resentment rolled over him. "I can't do this all at once," he whispered. "I can't . . . the show, the Okra Festival, Gwen." He looked at her. "You."

She nodded as if she'd expected that. As if she'd come here knowing she would be hurt, knowing disaster would befall her, and he couldn't believe it. He couldn't wrap his head around it.

"We're all connected, Jackson. All these people in your life who love you and who you try to hold at arm's length. We're connected and we're messy. And we can't live in the little compartments you want us to stay in. And I know you might not let me in, I know that might be too hard for you. I don't fit into the idea you had for your life, and that's too bad—mostly for you, because I could have been the best thing that ever happened to you. But I pray, Jackson, I pray you let your sister in, before you end up all alone. Before *she* ends up all alone."

She took a coffee, left the other for him, and walked away, her head held high, her shoulders back, as if she were free. As if there was nothing tying her down anymore.

He wanted to call her back, ask her how she did it. How she found the courage to be so open to the world. To make mistakes and let mistakes be made. To let pain happen. Disappointment.

His whole life was a sandbag effort to keep those things out. Away. Accepting that devastation, welcoming it even, sticking out her chin and asking for it . . . it was the bravest, craziest thing he'd ever seen.

The next forty-eight hours stretched in front of him with the potential for disaster at an all-time high, and he didn't know how to handle it with her at his side.

Or with her *not* at his side.

But he didn't know how to love her, either. The chaos of her, of love—it was terrifying. And he was shit at it.

The girl inside was proof of that.

The clouds burned off by nine a.m. and the day was brilliant with sunshine. And Jackson's cell phone was ringing nonstop. His in-box was full, and he was being texted and tweeted and tortured.

"Why the hell aren't you out here?" Sean asked on the phone. "I'm setting up these booths for the street fair all by myself."

"I'm on my way," he assured Sean and ran up the stairs to pound on Gwen's door. Bubba was a snoring sentinel guarding it.

"Go away!" Her voice was muffled.

"Look, I've got . . . I've got a lot of things going on today but you and I aren't over, Gwen."

Silence answered him.

"I'll be back to take you to the pageant tonight, but until then, you don't leave this house. Do you understand me?"

The door opened. Gwen, stony in her anger, stared at him.

"I'm going to Shelby's before the pageant," she said. "Monica is doing my hair and makeup."

Even the sound of her name stabbed at him. Called up some assurance buried in his gut that he was wrong. He was making mistakes, irrevocable and regrettable.

"Fine. I'll take you there. But we have—" The door slammed in his face. "We have unfinished business, Gwen."

The day roared by fueled by coffee and exhaustion and stress. The work was never-ending and he took a personal stake in all of it. He felt the weight of every single decision.

"Don't you have more important things to do than this?" Sean asked as they hung parade signs that would direct traffic in the morning.

"Everything is important," Jackson said, biting off the tape he used to hang a sign on a streetlamp.

"That's your problem," Sean said.

"Oh Christ. Not you, too."

"You know, the rest of the world figures out what's important. Not every single thing has to be code blue."

"Yeah, maybe in your life," Jackson said. "I mean, it's got to be a real dilemma figuring out which beer to put on special."

"That's not fair," Sean said.

Jackson knew it and he didn't care. "This town is my responsibility, Sean."

He barely got the words out before Sean was laughing.

"What the hell is so funny?"

"You. Well, not funny really. Sort of sad. After your folks died there wasn't a person in this town who wouldn't have helped you. But you wouldn't let it happen." His face screwed up in bewildered confusion. "And then you started trying to take care of everyone else. Like you didn't have enough shit on your plate. The world won't stop if you take a break, or mess up. Or just . . . I don't know, act normal. You can't fix everything. Some things just are."

That nonsense again.

"Hilarious you would say that the day before we win this contest that will in fact save this town. You're the one who said I swing for the fences—you can't be pissed when it works out."

"Well, when was the last time you swung for the fences for yourself? You're so willing to take risks for this town and such a coward for yourself."

"I'm fine."

"Really? Things are just great with your sister and you and Monica . . ."

"There's nothing between me and Monica." He'd taken care of that.

"Now you're lying." Sean shook his head. "And if you blew that, then you're an idiot. A bigger idiot than I thought."

"Fine," Jackson muttered, frustrated and furious that suddenly everyone had an opinion on his life and how he lived it. He gave Sean his handful of fliers and the tape. "You set the rest of this up."

He checked his watch. It was time to go grab Gwen for the pageant.

Twenty minutes later he took the steps two by two to the second floor of the Big House. Just as he put his hand up to knock, the door swung open and a stranger stood there. A young woman, radiant in gold.

Only her eyes—furious and belligerent—were his sister's.

"You . . . ," he gasped, feeling his head leave his body, his heart punch his lungs. "You look amazing. That dress—"

"It was Mom's."

He gasped again, couldn't help it—the pain slipping through his rib cage was acute. Sharp and precise. He missed his mother, his father. He missed his sister as a girl. Himself as a boy. He missed every chance he didn't take, every risk.

You can't fix this, you can't change it. You can't control it. It is time and it's moving by and you're losing everyone.

"I'm so sorry," he told her. "For what I said, earlier. About giving up my life—"

"It's the truth, isn't it? Just because you never said it doesn't mean I didn't know it. Let's go," she said, moving past him, leaving him broken in her wake.

On the drive over to the Art Barn silence filled the car, the kind of silence that couldn't be punctured with words, though he tried.

"I'm sorry about going through your room," he said. "I was just so worried."

Her thumbnail got more attention than he did.

"I wasn't looking for anything," he said. "I wasn't. I mean . . . maybe I was. I don't know."

She shifted, looking away from him, but he refused to be stonewalled again.

"Do you want to talk about the condoms?"

She laughed. "No."

"Do you want to talk about Jay?"

"Double no."

He sighed, wishing the ride to Shelby's could be longer, but they were there already, and the moment he put the truck in park, she was halfway out the door. Before thinking about it, he'd grabbed her hand.

"I want you to talk to me," he said. "I want . . . I mean, I know I'm not Dad. Maybe I'm not even much of a brother, and I know I'm not as smart as you, but no one is, Gwen. And . . . I'd like to be your friend."

"Fine. You want to be a friend, how about *you* talk to *me*?" She shook back her hair and gripped his hand, her fingernails digging into his skin, surprising him with their ferocity. "When were you going to tell me you were going to leave? Where are you going to go? What's happening between you and Monica?" She tilted her head and he realized he was gaping at her. A thousand words rushed through his brain and got caught, just there at the edge of his tongue.

"Why is this so hard for you?" she asked, clearly be-fuddled.

I wish I knew, he thought.

Monica stood at the door to the barn, waving Gwen in, and at the sight of her he was driven by a terrible need to make things right. Just one thing in his life. He had to make sense of what she'd revealed. He had to try to shove it back in its box. Make it manageable for him, so he could understand it.

He hopped out of the truck just as Gwen slipped inside the door and Monica turned to follow. "Wait," he called. "Wait, Monica."

She paused and turned to look at him, her expression stone.

I tricked you, he thought. *I duped you.*

"You love something that isn't real," he blurted, and her eyebrows rose.

"Maybe . . . maybe it's the sex, you know? The orgasm thing?"

Once, when Gwen was about thirteen and having a conniption about something he couldn't remember, he told her that she was overreacting because she was a girl and she was hard-wired that way.

Gwen had looked at him exactly the way Monica was looking at him now: with pity and fury.

"Your magic penis didn't save me, you jackass! I did, by being honest. Something I'm trying to do more of. And yes, the sex has a lot to do with it, but it's not why I love you. I love you because *you're* magic. You try so hard. You think of other people first. You don't back down from a fight . . . except for when it's on your own behalf. You're the most caring and compassionate and selfless person I know, while at the same time being the most closed-off and selfish person I know. You're a mess, and I love that about you, because I'm a mess too. But I'm figuring things out. But—and you'd better get this through your thick skull—I am not something that needs to be fixed."

She closed the door in his face.

Chapter 24

Monica leaned back against the door and closed her burning eyes. Her heart, too heavy to carry on her own, slipped from her hands and shattered against the floor.

The orgasm thing?

Never in her life had she been more reduced. More marginalized.

"My brother is stupid."

Monica opened her eyes to see Shelby and Gwen staring at her.

"I'm with Gwen," Shelby said. "Jackson is an idiot."

"I think maybe *I'm* the idiot," Monica said. "I knew going in that this was just temporary for him. That . . . he wasn't going to love me. And frankly, I wasn't going to love him, so I can't blame him for how I feel."

"That's awfully diplomatic of you," Shelby said. "For a woman who looks so heartbroken."

"Love sucks," Gwen said emphatically.

Monica's heart wrenched at the words, and she hated the idea of Gwen building herself a life behind walls like the ones that Monica had built for herself, or worse, the walls that Jackson had built. She pushed herself away from the door. "No, Gwen, it doesn't. It's . . . great."

"Yeah, it looks like a whole lot of fun."

Monica laughed at the girl's razor-sharp sarcasm. "I'm . . . grateful that I love Jackson, because I don't know what would have happened to me if I didn't meet him. I was really alone. And I'd convinced myself that I liked it that way."

"But . . ." Gwen looked puzzled. "Aren't you still alone?"

"No. Look at us. Right now. I'm going to do your makeup and Shelby is going to pour me a stiff drink in a mug. And Reba's all dressed up."

All three women looked to where Reba slept in the corner, pink ribbons in her fur.

"She does look nice," Gwen said. Monica laughed, though it hurt. She smiled, though she wanted to cry. It was like being torn in half by happiness and grief.

"I'm here because I was able to be in love. And I wouldn't change that for the world. Now, let's make sure you win this pageant."

Three hours later, Jackson drove Miss Okra home. Her tiara, a gaudy number that had to stand about a foot off her hair, glittered in the headlights of the cars passing by.

"Congratulations," he said. His chest ached with affection. With pride. With the bittersweet reality that she was leaving him behind to have a new life.

"Thanks." She smelled the roses she carried in her lap. "I thought Ania had me there at the end."

"I had no idea she could juggle."

"I know, right?"

He turned left toward the Big House, through the square. "Whose idea was it for you to bring up the chalkboard?"

"Shelby's. Monica helped me write the speech."

His beautiful, genius sister, instead of playing the piano, which he'd expected, had stood up in front of the gymnasium full of Bishop residents, glittering and golden in the spotlight, and explained why there weren't more women in high-level math and science jobs.

"I could play the piano for you, like I have every year," she'd said. "But we all know I'm not very good. So . . . I'm going to show you my real talent."

And then she'd flipped over the blackboard in the middle of the stage and found the area of an ellipse using integral calculus, explaining it as she went.

The audience had politely clapped, but they were whispering behind their hands, embarrassed for Gwen and her big, awkward brain. Jackson wanted to charge into the audience and knock heads together—silence all those people intimidated by his sister.

But Monica, standing in the back, a dozen feet from him, had stomped and whistled; she'd clapped hard and loud enough for a dozen people.

And he realized, to his chagrin, a deep and painful truth: that he was one of the silent ones in Gwen's life—he was just as intimidated as those people rolling their eyes, whispering behind their hands.

Pinpricks of horror racing up and down his arms and back, he'd joined in with Monica, stomping and cheering for every single time he hadn't in the past. He hollered, "That's my sister!" through cupped hands.

Onstage, Gwen had bowed and done a funny little embarrassed curtsy, before running off the stage.

Monica had grinned at Jackson and for one second, one crystalline, fantastic second, it was just them, gathered and collected and bound together by Gwen's big brain, Monica's big heart, and Jackson's giant, crushing fear. Monica, Jackson, and Gwen—nothing else. No expectations, no looming failure—just them. And it was perfect.

But then Monica walked away, taking the perfect moment with her.

And it was as though she had taken the color with her. The scent and textures of his whole life.

"I hope it doesn't rain for the parade tomorrow," Gwen

said, peering up through the windshield as it started to sprinkle.

"It will be all right," he said, and Gwen laughed.

"You have a plan to stop it?"

He shook his head. He didn't want to talk about the rain, or the parade, or *America Today,* or even the factory. He wanted to keep driving around in his truck with his sister and her roses, her beautiful dress. Her beautiful self. Maybe they could find Monica and he could apologize for being an ass, for not being able to love as fast and as well as she could, and explain to her that it didn't mean he didn't feel anything.

They could all go to Masonville for frozen custard, see how much free custard Gwen could get if she wore her crown.

The fantasy was so deeply real that he smiled.

"Jackson," Gwen said, pointing out her window. "You're about to drive past the house."

"Right." At the last minute he braked and pulled into the driveway, up to the back of the house. "Wait here."

He got out of the car and ran up to the back porch, where he grabbed his umbrella. And then he ran back down to the truck and opened his sister's door, helping her down and running with her through the rain to the back porch. She touched her crown, then the glittering clip-on jewelry, as if to make sure it was all still there.

"Well," she said. "I'm going to go change and go to bed. Early morning tomorrow."

He nodded. "I'm so proud of you."

The chance was there—right there—for him to hug her. To erase some of the years and the distance by giving her a hug, and she stood there for a moment as if she knew it too, and he wasted the moment by wondering when he should stop hugging her.

"Good night, Jackson," she said, her voice quiet. And

then she was inside, gone through the house, and he was left in the rain.

The night was suddenly huge, the darkness oppressive. He felt miles of distance around him. His loneliness was a radio signal bouncing off nothing. And sitting on a beach somewhere, or backpacking through Europe—it wasn't going to fix what was wrong with him. Being out of this house, this town, he'd still be him. Carrying around all the mistakes he'd made.

The idea of never being enough was going to haunt him everywhere he went.

Almost frantic, he walked through the kitchen in wet shoes, his hair dripping into his face. He jogged up the stairs to his sister's door. Shut, of course. He touched the sparkly edge of a butterfly sticker she'd put there . . . God, years ago. A lifetime ago, before Mom and Dad died. When she was still a little girl.

He knocked, and the door opened. Gwen had changed out of the dress into a pair of shorts and a baggy tee shirt. But her hair was still up and her makeup was still on and she was part stranger.

The scared part of him recoiled, afraid of messing this up, afraid of getting it wrong. But the scared part of him had been in charge for way too long.

"Can I come in?"

She blinked in surprise but then opened the door.

He stepped in and, realizing he was soaking wet and couldn't sit on her bed or at her desk, he put his back to the wall and slid to the floor. Bubba waddled over and collapsed by his side. Jackson put a hand in his short fur.

"You all right?" Gwen asked.

"No."

The silence was thick and heavy, and he rested his head back against the wall.

"I . . . never knew how to love you," he said. "I felt

like . . . you needed something else from me. Something more, or bigger. You . . . you needed me to make things right. The fact that Mom and Dad died, the fact that you were stuck with me, that you . . . you weren't very good at making friends. I had to make all of that right for you, somehow. Make it okay. And I didn't . . . I was so ordinary. And you were so extraordinary." He was gasping for air. "Loving you wasn't ever going to be enough for you."

She collapsed onto her bed, the posts shimmying, sending the princess canopy swaying.

"And I'm so . . . I'm so sorry for that. I'm so sorry that I wasted so many years trying to fix what was wrong, when you were perfectly . . . you all the time." Was he crying? He was. He was crying. Exhaustion swept over him in a wave and he closed his eyes.

"It's okay, Jackson," Gwen breathed.

"No." He shook his head; his eyelids felt as though they weighed a thousand pounds. "It's not. I didn't give up my life for you—"

"You did. We both know it. And I'm sorry, but . . . it's not my fault."

He gasped in awe. In awe of this amazing girl with the strength to see that. He wiped his eyes, unable to speak.

"I'm sorry I called you stupid," she said.

"Well, you were right. I was so stupid toward you. Toward this whole town. And I know it's late and I know you're going off to school—"

"You're leaving too."

Right. His big plans. They seemed so shallow now. Sex with nameless women? Was he sixteen?

"Actually," he said. "I think . . . I think I might finish law school."

"At Ole Miss?" She sounded horrified.

"That would bother you?"

He was braced for a sigh, a shrug, a "whatever." He didn't know how he'd react if she did that, but he was braced for it. "Okay," she said without a sigh or a shrug. Her eyes were square on his. "We can try."

It wasn't perfect, it wasn't redemption or forgiveness for his mistakes, but it was a start. He'd take it.

"We've still got some time. Maybe, after the election, before school, maybe we could take a road trip together. Go see some sights."

"What kind of sights?"

"Anything you want."

"Washington, DC? I've always wanted to see the Smithsonian."

Really? "You bet."

She smiled. "I'm just kidding. How about the Grand Canyon?"

"Much better idea."

"What about Monica?" she asked.

The joy stilled in his chest—a fragile ball in danger of breaking. "What about her?"

"She should come. It would be good."

"It would, wouldn't it?" he said, pushing aside her concern, her question. But then he groaned and buried his head in his hands. "I was pretty stupid toward her, too."

"She loves you."

"She told you?"

"We're . . . we're friends." Gwen shrugged. "She says she's glad she loves you, that it changed her life. But you can tell she's sad."

The recrimination in his sister's voice was salt in a wound he didn't realize he had. "I didn't want to make her sad."

"Then don't," Gwen said, as if it were all that simple. "I'm starving. You want some cereal?" Gwen walked out of the room but Jackson was rooted to the spot, heavy and immobile.

Then don't. It was just that easy.

He sat there, moving aside boulders and obstacles put in place dozens of years ago, to get to the truth. His truth.

I don't have to leave this town to be happy.

I just have to be with Monica.

Was this love? It felt selfish; it felt like half of the equation. Wanting her around because she made him happy seemed one-sided. That she brought color and texture to his life seemed unfair. What did he bring to hers?

He suddenly felt hollow—unsure even of who he was. He'd compromised himself in the face of so many expectations and fears that he didn't even know what about him was worth loving.

Chapter 25

Shelby was at the parade start early, helping the Girl Scout troop get ready. Stuffing tissue-paper flowers back into the municipal float.

"Thank God it stopped raining, huh?" she asked the fire chief, who agreed.

Her art-camp kids were out in mismatched costumes, carrying banners and signs covered in glitter and stickers.

"You guys look great!" she said, helping a ninja with his mask.

Gwen, her crown perched on her loose hair and her face clear of all makeup, sat in the convertible donated by Sawicki Motors. Jackson sat beside her, dumping candy into baskets to throw at the kids.

"Something is different about you," Shelby said, tucking the edge of Gwen's strapless bra beneath the edge of the golden dress.

"No makeup," Jackson said. "Miss Okra is *au naturel*."

That wasn't it at all, but Shelby nodded. "You look beautiful."

"Thanks," Gwen said.

Jackson leaned behind his sister and grabbed Shelby's hand. Shelby was so surprised, she just stared. "Thank you," he said. "For how you helped her . . . that math thing?"

"Gwen's idea," Shelby said, delighted that something

had been knocked loose between the two Davieses. "I just helped with the details."

"I think . . . I think you helped us both. More than you know."

The motorcade started and Jackson rocked back, catching himself against the trunk of the car.

Gwen grabbed ahold of him. "We can't lose the mayor now!" She laughed, and they both waved as they drove away.

Wow, Shelby thought as she watched them go by with the rest of the parade. *Talk about unexpected!*

Finally it was just her, the sirens and the marching band fading into the distance.

"Hello."

She whirled around at the familiar voice, her heart sinking. "Dean!" she cried, stunned to see that handsome face, ruined by that smug, knowing grin. "Are you here for the taping?" Her heart soared. "Did we win? Is that why you're here—"

"America is deciding that." He stepped toward her and she fought the urge to step back, so repelled by him. He was still physically attractive enough—but that smile. It made her feel dirty. Slimy. Oh God, honestly, what had she been thinking, letting this man touch her?

"I came to see *you,*" he said.

"Me?"

"You sound so surprised. Why haven't you been returning my emails?"

"Why . . . why would I?" His eyebrows clashed. "We were a fling, Dean. Just . . . just a . . . fling."

"What if I want more?" *More. More? Oh.* Her stomach turned. "There's a good chance Bishop could win this, and then I'll be moving here and we can . . ." He reached for her, his hand glancing off her shoulder before she ducked away.

"Listen, Dean. Even if we win and you move back here . . . there's no 'more' for us."

"You said that before, remember?" He smiled. "And you changed your mind."

Images of herself on her hands and knees on the floor of her barn roared through her. Trying so hard to feel alive and sexy and desirable to a man she didn't like.

"I won't. Dean, I'm serious. I don't like you."

His face turned stormy. Not unlike one of the toddlers in her moms-and-kids class when she took away the glitter. "You liked me plenty when you had my dick in your mouth."

She recoiled, from the memory, his words, him. "Don't . . . don't talk to me that way, Dean. Not here. I want you to leave."

"Not many people tell me no, Shelby."

Her cell phone in her pocket buzzed and she fished it out, grateful to have a reason to get out of this conversation, away from his slightly poisonous presence.

"I have to go," she said, stepping backward, away from him.

"We're not done," he told her.

"Yes, Dean. We are."

The rain from last night had left puddles on the sidewalk, and Reba did not like getting wet. Fearing she'd be late, Monica picked Reba up and carried her in her arms across the street to the square, where the street festival was set up.

Oh my God. I've become one of those women who carry their dog.

Of all the small and large changes in her life since coming to Bishop, this seemed the most dire.

The parade had ended, and everyone filled the square. Businesses had closed for the day and it seemed like the

whole town was out in force. It was early for chili, but
that didn't stop people from eating it. Vanessa and Matt
from *America Today*, with a pretty, dark-haired reporter,
were setting up in the only empty corner of the square.

"We go live in twenty minutes, everyone!" Vanessa
yelled.

The crowd buzzed with a pained excitement.

"Monica." Jackson's voice sent ripples across her
skin; it was as if he'd touched her, and she backed away
from him, from his boyish grin and stern eyebrows.
Too late, as it happened—her heart had already been
sacrificed—but a girl had to wise up eventually.

"Good turnout," she said, putting Reba down in the
grass. "You must be thrilled."

"Looks good, doesn't it?" He surveyed his kingdom
with a half-smile, as if slightly surprised to see it all
sprung up around him. She took the moment to drink
him in with thirsty eyes. "Your mom is here," he said.

"What?" She stood on tiptoe to see over the crowd, to
catch a glimpse of white-blond hair. "That's ballsy even
for her. Is she . . . is she taping or something?"

"I don't think so. Look, Monica." He dropped his
voice and stepped closer, and every muscle in her body
clenched.

"Hey!" Vanessa cried, approaching with the camera
on her shoulder. "If it isn't the lovebirds!"

Monica and Jackson both turned to glare at her.
"Ohh," she said, stepping back. "Not playing it up for
the cameras anymore, I see. Too bad. Matt, let's go get
some footage of Cora and her chili."

Vanessa and Matt walked away and Monica stood
there, a terrible realization dawning.

*And I will do anything to see that happen, Monica.
Anything. I will lie, beg . . .*

"Are you kidding me?" she yelled.

"I swear I wasn't playing up anything," he said, knowing exactly what she meant, which was pretty damning in her eyes. "Everything I felt for you was real."

"Really?" she asked, on a painful laugh. "*Everything?* Lucky me."

She thought of that footage of them during the parade build, the footage that everyone saw and commented on and that she'd spent so much time denying. And he'd been silent about it.

It was as if the world had been ripped away under her feet and she couldn't breathe.

"If this was part of your plan, to use me like this—to use what we had, what I thought—" She stopped, her throat ruined, her stomach in knots.

He winced. "I didn't *not* use you."

"What the hell does that mean?"

His sigh said too much and she couldn't look at him anymore. *I am such a stupid idiot.*

"It means, if they thought our relationship would get votes . . . I let them use our relationship."

Her anger made her nauseous. Or maybe that was him. "Who are you, Jackson? Do you even know, really?"

"Listen to me," he said, reaching for her wrists. He touched her, briefly, and her body went up in flames before she could step away. "I don't care about this contest anymore. I don't—"

She laughed, yanking her hands away. "Now I *know* you're lying. I need to go." What she had to do, she wasn't sure. But she knew she had to get away from him.

Blindly, she walked past the tents, the crowds, to the edge of the festivities where she could finally catch her breath. She braced her hand against a tree, the only thing solid on earth. The only thing she could count on was this damn tree.

"Monica?" It was her mother, wearing a summer dress of red and blue and white Indian-print fabric. She looked normal. Beautiful, but normal.

Monica groaned and put her head down on the bark. If only it could be just her and the tree. Forever. Shelby could visit her here. Gwen. But no one else got to come to the tree.

"Are you . . . okay?"

She couldn't even flinch away from Simone's touch against her back.

"No."

"What can I do?"

Monica sighed and lifted her head, struggling to find firm ground inside herself. "Nothing. There's nothing anyone can do—I'm just another sad example of a woman falling for something in a man that isn't really there."

Simone's smile was an encyclopedia's worth of knowledge on just that subject.

From the corner of her eye, Monica saw Vanessa approach, the camera on her shoulder. Simone saw it too and swore under her breath. "I'll . . . I'll go."

She took a few steps backward, as if waiting for Monica to tell her to stay, but she couldn't do that. She couldn't have this day trumped by their strange mother/daughter reunion. There were so many holes in their relationship, she didn't know how to mend it, or what could possibly do the job. Or, frankly, if she was even interested in mending anything. But one thing was for certain: if she was ever going to be interested, some of Simone's garbage had to be swept out of the way.

"Simone!" she called. "You want to do something for me?"

"Anything."

"Quit the show. Stop it."

Simone nodded. "Done." And then she was gone, off the grass onto the sidewalk leading her to the house she'd made into an unlikely home.

Whether Monica was surprised or happy or worried

by her mother's easy agreement, she wasn't sure. Nothing felt sure.

Over the crowd, near the fountain, she saw Jackson helping Sean set up the television and speakers so everyone could watch the results on the square. He must have felt her attention because he glanced up, right at her.

And she knew—more than at any other time in her life—that when she left this place without him, she would truly be homeless.

"All right!" Vanessa shouted, rounding up some of the key players in front of the square. "I need Jackson and Shelby over here. Monica, you come too. Cora. Everyone over here—we're live in five minutes."

Monica stood next to Shelby, and when Jackson came to stand beside her, he felt her nearness like a nuclear blast, a gale-force wind.

What kind of man am I? Her words were pinging through his body, putting holes in the walls, scratching the floors. Making a mess. He thought of every single time he'd stayed silent when Dean was being disgusting, when he wondered, what would a better man would do?

The answer was—the opposite of what he did.

Jackson was ready to be done with this fantasy version of himself and equally ready to be done with the version of himself that was what everyone expected him to be.

Jackson was ready to be the kind of man who deserved Monica.

"Here's how this works," Vanessa said. "We're going to do a live pan of the event. Anne here," Vanessa pointed to the reporter, "is going to do a quick recap. Jackson is going to give one last pitch to the American public about why they should vote for Bishop, and then we break. America has one hour to vote. In two hours the results are revealed at the end of the show. We'll have a reaction shot and should you win, some interviews. We good?" Vanessa asked.

Everyone dutifully nodded.

"Monica," Jackson whispered, leaning toward her ear. "I really need to talk to you."

"I think it can wait," she said, giving him her best hairy eyeball.

"It can't." He touched her hand and he could tell she almost reached out to slap it away. She looked pointedly at the cameras.

"I don't care about the cameras, Monica. I don't care who is watching or what they think." He didn't bother to whisper, and his words pretty much guaranteed everyone was watching.

"Jackson . . . please."

"I love you."

"What?" Her purple eyes were wide and angry and beneath the anger . . . she was wounded.

"I love you." He stood as naked as he could be in front of her. No smile, no charm. Just him and his faults and his promises and his beating heart.

"Is this . . . is this for the cameras?"

Oh, the hurt on her face. It destroyed him, destroyed him to know he'd caused it. He shook his head. "I've wasted so much time trying to be everything to everybody and dreaming about some future version of myself that I stopped caring about who I was. That's over. I care about you. About Gwen. About . . . my family. And I know it's late and I've messed up and I still don't really understand how you can love me, what part of me I've shown you that's worth the faith you've given me. But I love you. And I want to be the kind of man you can love."

"Holy shit. Is that Dean?" Cora whispered and glanced back at Jackson.

"Where?"

Cora pointed toward the fountain where, yes, in fact Dean was walking across the grass toward them. "Does this mean . . . ?" Cora's smile was hopeful. Beautiful. Everyone began to murmur behind them, a whispering, gasping celebration gathering steam.

Vanessa, however, did not look celebratory. "What the hell is he doing here?" she asked.

"This isn't planned?" Jackson asked, going razor sharp in a moment.

Shelby moaned and Monica put her arm around her friend. "What's going on?" Monica whispered.

"He's here for me," Shelby said, and Jackson turned to face them.

"You?" he asked.

"We . . . had a thing."

"Again, with the thing," he muttered. He looked at Monica, the arm around Shelby's back. His Island Girl, his lone wolf, had managed to gather quite a group of friends around herself. It took courage to reach out to people. And she'd found that courage, and he'd love her for no other reason but that she'd taught him to have that courage too.

For him, it was no risk to be what people thought he should be. The risk was being himself.

"You knew about this too?" he asked.

Monica nodded.

"Honestly, we're going to have to have a discussion about all the secrets you were keeping for this town."

Monica couldn't say anything because Dean was right beside them, red-faced, his hands in fists at his sides. The frustrated lover was not an attractive role for the man.

"Dean," Vanessa said, wide-eyed and impatient. "What the hell, man? We're live in ninety seconds."

"I know. I just . . . Shelby? Can I talk to you?"

"No." Shelby shook her head. "You can't. I said what I had to say."

"Well, I haven't." Dean grabbed her arm and before Jackson could step in, Monica knocked Dean's hand away.

"Don't touch her," Monica said.

"Dean!" Vanessa cried. "You will ruin the shot and the whole damn contest. Get out of here!"

"Please just go," Shelby said.

"Not until you promise me we'll talk."

"Listen, Dean." Jackson stepped in with his calming, cooling influence. "Why don't you head on over to Cora's booth and have some chili—"

"I don't serve assholes who grab women," Cora said, her arms crossed over her chest.

Jackson swore under his breath. "All right. There are four other chilis to try."

"We're live in five seconds!" Vanessa cried.

Jackson reached out and tried to back Dean away, but the man was digging in his heels, all the asshole nature Jackson had guessed at suddenly on full display.

"You had plenty to say last week," Dean hissed at Shelby, the crowd behind them suddenly funeral quiet. You could hear a pin drop; Dean's words echoed through the square.

"Dean, don't," Shelby whispered.

"Four!" Vanessa cried. "Three!"

"Honest to God, Dean, leave," Jackson warned him, wrapping his hand in the guy's shirt. Dean strained against him. Jackson shoved him, trying to get him out of the shot, but Dean was a rabid badger going after Shelby.

"Why don't you tell them all what you said—" Dean cried.

"Two, and . . ." Vanessa groaned as the red light bloomed to life on the camera. "We're live."

"While I was fucking you like an animal. While you were sucking my dick."

The crowd was so silent, Shelby's sob sounded like a woman being torn in half.

Jackson punched Dean.

Hard as he could, right across the face.

That's what a better man would do.

Dean staggered back, the crowd parting around him.

"Ah!" Jackson cried, shaking out his screaming hand. "God, that hurts."

"What the hell?" Dean whispered, touching the blood trickling from his nose, before falling back on his ass.

"I should have done that a long time ago," Jackson said. And then, realizing the camera was still rolling, he turned to face it.

Oh. Shit.

Monica followed suit, and so did Cora—everyone pasting wide smiles over their shocked faces. Except for Shelby, who ducked quietly out of the picture.

"Vote Bishop," Jackson said.

Monica snorted with laughter. Cora's shoulders started to shake. Jackson tried to hold onto his mayoral cool, but he couldn't, and he started laughing too.

"And we're out," Vanessa said, and the camera turned off.

Chapter 26

"I don't care how America votes," Dean groaned, blood dripping down his chin onto his shirt. "You'll never get this factory."

"I don't care." Jackson stepped over the guy's legs. "Someone take this trash out."

Sean came forward, as well as some other guys from the bar, and grabbed Dean by the armpits. Dean struggled. "Don't touch me!" He shook the hands loose and started walking away, but Sean followed.

"That was pretty awesome television," Vanessa said.

"We lost the contest."

"Undoubtedly." Vanessa started to pack up the cameras.

Jackson sighed. He didn't regret it, not for a minute, but the consequences sucked.

The entire town was staring at him. Shocked, some of them angry.

I can't be what you expect anymore, he thought. *I have to move on with my life.*

"I'm sorry," he said, but people had already turned away from him to watch the drama of Sean kicking Dean out of town.

He felt Monica come to stand beside him and he wanted to grab her, lean against her, glean a little of her fiery strength. As it was, he felt better just having her there, a foot away, her purple eyes gazing up at him with equal parts laughter and worry.

"Boy, you weren't kidding, you really don't care about this contest anymore," Monica joked.

"Bastard," Jackson said, feeling the anger ripple up all over again. He hoped Sean was literally kicking that man out of town. "I can't believe I brought that asshole here—"

"Hey," she said, her hand slowly covering his fist. He winced when she touched the knuckles. "Oh, sorry," she sighed.

"Something's probably broken," he said; his knuckles were already swelling. "He has a face like a rock."

"You're quite a hero," she whispered.

He looked around him at the town, gathered, their hopes so high only to be crushed. He had to make the decision about the fire chief, the library. The schools would be next. Blowing it looked exactly like this.

"How can you say that? I ruined everything."

"Some things can't be fixed."

He turned away from the people he'd disappointed and stared down at her, the most perfectly imperfect thing to ever grace his life. "Some things don't need to be." He stroked her face with his unbroken hand. "I should have punched him in the face the second he started talking about your underwear."

"My underwear? Please, plenty of men talk about my under—"

"Stop." His thumb touched her lip. "I know you're making a joke. I know that's how you deal with things, just like I deal with things by trying to keep everything under control. But I love you. And I won't listen to anyone talk about the woman I love that way."

The distance between them thrummed and throbbed, and he grew uncomfortable with her assessing silence. In the movies, this was the part where Monica would throw herself into his arms. But Monica was never very predictable.

"You used me."

He nodded, knowing that was true. But determined that having come this far, he could still convince her. It might take some time—like twenty years—but the Wild Child would be his.

Someone shouted, and the knot of people around Sean and Dean shifted.

"I have to make sure they're not killing him," he told her.

"I'm going to check on Shelby."

"We'll talk later?" While he was painfully aware that she hadn't returned his love, it didn't stop him from loving her, and he realized standing there that he loved her despite how she felt. He was now the one courting disaster. It was a terrifying, heady feeling.

"We'll talk later," she agreed. And it had to be enough. For now.

Chapter 27

Cora's was full. Sean had brought over a cooler of beer and was handing out icy bottles. Cora was giving away pie, and the mood in the room swung from dejected to defiant and back again.

Shelby's absence was conspicuous. Monica had followed her friend to the Art Barn, only to find her sitting, calm and dry-eyed, at her desk, staring at the wall of pictures kids had created for her over the years.

"Who is going to send their kids to me?" she'd asked.

"No one will believe what that asshole said," Monica had assured her.

"Even if it was the truth?" Shelby asked, one eyebrow raised.

"You'll see, Shelby. Your reputation cannot be tarnished."

Shelby had declined Monica's invitation to come back into town to this informal meeting. And Monica had finally left Shelby alone after getting her promise that she wouldn't do anything drastic.

"Tourism is through the roof," Sean said from his spot at the counter. "I mean, poker night was full this weekend. And the mayor knocking down that asshole on live TV is going to bring us a few more people coming to see the sights."

"To the mayor knocking down that asshole," Monica said, lifting her coffee cup in a toast.

People smiled, but no one joined her.

"Look." Jackson took a deep breath and let it out

slowly. There was nothing like a loved one's pain. She would take it all if she could. Even though he'd dished out his fair share. "We've got some hard decisions ahead of us. Without the factory, we're going . . . we're going to have to either close the library . . ."

People gasped.

"Or retire the fire chief."

More gasps.

"What if we sell the house?" Gwen asked from the stool she was sharing with Jay. "And donate the money to the town."

Jackson smiled at his sister with so much love in his eyes, Monica had to look away or start crying.

"That's generous, Gwen," Brian Andersen, the city treasurer and, as Jackson called him, the real salvation of Bishop, spoke up. "But it's not what we really need to do."

Before anyone could ask what they really needed to do, the bell over the door rang and Simone walked in and then stopped, as if surprised to see all the people.

Monica stood up. "What are you doing here?" she asked, unable to work up any heat behind the words, just surprise. She was still in the lovely dress from before, and Charles was with her.

"I . . . I watched the show," she said, looking at Jackson. "You have a fine right hook."

Jackson lifted his coffee cup, an ice pack wrapped to his knuckles.

"I understand that the factory will go to that town in Alaska," Simone continued, "which leaves this town in a bit of a bind."

"You need a factory?" Sean asked. "We'll sell it cheap."

"No, but I had planned to stop filming my reality show, *What Simone Wants*. But Charles, here, had a fabulous idea for one more season. Just one." Simone glanced toward Monica, as if gauging her reaction. "What if I returned to my hometown, to Bishop?"

The room perked up. Monica felt her heartbeat in her ears. Her mother was doing this for her. It was a gift she didn't know how to accept.

"We would, of course, pay your ridiculous permit fees, but we would actually have to tape in the town."

"You can tape here," Cora said.

"My place, too," Sean agreed.

Other people nodded along.

"Parts of it will be awful," Simone said. "I mean . . . *I* will be awful, to most of you. For whatever reason, the world likes that. But I think between the increased tourism, the small amount of industry the show brings with crew and staff, and of course, your permit fees, the town could make a bit of money."

Jackson and Brian shared a look and, as if in answer, Jackson held out his hand to Brian, indicating the decision was his.

"We'll need to discuss the details," Brian said, sounding very mayoral.

"Of course," Simone said. "That is what lawyers are for. But I thought it would be an interesting idea."

"I'd watch it," Sean said.

"You and my many millions of fans." Simone took a step back, and Charles opened the door so they could leave.

"You want to stay for some pie?" Cora asked, offering a delicious olive branch. "It's free today."

Simone shook her head. "Not today, thank you."

And then the bell was ringing as they left.

Monica looked at Jackson, unsure of how to process what Simone had just done, but he seemed equally surprised. Floored. But when she stood up ready to follow her, Jackson was right behind her.

And she was glad. So glad.

"Simone," she said, as she walked out onto the sidewalk. Simone and Charles had just crossed the street to the square, where the remnants of the street fair were being taken down. "Wait a second." Monica jogged across the road.

"I'm sorry I'm not stopping the show," Simone said, opening her purse and pulling out a big pair of sunglasses. When she put them on, they obscured half her face. "But I thought this town was important to you."

"It is . . . it's . . . you're doing this for me?"

"Who else would I do it for?" she asked, looking regal and imperial and like she just didn't give a shit, at total odds with her words. If Jackson tried to control things, and Monica tried to make jokes, then Simone pretended she just didn't give a shit.

"I may not be here," Monica said. "I mean, if you're doing this so you can have that big on-air reunion, you're going to be disappointed."

"I didn't expect that," she said, sniffing. "I didn't expect anything."

"I'm still going to write the book. About Dad."

Simone was silent, her hand reaching out for Charles's just as Jackson's hand curved over Monica's shoulder.

Love was a powerful support.

"Thank you," Monica said. "For doing it."

"I'm sorry I don't remember Greece," Simone said, and Monica squeezed Jackson's hand, so hard she heard him whimper. "I realize I can't take that year away from you. But I want you to know . . . I'm sorry. Now, if you'll excuse us, we need to go make some phone calls."

"Sure," she whispered, and then Simone and Charles, hand in hand, were gone.

Jackson was silent, as if he understood that there was nothing he could say that would change the bittersweet nature of what had happened. Instead, he just pulled her against his chest, into his arms. He rested his chin on her head.

"I love you," he said, and she let the words wash over her, a balm to all the old wounds. "I love your bravery and your heart. I love the mistakes you made, because they made you the woman you are now. I love your fierceness and your fear."

"Thank you," she whispered.

"And I am so proud of the way you just handled that with Simone."

She kissed his hand, the broken one that rested beneath her chin.

"I just . . ." he whispered. "I just want to be the man you love. The man who deserves you."

Her eyes closed at his words, the damage he'd done repaired.

"I'm sorry I didn't stand up for you earlier," he said. "I'm sorry I used you."

"I thought you didn't *not* use me." Forgiveness was easy when faced with so much love and support. Everyone was entitled to a misstep. Lord knows she'd made plenty and would probably make more. "Big difference, buddy."

"I get that I might have blown it, and that I might be too late, and I screwed up with the camera crew, and you can give me shit for that for the rest of our lives together—"

"You're damn straight I will."

He paused, and she felt him lift his head. "You . . . will?" He sounded so hopeful, so surprised.

"You didn't blow it."

"I didn't?"

"It was close," she said, pursing her lips, because she knew how he felt about her lips. "But then you broke Dean's nose."

He grinned, this handsome, caring man with the beautiful wild streak that no one got to see but her. "I could also punch Sean, if you like that sort of thing. It's long overdue."

She touched his chest, ran her hands up over his shoulders, and it felt like she was gathering him up, putting him back together but in a new order, a new way. The way he'd done to her. *Mine,* she thought, attaching neck to body, face to neck. "I love you, Jackson Davies."

His eyes fluttered, not quite shut. "Say it again," he whispered.

"I've been waiting for you my whole life. I'll love you forever."

The hug was a blessing. The kiss was a promise; the future glittered around them.

At the sound of another footstep on the pavement, Monica and Jackson turned as one to see Gwen beside them, wearing her mother's formal gown and flip-flops. Monica smiled at just the sight of her.

"Everyone okay?" Gwen asked, her anxious eyes looking from Monica to Jackson.

"Yes and no," Monica sighed.

"You know what you need?" Gwen said, taking another step and then another until she was close enough to touch. Jackson, who had clearly decided not to waste any more precious time with his sister, hooked Gwen around the neck, pulling her into his arms too.

"What do I need?" Monica asked, hugging the girl and the man as hard as she could.

"A road trip. Have you ever seen the Grand Canyon?" Gwen asked, and Jackson pressed a kiss to Gwen's head—perhaps the first time he'd ever kissed his sister, because they both looked slightly shocked.

"No," Monica answered. "I've never been."

"Well, we're going," Gwen said. "And you should come with us."

"Is that an invitation?" Monica turned slightly to face Jackson.

"Wherever I go, I want you with me, Monica."

It was the most profoundly beautiful and simple thing anyone had ever said to her.

"How can I say no?"

"And after that, I want to finish law school," he said.

She smiled, eager to support him in that. "I want to write fiction books for teenagers." She didn't realize the words were going to come out of her mouth, but once they did, she recognized them as the truth.

"Cool," Gwen breathed. Someone across the square called her name, and Gwen eased away from the group hug. "This is nice and all," she said, "but I gotta go."

"What if . . . what if I want to come back here sometimes?" she asked, as they watched Gwen run across the grass. Monica thought of Shelby and Cora. Sean.

"To Bishop?" Jackson asked. She nodded.

"It's just a town, Jackson. Not innately evil or innately good. It's not going to save us or ruin us. It's where our friends live, that's all. We can live anywhere, Jackson. But I'm going to want to come back here sometimes."

"Then we come back," Jackson said. "You're all I need. You're every daydream and fantasy I've ever had. You're my home."

He pulled her into his arms, and in front of the town and the fountain and every single face pressed to Cora's front window, the mayor kissed her. And the Wild Child kissed him back.

After a thousand wrong turns and near misses, Monica had managed to find her way back to herself, to the person she was supposed to be.

And the man she was supposed to be with.

She'd found her way home.

There's plenty of heat to go around
in Bishop, Arkansas,
as the characters in Molly O'Keefe's next novel
are about to find out.

Read on for an exclusive sneak peek at

NEVER BEEN KISSED

Chapter 1

For a man of few words Brody Baxter hated silence. Watching the waves crash on the beach, he wished his brother was there. Sean's chatter would make him focus.

At this point, the third hour in a four-hour shift with nothing but moonlight and dolphins in the ocean in front of the villa, Brody prayed for a three-man paramilitary attack from the water but would settle for camera-wielding paparazzi jumping out from the Tiare bush to his left.

Anything to break up the monotony.

Funny, but at one time he'd thought guarding shady politicians would be more exciting than guarding the earnest ones, but the years had taught him otherwise.

The screen door behind him slid open with a gasp and a swish. The short hair on his neck prickled in warning, but he didn't turn around. It was the woman Senator Rawlings had brought. The smell of sweat over perfume preceded her.

"Sorry," she said, her voice gaspy and breathy. "I forgot you were out here."

That's the idea, he thought and stepped further into the shadows of the balcony.

Perhaps knowing he was out here, she'd have second thoughts about enjoying the view from the balcony.

But no, the woman came to lean against the railing overlooking the bay. Her robe, barely tied at her waist, looked like a dark oil spill over her body. The color blended with her hair. The night sky behind her.

Quickly, he glanced away. She'd been loud in that villa. Lots of *Oh Daddy*'s.

"Is all this really necessary?" she asked, waving her hand around to indicate him and the other members of the team, silently guarding the senator and by proximity, her. Her accent was nearly nonexistent, but the alleys of Cairo clung to her vowels.

She'd come into the Senator's life suddenly. A friend of a friend of an aide at some political fund-raiser in D.C. Brody didn't particularly like how much they didn't know about her.

Choosing not to answer, Brody scanned the edge of the cliff to his left. If Brody was lucky, Senator Rawlings's wife would come rappelling over the edge with a submachine gun and he wouldn't have to engage in this conversation.

There were days he really missed the Marine Corp.

Out of the corner of his eye he saw her run her fingers over the silk edge of that robe, revealing her collarbone, the gravity defying inside curve of her breast.

"Maybe Doug gave himself the death threats, just so he could take me someplace."

Doubtful. Brody's team didn't come cheap. And Cook's Bay was a lot of effort for a woman who probably would have put on the very same show at The Four Seasons in Washington D.C.

"Does it bother you? Listening to us?" She tipped her head, her oil-spill hair falling down her neck. "Knowing he has a wife. A family. That he's cheating? Lying?" Her eyes glowed with a certain avarice. Obviously, it turned her on. The dirty illicitness of it. Of her role in it. It explained why she was putting on a show for a man twice

her age, three times her weight and with the morality of
a shark.

For a moment he thought about telling her she was
the cleanest thing in Senator Rawlings's life. That the
death threats could have come from the full spectrum of
extremist groups, the product of a lifetime of double
dealing and lying in the name of politics.

But, lately, he was pissing off the Syrian Ba'ath party
in vocal support of the rebels.

He didn't bother explaining any of this to her, because he doubted she cared. Instead, he looked back
over the ocean. The dolphins, the moonlight. *Bother
him?* As a rule, Brody didn't get bothered.

"Gina?" The senator yelled from inside the door.

She shrugged, her lips twisted in some kind of coy regret.

"Duty calls," she whispered and vanished back into
the villa.

The world issued an open invitation to humanity to
fail itself. To be selfish and small. Mean, even evil at
times. And most people, in Brody's experience, found it
impossible to turn down that invitation.

The Senator and his lies were just another example in
a long line.

His ear piece buzzed in the split second before he
heard Colin's voice. "Brody? Bill is coming up on your
six. You have a visitor at HQ."

A visitor? Here?

Suddenly he thought of Ed, sick and alone in that
house. Too stubborn to ask for help if he needed it.

Christ.

He and Sean should have gotten him a nurse. They'd
been talking about it, but Ed was so stubborn and
Brody, in the end, didn't know how to fight him. Or
maybe he just didn't care enough.

But Sean didn't know where Brody was, or how to
find him.

So, not Ed.

His diaphragm relaxed.

Bill, a thick squat man Brody had worked with for years and managed to know nothing about, came up through the shadows. They nodded at each other and Brody slipped down the path through the ferns and wild banana trees to the guest house where the team had set up headquarters.

Tropical bugs hovered around the light of the guest house veranda. To the left of the light and the cloud of bugs stood a man sweating through an expensive white button-down shirt, his suit jacket was tossed over the railing. Brody couldn't get a good look at the guy's face, because his head was bent as he rolled his sleeves.

The intricate warning system of adrenaline, Brody's gut and the hair on the back of his neck began to buzz. Whoever this guy was, he'd gone to great lengths to find him.

And people didn't work so hard to bring good news.

"You're here for me?" Brody asked, stepping to the edge of the light, but no further.

"Brody Baxter?" the man asked, peering into the shadows where Brody blended into the darkness.

Something niggled in the back of his head. A memory. This guy wasn't a stranger. His All-American, confident-of-his-place-in-the-world looks were familiar.

"Yes," Brody answered.

"You're not an easy man to find."

Once again, that is sort of the idea. Brody cut through the bullshit. "Who are you?"

The guy smiled, wearily. Whatever had brought him to the islands of Polynesia to find Brody, it wasn't anything good.

"It's been a few years," the man said and held out his hand. "I'm Harrison Montgomery."

Brody felt deep ripples of recognition, memories of

this guy and his kid sister came running from the corners where he'd shoved them years ago.

Ashley.

Brody shook Harrison's hand. Last time Brody saw him he was an eighteen-year-old asshole. Almost as bad as his father, but miles away from his mother's very special brand of asshole.

But it explained how he managed to find Brody. Harrison had all the right connections. The Montgomerys were a four-generation political family out of Georgia. The Kennedys without the president, the assassinations, or the sex scandals.

If Harrison wanted to find someone, he had enough money and power to see it done.

Interesting, Brody thought. *But why me?*

"What can I do for you, Harrison?"

Harrison sighed and braced his hands on his hips. "We . . . need a man of your talents."

"I'm not all that special." Brody was not in any hurry to get tangled with the Montgomerys again.

"Ashley's been kidnapped."

All of his internal organs recoiled at the mention of her name, and then again at the thought of her in danger.

"Or taken hostage, I'm not . . . I'm not sure what the proper term is."

Quickly, his mind recovered for his heart's shortcomings. "By who?"

"Somali pirates. She'd been working at a refugee camp in Kenya, had gotten sick and a friend convinced her to take a vacation in Seychelles. They hired a boat for the day, and I don't know if they got off course, or the guys on the boat were connected to the pirates—"

"They've held her for ransom?"

"Yes." Harrison shook his head as if he realized he'd been rambling and he was grateful to be shoved back on track. "We've been negotiating—"

Of course the Montgomerys would negotiate.

"How long?"

"Three weeks."

As a rule the Somali pirates didn't hurt their hostages—it was bad for business. But three weeks was a very, very long time to be scared.

The thought of Ashley held at gunpoint and mistreated rearranged him. Reduced him to some instinctual, animal level. It wasn't right and he needed to do something about it.

It had been ten years, but in his mind she was seventeen—a protected child, stepping into womanhood. Precocious and ludicrously optimistic. Her presence in a Somali village, surrounded by armed pirates, made about as much sense as that of a unicorn.

"We'll pay of course. Whatever your fee—"

"What do you need?"

Harrison blinked at Brody's implied agreement, but then Brody had to give the man credit. He sharpened. Focused. Maybe he'd outgrown that genetic asshole problem in his family.

"We've been working with a translator, Umar. Cell phone reception on their end has been a problem but Umar has a satellite phone. And I've got a pilot on the ground outside of Garoowe."

"What do you need?" he repeated.

"We need someone to go get her at the drop-off coordinates. I'd go, but we've been advised that things could get ugly. And we need to keep this . . . quiet."

Of course they did. Harrison's father was up for re-election as governor of Georgia and, if the rumors were true, Harrison was going to make a shoe-in run for the senate.

Whatever emotional reaction thoughts of Ashley created in him, he managed to bury under logistics.

"What's the timeline?"

"We're supposed to get the coordinates in twelve hours. But they . . . the pirates haven't exactly been reliable."

"How will the money been exchanged?" He didn't want to carry around a briefcase of money through the tribal lands of war-torn Somalia.

"We'll transfer to an offshore account when we get the coordinates and proof that Ashley is alive and safe."

Electronic banking. Offshore accounts. The pirates have come a long way.

"How much?"

"One point two million."

Brody laughed, though none of this was funny. "Down from one and a half?"

Harrison stiffened, reading insult where there was plenty. "Brody, we need you, but you have no idea what this process has been like."

Brody's esteem for the man went up another notch.

He checked his watch. It was two a.m. Brody and the team were flying out of here with the senator at eight a.m. "You have a plane standing by?"

"The family jet. I can get you as far as Mogadishu, my pilot will pick you up there and fly you to Garoowe, where they've been keeping her. Umar will meet you and take you to Ashley."

"I'll need the satellite number Umar is using."

Harrison, again proving his mettle, handed him a phone. "It's programmed with all the numbers of people we've been in contact with. As well as a timeline, as complete as we could make it with the little bit of information we have."

Brody took the phone and slipped it in his pocket. He had to finish the Rawlings job, as repugnant as it seemed.

"Have you talked to her?"

"Once briefly. They'd been sending photographs, but a week ago I said unless I could actually speak to her—"

"You negotiated."

"Should I have let them shoot her?"

No, he thought, *you should have come and got me three weeks ago*.

"She said she hasn't been hurt," Harrison said. "But was well-fed. Bored, mostly. Scared."

Again, the thing with his lungs.

"We can leave in six hours," Brody said.

Harrison sighed like he'd been holding his breath for days. "Thank you."

Accepting Montgomery gratitude was heavily ironic and oddly difficult, like swallowing a golf ball. But he managed a nod.

"You can wait here in the guest house. Try to get some sleep."

"We haven't discussed any payment."

"We will."

Brody was about to knock on the front door to fill Clint in on some of the changes he was going to need to make to the itinerary. But he stopped at the edge of shadow and looked over his shoulder at the golden Montgomery child. Man now. It had been ten years.

Ashley would be a woman.

He pushed the thought, errant and useless, away. "Why me?"

Harrison's eyes were older and they told a story about the last ten years, and it wasn't a happy one. "We know you'll keep it quiet."

Brody nearly laughed. Yes, he'd proven he could keep the Montgomerys' secrets.

He pushed open the door, but Harrison's voice stopped him. "Brody. Get her and get her home and . . . keep her safe."

So much easier said than done with Ashley Montgomery.